TITLES BY DAWN ADDONIZIO

Novels Of The Faerie Realm:

A RISKY PROPOSITION, Book 1 of
The Third Wish Duology

SOUL SEDUCTION, Book 2 of
The Third Wish Duology

PASSIONATE MAGIC

GREY'S MAGIC

Published by Nouveau Ventures Unlimited
3606 Woods Walk Blvd
Lake Worth, FL 33467

Edited by DM Eburn
Cover Image courtesy of Can Stock Photo Inc / mimagephotography

GREY'S MAGIC

First paperback printing February 2014

For information contact:
Dawn Addonizio
Dawn@DawnsBoutique.Org

This is a work of fiction. All of the characters, organizations, locales and events portrayed in this novel are either products of the author's imagination, or are used purely for fictitious purposes.

Table of Contents

"...and while we wait in silence for that final luxury of fear-lessness, the weight of that silence will choke us."
-Audre Lorde

<u>Chapter 1</u>

Scarlett lowered herself onto a barstool and ordered a shot of whiskey from a Hawaiian-shirt-clad bartender. She tilted her head back as she tipped it past her lips, closing her eyes as it burned a fiery path down her throat. She sighed in appreciation, thankful that her father had insisted on paying for a full bar.

Tapping the empty glass with two fingers, she signaled the bartender to make the next one a double. She gave the dark purple hem of her bridesmaid's dress an irritable yank as she waited for him to finish with another order.

She supposed she should be grateful that her new sister-in-law hadn't chosen one of the more frilly contraptions she'd seen at the bridal shop. Whoever had designed some of those dresses bore an unhealthy obsession with making women look like cupcakes.

At least this frock had a simple cut and was short enough to give her a full range of movement. But Scarlett still preferred the loose robes that her people, the *sidhe*, wore for such ceremonies.

Or even better, her favorite jeans and leather vest.

Not that the pointy heels her mother had insisted she wear didn't have some intriguing possibilities...too bad they all involved using them as weaponry instead of shoes.

Scarlett's face ached from the strain of forcing a smile for the pictures. And it was going to take a week of sparring with her cousins to work out the knots in her shoulders and neck from sitting through getting her hair and nails done.

Being surrounded by all of these humans made her tense as hell.

She downed the second shot, the warmth in her belly taking root, and reached up to massage the base of her neck. A man in a rumpled suit grinned at her from down the bar. She glared at him, but it wasn't the deterrent she'd hoped.

He slid over to sit on the stool next to hers, the crinkles around his eyes glowing white against his too-tanned face as his smile widened. Combined with his shaggy, sun-streaked hair, it was a sure bet that he was one of her brother's beach bum friends.

"You're Doyle's sister, right?" he slurred, confirming her observation. "He never told me how pretty you are. Let me buy your drink, I insist."

He laughed at his own joke and Scarlett cringed. He was obviously some piss artist who'd been drunk long before the free wedding bar opened.

"No," she growled, adding a grudging, "thank you," as she remembered her mother's dire warnings to be nice to Doyle and Violet's guests.

"I'm Joe," he continued, unfazed by her refusal. The human leaned forward and brushed against her shoulder, the alcohol fumes on his breath wafting into her face as he called out to get the bartender's attention.

Scarlett jerked away, sweat trickling an uncomfortable path between her breasts. He was oblivious to her anxiety as he accepted a fresh drink and pointed for hers to be refilled. Then he clinked his glass against hers with a hearty, "To Doyle and Violet!"

Nearby guests cheered and raised their glasses in salute. It seemed Scarlett was expected to do the same, and she tried to steady her shaking hand as she lifted her own drink.

People crowded closer to tap her glass, a suffocating mass of bodies hemming her in. Their voices crashed against her senses, loud and unintelligible through the blood pounding in her ears.

Scarlett looked up toward the rustic wooden planks of the ceiling and tried to suck more air into her lungs. Her vision wavered as she blinked at the roof timbers, decorated with white paper garlands and strings of tiny lights. The myriad twinkling points grew brighter and coalesced into a dazzling supernova.

Scarlett swayed on her stool.

Suddenly there was a hand at her elbow, pulling her to her feet and leading her away from the cluster of humans.

Pat Sparrow's familiar scent of woodland spice enveloped her and she almost sobbed with the relief of it. He was her brother's best friend, and one of the few men outside her family that she trusted.

"*Easy there, Letty,*" he murmured in Gaelic as he steered her from the restaurant and toward a quiet bench on the docks. Tiki torches lent a velvety glow to the walkway. They flickered in the breeze, their fiery reflections shimmering on the rippled surface of the water.

Pat urged her to sit.

Scarlett's panic faded to annoyed embarrassment. "*I'm fine,*" she snapped in their home tongue.

He sighed and gave her a look so filled with pity it made her want to scream. "*Letty, you haven't been fine for almost two hundred years.*"

She scowled at him. "Well, I would be if I didn't have to visit the blasted human realm every time I want to see my own brother. Now that he's taking one of them as his soul mate, he'll probably never come home," she predicted with disgust.

Pat arched a brow at her. "Violet is perfectly lovely, and she makes Doyle happier than I've ever seen him. Besides, you know we don't choose our soul mates. If we're lucky, fate allows us to find them."

Scarlett knew he was right. She had even developed a grudging affection for her brother's human. But the look in Pat's eyes when he spoke of soul mates left her no doubt that he was thinking of his own date.

"I suppose you think you've found your soul mate as well," she scoffed.

"Though, in that sleeveless dress of hers, it's hard not to notice that your Aegishjalmur tattoo hasn't imprinted on her yet. At least Doyle's human can claim that much."

The warmth in Pat's eyes fled. "You and I have been friends for a long time, Letty, but I'm warning you to tread lightly on the subject of Sydney. She is my soul mate. My tattoo reacts to her touch. You know my human blood has always interfered with my sidhe magic. That must be why the Aegishjalmur didn't imprint on her skin."

"Sparrow?" called a concerned female voice. "Is she okay?"

Scarlett smiled sourly at the human in question. Sydney appeared ethereal in her ankle length, strapless gown. Her long, golden-brown hair floated in a cloud around her pale shoulders, and she looked softer and more feminine than Scarlett would ever be.

"Yes, love, just give us another minute," Pat replied.

"No problem." Sydney smiled at him, her eyes sympathetic as they travelled to Scarlett before she turned and went back inside.

Humiliation stained Scarlett's cheeks as she wondered what Pat had told his human about her. *"Sparrow?"* she mocked. *"Do you think you and your 'soul mate' will graduate to a first name basis any time soon?"*

Pat's jaw clenched. "You need to stop pretending you're jealous of her," he snapped in English. "You've used me as an excuse not to live your life for far too long."

He got up and followed Sydney back to the reception, leaving Scarlett feeling as if he'd slapped her. She squeezed her eyes shut, refusing to allow the tears to escape them.

She needed to get out of there. But she'd never hear the end of it if she left her brother's wedding this early.

Maybe she had time to slip away for a calming walk on the beach. She rose from the bench, hoping her mother hadn't already noticed her absence. The heel of her shoe snagged on a wooden deck plank and she expelled a vivid curse, barely catching herself from toppling over.

She'd give both pinky toes to be able to conjure her favorite pair of leather boots right now. But unlike Pat, she didn't have Seelie clearance to use gratuitous magic in the human realm.

Muttering to herself, Scarlett yanked off the ridiculous shoes and set out barefoot down the ramp and away from the party.

The solitude and salt air was a balm to her frazzled nerves as she meandered along the deserted sidewalk. If this place wasn't infested with humans, she might actually enjoy spending time here.

She turned down a residential street that bordered the beach, Pat's parting words replaying in her mind. He'd accused her of using him as an excuse not to live her life. And if she was honest with herself, she knew it for truth.

When she was younger, she hadn't had eyes for anyone but him. Though she hadn't been just another village girl swooning after his mouthwatering looks. She'd been a terrified teenager who idolized the boy that had saved her.

She closed her eyes and slammed her mental shutters down against the memory. Shaking her head, she drifted to a stop and peered across the unfenced yard of the house to her left.

It looked like cutting through the property would bring her straight to the ocean. There were lights on behind the windows of the house, but the curtains were drawn. She was debating the wisdom of trespassing, when she sensed that she was being watched.

∞ ∞ ∞ ∞ ∞ ∞ ∞ ∞ ∞ ∞

Grey stood in the shadows outside the quaint beachside cottage. Ceramic garden gnomes peaked out from the colorful hibiscus and bougainvillea blooming along the fence-line. A welcome mat embroidered with butterflies beckoned visitors onto the front porch.

The cheerfulness felt grotesque, considering the profanities that had been committed inside the cottage less than forty-eight hours ago. The profile fit the unsub he'd been chasing for three months now. He'd been to three other crime scenes, just like this one, spread across the country from New Hampshire, to Colorado, to Texas, and now Florida.

He couldn't figure out how this psycho was choosing his victims. Much less how he found the time to travel across North America stalking them.

Grey sighed and shook his head, trying to push his frustration aside and get into the mind of the killer.

Key Largo was a beach community. It thrived on tourism. None of the residents would think twice about a stranger hanging around this neighborhood.

The perimeter of the yard was a thick mass of foliage. Normally it would provide an ideal place for a predator to lie in wait. But the thorns on these bushes would scratch the hell out of anyone who tried to use them for cover.

There was no sign of forced entry. Nor was there any sign of a struggle near the front or back doors. And all the windows were locked tight from the inside.

It had been the same at each of the other crime scenes. Perhaps this victim had felt safe enough to leave her doors unlocked? But not all of the women had lived in such casual neighborhoods.

Which meant that they had to be inviting him in. Or he had keys.

Grey gritted his teeth at the all-too-familiar theories, wishing his brain would pick up something new. An unsub who had killed in four states in as many months would need access to a chain of inter-state businesses to maintain local professional ties in all of these cities. But Liza, Grey's technical analyst, hadn't found evidence of any victims having recent contact with professionals who had access to their customers' keys.

And when a tech as good as Liza found nothing, there was usually nothing to find.

Maybe Grey would get lucky and something about this poor woman would finally give him a bead on the bastard.

A faint sound interrupted Grey's musings, and his eyes narrowed as they scanned the surrounding darkness for its source. A lone figure approached along the sidewalk. The moon slid from behind a cloud, its light gilding strawberry blonde hair, and revealing the most incredible woman Grey had ever seen.

Tall and lithe, she moved with the grace of a panther. Her sheath dress clung to her lean curves, flaring to a stop at mid-thigh, and showcasing toned legs with a sexy bronzed glow. Her eyes flashed with awareness as she slowed her walk, her full lips gleaming beneath the caress of her tongue—as if she was tasting the air for danger.

Grey's heart jumped inside his chest and he inhaled sharply. Her eyes flew toward the pool of shadows in the yard, zeroing in on him. Though he knew she couldn't possibly see him from her vantage point.

He stood immobile, staring at her in fascination and feeling an odd pang of regret as she moved forward, seeming to dismiss his presence.

∞∞∞∞∞∞∞∞∞

Scarlett's pulse sped up as she scanned her surroundings. She felt, more than saw, a lone man standing motionless in the next yard. Adrenaline spiked in her blood, fueled by anger.

This was the first moment of peace she'd had all day. She'd be damned if she let another human ruin it. She moved closer, pretending as if she didn't see him. Then she stopped and pivoted on her heel, her stance defensive as she faced him.

"Do you make a habit of hiding in the bushes and spying on women?" she demanded.

Chocolate brows rose in surprise above dark eyes brimming with intelligence. He recovered quickly and flashed her a chagrinned smile, revealing an intriguing dimple in an otherwise smooth cheek. As her vision adjusted to the gloom, she saw that he had a trim, muscular physique and skin the color of coffee with a hint of cream.

"Do you make a habit of walking the streets alone at night?" he countered. "This isn't the safest place to be," he added, his expression turning grim.

Scarlett narrowed her eyes at his change in tone. He had a familiar scent about him. Her nose tingled with recognition as she realized it was a pungent combination of herbs that her people used to make a particularly potent sleeping draught—a Morpheus potion.

Her body tensed. "Is that a threat?"

He gave her an odd look. "No, I'm …"

He reached into his pocket as he spoke, and she leapt at him before he could complete the sentence. She wasn't about to give him a chance to dose her with Morpheus.

Grey grunted in shock as the woman came at him full force, sweeping his leg and sending him crashing to the ground. She landed atop him with one arm braced against his neck. Her other hand rose in a powerful arc behind her head, and he had a split second to realize that it was clenched around a stiletto heeled shoe.

With the pointy end aimed at his face.

Years of martial arts training kicked in, and he sent an uppercut flying into her ribs. He took advantage of her surprised gasp and deflected her chokehold, flipping her onto her back.

Then she began to fight in earnest.

They rolled across the lawn in a wild tussle of limbs, each landing punches heavy enough to bruise bone and steal breath. She refused to be subdued, and he realized with shock that she might be able to best him in a fight.

"FBI," he panted, groaning as she landed a brutal blow to his kidney. "I wasn't threatening you. I was trying to show you my badge. I'm FBI."

He rolled off of her and held up his hands, hoping she would accept the truce. But he kept his elbows tucked into a defensive position just in case she wasn't in the mood for diplomacy.

She leapt to her feet, nimble as a cat, and took a step backward. Her wary eyes never left his face as she towered over him.

"Do you want to see my badge?" he asked, pointing to his pocket. When she didn't respond, he slowly reached for it, keeping one hand up in supplication.

She took another step back, almost stumbling on one of the garden gnomes. Her face was smudged with dirt and her fancy dress was probably ruined. But her sharp, sea-green gaze tracked his every move.

"I'm Special Agent Greyson Derrington," he explained. "I'm investigating a murder that occurred here two days ago. That's why I said it wasn't safe for you to walk alone at night."

He watched her face as her mind processed his words. She glanced at his badge, but seemed to be more interested in discerning the truth from his eyes. The tension she held in her muscles relaxed and he felt his own tension begin to drain away.

"Who are you?" he asked, still incredulous that she'd almost beaten him at hand to hand combat. She was a skilled fighter, and quite possibly the sexiest woman he'd ever seen. It was a dangerous combination.

"My name is Scarlett Thresher," she answered softly.

Desire shot through his groin at the intense way she held his stare as the musical cadence of her Irish brogue washed over him.

She retreated another step and shook her head, silky strands of hair caressing her cheek where they'd escaped from their array of pins. "I'm sorry. I have to go," she murmured, looking as bewildered as he felt.

She bent to grab her shoes, then turned and fled back up the sidewalk, slipping away into the darkness before he could formulate a protest.

Grey sat back on his haunches in the grass, stunned. A shimmer of light caught his eye, and he reached down to pick up an earring with a large teardrop diamond glistening in a gold setting. He'd seen its mate resting against the delicate earlobe of the amazing woman he'd just let get away.

He stuck it in his pocket, wincing at the twinge in his ribs. She'd kicked his ass and then bolted without so much as an explanation. He wasn't sure whether to feel impressed, offended…or turned on.

∞∞∞∞∞∞∞∞∞∞

Scarlett ran, her legs pumping faster and faster, her mind a haze of confusion. She faltered to a stop when she found herself back at the docks by the wedding reception.

Agent Greyson Derrington of the FBI, her brain whispered as she made her way over the wooden planks and past the row of tiki torches. He'd said he was investigating a murder, so he must be part of the human police force.

She puffed at the loose hair on her cheek as she pushed open the door to the building. A cool blast of air hit her, drying the perspiration on her forehead. Scarlett grimaced as she realized what a mess she must look with her sweaty face, torn dress and bare feet.

She sprinted for the washrooms, avoiding the gazes of the other guests, and hurried through the door with the crepe-paper bride taped to it. She locked herself in the largest stall with the sink and steadied her hands on the basin as she tried to calm down.

She couldn't believe what had just happened. She never should have engaged the man. She should have turned and walked away. But she'd been upset and itching for a fight.

And what a fighter he was. She was almost disappointed that he'd surrendered before she found out if she could beat him. How insane was that?

He'd defended himself against her attacks, yet he lacked the arrogance of many fighters who could claim his skill. He'd attempted to subdue her, but none of his moves had been designed to truly hurt her. And there was something in his eyes that made her want to trust him, despite the fact that he was human.

That had to be the most insane part of all.

And it wasn't the only disturbing thing about their encounter. There were also the herbs she'd smelled on him. If Agent Greyson Derrington of the FBI had picked up the scent of her people's most potent sleeping potion from his crime scene, in all probability, his criminal wasn't human.

She couldn't allow herself to keep that knowledge a secret. Not if it could help catch a murderer.

She cursed and gave the tap a hard twist, yanking some paper towels from the dispenser so she could wipe the dirt from her face. The careful design that the human hairdresser had taken so much time creating was wrecked.

She began pulling out the remaining hairpins, and groaned as the mirror revealed her bare earlobe. *Damn it.* She'd lost one of the special dwarven-made diamond earrings that her father had given her for her birthday.

"Scarlett?" her mother's voice called from outside the stall.

She groaned again. "Yes, Ma," she replied, trying to sound composed.

"Are you alright? Paddy said you weren't feeling well." Marjorie Thresher's tone was concerned, but there was a strain of exasperation in it. It wasn't much of a leap for her mother to assume that Scarlett was hiding in the washroom to avoid mingling with the human guests.

Scarlett hesitated. One look at her dress told her that she needed to avoid opening the stall door at all costs. Nothing but faerie dust was going to fix the torn and stained cloth, and she didn't have any with her.

"Not really, Ma. I think I had a bad oyster from the raw bar," she improvised. "I've been in here wondering if I'm going to be sick."

Marjorie paused and Scarlett felt her disbelief thick in the air.

"Paddy said you were going for a walk."

Scarlett dropped her head back and exhaled. "I thought the fresh air might make me feel better," she answered truthfully.

There was another moment of silence, as if Marjorie was torn between wanting to comfort her daughter, and not truly believing she was ill.

"Do you want me to come in there?" she asked finally. "I may have a soothing potion in my purse…"

"No," Scarlett replied quickly, and then added, "Thanks, Ma. I'd really just like to blink home and go to bed, if you and Da don't mind."

Marjorie sighed. "It's not your Da and me you should be asking. It's your brother's wedding you'll be leaving early."

Scarlett swallowed a lump of guilt. But Doyle probably hadn't expected her to stay as long as she had. He was well aware of how she felt about humans.

"Please tell Doyle and Violet that I'm sorry," she said softly.

Her mother hesitated, as if she wanted to say more, but then she sighed again and left Scarlett alone in the bathroom.

Scarlett released a breath and thanked the goddess that she hadn't had to explain to her mother how she'd ruined her bridesmaid's dress. She loved Ma, but no matter how old Scarlett was, Ma could still make her feel like a disobedient child.

She thought about retracing her steps to look for her earring, but decided against it. She didn't want anyone to see her in such a disheveled state. And she'd had more than enough of the human realm for one day.

Not to mention she'd probably lost it during the fight, and Agent Derrington might still be hanging around his crime scene. The thought of seeing him again made her belly do a weird little flip.

She told herself that her stomach was reacting to her lie about eating bad oysters, and put him from her mind as she gratefully blinked home to the faerie realm.

But later that night, as she tossed in restless sleep, a hard bodied fighter with smooth, brown skin and a dimpled smile watched her from the shadows in her dreams.

Chapter 2

Scarlett yawned as she rolled out of bed and headed for the kitchen. Bradan, the brownie who shared her cottage, had already put on the tea kettle.

"Mmm," she sighed as she took the first sweet, scalding sip.

Even though brownies tended to stay out of sight and shunned compliments, Scarlett knew that Bradan secretly enjoyed it when she acknowledged his efforts.

Her lips twitched as she replaced the lid that he'd left off the honey jar. Anyone who didn't live with a brownie might think it was carelessness. But it was really a silent message that she needed to stop by the local apiary for a refill.

As a rule, Brownies refused to take payment for their housework. But they loved honey and became miffed if the owner of their house allowed the supply to dwindle.

She cradled her steaming mug in her hands and carried it to the open back door. Leaning against the frame, she surveyed her wildflower garden.

The air smelled of fresh rain, loamy soil, and green, growing things. The blue-eyed-grass and golden-samphire were blooming, a sea of purple and yellow creating a tranquil setting for her first workout of the day.

She rolled her neck and shoulders to loosen the muscles, then drained her cup and jogged through the misty morning drizzle until she was beneath the cover of her workout area. She stretched and gave her rack of weapons a cursory glance before opting to practice her hand fighting. She obviously needed it since she'd almost allowed a human to best her last night.

Agent Derrington's image flashed through her mind. Skin as smooth and rich as caramel softened the rugged planes of his face. Deep mahogany eyes pierced her with their intelligence. But there had been something gentle about them as well. Something that calmed her and stirred her pulse at the same time.

She shook off the thought and dropped into a stance, beginning a set of alternating punches and kicks and trying to lose herself in the rhythm. She'd been training every day since she was seventeen years old. It gave her confidence and strength knowing that she could fight her way out of any situation.

Her people, the sidhe, were immortal warriors who traditionally began sword practice at age eighteen. But she'd started a year early. Pat had been training for the Seelie Police Academy, and she'd begged him to teach her the sword, as well as the other martial arts styles he was learning.

All of the hours they'd spent training together had set the village rumors about them flying. But they'd never been romantically interested in one another. It was just that being with him, and learning how to defend herself, had been the only things that made her feel safe after the rape.

She fumbled a kick and nearly lost her footing.

She cursed under her breath, hating her mistake, and hating even more the memories that came to the surface whenever she spent time in the human realm.

They were like poison lurking in the darkest corners of her psyche. Sometimes she flushed them out of her system for a while, but they always came seeping back to torment her.

The thought of the rape itself made her want to squeeze her thighs together and never let anyone touch her between them again. But just as bad was the humiliation. The self recrimination over putting herself in a situation where it could happen in the first place. And the helpless shame that she hadn't fought harder and gotten away from the men before they could debase her like that.

She was an immortal warrior, for goddess' sake. If she couldn't fight them off, she should have at least blinked away from them. But she'd frozen. How stupid was that? She was a magical being, and she'd let a couple of disgusting humans rape her.

Scarlett felt a sharp pain in her finger and looked down to see that she'd picked at her cuticle until it was raw and bleeding. She sighed and walked over to the shelf where she kept her healing dust.

It was always like this. As if once the memory resurfaced, her mind wouldn't let it go until it played through every miserable angle of the experience, leaving her a quivering pile of nerves in its wake.

It was her day off from teaching sword techniques, but she knew better than to sit at home and stew in her memories. She had to find something to keep her busy.

Preferably something that would tire her out enough to ward off the inevitable insomnia, and the reliving of her torment behind closed eyelids that refused to conjure sleep. It was nights like those that had led to her escaping into the oblivion of Morpheus far more often than she knew she should.

She showered, pulled on clean workout clothes, and headed to the center of her village to find a sparring partner.

∞∞∞∞∞∞∞∞∞∞

"What up, G-man?" Liza's cheerful voice chirped through the cell phone.

"How's my favorite crime analyst this morning?" Grey asked.

"Jealous," she pouted. "How's F.L.? You bang any surfer chicks yet?"

Grey chuckled. What did he care about surfer chicks? The newest star of his fantasies was a tough strawberry blonde with sea-green eyes and a soft Irish brogue.

"You know I only have eyes for you, Lizzie," he teased.

Liza snorted. "Right. I've heard that before…usually around the time a guy decides to cheat on me and dump me."

"You are far too young to be that jaded," Grey replied with a shake of his head.

"Pfft," she scoffed. "I'm an old soul. It's the only thing that gets me through in this line of work. Besides, you know I never let them get away with it. The last guy ended up with his bank account flagged for fraud and his credit cards cancelled."

"I did not just hear that, Liza."

She sniggered. "Don't worry G-man. My hacks are tasty *and* untraceable. You couldn't prove it even if you tried."

Grey pushed air through his teeth to make a static sound. "Sorry, I didn't catch any of that. I think we have a bad connection."

"Fine," Liza relented with a laugh. "You can stop now, Captain America. I won't say anything else to incriminate myself."

"Oh, there you are," Grey said with feigned relief. "I thought I'd lost you."

"Hysterical," Liza replied drily.

"I try," Grey said with a grin. "So, what do you have for me today?"

"It's not good," Liza answered, her tone turning somber. "We have another vic. And this time she's right here in Virginia. Woodbridge, to be exact."

"Damn it to hell," Grey cursed. "Are you sure it's him?"

"She lived alone and her house was locked up tight. Same lack of evidence at the scene and on the body. And same weird, herby smell," she replied quietly.

"Can you call the office and ask them to book me a flight back this morning?" he said in a tight voice.

"Done and done. You're on the ten thirty from Miami to Dulles. The county Sherriff is expecting you this afternoon."

"Thanks Lizzie." He hung up and let out a chain of expletives.

Could the bastard be taunting him, choosing a victim so close to his home base?

He shoved his toiletries and change of clothes in his travel bag and headed out the door. He would have liked to spend a little more time at the Key Largo scene, but he'd have to rely on his notes.

It was more important to hit this new scene while it was fresh. And it was an hour's drive to the airport—he barely had time to make his flight.

∞∞∞∞∞∞∞∞∞∞

Quinlan frowned at the glint in Scarlett's eye as she strode purposefully toward the training center. He'd seen that look before, and it usually meant he and the boys'd be in for a rash of bruises before the day was done.

"Hiya, Letty. I thought ya were off today."

"I am," she replied with a thin smile. "But that's no reason to let you gobshites get soft in the sparring ring."

"Uh oh, we're in trouble now," her cousin Thom sniggered, earning a laugh from a few of the younger trainees who were visiting from a nearby village.

She arched a brow at him. "You're first then."

Thom's eyes widened, and then he shook his head in defeat, sending his boyish blonde curls bouncing. "Have it your way cousin. But take it easy on me, will ya? Ya know I was only codding ya."

Scarlett flashed him a grin. "Don't worry Tommy Boy. I'll stay away from your delicate parts this time."

"All o' Thom's parts are delicate," razzed Aedan, a grizzled old warrior who'd fought with her father in the last Unseelie uprising.

She'd only been a baby at the time, but Pat's father had been killed in that battle.

Aedan chuckled at the younger man's scowl. "Don' worry, Thom. Letty'll toughen ya up. Spend enough time sparrin' wit her an' yer calluses'll have calluses."

"Aye. That's what I'm afraid of," Thom muttered as he made his way toward the middle of the ring.

The training center was a large, open air arena at the heart of the village. Circled by colorful local shops, it was a daily hub of activity for the residents.

Earth magic kept its grassy carpet verdant and thick, which served to soften a fall as well as any sparring mat. And though it lacked a roof, it was spelled against the elements so that classes and matches could be held in comfort during summer rains and winter snows.

Five fighting rings were clustered at its center, and Scarlett always went for the one in the middle. When fists and weapons were flying in all five rings, she loved to be at the core of all that energy, pretending she was in the midst of a great battle.

"What's your poison, Thom?" she asked as she strode to the nearest rack of sickles, knives, axes and other assorted weaponry. "Swords?" She trailed her fingers over the hilt of a dull edged practice blade.

Thom scoffed. "Against you? Not bleedin' likely."

Their cousin Quinlan laughed, and Scarlett hid a smile. Only the most seasoned warriors would spar swords with her and the entire village knew it.

Every sidhe learned to summon their own soul bound long sword as part of their passage into adulthood. When she'd gotten hers, she'd honed her technique to a razor's edge. It was her personal guarantee that she'd be able to defend herself whenever she needed to.

"The shillelagh, then?" she asked, half teasing, and Thom groaned. The last time they'd practiced stick fighting his dangly bits had gotten a wee bruised. It wasn't intentional, but nor was it something he was likely to forget.

"Can't we just have an old-fashioned hand to hand match?" he pleaded, his eyes flickering toward the group of visiting trainees. A pretty lass, about his age, was watching their proceedings with interest.

"Fine then," Scarlett agreed on a laugh as she abandoned the weapons rack and joined him in the center of the ring.

She eyed him critically as they circled each other. "Your defensive form has improved," she complimented in a quiet tone.

Pleasure flashed across Thom's face and she smiled. He matched her in height, but she was lean and lithe compared to his awkward mix of youthful softness and burgeoning muscle.

He struck out with a quick jab, which she easily ducked. "Good speed," she encouraged, "but don't drop your guard," she added as she snapped a hook at his exposed cheek. She purposely didn't make contact, but it was enough to startle him and make him pay attention.

She went round with him until he was winded, giving him a few thumps and allowing him to make a show of coming close to hitting her. Finally she took advantage of his waning concentration and swept his leg, maneuvering him into a wrist lock as he stumbled.

Should have led with that move on Agent Derrington last night, she thought with a smirk as Thom submitted to the threat of a broken wrist. Might have saved me some sore ribs.

"It was a fine match," she said, patting Thom on the back as he rose.

He gave her a good natured grin despite his bruises and rejoined his friends, who were gazing at her with newfound respect. The pretty young girl leaned in and said something to him, and the other visiting trainees nodded in excitement.

"Uh, Cousin Letty," he began, looking torn between wanting to please the girl and not wanting to provoke Scarlett, "they want to see ya fight the swords. With one of the older warriors," he added quickly.

Scarlett laughed, resisting the urge to tease him again in front of his friends. "Come join me with a sword, Quin," she called, tipping her chin in a beckoning motion.

She felt limber and warmed up after sparring with Thom, and she wanted to keep going. Physical distraction was exactly what she needed today.

"Why is it always me ya choose to show up in front of an audience?" Quinlan jibed as he strode over to the weapons rack and grabbed a couple of practice blades. His meaty, tattooed fists tested them for heft and balance, and then he tossed one to Scarlett.

"You know it's only because I love you, cousin," she replied, snatching the blade deftly out of the air. "And perhaps you'll beat me this time."

Quin snorted and shook his shaggy orange head. "Perhaps with an axe. But with a sword? That hasn't happened in nigh over a hundred years."

"Maybe your skill has surpassed mine since last we tested it," Scarlett replied with a shrug.

"Remember that, lads an' lasses," Aedan called to their young audience from an adjacent sparring ring. "A wise warrior envisions victory without allowin' overconfidence ta cloud her judgment." The aged veteran winked at Scarlett as he deflected a swing from his opponent's sickle.

She grinned at him as she adjusted her grip on her practice blade and settled into a relaxed stance a sword's length from Quin.

"I don't think wise platitudes are going to aid me against ya today," Quin murmured as he struck an opening thrust.

She intercepted it and pulsed her blade against his to push it out of the way. "Oh no? I always find Aedan's advice to be sage and helpful."

She smiled faintly, refusing to be distracted as she adjusted her field of vision to take in Quinlan's massive frame, trying to anticipate his next move.

He feinted a downward cut to open up her guard so he could strike her from the side. His thrusts were swift and powerful, but she wasn't fooled. Her blade met his with a ringing clash as she pivoted to step behind him.

Quin rushed to regain his fighting distance, barely managing to deflect her answering attack, his ribs receiving a hard jab from her sword pommel for his trouble. He winced and their young audience sucked in a collective breath. Scarlett was so fiercely focused, she barely heard them.

"That's what I mean. Ya have that look in your eye today, Letty—the one that says no one who joins ya in the ring is going to leave unscathed."

She frowned at him, keeping her footwork nimble in case he was trying to distract her for his next attack. "And just what do you mean by that? Are you saying I'm being too hard on you, Quin?"

She saw an opening and sent a quick, playful jab toward his chest. It wasn't meant to connect, merely to illustrate his carelessness. He leapt back with a rueful laugh, shaking his head as he rejoined her.

"That wasn't too rough for you, was it?" she whispered with a smirk.

"Ya know I wouldn't suggest ya downplay your combat skills for anyone," he chided softly. "All I'm saying is that I can always tell when something's on your mind."

He twisted his wrists and his sword swept around in a lightning fast arc, almost catching her off guard. She met his blade just before it struck her shoulder, her arms straining as she bound its momentum with her own in a resounding clash of metal against metal.

Knowing she was no match for his brute strength, she sidestepped and allowed her muscles to go slack. His sword flew downward, missing her by a hair, and she jabbed him angrily in the ribs with her pommel again.

She glared at him as they regained their distance and faced each other once more.

"I'm not trying to piss ya off, Letty," Quin said with a sigh. "I'm telling ya I know something's wrong and I wish ya'd tell me what it is. Every so often ya show up here with that steely glint in your eye, your finger bloody like ya've been worrying it with your teeth," he tilted his head toward her hands where they gripped her sword. "And ya leave everyone ya spar with a bit more bruised than usual."

He glanced meaningfully down at his ribs and she gave him an apologetic grimace. Her last jab had been vicious and angry, aimed at the spot where she'd hit him before. It wasn't in the spirit of a practice match, especially one with weapons.

Even if he'd been distracting her with observations she didn't care to hear.

She had never imagined her emotions were so transparent to him. It made her uncomfortable to think someone else might have noticed.

"I'm sorry, Quin," she replied softly. "My lack of control was careless."

She sliced at him in a quick, threatening attack, anticipating his counter thrust and using its power to push her blade back in the opposite direction. Her sweeping upward circle landed the blunt edge against the pulsing vein in his neck.

There was no doubt it would have been a deadly strike in a real fight, and Quin smiled wanly. "I believe the match is yours as usual, cousin."

Thom and his friends cheered, and Quin bowed to her as he stepped back. "Shall we go again?" he offered.

Normally she would have accepted, but her mood for sparring had soured. "I think I'm done for the day."

He frowned as he followed her out of the ring. "What I said wasn't meant to upset ya, Letty," he told her quietly. "It's something I've noticed for years, but I've seen it in ya more often of late. I just wanted ya to know that I'm here if ya need to talk about anything."

Scarlett closed her eyes for a moment and then turned to face him. "I appreciate your concern, Quin. But it's probably just the stress from Doyle's human wedding ceremony."

He arched an orange brow at her. "Ya expect me to believe ya're all narky from having to put on a pretty dress and get your hair done?"

Scarlett couldn't help but laugh, though it was partially true. "As if that wouldn't make you narky?"

Quin snorted, his gray eyes sparkling with humor. "I dunno. I think I might quite like having a bonnie lass fuss over me with a comb. And as for wearing a skirt, my Scottish friends seem to find them downright comfy."

Scarlett gave him a playful shove and he grabbed her hand, pulling a small bag of faerie dust from his pocket and sprinkling some over her finger where she'd started to pick at it again.

"Why don't ya tell me what's really botherin' ya?" he suggested as he released her.

She sighed, knowing he wasn't going to let it go unless she gave him something more believable. "It wasn't just playing dress-up, it was also having to sit through about a hundred posed photographs with camera lights flashing in my face."

He looked at her expectantly, waiting for her to continue.

She groaned at his persistence. "And then at the reception, as soon as they opened the bar, some piss artist who was already in his cups wanted to get friendly with me."

Quin's eyes darkened. "I hope ya told Pat. If I'd have been there...*Oof*," he grunted and clutched his side where she'd punched him.

"I don't need you or Pat to rescue me, Quinlan Ursan. I can take care of myself."

She gave him a stormy look and he held his hands up in surrender. "That I know ya can, Letty Thresher. But I'll never *not* want to thrash some sot who tries to paw ya at a pub."

She sighed irritably. "He didn't try to paw me, exactly. He was just lushing and being generally annoying."

Quin nodded and clicked his tongue at her. "I see. Well what is it that has ya so out of sorts, then? Because nothing ya've said so far sounds particularly dire."

Scarlett hesitated and Quin's eyes softened. "Ya know ya can tell me anything, Letty."

She knew it was true. Quin had a kind heart and could match wits with anyone in their village, despite his fierce appearance. He would probably even keep her secret if she asked him to.

But she couldn't bring herself to tell him. It was bad enough to admit how powerless she'd been. But it was downright embarrassing to admit that she was still having panic attacks over something that had happened almost two hundred years ago.

She massaged her temple and tried to think of an explanation he'd accept. Before she realized what she was doing, she found herself telling him about Agent Derrington.

"I went for a walk to clear my head and I came across a man. He was lurking in the darkness near some bushes, and I assumed he was up to no good, so I attacked him. He turned out to be a policeman."

Quin's eyes widened. "Ya attacked a human peeler?" he asked

incredulously. "What did he do?"

Scarlett nibbled her lip and tried not to smile. "He defended himself. Quite vigorously."

Quin roared with laughter, startling a nearby class of trainees and earning a stern look from old Fianna, who was leading them in a meditation exercise. Quin mouthed an apology and placed a hand on Scarlett's back to lead her to a more secluded corner.

"Bad craic, Letty! Was he very angry? He didn't try to arrest ya did he?" He snorted with mirth, as if the thought amused more than concerned him.

Scarlett chuckled. "No. We had a bit of a tussle. Then he backed off and tried to reassure me that he was no threat."

"I'll bet he did," Quin grunted, pride and affection shining in his eyes. "Mustn't have taken him long to realize he wouldn't best ya in a fight. But why was he lurkin' in the bushes in the first place?"

Scarlett shifted uncomfortably. "He said he was investigating a murder. But the strange thing is, Quin, I smelled a Morpheus potion on him. I use it for insomnia sometimes and it's very…distinctive. That's why I was so quick to attack him. I thought he meant to use it on me."

A deep crease appeared between Quin's bushy brows. "What the bollox would a human policeman be doin' with a Morpheus potion?"

"I don't think he had one," she replied quietly. "I think he picked up the scent from his crime scene."

Quin's eyes widened in understanding. "Shite, did ya tell Pat?"

Scarlett shook her head. "Not yet," she admitted. "We got into a bit of a tiff at the wedding and I haven't spoken to him since."

"Ah, Letty," he said softly, "I know ya don't want to admit how hard it was for ya to see Pat with his new lady friend at yer brother's weddin'. But if ya think someone from our realm murdered a human, ya've got to tell him."

Scarlett blinked at him with the dawning comprehension that he thought the cause of her 'narkiness' in the sparring ring was her supposed unrequited love for Pat. The realization both relieved and annoyed her.

She'd never seen fit to correct the assumptions that she was holding a torch for Pat. Letting her kin believe that was easier than explaining why she'd never been interested in dating someone else.

But for Quin to believe that she'd withhold information from Pat about such a horrible crime because of it…well, that was just insulting.

"I'm not bajanxed, Quin," she snapped. "I have every intention of telling him."

"Of course ya do," he agreed quickly. "I didn't mean to suggest…" he faltered, his massive, heavily inked shoulders drooping in resignation. "I'm sorry, Letty. I've upset ya again, and I didn't mean to."

Her scowl melted away and she sighed. "I know you didn't, Quin. And I'm on my way to tell Pat today."

He smiled in relief and pulled her into a bear hug. "I'm glad we had this talk," he rumbled.

"Me too," she murmured, her remaining annoyance dissolving as she hugged him back.

It was impossible to stay mad at her cousin. Even if he was a giant idiot sometimes.

Chapter 3

Grey stood at the window, looking out at a tall sugar maple that shaded the west side of the house from the afternoon sun. The local police had gone, and the interior was dim and silent.

It was strange how the place already felt stale and uninhabited, as if the house's life-force had been snuffed out with its owner's.

He sighed and walked over to the fish tank. It rested on a long table behind the couch, level with the top of the cushions. He imagined the latest vic, Heather Peters, stretching out and relaxing as she watched its colorful denizens go about their lives behind the glass.

Purple anemones, red sea stars and tiny stalk-eyed crabs littered the sandy floor, while tropical fish of all sizes and hues darted through the rocky coral labyrinth above. A small blue eel and a frilly lionfish were two of the more impressive specimens inhabiting the little underwater universe.

The fish whizzed around erratically when they saw him and he wondered when they'd last been fed. He found containers of flakes and dried shrimp on the shelf below, and sprinkled some of each into the water. He watched as the food was quickly devoured and added some more.

Ms. Peters had obviously taken pride in the saltwater tank. It was well maintained, and probably worth thousands of dollars. It saddened him to think what would happen to all of the beautiful fish now that she was gone.

Hopefully her family would make sure it was taken care of. But in cases like these, maintaining a home where a loved one was murdered was often the last thing on a family member's mind.

Grey had arrived on the scene in time to snap some shots of the body before it was taken to the morgue. He'd also arrived in time to witness the heart wrenching spectacle of Heather Peters' mother driving to her daughter's house in a state of panic and denial.

The local uniforms had tried to keep her away, but they hadn't been able to prevent her from seeing the black body bag rolled out on a stretcher by the coroner. Grey clenched his jaw and rubbed his forehead at the memory.

He knew it wasn't the sheriffs' fault. It wasn't as if they could restrain a terrified mother from driving to her own child's home. It wasn't anyone's fault but the piece of shit psycho who was doing this.

And his.

He'd been chasing the bastard for three months and didn't have a damn thing to show for it but a laughably general profile: white male, age 25-35, probably employed in a position calling for regular interstate travel.

Grey had yet to find any solid connections between the victims. They had different physical characteristics, different jobs, different interests, and lived in different states. They were all raped and strangled by hand, but there were no prints and the crime scenes were all infuriatingly clean. There was an unusual herbal odor at each one, but no residue had been found for the lab to identify.

Grey shook his head and jogged up the stairs to take another look at the bedroom where Heather Peters' boyfriend had found her body. The walls were painted a deep sage green. The color reminded him of light filtering through the trees in a forest.

Book shelves lined the walls on either side of the king sized bed, and a flat screen tv sat inside a large cabinet across from the footboard.

He squatted in front of one of the book shelves, perusing the titles. They were mostly fiction, ranging from romance to fantasy to horror, with a few titles on lucid dreaming and astral travel. So Heather Peters had at least a passing interest in the occult.

That was interesting. He'd found an old Ouija Board at the home of the vic in Texas, and a well-used deck of tarot cards in the nightstand of the New Hampshire vic. The woman in Key Largo had a large dream catcher hanging over her bed, and the one in Colorado had an impressive collection of Native American Kachina dolls displayed throughout her house.

They were all relatively common items, but collectively they might add up to a connection between the victims that he had missed. Or maybe he was just grasping at straws.

A soft thump sounded behind him and he spun around, remaining in a crouch as he scanned the room, his heart kicking in his chest. He straightened, trying to identify the source of the noise, and saw a hand written journal lying open on the wood floor near the book shelves on the other side of the bed.

He crossed the room and bent to pick it up, realizing it must have fallen off the shelf. He smirked at himself for being so jumpy and began reading the flowing script on one of the pages. It was a dream journal. And unlike the tempting fantasies his subconscious had cooked up about his mystery woman while he slept last night, Heather Peters had been having some pretty nasty nightmares.

An entry dated only two days before her death spoke of being trapped in a deep pit in the earth that was slowly being overrun by spiders. It sounded unpleasant to him, but apparently it had filled her with the stark, mindless terror that only a phobia could inspire.

He flipped through and saw that she'd been having similarly horrific dreams for more than a week before her death. Whereas before that, the dreams she'd recorded had been sometimes odd, but mostly mundane reconfigurations of daily existence. Albeit with a few erotic fantasies thrown in.

Grey wondered if she had somehow sensed the coming violence that had ended her life. It was an eerie thought to consider, in the stillness and silence of the room that had been her sanctuary before it had become her death chamber.

His cell phone vibrated in his pocket and he jerked, cursing at his reaction. He needed sleep. His nerves were shot.

"Agent Derrington," he barked, not bothering to check the Caller ID.

"Hey Captain America. You still at the Peters house?" came Liza's steady voice.

Grey released a weary breath. "Yeah."

There was a beat of silence, and then, "I heard her mom came by as they were taking her body out."

Grey ran a hand over his face and sighed. "Yeah. It was a bad scene Lizzie. I really wish it could have been avoided."

"I'm sorry Grey, me too," she replied softly. "Did you find anything new?"

He cleared his throat and reached for the detached professionalism he needed to work the case. "I want you to check for any connections between the victims and the occult. Magic, witchcraft, voodoo, alternative spiritualism...check the websites and forums they visited on their computers, check their credit card receipts for new age type stores, anything you can think of. Try to find something that links all five of them."

"If it's there, I'll find it," she assured him. "Anything else?"

He hesitated and then asked, "Aren't salt water fish tanks one of your hobbies?"

"Yep. I have three at home."

"Well, there's a beautiful one here. And I'm pretty sure taking care of it is the last thing on anyone's mind. If the family wants it, of course it's theirs. But in the meantime I was wondering if you'd be interested in trying to keep the fish alive."

"Love to. I have extra tanks and equipment in my garage. I could come over with a couple of buckets to transport whatever's there."

"That's great, Lizzie. Thanks."

Maybe it was silly to try to save Heather Peters' fish, when what he should have done was catch her murderer in time to save *her*. But it eased his mind to know that at least something she'd cared about, something beautiful and alive, would have a chance to survive.

"Do you want to meet me here after work?" he asked.

"I hate being the bearer of bad tidings again," Liza said with an audible groan. "But there's been another murder, Grey. I'll make arrangements to pick up the fish, but you're on your way back to Florida in an hour—Palm Beach this time."

"How the hell is he doing it?" Grey murmured, torn between anger and despair.

"I don't know, Captain America, but if anyone can catch him it's you."

She sounded as if she truly believed it, and Grey wished his waning confidence matched hers. "He's escalating," he said grimly. "That means he's more likely to make a mistake."

"They all do...eventually," she replied in a bleak tone. "But you'd better get to the airport. I'll text your trip details, but there's some kind of convention going on down there and they haven't found you a hotel room yet."

"Great," he mumbled sourly. "Maybe I can grab a cot at the local police station."

∞∞∞∞∞∞∞∞∞∞

When Scarlett was showered and changed, she blinked to the Peg Station at the outskirts of Seelie City. The city was a bustling metropolis, the largest urban area in the faerie realm, and home to a diverse population of immortal residents.

It was also home to the Seelie Police Station, which was why she couldn't blink directly there. The entire district was protected by a binding spell to keep prisoners from escaping during transportation and confinement. Only high level Seelie employees, like Pat, could bypass it.

Scarlett waited her turn at the Peg Station, nodding politely at a hale dwarven woman with twin half-moon axes strapped to her leather cuirass. The stout warrior leapt onto the back of a kneeling pegasus, giving Scarlett a wave as they trotted past.

A handsome blue roan stepped forward and knelt low for Scarlett to mount, his wings folded tight to his sides. She asked him to drop her at the police station as he rose, and he settled into a comfortable canter with her astride.

Pegs never flew with passengers on their backs unless it was an emergency. Although it was undoubtedly a faster method of travel, they considered it demeaning.

At first there were only soft grasses as far as the eye could see, pegs dotting the meadows as they grazed between fares. Then gradually the city came into view. Its towering buildings of white marble and quartz glistened in the afternoon sunlight, its perpetual haze of faerie dust lending a mystical shimmer to the air.

Scarlett hadn't been to Seelie City for ages, and she murmured softly in appreciation.

"Lovely, ain't it?" rumbled the peg beneath her.

"It's been a while. I'd forgotten how the buildings, and even the air itself, sparkle with faerie magic."

The peg chuckled, the sound vibrating through his barrel chest and into her legs. "It certainly is a sight to see."

"Is Cybele's honey shop still on the main thoroughfare?"

"Yes ma'am."

"Do you mind if we make a pit stop there on the way to the police station? I have a brownie at home who'd love a special treat."

He tossed his head and replied, "Not a problem. You gotta keep the wee folk happy."

Scarlett smiled and nodded in agreement, falling back into silence as the dirt road gave way to even, brick paved streets. Ancient trees with thick, knobby trunks grew in the grassy median. They towered above the tallest buildings, their massive branches spreading out in leafy canopies above the traffic.

Sprites flitted overhead, leaving colorful trails of faerie dust floating behind them to sprinkle down onto the pegs and their riders. As they approached Cybele's shop, *The Queen Bee*, roses and herbs scented the breeze and the buzzing from the charmed bees grew into a steady, musical drone.

The peg slowed to a stop at the curb beside the shop and knelt for Scarlett to dismount.

"I'll only be a few minutes," she promised as she peppered his muzzle with some of the oatcake spell she'd brought.

"Take your time," he replied, whickering his thanks.

She passed beneath a trellis blooming with lavender and white roses and entered the shop. From the outside it appeared to be a small storefront bordered closely by its neighbors. But expansion spells and other enchantments transformed the inside into a bright, sprawling flower garden with walking paths and whimsical stone fountains that watered the blooms.

Honeybees darted about, gathering pollen and returning to their hives, one of which was perched atop the shop-keeper's head like a giant, fanciful hat.

"Welcome, daughter of the sidhe," Cybele greeted, her voice carrying a wavering vibrato reminiscent of her bees. "Can I help you find anything?"

Scarlett dipped her head in respect as she approached the tall, robed woman. Legend had it that long ago, when the veil between the faerie and human realms was thin, Cybele had taken up the mantle of a warrior goddess to the humans. It was said that later she forsook her axe to become one of their most potent fertility goddesses.

The tales were steeped in the mists of time, but regardless of their veracity, she was a mysterious and powerful being. Her aura pulsed with strength, and standing beside her was a bit like standing at the foot of an ancient mountain.

"Well, my brownie friend 'forgot' to put the lid back on the honey jar this morning," Scarlett explained with a rueful smile. "So I guess I'm getting a little low on supplies."

Cybele gave a hearty laugh. "Is there any variety in particular that your wee friend prefers?"

"I usually just buy the local clover honey for our tea. But I was hoping to surprise him with something a tad more exotic."

"You've come to the right place," Cybele assured her. "I have some gorgeous herbal varieties at the moment. The rosemary in particular is quite lovely. Come, let me give you a sample."

Scarlett followed her to the honey bar and accepted a tiny spoon of the ambrosial nectar, groaning at the amazing impression it left on her tongue. She tried a few more, thinking she'd love to linger in the beautiful gardens and taste honey all day. But she was aware of the peg waiting for her outside.

Reluctantly, she wrapped up her selections and exited *The Queen Bee* with her coin purse lighter and her sweet tooth satisfied. Any moment now, a large box with an assortment of gourmet honeys and biscuits would appear on her kitchen counter.

She had no doubt it would be unpacked and Bradan would have a blissfully full belly by the time she arrived home.

The blue roan peg remained patiently at the curb, and she sat astride him once more as he carried her on to the Seelie Police Station. She thanked him for his service and gave him some more of the oatcake spell before he trotted away.

She hesitated on the sidewalk in front of the entrance to the official-looking building. The Seelie Police Station was the largest complex in the city, housing not only the station, but also the prison.

As with most of the city's structures, it was laden with spells and enchantments that allowed it to take up far less space on the outside than it did inside. And it was easy to forget that a high security prison lay just behind it, since the austere penal complex was only visible when exiting from the back of the station house.

She took a nervous breath and went in. She knew she'd been a git to needle Pat about his soul mate. She hoped he wasn't too mad at her.

"Well, if it isn't young Scarlett Thresher!" exclaimed the shaggy-bearded dwarf behind the front counter. "What brings you to our fair city, lass?"

Scarlett grinned and leaned forward to kiss his wizened brown cheek. "Galen. It's wonderful to see you. How are you?"

"Can't complain, lass, can't complain."

"Not even about the troubles with goblins and the depredations of dragons?" Scarlett asked with a mischievous glint in her eye.

Galen snorted. "You always were a bit of a wise ass, Letty."

Scarlett laughed. "How's your sister doing?"

"Galena? She's as ornery as ever. Still runnin' covert missions for the force. She's gotten so good at disguises, I swear sometimes even I don't recognize her."

"She always was clever," Scarlett said fondly.

"Don't tell her that," Galen grunted. "It'll go straight to her fat head."

Scarlett scowled at him.

"You know I'm just teasin', lass," he said with a chuckle. "So what is it that brings you to the police station this fine afternoon? No crimes to report, I hope."

"I'm not sure," she replied with a sigh. "I need to speak with Pat about something that happened in the human realm. I think an immortal may have killed a woman there."

Galen blew a breath out through his teeth. "Breaches between our worlds seem to be happenin' more and more of late. Makes you wonder if the veil between the realms might be slippin', whether the Seelie Court likes it or not."

He shook his head. "I'll get Pat for ya. He's locked himself in his office to finish up some paperwork, but I'm certain he'll be glad to see you."

"I'm not so sure," she muttered as he hopped down from his stool and disappeared through the doorway behind him.

Scarlett fidgeted as she waited, questioning her plan to show up unannounced at Pat's workplace. She'd almost lost her nerve by the time Galen returned to the lobby with Pat in tow.

"Letty? What are you doing here?" Pat asked, looking concerned.

"I need to talk to you about last night."

He raised a dark brow and crossed his muscular arms over his chest. "What about it?"

Scarlett puffed in annoyance. He obviously wasn't in the mood to make things easy for her. "In private, Pat." She looked at the dwarf apologetically. "No offense, Galen."

"None taken," he replied in a gruff tone as he nimbly climbed back up onto his stool. He looked askance at Pat. "Give the lady a break, Sparrow, she came a long way to see you."

Pat rolled his eyes and dropped his arms to his sides. "Fine. Follow me, Letty."

He strode back through the doorway behind the counter and she rushed to catch up with him before he disappeared from sight. A few of the younger police officers were hanging out at a cluster of desks in the room beyond. The smell of burnt coffee was heavy in the air.

She followed Pat toward his office, holding her tongue as she hurried down the hallway behind him. He opened a door at the end of the corridor, and led her inside a small room with two desks and a rolling leather chair positioned between them.

"I'm sorry, Pat," she said as soon as he closed the door.

He looked like she'd caught him off guard, so she pressed on.

"Whatever is between you and your human...*Sydney*," she added at his warning look, "is none of my business. I was feeling a bit off my nut after being surrounded by humans all day. But that's no excuse. You're one of my oldest friends, and I shouldn't have bashed your relationship."

Pat's office chair groaned beneath his weight as he dropped into it. He exhaled, his blue eyes boring into hers, as if he was trying to figure out how to respond.

"Letty," he said finally, "I know how you feel about humans. And I know why you feel that way. But Sydney is my soul mate. I've waited my entire life to find her, and I don't have the words to tell you how important she is to me. You're going to have to accept that, when it comes to her, I have no patience for your prejudices."

Scarlett swallowed and nodded. "I know, Pat. I'm going to try harder to get my head straight about the human thing." She grimaced. "Between you and Doyle, I'm going to have to. It's just that it's...difficult for me to spend time in their realm. It brings up memories that I can't seem to let go. No matter how hard I try."

The sorrow in Pat's eyes was so sharp it should have cut her. "You've never told anyone what happened, have you?"

She looked away, unable to hold his gaze. "I can't. It would make it too real. It's bad enough that you know." She realized she was picking at her finger again and she wrapped her other hand around it, hiding it from view.

"It *is* real, Letty," he said softly. "It happened. You were only sixteen, and you were raped. It shouldn't have happened, and it wasn't your fault, but it did happen. And it's not something you're just going to be able to 'let go'. Keeping it a secret is like leaving an open wound untreated. It can't help but to fester. Don't you know that by now?"

She took a shaky breath, and admitted to herself that he might be right. But when she played through the scenarios of talking about it with her mother, her father, her brother...it was simply too awful. She shook her head in denial. "I can't. I just can't, Pat, okay? Not right now."

She hadn't seen him move, but suddenly he was standing beside her. He enfolded her in a fierce hug and she stiffened in his arms.

"I'm so sorry, Letty," he murmured brokenly. "You'll never know how sorry I am that I didn't get there sooner. But you have to promise me you'll deal with it. You can't let it fester any longer. It's like a shadow that's been hanging over you your entire life, and I can't bear to see it anymore. I want to see you happy."

His words hit her with quiet force, his sympathy breaking apart the fragile barrier she'd been working all day to erect against the memories.

A sob shuddered through her frame and tears rolled down her cheeks, soaking into his white cotton shirt as she hid her face from him.

Her muscles began to shake, as if the past had become a physical weight she could no longer carry. Finally she relented and sagged in his embrace, allowing him to hold her as she wept.

She didn't know how long she cried, but as her tears began to subside, she was mortified that she'd broken down in front of him. She cleared her throat and tried to pull away.

"I'm sorry," she whispered raggedly.

He grasped her shoulders and gave her a stern shake. "Don't you do that, Letty Thresher," he insisted. "You've had nigh on a hundred and eighty years of holding that shite in, and you deserve to let it out."

There was a catch in his voice, and when she lifted her gaze, his eyes were moist. She let out a fractured laugh, loving him more in that moment than she ever had.

"You sappy wanker," she sniffed, giving him a tremulous smile. "Is this what I can expect from you and Doyle now that you're both in *love*? A bunch of talking about our feelings and weeping like little girls?"

He chuckled. "You are such a hard ass. And I'm so going to remind you of it when you find your soul mate and turn into a big, sappy puddle of goo every time he comes near you."

Scarlett snorted. "Please. Never going to happen."

"I'll bet you a shot of whiskey you will," he goaded.

"You're on," Scarlett agreed confidently as she brushed away the last of her tears.

"We'll see," he taunted. He tweaked her nose and retreated behind his desk before she could retaliate. "And one more thing, Letty," he added.

She raised a brow at him.

"Crying doesn't make you weak." He held her gaze stubbornly until her lips twitched and she accepted his words with a slight nod.

He grinned. "Well, now that that's sorted, didn't I interrupt you groveling for forgiveness or something?" he asked, dodging her half-hearted punch.

"Actually, there is something…" she sighed. She told him about her encounter with Agent Greyson Derrington of the FBI and the Morpheus potion she'd smelled on him.

"He must have picked up the scent at the murder scene," she insisted.

Pat frowned at her. "Are you certain he was human?"

She gave him a dry look.

"Right. Stupid question," he apologized. "But has it occurred to you that he might not have been who he said he was? Maybe he made the whole thing up, or maybe he *was* the killer, and you scared him off when he realized he couldn't subdue you."

Scarlett shook her head slowly. She could still see Agent Derrington's dark, mesmerizing eyes as he tried to show her his badge and explain what he was doing standing in the shadowy yard.

"He was telling the truth. I'd bet my life on it."

Pat leaned back in his chair, astonishment etching his features as he stared at her. "You'd bet your life that a *human* was telling you the truth," he repeated.

She squeezed her eyes shut, knowing how crazy that sounded coming from her. Her reaction to Agent Derrington confused her, but she knew she was right about him.

"Just run a check on him, will you?" she demanded in exasperation.

Pat leaned forward to type something into his computer system, glancing up at her as he waited for the results. The calculating gleam in his eyes made her feel edgy.

"Greyson Derrington," he read, taking in the features of the rugged black man pictured on the screen. "Male, age thirty-seven, Lead Investigator for the Federal Bureau of Investigation's Behavioral Analysis Unit Two, specializing in serial and mass murders, sexual assault, kidnapping, and other crimes targeting adults…"

"Let me see that," she interrupted, hopping around his desk to read over his shoulder. "Military background consisting of eight years in the United States Marine Corp," she continued reading in a murmur, "six of which were spent in Forces Special Operations Command."

Pat whistled. "No wonder this guy almost kicked your butt. Those Special Ops guys are bad ass."

She jabbed him in the shoulder. "I didn't say he almost kicked my butt; I said we were evenly matched," she huffed. "And he said he was with the FBI—what's that?"

"That's the Federal Bureau of Investigation." Pat grunted at her blank look. "He's like a detective that has jurisdiction over his entire country. It's an elite human law enforcement organization for the United States."

Her lips rose in a slow smile. "So he kind of has the human realm's equivalent of your job. Scroll down. What else does it say?"

He tapped a key and the screen went blank. "Why are you so interested?" he asked with a smirk.

"I'm not!" she exclaimed defensively. "But I was obviously right about this guy telling the truth, so why don't you quit wasting time and see what you can find out about a woman being murdered down the street from Doyle?" She crossed her arms over her chest and glared at him.

Pat snorted, his smug expression making her want to smack him. He tapped another key and the screen on Agent Derrington popped back into view. Then he typed a quick command and they were looking at a summary of Derrington's current case files.

The names of five women were highlighted in red with the word DECEASED next to them in all capital letters. The teasing look faded from Pat's eyes as he scanned through the details of each file.

"Dragon dung," he cursed softly. "This is bad, Letty.

Chapter 4

Bile rose in Scarlett's throat as she read the bullet points that tied each of the five murders together. The women had all been raped and the man had strangled them to death with his bare hands. A 'distinctive herbal odor' had been noted at each crime scene, but no residue had been found to enable an identification of the substance.

"Let me show you something," Pat said. He clicked on a small icon in the upper corner of the screen and the image changed before she could get into the more grisly details.

A map of the human globe appeared, with tiny red dots flashing across every land mass. He zoomed into the western hemisphere, then zoomed further down to a map of North America, and finally settled on the United States.

"What is this?" she asked, her gaze travelling over what must have been hundreds of thousands of blinking red dots scattered across the country.

"It's a tracking program that some of the mages put together for us. Each of these dots represents a human who is aware of our realm in some way."

Scarlett's eyes widened. "All of these humans know we exist?"

Pat chuckled. "No, not exactly." He clicked on Florida and the map zoomed in to an image of the state. He pointed to a cluster of red dots along the southeast coast. "Do you see a green dot in there somewhere?"

Scarlett squinted and shook her head.

He clicked twice more, finally zooming in to a map of the town of Palm Beach. And then she saw it, a lone green dot amongst all the red.

"That's Sydney," he said with a vague smile. "Some humans, like Sydney and Violet, are fully aware of our realm and have even visited it. But they are only a tiny percentage.

"The rest are merely aware on a subconscious level. Some are fascinated by legends of Faerie and a part of them accepts the stories as truth. Some have dabbled in spellcraft and possess the ability to become mages, whether they realize it or not. But whatever the reason, the veil between our realms is thinner for them than it is for other humans."

"I had no idea so many of them were so close to believing in us," Scarlett said faintly.

Pat leaned back and sighed. "It's of grave concern to the Seelie Court. Most of them believe the balance between good and evil would be thrown into chaos if the veil were lifted for so many."

Scarlett didn't know what to say. She had never imagined such a thing was possible. "So what does this have to do with Agent Derrington's investigation?"

Pat reached forward to click on another icon and all of the red dots, as well as Sydney's single green dot, were replaced by black ones.

"What are those?" Scarlett asked, a sense of foreboding pricking at her spine.

"They represent all of the humans who once had red or green dots on the map, but who are now deceased. There's a symbol, only viewable by someone using this system, next to each of the names of the murdered women your Agent Derrington is investigating."

He reopened the screen with the case files and pointed out the small star-shaped emblems next to each name.

"Those symbols tell me that each one of these women is pinpointed on our map. They would have once had either red or green dots, but now they'll have been added to the map with the black dots."

Scarlett blinked at him. "So you're saying that all five of them either knew about us, or were close to believing in our realm?"

Pat nodded, looking troubled.

"The woman in Key Largo was certainly fascinated by garden gnomes," Scarlett murmured as she recalled almost tripping over one of them after her fight with Agent Derrington. "So what does this mean?" she asked. "Do you think someone from our realm is targeting human women because of your map?"

"Highly unlikely," he said. "Only a few of us have access to it, and you've seen how many humans are marked on it. No, what I'm thinking is that someone from our realm is targeting human women through his own connection with them. The map simply proves that the connection exists."

"Oh no," Scarlett breathed, her eyes fixated on the screen.

"What?" he asked, his concerned gaze following hers.

"Another name just appeared on the list of victims."

"Sarah Wentworth," he read in a startled voice. "And she has a symbol by her name too. I think you're right, Letty. I'm definitely going to have to look into this. If an immortal is committing these crimes, and using magic to subdue his victims and hide his tracks, the human police will never be able to stop him."

"Is all of this happening right down the street from Doyle?" she asked in alarm.

Pat clicked the first name on the list. "Nashua, New Hampshire," he murmured as he returned to the previous screen to click on the second name. "Denver, Colorado," he continued, going back for the rest of the names. "Fort Worth, Texas...Key Largo, Florida...Woodbridge, Virginia... and...holy shite," he cursed, turning pale.

"Palm Beach, Florida," Scarlett finished for him.

He stood abruptly. "That's right down the street from Sydney's penthouse. I have to go."

He grabbed his sports jacket from the back of his chair and shrugged it on, looking more panicked than Scarlett had ever seen him.

"Wait," she demanded, placing a hand on his arm. "Are you going to check out the crime scene?"

"As soon as I check on Sydney, yes," he replied impatiently.

"I'm coming with you."

"The hell you are!" he scoffed. "This will probably turn into an official Seelie investigation, not to mention you hate going to the human realm."

"What are you going to say if you run into Agent Derrington?" she challenged. "He'll recognize me from Key Largo. We can say we're with the local human police and wanted to investigate both crime scenes since they're so close to each other."

"Of all the troll brained ideas you've ever had, Letty, that has to be the worst! There will be no 'running into' Agent Derrington. I've had run-ins with the human authorities in the past, and I learned long ago that the less contact we have with them, the better it is for everyone involved."

Pat shook his head. "No. I'll go check out the scene after the human police leave."

She crossed her arms over her chest and her eyes narrowed with a steely glint he knew all too well. "I'm coming with you."

He cursed in frustration. "Why is this so important to you, Letty?"

She looked flustered, as if she wasn't sure of the answer herself. Then she glared at him as if it was his fault for asking. "I have my reasons," she insisted stubbornly. "Not to mention, I have the address. So I'll find my way there with or without you."

"You are a giant pain in my ass," he accused. "I'd lock you in a cell 'til I get back, but Galen would probably let you out."

She arched a brow at him. "Galen would definitely let me out. And that's assuming you could get me in a cell in the first place."

He curled his lip at her. "Fine. Come on then, I don't have time to argue with you."

He held his arms out and she stepped into them. "But you will be nice to Sydney, and you will follow my lead at the crime scene. And *not touch anything*," he emphasized.

"Agreed," she conceded.

"Why do I have the feeling I'm going to regret this?" he muttered as he blinked them out of the station.

They touched down in a bright, enclosed space between two doors. Scarlett's brow knitted in confusion as she took in the tiny, cheerful room. Oddly, the paintings, candles and welcome mat all depicted frogs.

Laughter spilled from beyond one of the doors, and on closer inspection, Scarlett realized that the second door led to a human contraption called an 'elevator'.

Pat knocked and there was a shushing sound, followed by a few beats of silence. Then a renewed bout of giggles grew louder as someone neared the door. Pat's human, Sydney, threw it open and rushed into his arms.

"Sparrow, I didn't expect you until later!"

He pulled her into his chest and held her for a moment, then bent his head to claim her lips in a slow, heated kiss.

Scarlett averted her eyes, wondering why Pat's soul mate insisted on calling him by his last name, as she waited for their kiss to end.

"Not that I'm complaining, but what was that for?" Sydney murmured finally.

"I'm just very happy to see you." He reached up to brush a strand of hair from her face. "And I wanted to make sure you were alright. Scarlett gave me some disturbing news today about the possibility of an immortal preying on human women."

"Another death djinn?" Sydney asked in disgust.

"We're not sure," he replied. "But there was a murder not far from here and I need to take a look at the crime scene. I brought Scarlett along."

He stepped to the side so that the women could see each other. "I believe you two met at Doyle and Violet's wedding."

Sydney's cheeks colored as she smoothed the hair that he had rumpled during their kiss. She managed to look charming even in an old t-shirt, shorts and bare feet. "Oh, hi...come on in!"

Scarlett started past the woman, but Pat nudged her with his elbow. She realized she was being rude and muttered, "Sorry." She was so used to avoiding contact with humans that being silent around them was a default behavior for her.

She cleared her throat. "Thank you for inviting me into your home, Sydney," she said in a stilted voice. She glanced at Pat for approval and his lips twitched as if he was trying to hide a smile. She glared at him and strode into Sydney's dwelling.

A wooden table lay to the right, its surface littered with papers, files and small machinery.

"I use the dining room as my office, so it's kind of a mess," Sydney apologized as she followed Scarlett's gaze. "Why don't we sit in the living room?" She pointed toward the area beyond.

"Where are we?" Scarlett murmured as her eyes widened to take in a wall of glass that looked out on the ocean, glistening far below them in the fading afternoon light.

Sydney gave her a confused look.

"Your home is as high as a pegasus' aerie!" she exclaimed.

Sydney grinned. "Oh, that! We're in the tenth storey penthouse of a hotel. I guess it would be disconcerting, blinking up here for the first time and not knowing that."

"You live in a hotel?" Scarlett asked in surprise.

"I know it's a little strange, but this penthouse is one of my ill gotten gains from my death djinn contract," Sydney replied with a laugh as she padded over to a corner bar and grabbed a couple of tall, stemmed glasses. "Would you like some champagne?"

"Death djinn contract?" Scarlett echoed, glancing at Pat in alarm. He'd lost his mother to a death djinn when he was only a child. She couldn't believe he would be so relaxed about them having a contract out for his soul mate.

"She got hers voided," piped a smug voice.

Scarlett followed the sound until her gaze rested on one of the strangest sights she'd ever seen. A sprite sat on a glass tabletop in front of the sofa, her bare feet swinging over the edge. She was dwarfed by the bottle of wine she leaned against, and as she took a dainty sip from a tiny earthenware jug, she erupted into a fit of hiccups.

A stream of miniscule bubbles floated from her mouth, drifting down toward a black cat that lay on the carpet below her. It rolled playfully on its back, batting at the bubbles with a fluffy paw.

The sprite giggled and then shot up into the air, jarring the bottle so that it teetered on the edge of the table. Sydney grabbed it before it could tip over, curling her lip at the faerie as she poured two more glasses and set the wine safely out of the way.

The sprite flew toward Scarlett, green dust sprinkling in an unsteady path behind her. "Hi, I'm Lorien. I'm Sydney's faerie guardian." She lifted a hand to cover another hiccup and grinned, her silvery skin glowing with mirth.

"Good day, little sister, I'm Scarlett." Her lips twitched in humor. "I see it's happy hour here in the human realm."

"I'm afraid I have a bit of a weakness for champagne," Lorien admitted on a loud whisper. "But the effects don't last long—quick metabolism. Come have a drink with us. I hear you're something of a legend with a sword."

Scarlett gave the faerie a wary look as she followed her to the sitting area. She lowered herself onto the smaller sofa, while Pat and Sydney shared the larger one.

"Who told you that?" she asked, wondering, not for the first time, what Pat might have told his human about her.

Sydney handed her a glass and she murmured her thanks as she stared curiously at Lorien.

"I was at your brother and Violet's bonding ceremony in our realm," Lorien explained. "My sister is Violet's faerie guardian."

Scarlett had avoided Sydney during that event, so it wasn't surprising that she hadn't met the cheeky sprite who watched over her.

Lorien grinned. "Your kin were bragging about you."

"She can kick my ass with a sword, that's for sure," Pat said drily.

"I can kick your ass *without* one," Scarlett retorted.

Lorien snickered and Sydney let out a bark of laughter.

Scarlett's cheeks heated and she added, "I teach sword technique to our young warriors, so I have to keep my skills sharp."

"Really?" Sydney asked. "My best friend Sunny teaches college, so her students are probably about the same age group as yours. Is that your full time job?"

"Yes," Scarlett replied in a guarded tone. She was surprised at the genuine interest in Sydney's expression.

Pat made a face at her behind Sydney's back and motioned with his hand for her to keep talking.

Scarlett cleared her throat, unused to conversing with humans, but aware of the promise she'd made to be nice to Sydney.

"I teach five days a week, primarily the young warriors from our village, but sometimes trainees come in from the surrounding villages as well."

"Cool. Sunny specializes in medieval literature. So I guess you teach your students how to use swords, and she teaches hers about people who fought with them long ago," Sydney said with a smile.

"Your histories are littered with tales of humans who unknowingly fought alongside the sidhe," Scarlett replied stiffly. "Many of the sword techniques your people used were learned from us."

"Really? You'll have to sit down with Sunny some time and let her pick your brain. I'm sure she'd love to hear anything you have to say about that time period."

Scarlett shifted uncomfortably at the thought of allowing another human to 'pick her brain'. She took a sip of her drink to avoid answering, and made a surprised sound of pleasure at the taste.

"It's good, right?" Sydney commented. "This penthouse came with a case of it and Lorien and I have been addicted ever since. It's pricey but, since I don't have a mortgage payment anymore, I can justify splurging on it."

"I think you go through about a case of that stuff a week," Sparrow teased.

"I usually have help," Sydney defended laughingly.

"Yeah, Sunny's usually here to drink with us," Lorien said. "Speaking of which, when's her next visit?"

"In a couple of weeks," Sydney replied. "She's presenting an academic paper at a conference in France in a few days, and she may extend her stay to hang out in Paris. I'm so jealous!"

"Have you ever been to Paris?" Sparrow asked, his thumb idly brushing her shoulder.

"No, but my mom says it's beautiful."

"Maybe we can meet Sunny there for dinner one evening," he suggested.

Sydney twisted on the sofa to face him, excitement lighting her eyes. "Seriously?"

Sparrow smiled at her and nodded.

"They can be a little nauseating, can't they?" Lorien asked from the side of her mouth.

Scarlett transferred her startled gaze to the faerie. She realized she'd been staring at the couple, but it was intriguing to see Pat acting the man-in-love. She was used to his tough detective side, and his teasing brotherly side, but this was a side of him she'd never witnessed.

It was just as strange to see her beach-bunny-chasing brother suddenly all doe eyed over his new wife, Violet. The fact that both women were human only added to the surrealism. Not that she disapproved, exactly. She was surprised by how much she liked them.

An image of Agent Derrington popped into her mind, and she wondered why she couldn't seem to shake him from her thoughts.

Not that it mattered. She would probably never see him again. Pat had made it clear that he had no intention of making their presence known to the human authorities.

Perhaps she was just feeling a little adrift because Pat and Doyle had found their soul mates. The last time she'd felt such an inexplicable fascination for a male had been when she was a teenager.

Acting on that feeling had been the worst mistake of her life.

This felt much different though. Back then she had been focused solely on how *he* reacted to her. With Agent Derrington, it was more that something deep within *her* reacted to him.

A soft *wuffing* sound escaped her throat as the hefty black cat jumped onto her lap, effectively derailing her unsettling train of thought.

"Oh sorry! That's Jasper," Sydney apologized as she extricated herself from Sparrow's embrace and started to lunge for the feline.

"No. It's okay. I like animals." Scarlett maneuvered the cat into a more comfortable position and stroked his silky fur.

"My brother has an Irish wolfhound," Scarlett murmured as she ran her palm along the cat's long, white-tipped tail. "He's as big as a baby peg. He loves to play with the fallen palm fronds in Doyle's back yard."

"Well, Jasper certainly seems to like you," Sydney remarked as she refilled their glasses and dropped back onto the couch next to Sparrow. "Do you have any pets?"

Scarlett shook her head. "We don't have the same issues with animals needing homes as you do in your realm. Most of the animals of Faerie possess a certain...magical awareness. They are independent creatures in their own right. Some may choose to live with us, but we do not own them or make such choices for them."

Sydney turned to the hiccupping sprite and asked, "What about your nephew's pet frog? Is he magical?"

"Buster?" Lorien asked in amusement. "He's not magical in the sense that he can cast spells, but he's unlike any frog you'd find in the human realm. He injured one of his back legs years ago and my sister cured him. He never strayed far from our home after that. When my nephew was born, they developed a bond, and Buster chose to live as part of our family."

Scarlett grinned at the faerie. "So the sprite child riding the frog across the aisle in the middle of Doyle and Violet's bonding ceremony must have been your nephew."

Lorien rolled her eyes and covered her mouth to stifle a stream of bubbles. "He can be a handful. Turn your back for a second and he's halfway to Seelie City—drives my sister batty."

Scarlett chuckled and took another sip of her drink. She scratched the purring cat under his chin and looked out the wall of glass at the bruised purples and oranges of the darkening sky.

It was strange to realize that, despite being in the home of a human, she was actually beginning to relax and enjoy herself. It made her regret leaving her brother's wedding events early and missing out on celebrating with him.

Perhaps she could have made more of an effort to get to know Pat and Doyle's human women, especially when they had been guests in her own realm.

"It's getting late," Pat commented. "The human authorities may have left the crime scene for the night. I should blink over and check it out."

"You said a woman might have been murdered by someone from the faerie realm," Sydney said with a frown. "What happened?"

Sparrow sighed. "Scarlett brought it to my attention today. There have been a series of rapes and murders across the country and the FBI believes they were all committed by the same man. When I ran the case through a program at Seelie Headquarters, I realized that all of the women had a periphery connection to the faerie realm."

"That's horrible!" Sydney exclaimed. "What kind of connection? And how did you find out about it, Scarlett?"

Scarlett glanced at Pat, unsure how much she should tell his human. "I stumbled across it by accident," she replied evasively.

Pat smirked at her. "Scarlett got into a fistfight with the FBI agent who's heading up the case. She got suspicious when she smelled a magical sidhe sleeping potion at his crime scene."

"A fistfight?" Sydney asked in disbelief. "With an FBI agent?"

"Yes. And apparently he was a skilled enough opponent to pique her interest. Right Letty?" Pat teased.

Scarlett glared at him. "That has nothing to do with anything," she stammered her accent thickening with embarrassment. "And I gave you that information so you could stop a crime, not use it to take the mickey out of me."

Sydney punched Sparrow in the shoulder. "Yeah. Leave her alone, you big bully."

Scarlett gave her a startled look, as if she couldn't understand why Sydney would side with her over Pat.

Sydney snickered at Sparrow's indignant expression and the other woman's confusion. "What? Haven't you guys ever heard of female solidarity?"

Pat shook his head at Scarlett. "I knew I was going to regret bringing you with me," he accused.

Sydney narrowed laughing eyes at Scarlett. "Don't get me wrong. I definitely want to hear more about your FBI agent. But first tell me how these women were connected to the faerie realm," she said with a concerned look at Sparrow.

"We're not sure yet. And I want you to be very careful until we figure it out," he replied in a serious tone. "If this psycho is choosing his victims based on that connection, you could be at risk."

He turned his worried gaze on Lorien. "So both of you, keep an eye out for any sign of danger. And let me know immediately if you sense something. Okay?"

"Consider us on high alert," Lorien replied with a jaunty salute.

"And be sure to let your sister know what's going on," he added, "since Violet could be a target as well."

"Oh, dragon dung," Lorien murmured unhappily.

"What's wrong?" Sydney asked.

Lorien sighed. "This is going to put my sister into a complete panic. Her ability to sense danger tends to go on the fritz when another immortal is involved."

Sydney grimaced in sympathy.

Pat looked askance at Scarlett. "Are you sure you wouldn't be more comfortable hanging out here? I won't be long."

"Don't even try it," she said as she stood. "I told you I was coming with you, and I haven't changed my mind."

"Fine," he replied in a resigned voice. "We'll see you ladies later." He winked at Lorien and kissed Sydney soundly on the lips.

"Do you know where we're going?" he asked Scarlett.

"Committed it to memory." She smirked. "In case you tried to ditch me."

"Of course you did," he drawled in a long suffering tone. "While you're at it, commit *this* to memory—there may be people around. So stay out of sight when you blink in."

"*Thanks, Captain Obvious,*" Scarlett muttered beneath her breath.

Chapter 5

Burr sneered as he watched the blonde fold a fluffy white sweater. This one was called Marianne, and from what he'd seen, most of her dreams were pathetic and mundane. It was as if her dull human mind was caught in a loop of repetitive tasks from her life.

This time she was packing a suitcase, her ponytail bobbing as she muttered to herself about how she was going to miss her flight. Burr felt her anxiety and breathed its essence deep into himself, feeding off of it and shivering with pleasure as her panic escalated.

But it was too soon in the game to get her worked up. And this wasn't the type of primal fear that he savored most. He fed her a calming suggestion and showed himself to her in a form that he knew she would find pleasing.

She started, unsure what to make of a strange man appearing in her bedroom, clad only in jeans. She wasn't afraid though. It was as if a part of her knew this was a dream. Or perhaps his facade was so attractive that the little slut didn't care.

Burr smiled at her, throwing off languid waves of seduction. "Marianne," he said in a throaty voice, "I've been looking forward to seeing you all day."

She stepped toward him, the suitcase disappearing and her imaginary flight forgotten. "You have?" she asked, clear green eyes sparkling with hope and uncertainty.

He gave a slow nod and extended a hand to her. "Come here, my love," he whispered.

Burr felt her responding to him, felt the moment that she began to accept the fantasy he offered. In turn he made subtle changes to his appearance as he sensed the finer tendrils of her desires. A darker shade of hair, a slightly fuller lip, a gentler arch to his brow...

Her pupils dilated in response and he knew he had her ensnared. He pulled her into his arms, and she exhaled in a soft puff as he slowly lowered his head to kiss her.

He brushed her tongue with his, teasing, not going too deep, just the way she liked it. He cupped her neck with one hand, his thumb caressing her slender nape, his other hand stroking the small of her back. He gave her exactly what she yearned for, and her passion bloomed at his touch.

Her emotion tasted sickly sweet to Burr, an unpalatable mush compared to the deliciously sharp flavors of fear and pain.

But he reigned in his own desires and continued to indulge hers. He hated this stage of the game, but it was necessary. If he played his part with skill, the bitch would begin to crave him in her waking life as well as her dreams.

She would invite him into her psyche, laying herself open to him like a banquet. And then it would be her fears he fed from, instead of her filthy desires. He would touch her lithe, little body the way *he* wanted.

And that fragile neck of hers? He would enjoy watching her gasp and choke for air as he squeezed it.

∞∞∞∞∞∞∞∞∞

Fat, round seagrape bushes dotted the yard of the small white-washed house. It was a throwback to Florida's yesteryear, with its low, flat roof and dated jalousie shutters. But it was on prime real estate, tucked into a corner lot across the street from the pristine shores of Palm Beach proper.

Scarlett and Pat blinked to an inconspicuous spot further down the sidewalk. They started casually toward the property, like any other couple out for an evening stroll.

A silver Bentley convertible was parked beneath an old fashioned carport on the side of the house, but there were no other vehicles in sight. Yellow crime scene tape crossed the front door, fluttering softly in the breeze.

Pat paused to listen, murmuring a detection spell beneath his breath. "There's no one inside," he said after a moment.

"Here, put these on." He pulled a thin pair of latex gloves and shoe covers from an inside pocket of his jacket and handed them to her. "The human lab techs have probably collected their evidence already. But just to be safe, when we blink in, don't…"

"Touch anything, I know," Scarlett finished for him, as she pulled on the latex. She was beginning to feel antsy and unsure about her insistence to come along. There was an uncomfortable aura about this place, as if the murdered woman's horror and pain lingered in the air.

Pat's gloved hand landed on her shoulder and she inhaled sharply. His eyes flickered to hers, heavy with concern.

"Let's just get inside before someone sees us," she muttered, blinking into the house before either of them could further question the wisdom of her doing so.

The place was as tiny as her cottage in the faerie realm. The floors and baseboards were done in distressed white wood that looked crisp and clean against walls painted a foamy sea-green. Beautiful fans of coral were mounted throughout the space as decorative sculptures.

A sliding glass door along the back wall opened onto a quaint patio garden with a canvas umbrella above a wicker table. Flowers bloomed neatly in baskets hanging from upright metal stands.

Pat nudged her and pointed to a small bookshelf built into one wall. Titles like *Supernatural Realms* and *Shamanistic Healing* populated its length.

"Come on," Pat said, motioning toward the door to the bedroom. His voice fell flat against the silence.

Scarlett trailed behind him, stifling a gasp at the sudden, oppressive atmosphere when she crossed the threshold of the room.

"I've felt this at violent crime scenes before," he remarked quietly. "This woman's spirit is not yet at rest. It loiters here, searching for closure, instead of crossing over to the Sea of Souls."

"Is there a way to speak with her?" Scarlett asked, taking measured, calming breaths.

Pat shook his head. "Not likely. Mediums are rare. And when we've used them in the past, the victims' spirits were usually too terrified and confused to give us any intelligible information."

"Do you smell that?" Scarlett asked.

Pat moved closer to the tousled bedcovers and sniffed. "Definitely a Morpheus potion. And it's stronger by the bed."

"You don't think it's one of the sidhe, do you?" Her chest tightened at the thought of one of her own people committing such terrible crimes.

"There's no reason to assume that," he assured her, though his eyes were troubled. "Anyone from our realm could get their hands on a Morpheus potion. I'm going to have to bring a mage in on this to tell for sure though. Between all six crime scenes, hopefully she can pick up on something that will tell us what kind of being we're dealing with."

Scarlett heard a faint click from the other room and her gaze flew to Pat's. "Did you hear that?" she whispered.

She lifted her hand to summon her sword, and Pat grabbed it out of the air with a curt shake of his head. She jerked her fingers away from his, but before he could warn her to blink out, there was a man crouched in the doorway pointing a gun at them.

"FBI. Hands where I can see them," he barked. "NOW!"

Pat lifted his palms in supplication and motioned for Scarlett to do the same. He could see that she was having trouble with the idea, and silently prayed that she didn't do something stupid. Like summon a sword out of thin air in front of an armed human.

"Identify yourselves," the agent demanded.

"Pat Sparrow, Palm Beach PD," he replied calmly.

He hated impersonating the human police, especially to other police officers. But talking to their FBI might reveal useful information. Not to mention Pat recognized him from his online mug shot.

Dark skin, a fighter's physique, and intelligent, piercing eyes beneath a neat skull trim. This was Scarlett's Agent Derrington. And the temptation to bring them together was too much for him to resist. He hadn't seen her show interest in a male in almost two hundred years.

"This is Scarlett Thresher." He jerked his head toward Scarlett. "She's a friend of mine with the Key Largo PD."

It was obvious from the confusion on Derrington's face that he recognized her from their front yard brawl.

"Listen man," Pat continued, trying to create a plausible scenario before Scarlett said something to add to the agent's suspicion. "I know we're not supposed to be here, but I heard about it on my scanner and it's less than a mile from my girlfriend's place.

"Scarlett's in town visiting and we decided to go for a walk and check it out. She said there was a murder a lot like this one down in Largo recently."

Pat could practically see the wheels turning in Derrington's mind as he weighed the probability of the story.

"How did you two get in here?"

Pat gave a chagrinned smile. "I don't want to get anybody in trouble, but the back slider was unlocked. We figured the lab techs had already been through the place, but we were careful not to touch anything." He waggled his gloved fingers at the FBI agent.

Derrington's gun remained pointing steadily at them. He was obviously having a hard time swallowing the coincidence of Scarlett showing up at both crime scenes. Pat couldn't say he blamed the man.

"You two have your badges on you?" the agent challenged.

Pat nodded and glanced down at his jacket. Luckily he never entered this realm without a spell designed to fool human eyes into believing they had seen whatever identification he needed them to see. He might hate situations like this, but he was prepared for them.

"Let's see them. Slowly. One at a time. You first," Derrington told Pat.

∞∞∞∞∞∞∞∞∞

Grey could scarcely believe his eyes. The badass woman of his dreams was here at another one of his crime scenes. It occurred to him that it might not be real. He might still be snoozing on the plane right now. He was certainly sleep deprived enough.

She had looked delectable in that thigh length couture she'd worn while kicking his ass. But she looked even more amazing in skin tight jeans, a black leather vest and boots.

Her presence was making it difficult for him to concentrate. And that was dangerous in his line of work. He narrowed his eyes on her companion and tried to focus.

The man kept one hand up as he slowly reached inside his jacket and pulled out a leather wallet, flipping it over so Grey could see. The badge blurred before his eyes for a moment, and he blinked.

He really needed to get to a hotel and get some sleep.

His vision cleared and the badge resolved into what he recognized as a PBPD shield beneath a card identifying the man as Patrick Sparrow.

He nodded, relaxing his guard. "Sorry about the weapon, Officer Sparrow. You can't be too careful. Especially when you're dealing with an unsub like this one."

"No need to apologize, Agent. As I said, I know we're not really supposed to be here."

Grey holstered his gun and raised a brow at Scarlett. "Officer Thresher? I believe we've met," he said with a lopsided grin.

Pat's eyes widened in an admirable semblance of surprise. "Holy shite. You're the FBI guy she attacked down in Largo?"

"Oh she told you about that, did she?" His curious gaze travelled back to Scarlett. "Why didn't you identify yourself as a police officer the last time we met?"

Scarlett cleared her throat, trying not to appear as nervous as she felt. She was still reeling over seeing him again. Not to mention she had no idea what to do if he asked to see her badge. She didn't know what kind of Seelie magic Pat had up his sleeve, but she was pretty sure she wasn't going to be able to pull one out of her ass.

Pat nudged her and she realized Derrington was still waiting for her to respond. "Uh. I was at my brother's wedding," she said huskily. "I wasn't on duty and I'd been drinking. And to be honest, I was mortified that I'd attacked an FBI agent. I just wanted to get out of there before there was any more trouble."

The words flowed easily from her lips because they were mostly the truth. She silently thanked Pat for his quick thinking in setting up such an easy story for her to play along with.

"Do you do that a lot?" Grey asked with a dimpled grin.

"What? Drink?" Scarlett asked defensively.

Grey's laughter was a rich, smooth sound that resonated in her core. "No. Get into trouble," he clarified.

Scarlett realized he was teasing her and a slow warmth infused her as she drank in his smile and returned it with one of her own.

"I *am* trouble," she returned softly.

"I don't doubt that for a second." Something flashed in his dark eyes that made her heart skip a beat. "And I definitely want you on my side the next time I'm in a fight."

"You just name the time and place, Agent Derrington," she replied.

"Please, call me Grey," he requested.

"Grey," she intoned, "I'm Scarlett."

Jesus, it made him a little hard just to hear her musical brogue caress his name. Grey swore to himself. If she ever physically caressed him like that, he'd probably explode.

Pat watched as Scarlett flushed prettily beneath Derrington's gaze. Well he'd be damned. She was actually flirting with a male—a *human* one. He'd have never believed it if he hadn't seen it for himself.

And from what he'd seen of Derrington's bio, the guy might just be perfect for Scarlett. Now how to keep the two of them together for a while?

Pat cleared his throat. "I don't want to step on any toes," he hedged, "but it's obvious this case and the Largo one are serials. Otherwise the FBI wouldn't be involved."

Grey sighed and ran his hand over his skull trim. "I usually work with the county sheriffs instead of the local PD's. But it's no secret what kind of monster we're dealing with here. And frankly, the more local cooperation we have, the easier it's going to be to catch this guy."

Pat smiled. "I'm real happy to hear you say that, man. Like I said, my girlfriend lives right up the street from here, and Scarlett's brother and sister-in-law live less than a mile from the victim in Key Largo. We'll do anything we can to help. This psycho is hitting a little too close to home for all of us."

He frowned as if a thought had just come to him. "Hey, I don't know where you're bunking tonight, but can Scarlett and I buy you a drink before you head out?"

"I may not be the best company," Grey warned. "I've had about three hours of sleep in the last three days."

The FBI agent looked uncertain. But Pat could tell from the smile he flashed Scarlett that he didn't want to refuse a drink with her no matter how tired he was.

"That's rough," Pat sympathized. "My girlfriend's waiting for us to get back, and her penthouse is in the hotel just up the street. A drink there would be quick and we've got an idea about the case we'd like to bounce off of you. I promise we won't keep you long."

Grey glanced around the bedroom. That familiar herbal smell lingered in the air. It was driving him crazy that they hadn't been able to identify it yet. But he couldn't do anything about it tonight.

His flight had arrived too late for him to meet with the lead detective at the sheriff's office. And he would probably be better off waiting until tomorrow to look at the scene with fresh eyes.

He was about to accept their offer when his phone rang. "Excuse me," he said, leaving the room to take the call in private.

Scarlett waited until she heard Grey talking in a muffled voice from the other room, and then turned on Pat with a hiss.

"What the hell are you doing?" she demanded in a tight whisper. "First you swore we wouldn't get involved with the human police, and then you go and offer to show him my badge?" she spat incredulously.

"Calm down," Pat insisted in a low tone. "If he'd wanted to see your badge, my spell would have made sure he'd seen it. I told you I didn't like impersonating the human police, but sometimes it's necessary.

"Besides, don't act like you don't want to have a drink with him," he added with a grin that she wanted to knock right off his face.

She clamped her mouth shut when she heard Grey's soft footfalls returning to the room.

His eyes were drawn to her as soon as he walked through the doorway. She was so damned beautiful it took his breath away. Right now her sea-green gaze was narrowed with dangerous intent on Sparrow. She flicked at a strand of silky, strawberry blonde hair that had escaped her ponytail as she glared at the other man.

Grey frowned, hoping she wasn't pissed that Sparrow had invited him along for a drink. But when her eyes moved to his, her gaze softened. Hopefully that was a positive sign.

"Well, if the offer still stands, I guess I could use a drink," he said. "I've just been informed that I have my choice of a third-rate motel about a half hour from here, or a second-rate one an hour away. Apparently some damned convention is in town and they've booked all the decent rooms."

"You mean to tell me they can't find space for the FBI?" Sparrow asked incredulously. "This country's gratitude toward law enforcement is overwhelming."

Grey chuckled.

"Seriously, though, we can do better than that. I'll have my girlfriend, Sydney, see if she can get you a comped room at her hotel up the street."

Grey lifted a brow. "I wouldn't turn my nose up at that offer. But don't trouble yourself, Officer Sparrow. I'm used to living rough when I work a case."

"We'll consider it even if you give us a ride back to the hotel," Pat replied with a smile. "And by the way, my friends call me Pat or Sparrow—you can take your pick, as long as you drop the 'Officer'."

"I'll keep that in mind, if you'll lose the 'Agent' and call me Grey," he said with a grin.

Chapter 6

Grey whistled in appreciation as they strode through the cavernous lobby of the sprawling beachfront hotel. Marble floors, frescoed ceilings and gilt trim out the yin yang. This was old Palm Beach at its finest. And its most expensive.

"Thanks again for setting up the room," he said to Sparrow. "I doubt my office even tried to book this place. It's not exactly in the FBI's daily travel budget."

Sparrow laughed. "No problem. Sydney has connections with the staff. And here she is," he added, his expression gentling as they approached a smiling woman sitting on a leather barstool.

Grey didn't know what he'd expected, but it wasn't the unassuming, jean clad beauty waiting for them. She had a free spirited, bohemian look with her long hair and loose, colorful top.

And if their lingering hello kiss was anything to go by, she and Sparrow were crazy about each other. She broke it off with a laugh and gave Sparrow a playful swat when he continued to nuzzle her. Leaning around him, she said hello to Scarlett, and then stuck her hand out to Grey.

"Hi. I'm Sydney."

"Greyson. But my friends call me Grey. Pleased to meet you." Her smile was infectious and he couldn't help but grin back at her. "I was just thanking your man, Sparrow here, for getting me the free room. But I hear that was really your doing."

She waved it off. "Live in a place like this and you get to know people. Besides, do you have any idea how much they make here in a single season? They can afford to comp a room for an FBI agent working a local case."

"Well, I thank you nonetheless," he said sincerely. "How does one get to live in a place like this anyway?"

She gave a wry laugh and glanced at Sparrow. "It's a long story. And you wouldn't believe me if I told you. But that's neither here nor there," she said, hopping off the barstool. "How do you feel about champagne and Chinese food, Grey?"

"I feel pretty good about champagne and Chinese food," he replied with a bemused look at Scarlett, who shrugged as if to say she was just along for the ride.

"Good! Because the food and drink prices here are outrageous. And I happen to have a couple of bottles chilling up in my penthouse, as well as quite an assortment of little paper boxes of deliciousness on the way."

"How could I refuse an offer like that?" Grey replied.

"I was hoping you'd say that. Come on, we don't want to miss the delivery guy." Sydney shot Sparrow a self-satisfied smirk as she linked her fingers through his and pulled him toward the elevator.

He'd had about thirty seconds to explain what was going on when he'd called to warn her they were coming. And he had to hand it to her—he couldn't have planned a cozier, less threatening setting for Scarlett and Grey to get to know each other if he'd had an entire day to do it.

"Posh living," Grey commented as they exited the elevator into Sydney's private foyer. "I like it."

"Know what my favorite part is?" Sydney asked in a conspiratorial whisper.

"The amazing view?" he suggested on an impressed breath as he followed the trio inside.

Sydney shook her head. "The twice a week maid service," she replied giddily as she continued into the living room and dropped onto the couch with a blissful sigh.

Sparrow joined her, leaving the smaller loveseat for Scarlett and Grey.

"Wasn't there a chair here before?" Scarlett stood frowning at a space near the sliding glass door.

"Yes, but I'm having it cleaned," Sydney answered brightly as she leaned forward to pull a bottle of champagne from its ice bucket on the coffee table.

"I hope no one minds casual dining with chopsticks on the sofa," she said, smiling at Grey as she filled his glass. "I'm afraid my dining room has become my home office."

Scarlett lowered herself into the space beside Grey, trying to act as if his nearness didn't affect her. But he smelled amazing. She'd noticed it on the car ride over, sitting next to him in the front seat.

He didn't have the artificial cologne odor that many human men seemed to favor. He smelled simply of clean soap and warm skin, like her own people. But more appealing than any male she'd ever met.

His leg brushed against hers and she could feel the firm muscles of his thigh through the material of his slacks. It sent fissions of awareness prickling across her skin, and tingles of heat cascading through her blood stream.

The sensation was entirely new to her, and she had difficulty ignoring it as she tried to focus on what he was saying to Sydney.

"…working from home. I'm on the road so much. I have to say this is a nice change from eating out of boxes alone in my hotel room."

"You're still going to be eating out of boxes in a hotel room," Sparrow joked, "but at least you're among friends."

Grey turned to Scarlett. "So, how long have you and Sparrow known each other?" he asked, his lips quirking upward. "A buddy from Australia once told me that he thought it was rude when people commented on his accent, but I couldn't help noticing yours and Sparrow's are similar."

"So you're sayin' all Irish people sound alike now, are ya'?" Scarlett quipped in an exaggerated brogue.

Grey held up his hands and laughed. "I wouldn't dare. I know what a dangerous woman you are to offend."

"She's a triple threat," Sydney warned him. "Are you aware that she's a master swordswoman, amongst all of her other talents?"

"Really?" Grey asked. "Fencing?"

Scarlett shook her head and took a sip of wine, her cheeks heating beneath the attention. "Long sword fighting."

Grey's eyes lit with respect and something deeper. It curled along Scarlett's nerve endings and made her entire body feel alive.

"I'd love to watch you some time," he said. "We had a little sword training in the Marines and it was something I always thought I'd be interested in pursuing. Is there a place down in Key Largo where you train?"

The question jolted Scarlett back into the reality that everything they'd told Grey was a lie. And she hated the reminder.

"Man, you were in the Marines?" Pat interjected, saving her from answering. "Which unit?"

"I did most of my time in Special Ops Command and went straight into the FBI from there," Grey said, wondering if the other man was about to burst out in a testosterone laden 'Oorah'.

Not that he wasn't proud of his service, but it seemed to bring out the adolescent one-up-man-ship in a lot of guys.

"How does it feel to be a bad ass G-man?" Sparrow asked with a deadpan expression.

Grey let out an amused snort. "Like half my life has been classified?" he replied, only partly joking. "Seriously though, I had a plan, I was dedicated to it, and my career has pretty much followed the path I charted.

"My only regret is that some of my relationships have fallen by the wayside because of it. Most people can't accept it when you tell them you have to keep such a big part of your life a secret from them."

Sparrow nodded in understanding. "That's tough, man," he said as he leaned back and put his arm around Sydney. "But I think when the right people come into your life, they understand."

Sparrow glanced at Scarlett as he continued. "And to answer your question from before, Scarlett and I grew up together in a small town in County Kerry, Ireland. That's where we learned to sword fight, though I have no problem admitting she can kick my ass at it."

"You're in good company then. I just met her and she's already kicked mine," Grey said with a grin.

"You haven't found a place to spar down in Largo yet, have you Letty?" Pat asked casually, trying to lure her back into the conversation.

"Uh, no," she replied, reminding herself that she needed to play along with their fabrication. "I've been training by myself out in the yard."

"Maybe you can help me brush up on my technique while we're here," Grey suggested. "I saw a gym downstairs with a good sized space covered in floor mats. Maybe they have something we could use as practice swords, or if not, we could just work on forms."

"Sure, if you want," Scarlett agreed without thinking. "How about first thing in the morning, before breakfast?"

"It's a date," he confirmed. "I'll pick you up at seven."

The thought of sparring with him was...exciting. Every cell in her body came to attention at the idea. Maybe she shouldn't have agreed, but she couldn't resist. All she had to do was blink back here before seven and pretend she'd stayed the night with Pat and Sydney.

Wait a minute, had he just called it a *date*? She studied him surreptitiously, wondering if he'd meant it that way.

Not that it mattered. Getting too close to him would be crazy. She couldn't tell him the truth about her world. And even if he somehow found out, he'd probably be furious with her for lying about it.

Although, from what he'd said, he understood the necessity of keeping secrets...

There was a knock at the door and Sydney exclaimed, "Finally, I'm starving!"

"I'll get it," Sparrow volunteered as they both rose.

Grey shifted so that he was facing Scarlett and smiled. The activity by the door faded into white noise as he caught her gaze. It was as if the entire surface of her skin vibrated with awareness at his proximity.

Being this close, touching him, having his attention focused on her—the feeling it gave her was akin to the electric buzz she got after downing a shot of smooth Irish whiskey. Yet so much better.

He gave her a curious look. "What were you thinking about just now? You had the strangest expression on your face."

"Whiskey," she answered huskily.

Grey lifted a dark brow, heat flaring in his eyes at her tone. "Not really a champagne kind of girl, then?"

Scarlett cleared her throat. "I suppose I prefer the burn from a shot of good blended Irish whiskey."

"I'll keep that in mind," he replied with a half smile. "I, myself, prefer to sip a rare single malt."

Her eyes lit with appreciation. "I enjoy that as well."

"I once had the pleasure of sharing a glass from an $1100 bottle of Knappogue Castle 1951 with a five star general. It was the most amazing thing I've ever tasted. The layers of complexity were unbelievable."

"I know that bottle, and you're right, it's incredible," Scarlett said with a grin. "My Da bought me one for Christmas a few years back."

It had actually been more than a few years back, when the bottle was not yet so rare. But it had still rivaled the finest offerings from the distilleries in her own realm.

And her family didn't really celebrate Christmas, but it was easier than confusing Grey by calling it a Winter Solstice gift.

He whistled. "I wouldn't mind finding one of those in my stocking. You must have been very good that year."

He leaned forward to grab his champagne glass from the coffee table and Scarlett sucked in a breath as his leg brushed hers and little shockwaves of sensation travelled up her thigh.

"Are your parents still in Ireland?" he asked as he leaned back and rested his arm across the couch cushions.

She nodded and took a sip of her drink to moisten her throat. Something about the way his shirt stretched taut over his chiseled pecs made the muscles beneath her stomach tighten.

"I've often wondered if the more collectible Irish whiskies are easier to come by in Ireland. Some of them are damn near impossible to get in the States," he said with a chuckle.

She didn't know the answer to that question. Her Da knew a dwarf who imported such treasures from the human realm, but she'd never considered the geography of where he got them.

Instead of answering, she asked, "Did you know that, in Gaelic, the term for 'whiskey', *uisce beatha*, means 'water of life'?"

"That sounds about right," he commented wryly. "Did you grow up speaking Gaelic?"

"Yes," she replied, watching golden bubbles coat the inside of her champagne glass as she swirled it. "My family mostly speaks English nowadays, for convenience. But Gaelic has a certain melodic rhythm and flow that I sometimes miss."

She looked up to find Grey watching her, his dark eyes intent with fascination and warmth. "Say something to me in Gaelic," he murmured.

Scarlett hesitated, unable to tear her gaze from his. The desire to lean into him and taste his lips was so visceral that she almost couldn't contain it.

"*Ní féidir liom a thuiscint cad is dóigh liom ar do shon,*" she said, her heart beating in double time.

"That sounds beautiful," he said softly. "What does it mean?"

The literal translation was, *I don't understand what I feel for you.* Heat rose to her cheeks and she forced her eyes back down to her glass.

"It means the food is here," she replied as Sydney and Pat returned with plates and bags of food. "Let's eat."

Grey frowned. He had the strangest feeling that she'd lied about the meaning of what she'd said. But he couldn't call her on it since he didn't speak the language.

He shook his head and let it go, accepting a plate and a white paper box with a red pagoda printed on its side.

Soon everyone's glasses were refilled and they were all dipping fresh eggrolls in duck sauce and tucking into plates of savory beef lo mein, spicy kung pao chicken, and sweet honey garlic shrimp.

"I'd like to propose a toast," Grey said when everyone had sated their initial hunger and the sound of chopsticks hitting plates began to slow.

"To three of the best people I've met in a long time. Thank you for making an otherwise unpleasant evening fun. And thank you for reminding me why I've been on two planes and had three hours of sleep in the last three days. Because all the good people of the world deserve to have nights like this without having to worry about the monsters on their doorsteps."

The women raised their glasses solemnly, and Sparrow lifted his with a, "Here, here, brother."

Scarlett jumped when Lorien whispered in her ear, "That is one sweet, hot man you've got there."

She glared as the little scamp of a faerie fluttered over to steal a tiny jug of champagne from her glass. When Sydney noticed, she rolled her eyes in commiseration. Lorien was invisible to Grey, so of course everyone else had to pretend they didn't see her either.

Lorien drained her cup and winked at Scarlett before blinking out, obviously enjoying her game.

"Speaking of monsters," Sparrow said, "remember I told you we wanted to bounce an idea off you?"

Grey nodded, glancing at Sydney.

"Don't worry," Sparrow said, "I know you can't discuss the details of the case in front of a civilian."

"No offense to Sydney," Grey replied apologetically.

"None taken," Sydney assured him.

"It's just that Scarlett and I noticed something and wanted to point it out," Sparrow continued. "You're probably already aware of it, and it may be nothing, but have you considered that the victims may have had some sort of interest in the supernatural?"

Grey's eyes narrowed. He'd mentioned the same suspicion to Liza. "What makes you say that?"

Sparrow shrugged. "Like I said, it may be nothing. But Scarlett noticed the garden gnomes in the Largo vic's yard, and then we noticed the supernatural book collection in the Palm Beach vic's house today. So we're just throwing it out there."

"You two have sharp eyes," Grey said. "And I appreciate the help." He wanted to tell them he'd had the same hunch and was already following up on it. He might have if Sydney hadn't been there, but he didn't feel right about discussing it in front of her.

"I remember those garden gnomes," he teased Scarlett instead. "They were an audience to our wrestling match on the lawn."

Scarlett snorted. "I know. One of them tried to trip me afterward."

Grey laughed as he took one last bite and pushed his plate across the coffee table. "Oh, that reminds me," he added. "Are you missing a diamond earring?"

Scarlett sat up, her eyes widening. "Yes. One of the ones my Da gave me for my birthday. I was dreading having to tell him I'd lost it."

"Now you don't have to," Grey assured her with a smile. "I have it in my room. I'll grab it for you after dinner."

Scarlett swallowed the remainder of the bubbly liquid in her glass and sank back into the couch cushions with a sigh of relief. "You have no idea how happy that makes me."

Grey beamed at her, feeling like a hero. She had to be the loveliest woman he'd ever seen. Her cheeks were flushed from the champagne, and her hair curled into little wisps around her face where it had escaped from its binding.

She was an amazing blend of contrasts. She gave off a unique impression of strength and vulnerability, and it was a siren song to his senses.

He didn't know what there could be between them. But the thought of not taking the chance to find out made his heart squeeze inside his chest.

Sydney yawned, and Sparrow got up to start clearing dishes. "Why don't you two go on then," Sydney said with a smile. "We'll see you in the morning."

"Can I help you clean up?" Grey asked, standing as well.

Sydney waved him off. "Please. This will take five minutes. And besides," she said with a waggle of her brows, "twice a week maid service."

Grey laughed. "Well, thanks again."

"You're welcome," Sydney replied. "See you tomorrow."

Grey held out a hand to Scarlett, and she grasped his warm palm, allowing him to help her up. "I just need to use the lavatory, and then I'll follow you down," she told him.

Grey nodded and bent to give Sydney a quick hug before walking over to the kitchen to say goodnight to Sparrow.

"Thanks. I really appreciate the hospitality," he said earnestly.

"No problem, man." Sparrow dried his hands on a dish towel and extended one to Grey.

They shook and Sparrow patted him on the back, pulling him further into the kitchen. "Listen, Grey," he said in a low voice. "I know that Scarlett can come off like a bad ass, but..." he hesitated.

Then he shook his head and said, "There are things about her that it's not my place to tell you. But she's more fragile than she seems, okay? Just take it easy with her."

"Of course," Grey murmured in confusion. But before he could question the man further, Scarlett was there, waiting for him by the door.

"I'll be back in a bit," she called as they exited into the foyer and summoned the elevator.

"How often do you get up this way to visit Sparrow and Sydney?" Grey asked as they descended.

"This is actually the first time I've ever been here," Scarlett replied. "They've only been dating for a few months."

"Really?" Grey echoed in surprise. "They seem like they've been together for years."

Scarlett chuckled. "I know. It's hard to get used to. Pat's been a bachelor for as long as I can remember. But I guess it happens that way sometimes. It was the same with my brother and his wife."

"The one whose wedding you attacked me after?" he teased.

Scarlett groaned. "I'm never going to live that down, am I?"

"Doubtful," Grey replied as they stepped onto his floor.

"In my defense, I thought you were a pervert lurking in the bushes."

"I *tried* to show you my badge," he drawled.

"I thought you were trying to pull a weapon on me," she shot back laughingly.

"Just admit it," he cajoled as he inserted a keycard into his room's lock, "you were itching for a fight and you enjoyed kicking the crap out of me."

"I may have…enjoyed it a little."

Grey chortled. "The truth comes out. I never had a chance, did I? I guess we're just lucky it wasn't some other poor schlub out there for a stroll, unable to defend himself."

Scarlett scoffed. "Are you calling me a bully?"

"I refuse to answer that on the grounds that I might incriminate myself," Grey joked. "Hang on, let me go find your earring."

Scarlett snorted and dropped onto the couch in the sitting room. She propped her booted feet up on the coffee table and crossed her arms over her leather clad breasts.

"You think I'm a bully," she needled when he exited the bedroom and came to sit beside her.

He shook his head and smiled at her as he held up the sparkling teardrop diamond. "I found the back too," he announced proudly.

She took it and fitted it into her earlobe, her fingers lingering as if to confirm it would stay where it belonged.

"Making sure it still fits, Cinderella?"

"Thank you for bringing it back," she said earnestly. "They were a special gift."

"You're welcome. And no, I don't think you're a bully."

She smiled at him and he noticed the most intriguing indention in the middle of her lower lip. He tried not to stare, but the plump little curve drew his attention. He wanted to touch it with his thumb. And then with his tongue.

"We'll see what you have to say about whether or not I'm a bully tomorrow, after our sparring session," she said in an airy tone.

"That sounds like a challenge," he murmured, forcing himself to concentrate on her words instead of her mouth.

"Scared?" she taunted.

He shook his head slowly. "No. As a matter of fact, I can't wait."

A shock of awareness blossomed across her nerve endings at his heated look, and she realized they weren't teasing anymore.

She blinked at him, her breath coming faster. "I should go."

"Why don't you stay?" he asked in a languid voice, searching her eyes as his hand came up to caress her cheek.

It was as if all the sensation in her body centered around his touch, and she shuddered as she tried to reconcile the unfamiliar feelings coursing through her. His thumb brushed across her lower lip, lingering at its center, and she felt her thigh muscles clench as her lips parted on a shaky exhalation.

"Grey," she whispered his name uncertainly.

He held her gaze as he leaned forward, his smooth skin gleaming mahogany in the lamplight. His mouth looked soft and inviting, like something to be tasted and savored.

When his lips moved gently over hers, she wanted to groan at how good it felt. Pleasure sparked through her, stealing her capacity for thought and leaving her to rely solely on the coaxing glide of his mouth.

As she began to kiss him back, Grey thought he would die from the sheer sweetness of her response. There was a hesitance about it, like she wasn't quite sure what to do. As if this was her first kiss.

But that was impossible.

The thought melted away and he lost himself in a haze of desire as he sipped at her lips, slowly deepening the kiss.

Scarlett shivered as his tongue brushed into her mouth and she instinctively met the caress with a soft push of her own. It created a warm, delicious friction that she wanted to feel again. His tongue retreated and hers followed, venturing between his lips to search for the little rush of heat he'd given her.

Grey's quiet groan of pleasure vibrated through her, heightening her excitement. She pressed closer, her knees lifting onto the cushions as she leaned into him, her palms braced flat against the hard contours of his chest.

Grey's arms banded around her, easily lifting her weight and pulling her across his lap so that she straddled him. It was as if she had him pinned from above, and the power of the position was heady.

As she tilted her face to meet his lips, his hand slid up her spine to cup the back of her neck, his fingers massaging lightly as they tasted each other once more.

A low ache began to build between her thighs and she shifted against him, trying to relieve the almost-pain of it. Grey lifted his hips, his hardened heat pressing into the vee of her jeans. She exhaled in surprise as the pressure of his touch eased the feeling, transforming her core into a tingling mass of sensation.

God. She was killing him, Grey thought as she moaned softly and ground herself against him. He'd never felt so out of control from a kiss in his life. If he got any harder, he was going to burst.

His free hand moved between them to work at the top button of her vest. The leather was soft and supple against his fingers. But the creamy flesh beneath was infinitely softer.

He trailed his lips down her neck, nipping and licking at the sensitive skin, and she tilted her head, her pleasured rush of breath sending a shockwave of need straight to his groin. He lingered at the hollow of her throat, savoring her quickening pulse, before he moved lower.

He peeled away her vest to reveal a delicate camisole trimmed in black lace. Her fine, strawberry blonde hair hung in careless wisps around her face, its band having come loose. He reached up to pull it the rest of the way free, and the vision of her rising above him like that, her cheeks flushed and rosy, was by far the most arousing thing he'd ever seen in his life.

His fingertips grazed the silk hugging her breasts as he dipped his head to kiss the valley between them. Her nipples pebbled into hardened little gems beneath his attention. He laved his tongue across one, moistening the silk that covered it and bathing it in warmth.

A quiet cry escaped her throat and one hand left its perch on his shoulder to cup the back of his head, easing him closer as she arched her back. He drew the tip of her breast into his mouth with a gentle pull, his fingers tracing lightly over the outer curves.

Scarlett was lost, her senses awash in Grey's touch and the heated caress of his breath. She wanted to taste him again, but what he was doing to her sent indescribable frissons of pleasure searing straight from her nipple to the aching flesh between her thighs.

It was almost too much, yet she didn't want it to stop. She circled her hips against his, seeking the exquisite pressure that had eased her before.

Grey groaned and twisted around to lay her on the couch beneath him.

A spark of apprehension fluttered through her as his body pressed down into her, leaving her partially immobile. She closed her eyes, trying to ignore her disquiet and lose herself in his touch once more.

But the pleasure of his fingers moving gently over her skin was lost to the rising panic of being trapped beneath his weight. And his breath, which had tasted sweetly of champagne before, began to remind her of the hot alcohol fumes on another man's breath long ago.

Scarlett whimpered softly, and the cadence of the sound made Grey lift his head. Her beautiful sea-green eyes were no longer cloudy with passion. They were open wide and staring blindly through him, as if she was seeing something that wasn't there.

He felt her body stiffen beneath him a split second before he found himself flying off the couch and crashing into the low wooden coffee table.

"Scarlett?" he called in alarm as he pushed himself off the carpet. He scanned the room and found her crouched in the opposite corner, arms wrapped around her heaving chest.

"What the hell? Are you alright?" he asked as he started toward her.

She shot to her feet and backed toward the door, her eyes wild and haunted. "I'm sorry, Grey," she whispered. "I have to go."

"Wait!" he called, but the door was already slipping closed behind her. He stared at it in blank shock for a moment, and then dashed after her.

Grey cursed as the door clicked shut behind him and he realized he didn't have his key. She was headed for the elevator and he followed, the thick hallway carpet muffling the pounding of his bare feet as he tried to catch up.

But he got there too late. He caught a glimpse of Scarlett's stricken face as the doors slid closed between them. With a few choice words, he punched the bronzed façade, but succeeded only in denting his knuckles.

He watched as the light signaled that the car was going up, and some of the tightness in his chest loosened as he realized she must be going back to Sydney's.

He wanted to go after her, but he knew he couldn't get off the elevator at the penthouse without a key.

"May I help you, Sir?" asked a feminine voice. It had a husky quality that was oddly soothing to his nerves. He turned and blinked to find a blonde in a skimpy French maid's outfit standing behind him.

He glanced toward the elevator, but quickly realized his only choice was to go back to his room and call up to the penthouse to see if Scarlett was alright.

"I, uh, locked myself out," he said hoarsely.

The woman smiled. "No problem, Mr. Derrington. I can open the door for you."

He fell into step behind her, frowning at her slender back as she headed for his room.

"How do you know who I am?"

She pulled a key card from her apron and answered, "The hotel's staff make it a point to know all of our guests." Her crystal blue eyes sparkled at him as she looked up with a wink. "Not to mention, I helped Sydney arrange your room earlier."

"Oh, right," he replied with a chuckle. "Well, thanks for your help."

"Any time. If you need anything, just call down to Cleaning Services and ask for Angelica. Will you be alright now?" she asked, the serenity in her voice washing over him again.

"Yes, thank you," he said in bemusement. "Good night."

"Good night, Mr. Derrington," she said, giving him a brilliant smile as she turned to go.

He shook his head, taking a deep breath as he called the front desk and asked to be connected to Sydney's penthouse.

What the hell had happened? One minute Scarlett was melting in his arms, and the next she was in a blind panic to get away from him. He'd recognized that faraway look in her eyes. He'd seen it in vets suffering from PTSD.

What had Sparrow said to him before he and Scarlett had left the penthouse earlier? That there were things about her that it wasn't Sparrow's place to discuss. That she was more fragile than she seemed and he should 'take it easy' with her.

A heavy weight settled in the pit of Grey's stomach. He'd thought the man was just giving him the standard 'don't hurt my friend' speech. But now he was afraid the warning went much deeper.

He lost count of how many times the phone rang before Sydney picked up with a strained, "Hello?"

"It's Grey. Is she there?" he demanded.

He heard voices in the background, but Sydney must have carried the phone to another room because they faded to silence as a door closed.

"She's here, Grey. And she's fine," Sydney assured him.

"She is *not* fine," he said in a clipped tone. "She had a panic attack and nearly tossed me across the room. She ran out of here like there was a demon on her heels."

"She's talking to Sparrow now. She'll be okay," Sydney insisted. Then she sighed and said, "It's not your fault, Grey. But you should probably give her the night to calm down."

"Was she raped?" he asked bluntly, fearing the answer but needing to hear it anyway.

There was a long moment of silence, and then Sydney said, "I'm not the one you should be talking to about this."

His helplessness and anger seethed through the phone. He took a breath and said in a tight voice, "You're right. Tell her I'll see her in the morning. Good night, Sydney."

Grey hung up the phone and sat on the edge of the bed, staring blankly at his reflection in the darkened television screen. His mother had been raped. His need to understand the pain she'd kept hidden from him for years, and to find justice for other victims, had been part of what led him to pursue a career with the B.A.U.

God damn it. He would never forget the desire in Scarlett's eyes being replaced by that frozen, haunted look. He wanted to murder whoever had put it there.

Preferably slowly, and with the maximum amount of suffering it was possible to inflict.

Chapter 7

Sydney exited the bedroom to find Angelica pacing the hall in her French maid's uniform. She could hear Sparrow and Scarlett's voices beyond, but couldn't make out what they were saying.

"What happened?" Sydney asked her friend.

"I felt them," Angelica replied wistfully. "Their blossoming passion for each other was so beautiful. I haven't experienced its like since you and Agent Sparrow first made love."

Sydney smiled self consciously. She should have been used to the succubus' frank manner concerning all things sexual, but it still put a blush in her cheeks.

"And then it was as if the fire inside her simply went out," Angelica continued sadly. "I could sense her panic and his confusion. I didn't know what I could do, but I blinked to his floor to see if I could help.

"He had locked himself out of his room, so I tried to calm him and I let him back in. Then I found her in the elevator. I think she was trying to blink back to the faerie realm, but she was so distraught she couldn't get her magic to work."

"This is partly my fault," Sydney groaned. "Sparrow and I tried to push them together tonight, and I guess Scarlett wasn't ready for it."

She glanced guiltily at the chair she'd moved out of the living room. She'd lied about having it cleaned. She'd moved it into her bedroom so that Scarlett and Grey would be forced to sit on the loveseat together.

Angelica shook her head. "If you had felt the sexual chemistry between them..." the maid shivered. "Something terrible blocked her from fulfilling her pleasure with him, but she was so close to taking it. It would be a shame if those two did not come together."

"That actually makes me feel a little better," Sydney replied with a crooked grin. "I'm going to see if I can get her to talk to me. Thanks again for helping out, Angelica."

"Anytime," the succubus said with a luminous smile. "I'll see you soon."

Angelica blinked out and Sydney took a deep breath before following Sparrow and Scarlett's voices into the living room.

"Please stay, Letty," Sparrow pleaded softly. "I don't want you to be alone tonight."

Good, Sydney thought. She'd told him to offer Scarlett the second bedroom. Hopefully Scarlett would take him up on it. She ran back to her room for a spare set of pajamas just in case.

"This wouldn't have happened if I hadn't told Derrington we were with the human police," Sparrow was saying angrily as she returned. "I should have wiped his memory and been done with it."

Scarlett's jaw took on a stubborn set and something akin to a protest flickered in her eyes, but she remained mute.

"There are fresh towels in the guest bath and my friend, Sunny, tells me the bed is the most comfortable thing she's ever slept on," Sydney said, alerting them to her presence.

"I spoke to Grey," she continued, ignoring Sparrow's warning glare. "He said he'll see you in the morning. You guys said seven, right?"

Surprise flitted across Scarlett's wan features.

"Come on," Sydney encouraged, motioning toward the guest room. "I'll show you how to set the alarm. These pajamas are tight on me, but they should fit you fine."

Scarlett got up, looking dazed, and followed Sydney down the hall.

"What happened there?" Sydney asked with a wince at the raw, bloody skin on one of Scarlett's fingers.

"Nothing, just a hangnail," Scarlett murmured.

It looked painful, but Scarlett hid it from view with her other hand. "What time do you want to wake up?" Sydney asked.

"Around six," Scarlett replied, "but I don't need an alarm."

"Are you sure?" Sydney asked.

Scarlett nodded.

"Okay, well I'll let you get changed. I'll be back in a minute with a band-aid for your finger." Sydney closed the door behind her before Scarlett could refuse that as well.

Sydney was bent over, looking under the guest bathroom sink for the box of bandages, when Sparrow's whispered voice behind her made her jump.

"Why are you pushing this?" he hissed. "Trying to get the two of them together was a mistake, or hadn't you noticed?"

She straightened with the box of band-aids in her hand and raised a brow at him. "She wants to see him again, or hadn't *you* noticed?" she shot back quietly.

"I told you what happened to her. Didn't you see the state she was in when Angelica brought her up here?" he asked incredulously. "I should go wipe Derrington's memory right now and put an end to this."

Sydney reached out to brush her knuckles over his stubbly cheek. "Sparrow, I know she's like a sister to you, and it's hard for you to see her like this. But even you said that it's been almost two hundred years and she needs to work through it.

"That's not going to be easy for her, no matter who she's with. But I think the connection you sensed between her and Grey is a strong one.

"And she shouldn't go the rest of her life without falling in love or having a healthy sexual relationship with someone. Forever is a long time for an immortal."

Love and uncertainty swirled behind Sparrow's eyes as he searched her gaze. Then he took her hand and pressed his lips into her palm. "Alright, Sydney. I'll try to trust your judgment in this. At least until we see what happens tomorrow."

She grinned and rose onto her toes to give him a quick kiss. "Good. Now wish me luck," she murmured. "I'm about to go in there and try to get her to open up to me."

Sparrow cringed, at both her plan and her use of the word 'wish'. That particular utterance was still a sore spot from her time under the threat of a death djinn contract.

"Do you really think that's the best idea?" he asked. "She's been prickly around you since you met. And she's not in the friendliest of moods."

"She needs to talk to someone," Sydney replied. "And wounds should be tended while they're fresh." She rattled the band-aid box at him as she sidled past and went to knock on Scarlett's door.

He shook his head as she disappeared inside. Sydney had become increasingly philosophical since her narrow escape from having her soul enslaved for eternity. He silently lent her his support in dealing with Scarlett, but fully expected his old friend to toss his soul mate out on her ass.

Scarlett heard Sydney's soft knock and called for her to enter. She knew the woman was only trying to help, but she wished Sydney would just leave her alone with her misery.

She rolled over to accept the bandage Sydney offered and murmured her thanks. She felt mentally and physically exhausted. But she feared she wouldn't be able to stop reliving the mortifying scene with Grey long enough to fall asleep.

He must have thought she'd completely lost her mind. She couldn't believe he still wanted to meet her in the morning.

"Sparrow told me you were raped when you were younger," Sydney said quietly.

Scarlett couldn't muster the energy for the anger she wanted to feel. A part of her accepted that Pat would tell his soul mate what had happened. It was part of his history too.

Scarlett curled back into the pillow and remained silent.

"It's a terrible thing, Scarlett. Enough to make anyone freak out at the prospect of sex." Sydney paused as if to gather the right words. "I don't want to push you, but holding that inside you is like swallowing poison. Don't you want to talk about it?"

Scarlett considered Sydney's words. *Did* she want to talk about it? She wasn't sure anymore. There was a part of her that had always believed that not talking about it made it less real.

But if that were true, she should have been able to put it behind her by now. It had happened so long ago, yet here she was, still trapped by the memory of it.

"Scarlett?" Sydney pressed.

Scarlett flipped over to face her, eyes flashing with frustration. "Why should I share this pain with you, human?" she spat. "You know nothing of me, and I know even less of you."

Sydney didn't recoil as Scarlett expected. Instead she said, "My friend's older brother raped me when I was sixteen. I'm in no way trying to compare what happened to me with what you went through. But it fucked me up, and it took me years to accept that it even happened."

Sydney's words and the quiet strength in her voice diffused Scarlett's irritation. She propped herself up on the pillows, her brain whirling with questions and regrets. She gave Sydney a searching look.

"How did it happen to you?" Scarlett asked finally.

Sydney's lips curled into a winsome smile. "My friend told me her brother liked me, and I was flattered because he was a few years older. Their parents were out of town and some of us decided to spend the night at their house. I felt safe there with my friends and I drank way too much."

Sydney closed her eyes and took a deep breath. "When my friend and her boyfriend went to her parents' bedroom at the end of the night...I was wasted. I threw up in her bathroom and collapsed on her bed. I was nauseous and I just wanted to pass out. But her brother lay down next to me and started kissing me. At first I was into it."

She swallowed. "I was a virgin, and I told him over and over that I wasn't going to have sex with him, but he wouldn't stop trying. The room was spinning and I passed out a couple of times. But he kept waking me up, trying to get between my legs."

A pained look crossed Sydney's features, but she continued.

"I begged him to leave me alone. I kept thinking that if I could muster enough strength to roll off the bed and crawl out of the room, maybe I could find somewhere else to sleep. But I was shivering with cold, and so sick and weak that I could barely move.

"He wouldn't listen to me telling him 'no'. So every time he tried to force himself inside me, I squeezed my muscles tight to keep him out. I don't know how long it went on before he gave up. It felt like hours. He'd stop for a while and I'd pass out, then I'd wake up with him trying again.

"Finally he just decided to finger me. He was rough, and I was moaning in pain, but he didn't stop. I didn't complain more than that because I was grateful that he wasn't trying to have sex with me anymore. And to be honest, I didn't have much fight left in me."

The shame in Sydney's eyes reflected Scarlett's own.

"I used to tell myself that it was my fault because I was so drunk. That maybe he thought I was moaning in pleasure instead of pain."

Her forehead wrinkled in consternation. "But how could he have thought that? He saw me throw up. I was in and out of consciousness. I repeatedly begged him to leave me alone. How could anyone think that felt good?"

Sydney shook her head as if to rid herself of the confusion. "The next morning I woke up sore and there was blood on my thighs. I thought I'd started my period, but it wasn't time yet. I didn't realize he'd broken my hymen with his fingers until I actually *wanted* to have sex with a guy for the first time. When I told him he was my first, he didn't believe me because I didn't bleed. Which was a dick move in itself, because not all girls do, but I still felt robbed."

She tried to smile, but the expression didn't make it to her eyes. "The morning after it happened, the bastard pulled me aside and said, 'When you get older, you'll realize what happened here.'"

Sydney scoffed. "I still don't know what the fuck he meant by that. All I know is it makes me furious every time I think about it, because the only thing I *realized* when I got older was that he raped me."

"Did you tell anyone?" Scarlett asked softly.

Sydney shook her head. "I was too humiliated to explain it to anyone. I knew I was angry and upset. I knew that what had happened was wrong and that it made me feel helpless and ashamed. But I felt like it was my fault.

"Years later I told my friend, Sunny. She said that when someone forces their fingers inside you like that, it's called 'digital' rape. It started to make sense then, but when I was younger, I wasn't able to see it for what it was. All I wanted was some semblance of revenge, and to never have to see him again.

"What I ended up doing still pisses me off—I asked him to go to my senior prom with me."

Scarlett frowned at her. "Your what?"

Sydney gave a humorless laugh. "The last year of human high school is called 'senior' year, and 'prom' is like the farewell dance. Everyone gets all dressed up and has pictures taken with their dates and their friends.

"But my prom wasn't free. You had to buy tickets for it. He said he'd pay me back for his, so I used the money my mom had given me for my senior yearbook to buy an extra ticket."

Scarlett looked confused again and Sydney added, "A yearbook is a big memory book with pictures of all your classmates and spaces for them to sign and write messages.

"I knew he wouldn't repay me for his ticket," she continued, "but all I could think about was getting back at him somehow."

"How was inviting him to your special dance getting back at him? And why would you want to include him in something so important to you?" Scarlett asked, puzzled.

Sydney's expression was resigned. "Did you know that over forty percent of rape survivors have sex with their rapist again?"

Scarlett gave her a look of mingled horror and disbelief.

"I know. It sounds crazy," Sydney said with a sigh. "I called a Rape Crisis Center to talk to a counselor a few years ago. I was struggling with what happened and why it still affected me so much.

"The woman who answered the phone was really helpful. She's the one who told me the forty percent statistic. It happens because so many rape survivors know their attacker. And it starts to make more sense when you think about how many women stay with men who beat them.

"But that's actually not what I was doing. I had no intention of ever having sex with that bastard. I was more like…" she trailed off, sucking in a breath as she searched for the right words.

"Have you ever cut yourself on purpose, or held your hand over a flame, just to prove to yourself that you had control over the pain?"

Scarlett shook her head, but her eyes were filled with a kind of disturbed empathy. Her torn finger wasn't a conscious infliction of pain. But she could see a morbid logic in what Sydney was talking about.

"See, prom was supposed to be this huge event, this big milestone," Sydney explained. "And I thought that by going with him, and forcing myself to ignore how awful it made me feel, I was proving that what he'd done to me hadn't really hurt me.

"Not to mention, prom night notoriously ends in sex, and I was pretty sure he'd expect it. So I saw it as my chance to say 'No' and actually have it mean something. I couldn't think of any other way to take back the power he'd stolen from me."

Sydney's eyes searched Scarlett's. "Rape isn't really about sex. It's about power and control. I think I knew that, at least subconsciously, even back then."

Scarlett's brow puckered. "I hadn't thought of it that way," she admitted. Goddess knew she'd been trying to take back her own power and control for her entire life. "So did it make you feel any better? Did you feel as if you'd regained some of your power afterward?"

"Honestly, it was a pretty pathetic revenge plan." Sydney's chuckle held no humor. "Everyone went to a hotel to hang out after the dance. He paid for a room and I knew he thought I'd have sex with him—willingly this time.

"So when he suggested we go back to the room alone, it was what I'd been waiting for all night. I laughed in his face and said, 'yeah right'. He spun away from me, looking furious, and I just smirked at him.

"And yes, in that moment, I felt more powerful than I had before."

Sydney's eyes lit with the first honest amusement and pleasure she'd shown since beginning the story.

"Afterward, I sat alone by the pool all night while everyone else hung out with their dates. Some kids I didn't know let me bum half a joint, and I smoked it while I watched the sun come up over the ocean. Then I caught a ride home with one of my friends.

"I never saw him again. And of course he didn't repay me for the prom ticket, so I couldn't afford to buy my yearbook. Which sucked, because my family had scraped together enough money to surprise me with a page in it that was dedicated to me. My mom was pretty upset."

"And you never told her why?" Scarlett asked with a wince.

"Oh, I told her I used the money to buy a ticket for my prom date. But I'm sure it sounded like a piss poor excuse."

"I'm so sorry, Sydney," Scarlett said quietly.

"Thanks," Sydney replied with a sniffle. "Me too. I don't have the yearbook, but I still have those god-damned prom pictures."

Scarlett let out a surprised laugh and, after a moment, Sydney joined her.

"So," Sydney said when their mirth faded, "now that you know the darker corners of my soul a little better, I'm dying to know what happened with you and Grey tonight. May I?" she indicated the space on the bed next to Scarlett.

Scarlett sighed and scooted over. She couldn't help but respect the woman's unflinching honesty. And truth be told, she no longer felt like being alone.

"I gather the two of you were…getting intimate," Sydney hedged, "and you had a bit of a panic attack?"

"A bit?" Scarlett groaned. "I went completely off my nut. I tossed him off the sofa and ended up crying in the corner like a sodding toddler in timeout.

"It could only have been worse if I'd blinked out in front of him. And if I could have, I would have." Her head sank back against the headboard and she stared up at the ceiling morosely. "I never thought I'd be grateful for my magic freezing up on me."

"Is he a good kisser?" Sydney asked.

Scarlett sent her a startled glance and snorted at her teasing expression. "Not that I have anyone to compare him to, but I'd wager he wouldn't place last in a kissing contest."

Sydney wanted to exclaim over Scarlett's first kiss, but she didn't think the other woman would appreciate it. Instead she joked, "'Not last' isn't exactly a glowing recommendation."

"Not at all," Scarlett denied quickly. "It was…" she lifted her fingertips to her lips and her eyelids fluttered close, "really quite good," she murmured.

"That sounds promising," Sydney replied with a grin. "Can you pinpoint what you were doing when you stopped enjoying it and started to panic?"

Scarlett opened her eyes and frowned. "What do you mean?"

"Well," Sydney said slowly, "sometimes I used to get panicky when my ex-husband fingered me. But I was okay as long as we were kissing while he did it. I guess because it made me feel like he was focused on what I was feeling.

"I think my panic was triggered when he touched me in a way that reminded me of what happened when I was younger. So I'm asking if you can pinpoint something that happened between you and Grey tonight that triggered your panic. If you can tell him what it was, maybe the two of you can avoid it in the future."

Scarlett shifted uncomfortably. Sydney made it sound so easy. And of course Scarlett realized that it was Grey's weight pressing down on her, making her feel trapped, that had caused her to panic.

But how could she tell him that? Wasn't that an integral part of making love? Why would he want to bother with someone who was so broken that she couldn't even handle having her lover's weight pressed against her?

"What are you thinking about?" Sydney asked with narrowed eyes. "Do you know what your trigger was?"

"Yes," Scarlett replied self-consciously. "But if I tell him not to do it anymore, he'll want to know why."

Sydney pursed her lips at Scarlett. "Grey catches serial rapists for a living. I'm pretty sure he's studied psychology, and he seems like a fairly sensitive guy. I'm betting that, after tonight, he already knows why.

"And even if he didn't, you couldn't keep it from him. Trying to keep something like that a secret wouldn't be fair to either of you."

Scarlett dropped her face into her hands. "He probably won't want to be with me after the way I reacted tonight anyway," she muttered.

"I don't think you're giving him enough credit," Sydney said softly. "I think if he wanted to bail on you he wouldn't have sounded so upset when I talked to him on the phone. And he certainly wouldn't still be meeting you in the morning."

Scarlett shook her head, her face remaining hidden in the cradle of her palms. "I don't know if I can tell him, Sydney," she whispered. "I've never told anyone. Pat's the only one who knows, and he only knows what he saw when he blinked in and stopped them."

Sydney flinched at the word 'them'. Sparrow had told her Scarlett was raped, but she didn't know the details. She steeled herself and suggested, "Why don't you start by telling me?"

Scarlett was silent for so long that Sydney wondered if she'd decided their conversation was over.

"What would be the point?" Scarlett finally asked in a weary tone.

"To practice getting it out," Sydney replied softly. "To tell someone who doesn't have a history with you that clouds their reaction. Hell, just to let someone help share a burden that you've kept secret for far too long."

Scarlett dropped her hands from her face and crossed her arms over her chest. "What do you want to hear?" she asked in an uneven voice. "About how stupid I was? About how I was so infatuated with the human realm that I kept sneaking into it, even though my parents told me not to?"

Scarlett shook her head in remorse. "At sixteen years old, I was still treated like a child in my realm. But in the human realm at that time, your mortal life spans were so short that I was considered a woman. It was addictive. It made me feel more grown-up than I ever had before, and I couldn't get enough of it."

Sydney gave her a silent nod of encouragement.

Scarlett sighed and looked up at the ceiling. "Cholera and famine were taking their toll among the human poor at that time, but the rich could still afford their amusements. And I was flattered when a wealthy young human showed an interest in me," she murmured.

"I met him at a human tavern with Pat. Afterward, I snuck back to see him a few more times alone. One night, he and another man invited me to go for a carriage ride. I felt so invincible in my magic that I didn't think twice about it.

"They took me back to the man's house to play cards and tried to get me drunk. All the while I was so certain I was in control," Scarlett scoffed, "right up until the man punched me in the face. The younger one, who I'd thought liked me, called me a whore. He held me down…"

Scarlett's voice grew hoarse and she cleared her throat into the heavy silence.

"Keep going," Sydney urged. "What happened next?"

Scarlett swallowed convulsively and tried to continue, but she couldn't get her voice to work. She cleared her throat again. "What do you think happened next?" she croaked finally.

"Tell me," Sydney replied with a steady gaze.

Scarlett's lips rose in a mirthless parody of a smile. "I froze," she managed in a husky tone. "I tried to blink away, and I couldn't. And two filthy, non-magical human men, with alcohol on their breaths and foul words in their mouths, ripped my clothes and put their fingers and their cocks inside me while I screamed and struggled and cried…and bled."

Sydney sucked in a breath and clenched her jaw. Scarlett saw the tears swimming in her eyes, but Sydney wouldn't let them fall.

"Then what happened," was all she said.

"I grew too tired to struggle and too numb to cry," Scarlett whispered. "And I let them do it again."

Sydney shook her head. "You didn't *let* them do anything," she said with vehemence.

Scarlett blinked at her. "I remember laying there on that rough, gritty floor, wondering if they were going to kill me...most of me wishing they would," she murmured softly. "And then, all of a sudden, Pat was there."

Sydney's grin was fierce as she swiped at an escaped tear. Scarlett saw the love and pride shining in her eyes, and thought she'd never seen anything so pure in her life. It made her chest tighten with an unfamiliar yearning.

"What did Sparrow do?" Sydney whispered.

Scarlett swallowed. "I was too in shock to move. I heard yelling and crashing. And the men screaming and pleading. And the next thing I knew Pat was blinking me home in his arms. He wanted to take me to my family, but I begged him not to. I was so hysterical that he finally agreed to take me to his place and let me get cleaned up there."

"How did he find you?" Sydney asked.

Scarlett's eyes rose to hers. "He didn't tell you any of this?"

Sydney shook her head. "He didn't tell me much. Out of respect for you, I'm sure."

"That was kind of him," Scarlett said with a self deprecating wince. "Pat treated Doyle and me like his kid brother and sister when we were growing up. He was always trying to tell me what to do under the guise of 'watching out for me'."

Scarlett curled her lip. "It annoyed me to no end and I did my best not to listen to him. So, of course, when he told me that the human I liked was bad news..." she trailed off.

Sydney nodded in understanding. "Any self respecting sixteen year old girl would have done the same," she said gently. "There was no way you could have known what would happen."

Scarlett lifted one shoulder in a half hearted shrug. "Still, if I'd only listened to him. If I hadn't been so stupid..." She dropped her gaze from Sydney's. "My magic still freezes when I get scared," she said in a small voice.

Sydney let out a sound that was half laugh and half sob. "I'm going to hug you now, Scarlett."

She leaned over and wrapped her arms around Scarlett's neck, resting her cheek against Scarlett's in a surprisingly comforting gesture. Sydney squeezed her tight for a moment and whispered, "None of it was your fault."

"Thank you," Scarlett said, swallowing the lump in her throat and looking away.

"It's the truth. And you're welcome," Sydney replied as she settled back into the pillows. After the silence went on a beat too long, she said, "Sparrow killed those men, didn't he?"

Scarlett gave her a considering look. "I only asked him what happened to them once. He told me he 'took care of it'. When I asked what he meant by that, all he'd say was that he pulled a favor to make sure the human police didn't ask too many questions."

Sydney's answering smile was tremulous. "Goddess, I love that man."

"Me too," Scarlett replied with a teary grin. "Like a brother," she added with a glance at Sydney.

"I know." Sydney chuckled. "But thanks for clearing it up anyway."

"I've been wondering," Scarlett questioned, "why you call him Sparrow instead of Pat?"

"He asked me the same thing once," Sydney replied, nibbling her lip, "and I told him it just felt better somehow. But I think the real reason is that we tried to keep our distance from each other at first, and I just got used to thinking of him that way."

Sydney grinned and sank further down into the pillows. "Or maybe it's just because 'Sparrow' feels sexier rolling off my tongue than 'Pat' does."

Scarlett laughed.

Sydney smiled and stifled a yawn. "Do you mind if I close my eyes for a minute?" she asked. "I normally wouldn't invade your space like this, but I'm so sleepy."

Scarlett hadn't slept beside another person since she and Doyle were children, and he had crawled into her bed after a nightmare. Yet she realized she was strangely loathe for Sydney to leave her side.

"It appears to be a night for sharing, sister," she conceded.

∞∞∞∞∞∞∞∞∞∞

Sparrow rapped quietly on the bedroom door when Sydney didn't return after over an hour. No one answered and he didn't hear voices, so he opened the door a crack and peaked through.

His chest swelled with emotion when he saw Sydney and Scarlett curled up next to each other, sleeping soundly.

If that wasn't a miracle, he didn't know what was. Sydney might have been right about giving Grey a chance to get through to Scarlett. Maybe the man did deserve another day with her before Sparrow wiped his memory clean...

Chapter 8

Marianne cut across the wide, manicured lawn of the college campus. The grass was so green it looked fake, and she was sure it must be full of pesticides.

Her sandaled feet would probably break out in hives later, but right now she was in a panic to get to class. Somehow she had forgotten about her exams and she was an hour late for a two hour history final.

She tried to break into a run, but the air around her began to shimmer strangely and black spots swam before her eyes as an eerie whispering filled her ears.

Oh god. It was happening again.

She tried to ignore it, but the voices only grew louder and more agitated. Darkness crept across her field of vision, narrowing it into a tunnel. She stumbled to a stop and bent over, propping her hands on her knees and taking slow, even breaths.

She was eleven years old the first time this had happened. Her parents sent her for tests, but the doctors couldn't find anything physically wrong with her. She finally told her deeply religious mother about the voices, and from then on she was shipped back and forth from psychiatrists to priests.

Her mother wasn't sure if she was crazy or possessed, but either way, she was going to make sure her only daughter was fixed.

The voices in Marianne's head receded to a whisper. She straightened cautiously and opened her eyes, blinking in confusion at her surroundings. The college campus was gone, and she was in the middle of an old, sprawling graveyard.

Was this a dream?

Age and ancient lichens stained the headstones and hoary trees towered above her, straggly beards of moss swaying gently beneath their reaching branches. She recognized this place. It was where her grandmother was buried.

Grandma died when she was fifteen. And it was only then—after four years of poking, prodding, pills and one truly frightening exorcism—that Marianne realized what the whispers in her head really were.

Because her dead grandmother's voice joined them.

She picked her way through the jumbled maze of tombstones. She had always loved this graveyard. Most modern cemeteries seemed obscene by comparison. There was something so impersonal about an open field plotted with mathematically neat rows of identical grave markers.

Death shouldn't be such an efficient affair.

Her gaze searched the pitted granite and marble sentinels. Most were traditional rectangles with squared edges or rounded tops. A few crosses were scattered amongst them, as well as the occasional double tablet commemorating a husband and wife whom not even death would do part.

But Marianne was looking for the distinct curve of a particular headstone. And there it was, several yards away…a thick granite heart rising up next to the gnarled roots of a huge oak.

The layered stone had a rosy tint and a faint sparkle from the tiny crystals that had formed deep within its surface. Grandma once told her that she picked out the headstone herself and used the money from Grandpa's life insurance policy to buy it.

She said that Grandpa never bought her anything fancy while he was alive. So when he died on her after sixty-two years of marriage, she decided the least he could do was finance the prettiest tombstone she could find to mark her eternal rest.

Marianne picked her way over the uneven ground and lowered herself onto one of the oak's broad, sturdy roots. She used to sit here as a teenager and soak in the calming silence. It helped center her mind so that she could focus on her grandmother's voice.

When she'd finally realized that the whispers in her head were the dead attempting to communicate with her, she'd begun having nightmares. Night after night she would dream about them coming back to life and trying to drag her down beneath the earth, the dirt suffocating her and worms wriggling against her flesh as the corpses pulled her into their graves.

It was strange, then, that she found solace in a graveyard. But it was here that her grandmother's voice came through the loudest, and it helped to calm her fears.

She closed her eyes and listened for it now. Again she had the thought that this was a dream, and she tried to imagine herself in bed with the fantasy lover who had appeared during her nap earlier that day. But when she opened her eyes, she was still in the graveyard, and the awareness that she was dreaming faded from her mind.

Burr remained hidden and watched the scene play out in the girl's dreamscape. Good—she was already beginning to crave him physically. And there was an unusual openness to her psyche that allowed him to access her thoughts and memories with surprising ease.

She had a primal fear that blended her anxiety over the dead returning to life with her terror at the thought of being buried herself.

He watched her unease grow as he fed her the suggestion that an odor of decay was rising from her grandmother's grave. He created the illusion of earthworms wriggling to the surface, writhing in the disturbed soil as if they were fleeing from something beneath.

Her eyes glazed with horror and she scrambled backward until her elbow slammed into the rough bark of the tree. Burr manipulated the whispers in her head, making them rise in a sinister swell until they coalesced into a perverted semblance of her grandmother's voice.

"I'm coming for you, Marianne," it keened softly.

She let out a strangled moan of denial and tried to flee, but the roots tripped her and sent her sprawling onto the fetid earth above the grave. Worms twisted beneath her, twining around her fingers, and squirming wetly against her cheek.

The soil became a shifting mire that sucked her deeper as she struggled to grab onto the heart-shaped tombstone and pull herself to her knees. Her grandmother's rotting face broke through the dirt, her fleshless smile leering and empty as her withered arms lifted in an embrace.

It was then that Marianne started to scream.

Burr watched in fascination, his tainted hunger and desire shuddering through him.

He was going to have so much fun with this one.

∞∞∞∞∞∞∞∞∞

Marianne woke with a shriek of terror. The sound was eerily loud in the stillness of the dark room and she snapped her mouth shut. Every muscle was stiffened in horror as she lay in her bed, afraid to move, listening to the soft clink of the ceiling fan chain as it bumped against the fixture overhead.

She prayed she wouldn't hear anything else. Like the scraping drag of a corpse pulling its wasted body closer and closer...

She scrambled to the edge of the mattress and clicked on her bedside lamp. Dim, yellow light flooded the room and she scooted back to the center of the bed, sitting up against the headboard and tucking her knees into her chest.

Her eyes took a panicked survey of her surroundings, skittering across the laundry piles cluttering the length of her dresser, to the shadowy space beyond her bathroom door, to the mirrored doors of her closet.

Nothing looked out of place. There were no rotting corpses dragging themselves toward her. A helpless tear leaked from her eye and she swiped at it, gathering her courage to lower her feet over the side of the bed.

As soon as they hit the stippled firmness of the rug, she sprinted to the bathroom to turn on the light, then locked the door to her bedroom and took a running leap back onto the bed. She was too afraid to look underneath it.

She exhaled a shaky breath and blinked at her reflection in the mirrored closet door. Her eyes were dark, haunted pools, and the skin beneath them looked bruised in her pale face. She glanced at the clock. 3 a.m. Tomorrow was going to suck if she didn't get back to sleep tonight.

She grabbed the tv remote from her nightstand and chose an episode of her favorite comedy, "The Big Bang Theory", from the on demand menu.

Just hearing the theme song was enough to drain some of the tension from her body.

What an awful dream. She was used to the corpse nightmares, though it had been a while since she'd had one. But she'd *never* had a dream like that about her grandmother before.

Thinking about it made her eyes water and she blinked angrily. It was unfair that her mind would play such a nasty trick on her. Grandma had always been a safe haven when it came to her fears about communicating with the dead.

The more she thought about it, the more impossible it seemed that her psyche would betray her by constructing such a horrible fantasy. It was almost as if some external evil had permeated the dream, purposely twisting the scenario into what would terrify her most.

The idea made her shiver and she pulled her grandmother's quilt up tighter to her chin. A normal person would dismiss the thought as paranoid and insane. But for someone who had been hearing the voices of the dead since childhood, it wasn't so farfetched.

She stared at the television, forcing herself to concentrate on the characters and the dialogue. The familiarity soothed her, and she relaxed into her pillow. Her eyelids drooped and a low hum rose in her ears.

At first she dismissed it as interference in the tv signal. But when it persisted, she paused the program.

The sound grew louder, expanding like a wet sponge between her ears. She froze, listening intently, and it resolved into a shaky whisper that she recognized as her grandmother's voice:

"*Danger. You're in danger, Mari. Must stay awake. Someone here needs to speak with you…*"

Chapter 9

Grey awoke to the soft hum of the hotel's air conditioning unit as it clicked on. Disoriented, he turned his head toward the red lighted numbers on the bedside alarm clock. They blurred and then resolved into 6:24 am.

He sat up and rubbed at the stubble on his chin. After what had happened with Scarlett last night, he was surprised he'd fallen asleep at all. Apparently the combination of exhaustion and an exceptionally comfortable bed had lured him into unconsciousness.

He rolled to his feet and plodded to the bathroom. He had half an hour to get ready for his workout and breakfast with Scarlett. His gut tightened at the thought, and he realized he was nervous.

He couldn't remember the last time he'd cared enough to feel anxious about a date with a woman. He wasn't cold-hearted, but he'd learned that romantic ties were tenuous at best in his profession.

What if she refused to see him again? Anger clouded his vision at the memory of her fleeing from him in panic. She was so damned strong. The thought of someone making her feel that helpless nearly blinded him with rage.

He took a deep breath and twisted the cold tap on full force, submerging his head beneath the water. He needed to get a grip. He was no good to her like this.

He swore to whatever God was listening that, if she agreed to see him again, he was going to be calm and rational. And gentle. And supportive.

Because the thought of her turning him away was so unbearable that it literally made his chest ache.

∞∞∞∞∞∞∞∞∞

Scarlett awoke at 6:03 am and frowned when she realized she wasn't in her own bed. The sound of soft, even breathing rose from the space beside her, and her gaze flew to Sydney's sleeping form.

Everything from the night before came flooding back. The mortifying scene with Grey. Sydney confiding in her about her rape. Scarlett recounting her own terrible memories.

She spent an uncomfortable moment searching her emotions, trying to decide how she felt. She'd feared that talking about it would make it more real. And in a way, it had.

But she realized that it had also diminished the intangible horror of it. It had helped turn it into something solid. And maybe solid things were easier to battle and, eventually, defeat.

Scarlett slid slowly off the bed, careful not to wake Sydney, and blinked home to shower and change into her sparring clothes.

"Good morning," Scarlett said quietly.

Pat looked up, startled. Sydney's fluffy black cat was curled on his lap. He had a steaming mug of coffee in one hand and a human newspaper in the other.

"Morning," he replied in bemusement. "Coffee?"

"I already had tea," she said as she plopped down onto the couch beside him.

"Is everything okay?" he asked, seeming at a loss for words.

Scarlett chuckled. "What's the matter, Pat?" she ribbed. "Are you afraid your girlfriend and I got a bit too chummy last night?"

He snorted. "What does it say about you that I find your snarkiness reassuring?"

"I don't know. But I believe it says *you're* a glutton for punishment."

The cat stretched and walked across their legs to settle on Scarlett's lap.

"Traitor." Pat smirked and took a sip of his coffee. "It's too early for verbal sparring with you, Letty. But I'm guessing your current attire means you're planning on keeping your date with Derrington this morning?"

"If he shows," she replied as she scratched the feline behind his ears. She sent a worried glance down at her tank-top and leggings. "Do you think this is appropriate for a human gym?"

Pat's gaze softened. "It's perfectly fine, Letty. Don't worry. You look great."

She nodded and they fell into a comfortable silence that was broken only by Jasper's contented purring.

"Sydney is not at all how I thought she would be," Scarlett murmured after a while.

Pat looked up from his paper. "What do you mean?" he asked.

"Humans have such short life-spans," she explained hesitantly, "I assumed that, as a species, their philosophies would be shallow and short sighted as well. But Sydney sees through to the heart of things in a way that spans beyond her narrow existence."

"She *is* my soul mate," Pat pointed out. "I'm counting on our connection to lengthen her life-span, despite my human side fouling up my sidhe magic."

Scarlett heard the fear behind his words and regretted her unthinking comment. "Of course her life-span will match yours," she scoffed. "Your magic is as strong as that of any full blooded sidhe I know."

Pat shot her a grateful look, then smiled and said, "She won you over last night, didn't she? I told you she was great."

Scarlett rolled her eyes at him. "Yes, she's great. Let's wake her up and tell her we think so."

Pat laughed. "I wouldn't try that for about five more hours."

Scarlett looked at him dubiously. "Are you telling me she's going to sleep until noon?"

Pat shrugged. "To know her is to love her. And her habits. Which include sleeping ridiculously late whenever possible."

Before Scarlett could come up with an appropriate response, the phone rang and Pat snatched the cordless handset from the coffee table. He gave an affirmative answer and hung up.

"Your date's on the way up," he told her.

Her stomach fluttered in response. She tried to take her furry ally to the door with her for moral support, but Jasper wasn't interested in being carted around. He jumped out of her arms as soon as she stood.

She opened the door just as Grey was getting ready to knock.

"Hi," she said, her stomach quivering with something other than nerves as she greeted him. She had only seen Grey in slacks and long sleeves. But today he wore gym shorts and a fitted cotton tank that molded his well defined chest.

Freshly showered and shaven, his clean scent teased her senses as her gaze drank in the firm, bare flesh of his muscled thighs and thick, toned arms.

The warmth in his dark eyes drew her, a hint of uncertainty flickering within them as they held hers. "Good morning," he replied softly.

"Hey brother, want some coffee?" Sparrow offered as he crossed behind Scarlett on his way to the kitchen.

Grey cleared his throat and glanced past her. "No thanks. Already had some and I don't want to be too jittery for my sword fighting lesson."

"Wise choice," Sparrow called.

Grey grinned at Scarlett. "Ready?"

Scarlett nodded. "Are you?"

Grey chuckled at the glimmer of challenge in her tone. "I was born ready," he replied as he held the door for her.

The hotel's gym was a large facility stocked with sturdy, modern equipment. Elipticals, stationary bikes and treadmills were grouped along one wall; while a collection of weight training machines and a free weight station took up the adjoining wall.

The remaining space was carpeted with spongy, interlocking mats. It looked like it was used for group exercise classes, but it was perfect for sparring.

Scarlett had snuck down earlier and left a couple of the practice swords she used with her beginning students. They were simple wooden staves and didn't seem too out of place amongst the other gear.

"Hey, these look a little like what we used to practice with in the Marines," Grey said, picking one up and testing its weight between his hands.

"Yeah, those should work," Scarlett replied with a smile.

"So Sparrow said you both trained with swords in Ireland. Were you in the military there?"

Scarlett used her stretching routine as an excuse to delay answering. Of all the things that had whirled through her mind as she'd gotten dressed this morning, the continuing lies between them were what bothered her most.

She sighed and looked him in the eye, giving him a half truth that she hoped would be enough for now. "Yes. Pat and I were both in the military."

As sidhe, they were warriors for the Seelie Court, and could be called upon to fight during times of war in the faerie realm.

"I don't know much about Ireland's military," Grey said thoughtfully. "What branch of service were you in?"

"I really can't discuss it," Scarlett replied, giving him a guarded look. "You said last night that it was difficult for some of the people in your life to understand your need for secrecy concerning your work. I get that," she said meaningfully.

Grey's gaze was considering as he absorbed her words and the implication behind them. He already knew that she was a highly trained martial artist. It made sense that she would have been in a specialized branch of the military.

But outside of his professional chain of command, he wasn't used to the people in his life playing the classified card on him.

"I guess I'm due for a taste of my own medicine when it comes to secrecy," he said drily. "So how did the two of you end up as cops in Florida?"

He pulled one ankle up behind him in a quad stretch and Scarlett's eyes followed the motion. There was something so tantalizing about the way the thick ropes of his leg muscles shifted beneath his smooth, dark skin.

She shook off her fascination with his body and tried to concentrate on his question.

"My brother, Doyle, moved here first," she answered truthfully. Then with a shrug she added, "Pat and I enjoyed visiting so much that we decided to stay."

"You make naturalization sound like an easy process," Grey remarked with a grin. "How long did it take you to become citizens?"

The question flustered Scarlett, but she quickly deflected it with, "Long enough. Now toss me one of those practice swords and quit stalling, Derrington."

"Yes ma'am," Grey said, his lips twitching with mirth. "You know, I kind of like it when you're bossy."

"Kissing up to the teacher won't get you out of this lesson without bruises," she replied silkily.

"Wait a minute, I still have the bruises you gave me the other night," he complained with a laugh. "I thought we were just practicing forms today."

"We are," she agreed with a smile. "But I've always been a proponent of practical application. So suck it up and show me what you remember from your training, soldier."

"Alright," Grey said, accepting her challenge. He moved through his guards and she stepped in to make minute adjustments to each stance. She explained the theory behind her corrections, showing him how they could affect his performance in a fight.

He was impressed as hell.

"Not bad," she complimented as she watched him flow through his five major strikes with attention to the improvements she'd suggested. He could easily hold his own in her intermediate class.

"Now let's put some of that into practice," she instructed, moving into sparring position with her own wooden sword.

"I knew you wouldn't be able to resist beating up on me for long," he said, his eyes twinkling with humor and respect.

"Just remember what I told you and you'll keep the bruising to a minimum," she replied, fighting a smile.

It didn't take long to realize she was only kidding. She was far too controlled to cause unintentional injury. And far too good to take any hits from him.

"You're doing very well," she encouraged when he shook his head at her effortless deflection of one of his thrusts. "If I were a lesser opponent, I wouldn't have been able to intercept that one."

Her ability to anticipate his moves was uncanny, while he couldn't read her intent at all. Her feints seemed to come from nowhere and her tactic changes were lighting quick. She was on to the next strategy before he could process what had happened.

But she always slowed down to recap her strikes and suggest ways he could have reacted differently to counteract her.

"How is it that you're not even winded?" he demanded on a breathless laugh.

"Honestly?" she replied as she pulsed his blade, once more foiling his attempt to get a strike past her guard. "You're still tensing up and over extending a bit. That'll tire you out fast."

Grey snorted. "It's pretty hard not to tense up with a master swordswoman like you coming at me. You realize how amazing you are, right?"

She pursed her lips at him. "Trying to distract me with flattery now, are you?" she teased.

"Is it working?" he asked hopefully.

She smirked. "Not a chance."

He was breathing hard, while she barely showed any sign of exertion at all. A fine sheen of sweat gave her tanned skin a healthy glow, and her eyes shone bright with her enjoyment of their sport.

"Of course, the ideal outcome of any sword fight is to disarm your opponent," she commented idly. "It's far less messy than running them through."

"I'm sure your opponents appreciate that outcome as well," he drawled.

"The simplest way to disarm someone with a long blade," she continued, "is to look for an opportunity to grapple with them. When you see an opening, you rush into their fighting space and engage them with your body and the pommel of your sword until they drop their weapon. Then you can get them into a joint lock and take them down. Like this."

It was all the warning she gave him. She stepped in and threw him off balance with a kick to his leg. Before he could recover, she jabbed the handle of her practice sword into his stomach, and as he doubled over, she knocked his own weapon out of his hands. A split second later he found himself lying on his back with her perched atop him, holding his wrist at an angle that would have broken it if he'd moved.

He blinked up at her in amazement, wondering if it was wrong that he was so incredibly turned on. Laughter danced in her eyes as she released his wrist and sat back, her hips rocking gently against his groin.

A quiet groan escaped his lips as he hardened instantly beneath her.

The thin material of their clothing did nothing to disguise his body's response to her. He shifted to find a more comfortable position, and reflexively pressed his erection upward into the vee of her legs. Surprise flitted across her expression and he froze as he realized what he'd done.

"I'm sorry," he murmured, searching her face and feeling like an insensitive jerk.

Her eyes were closed and her breathing was shallow. Concerned, he reached up to cup her cheek. "Scarlett?" he whispered questioningly.

She rocked slowly against him and her lids fluttered open, revealing sea-green eyes that were hazy with desire. Stark relief coursed through him, melding with the need that slammed into his gut.

He slid his hand to the nape of her neck, holding her gaze as he pulled her down and took her lips with a soft urgency the nearly shattered them both.

"This is crazy," she sighed against his mouth as he gentled the kiss. "I feel like I'm losing my mind whenever I'm around you."

"I know," he said simply. "I feel the same way."

He sat up, bringing her with him, and smiled as he pulled the loose band from her hair and combed his fingers through its length. "I think we should talk about what happened last night."

Scarlett took a deep breath and held it, releasing it slowly as she answered, "I know."

He nodded and brushed her mouth with a quick kiss. "But breakfast first."

"Breakfast first," she agreed with a relieved grin.

"I'm not sure they're going to let us in here wearing our sweaty workout clothes," Grey commented as he eyed the hotel dining room's delicate china, polished silver and hovering wait staff.

"Speak for yourself," Scarlett replied with a teasing smirk. "I feel as fresh as a daisy."

Grey smiled at her, his adorable dimple making an appearance in one smooth cheek. "I'm sure they'd let *you* in anywhere." The warmth in his eyes made her feel as if she was the only woman in the world.

"Two for breakfast?" inquired a pretty, young hostess.

Scarlett cleared her throat and tore her gaze from Grey's to nod at the girl.

"Will you be dining inside or out on the terrace this morning?"

"The terrace?" Scarlett suggested with a questioning look at Grey.

"That sounds perfect," he agreed. "You don't have a dress code, I take it," he remarked to the hostess as they followed her out onto a breezy patio with white linen clad tables shaded by enormous white umbrellas.

"Not for breakfast, Sir," she replied with a smile over her shoulder.

She led them to a table at the balcony's edge that overlooked a glimmering stretch of sandy beach below. Scarlett sighed as she sank into the thick cushions of a captain's chair and accepted a menu from the hostess.

Her entire body felt light. Her muscles were pleasantly limber from her workout with Grey, but it was more than that. It was as if a mental weight had been lifted from her as well.

She couldn't help marveling at her ability to relax amongst all of these humans, when just days ago eating at one of their restaurants would have made her a nervous wreck.

"What looks good?" Grey asked as he scanned the menu.

"I don't know," she murmured as she glanced over it. "I guess they don't offer a full Irish breakfast here?"

"Full Irish breakfast?" Grey repeated with a bemused grin.

She nodded. "You know, eggs, bacon, potatoes...blood pudding," she added, her lips twitching with humor.

He eyed her over the top of his menu. "You wouldn't be trying to test my food gross-out threshold now, would you? Because I grew up in the south, where people eat fried chitlins and pickled pigs feet."

"Chitlins?" Scarlett asked with a raised brow.

"Pig intestines," Grey clarified, "usually doused with vinegar and hot sauce."

"Mmm," Scarlett intoned on a laugh. "I don't see that on the menu either."

"I guess we'll just have to settle for the tamer pork byproducts, like bacon and sausage. I'll take you out for a hotdog later if you want, though," Grey offered, his dark eyes glinting with amusement.

"Make it tacos and I'm in," Scarlett countered.

"Are you asking me out on a date, Officer Thresher?" Grey teased.

Scarlett's heart skipped a beat at the unwelcome reminder that he believed she was a human police officer. She liked him far too much to want to keep the lie between them, but she didn't have any choice.

"Well," she replied finally, "you certainly weren't doing a very good job of asking *me* on a date. Hotdogs...pssh."

Grey chuckled at her quip, his grin widening as the waiter stopped and took her order for eggs over easy, crispy bacon, sausage, hash browns, and biscuits with strawberry jam.

She paused for a moment, one short, rounded fingernail tapping at the menu. "This omelet has tomatoes and mushrooms," she said thoughtfully, "so can I just get a side of sautéed tomatoes and mushrooms with my eggs?"

"Certainly ma'am," the waiter confirmed.

Scarlett thanked him and handed him her menu.

Grey placed his own order, a helpless smile playing across his lips as he returned his attention to Scarlett. He'd never seen such a beautiful woman ask for so much food with so little self consciousness.

"What's so funny?" Scarlett asked, her sea-green eyes searching his.

"Nothing," Grey replied with a shake of his head. "I'm just amazed to be sitting in this fancy hotel, having breakfast with the most beautiful, talented swordswoman I've ever met."

Her eyes narrowed and she tilted her head as if she was trying to figure out his angle.

"I'm serious," he told her softly. "You have no idea how rare a pleasure this is for me."

Scarlett swallowed and a pink tinge rose in her cheeks. Sunlight streamed across the deck behind her, gilding one bare shoulder and glinting in the silken strands of her hair. Her breasts rose and fell with her quickening breath, and Grey's mouth went dry at the picture of loveliness she made.

He wanted to touch her more than he'd ever wanted anything in his life. He wanted to make love to her slowly, savoring each inch of soft, creamy flesh. To taste her sweetness and watch her face as he gave her more pleasure than she had ever dreamed it was possible to feel.

Scarlett's lips parted on a shaky exhalation, her pupils dilating as if she could read his thoughts and was as aroused by them as he was.

Grey shifted his napkin in his lap, shielding his second erection of the morning from view.

A jarring clatter broke the charged silence as a waiter dropped a plate several tables behind them. Scarlett jumped and twisted in her chair to identify the sound, giving Grey a glimpse of the tattoo inked between her shoulder blades.

It was an intricate design, almost like a snowflake emblazoned within a shield of Celtic knot work. The green ink shimmered with an emerald glow as he studied it, and Grey blinked at the strange visual effect. She turned back around and he decided it must have been the way the sunlight hit it when she moved.

Her cheeks were still flushed, her expression uncertain. His candid admission before had obviously put her off balance.

"I like your tattoo," he commented, attempting to return them to a normal flow of conversation. "Does it have any special meaning?"

She lifted her elbow and reached back to rub her fingertips over the design. "It's an Aegishjalmur," she replied, a faint smile creasing her lips as he tried to mimic her pronunciation. "It's an ancient Norse symbol designed to provide warriors with protection in battle."

"Norse?" he repeated questioningly.

Scarlett nodded, grinning at his confusion. She'd thought it odd herself, until she'd studied ancient warfare. "Ireland's history is littered with Viking incursions. Celts and Vikings inevitably mixed, and my tattoo contains symbolism from both cultures."

"Very cool," he said with a nod of appreciation.

"And what of yours?" she asked, pointing to the words tattooed in large, curving script across his shoulder. "What does 'Semper Fidelus' mean?" she asked.

It was Grey's turn to brush his fingers over his ink. He was a little surprised that she didn't recognize the Marines' motto, but he supposed it wasn't as well-known in Ireland as it was in the States.

"It's a military tattoo," he answered. "It's Latin. It means 'Always Faithful'."

Her eyes lit with respect. "Very cool," she echoed.

Grey smiled. "It's a pretty common design. Go to a military base and you'll see it on every other arm."

"That doesn't diminish its meaning," she replied, her musical brogue turning soft. "Everyone from my village bears the Aegishjalmur. Yet each one is a sacred symbol of protection, unique to the warrior who carries it."

Grey gave her an odd look and she silently berated herself, realizing her talk of 'a village of warriors' might sound strange to him. The waiter brought their food and she fiddled with her napkin, struggling to regain her composure before she met Grey's gaze again.

"Tell me about your village," he requested, biting into a strip of bacon as he waited for her to continue.

She stuffed her mouth with egg, chewing slowly and thinking quickly. She was treading on dangerous ground with this topic. She needed to be far more careful about what she said to him.

"It's probably like a lot of small towns here in America," she replied finally. "The locals run all the businesses, there isn't much to do unless you travel to one of the bigger towns, and there isn't much privacy. Everyone always knows what everyone else is up to.

"But the people are the best you'll ever meet," she continued after another bite. "If someone's in trouble, the entire village pulls together to help."

Grey's grin was almost wistful. "What kind of house did you grow up in?"

"A small one," she replied with a laugh. "My brother and I shared a room until I was sixteen. Then I threatened to move in with Pat unless my parents let me convert the loft into a bedroom."

Her expression darkened, as if clouded by memories.

Grey frowned. "Did they let you have your room?" he pressed, the thought of her living with Sparrow making his chest tighten with something suspiciously akin to jealousy.

Scarlett took a deep breath and forced a smile. "Yes, I got my loft. I think I was at the age when a threat about shacking up with a boy was the most terrifying thing they could imagine." She smirked. "Not that Pat would have ever let me move in with him."

"Did you two ever date?" Grey asked.

Scarlett snorted. "No. But the entire village still thinks I'm holding a torch for him."

"Did you?" Grey asked, his intent gaze belying his casual tone. "Hold a torch for him?"

Scarlett caught his eyes and held them. "No. I never did. It was just easier to let everyone believe that than it was to explain to them why I wasn't interested in dating anyone else."

Grey nodded, the awareness that she was both reassuring him, and talking about her rape, twisting in his gut. He wanted to ask her more, but he didn't want to push her.

"Enough about me," she said, closing the window on the subject. "You said you grew up in the south. What was it like in your home town?"

"I was raised on the south side of Atlanta, Georgia, so I guess I'm more of a city boy," he drawled.

"Is it a very big city?" she asked, missing his raised eyebrow as she slathered a biscuit with sticky, red jam.

"It's a pretty major city," he said. "The Atlanta airport is one of the largest hubs in the country."

His tone told her that she should have already known these things, and her eyes flew to his as she tried to cover her ignorance. "I've heard of it, but I've never been there. What was it like growing up there?"

He shrugged. "Honestly? It was tough. It was the sort of place where the wrong choices were always easier to make than the right ones. And in my neighborhood, the wrong choices were the kind that got you arrested. Or worse."

"Did you get into a lot of trouble as a kid?"

Grey let out a humorless laugh. "I lost more friends than I care to count to the kind of trouble found on every street corner in that neighborhood. It was only by the grace of God, and my mother, that I didn't end up lost with them.

"My mom is the strongest person I've ever known. And I believe she kept me out of trouble with the sheer force of her will."

"She sounds like an amazing woman," Scarlett commented in a quiet tone.

"She is," he replied simply.

"And your Da?" she asked.

Grey's lip curled and his expression shuttered. "Never knew him."

"I'm sorry," Scarlett murmured.

"Me too," Grey replied.

"How often do you make it home to visit?" she asked.

"A couple of times a year for the holidays. Not often enough, as my mom is fond of telling me," Grey replied with a snort.

"Marietta, Georgia is home now. As soon as I started to make enough money, I moved Mom out of the old neighborhood. She refused to come to Virginia with me, said she was too set in her ways to pick up roots and move so far from everything she knew. So I bought her a nice little house on the outskirts of Atlanta."

"You're a good son," Scarlett said with a gentle smile.

"She's the best mom." Grey grinned at her as he sopped up the last bite of egg with his toast.

He pushed his plate to the side and glanced at his watch. "I hate to run, but I have a meeting at the Sheriff's office in forty five minutes. I wasn't kidding about that date, though. Can I take you out to dinner tonight? Assuming I don't have to fly out of here at the last minute," he added with a grimace.

She nodded. "I'd like that."

"Great," he breathed, signaling the waiter for the check. "I'll pick you up around 6:30 at Sydney's, if you don't mind asking her to call down to the front desk to get me elevator access?"

"Oh right," she said, remembering how Sydney's succubus friend had appeared and let her off the elevator the night before. "I'll do that."

"Will you give me your number so I can get in touch with you in case I'm going to be late?" he asked, taking his phone out of his shorts pocket.

Scarlett gave him a blank look.

"Your cell phone number," he prompted. "You do have a cell phone, right?" he asked with a laugh.

She shook her head, beginning to feel uncomfortable. She knew that Pat carried one for work, but she'd never found it necessary to have one of her own.

"You're kidding," he stated incredulously.

"I...left it at home," she fabricated.

"Seriously? What if there's an emergency?"

"I'm on holiday," she replied with a defensive shrug. "My family knows how to reach me."

Grey shook his head as he took some bills out of his wallet. "I can't even remember the last time I didn't have mine attached to my hip. I guess I need to go on vacation more often."

"Probably," she agreed, her mind reeling with the awareness that she wasn't going to be able to keep up this human charade with him for much longer.

But she couldn't tell him the truth and out her world to him. Pat would kill her. And who knew how Grey would react.

The best thing to do would be to end it with him now. She knew that. But the thought of never seeing him again made her feel like she'd been punched in the ribs with her sword pommel.

"Are you okay?" Grey asked.

She focused her troubled eyes on his and found him frowning at her in concern.

"You don't look so well all of a sudden," he said, reaching over to brush his knuckles across her cheek.

The tenderness of the gesture made her want to cry. She clenched her jaw against the unwelcome feeling, wondering what the hell was wrong with her.

"I'm fine," she insisted. "I think I just ate too fast."

"Okay," he replied uncertainly, his worried gaze still searching hers. "Well, I'm sure Sydney has something to settle your stomach."

She nodded and managed to smile.

"I really have to go," he said as he stood. "But thank you for the sword fighting lesson. And I'll see you around 6:30?"

"Yes. And thanks for breakfast."

"Any time," he murmured, dropping a kiss on her cheek before he left.

She put her fingertips to the place his lips had touched and watched the muscles in his broad back and firm thighs flex as he strode away. He really was one of the most beautiful men she'd ever seen.

She shook off her starry-eyed musings and glanced around for a private corner where she could blink out. She needed to get back to the faerie realm or she was going to be late to teach her first class.

Chapter 10

"I would be more useful if I could take a look at the freshest crime scene first," Villia admonished. Her short, white hair stood at attention, quivering with static electricity as she tried to pull information from the stale air.

Sparrow sighed, scanning the contents of the cozy living room with the west-facing picture window. An enormous fish tank rested on a low table behind the couch, empty of all but a few inches of sand and murky water.

"I know, Villia," he said apologetically, "but the human authorities are still looking at that house. We're much less likely to be interrupted here, and the scene isn't that much older."

The mage blinked her pale grey eyes at him and frowned. "It's faint, but a woman's voice is still bouncing around the ether in here. I might be able to cast a spell that will allow us to hear her final words."

Sparrow smiled. He had requested Villia for this specifically because she was a Sila djinn. She possessed an uncanny ability to sense disturbances in her natural element of air.

"See, you're already proving useful," Sparrow told her with a satisfied look.

The old mage snorted. "Don't get your hopes up just yet, Detective Sparrow. For all we know, Heather Peter's last words were her singing off-key in the shower. From the stink of that Morpheus potion, I'd be surprised if she was conscious enough to say anything before she died."

"You can smell it from here?" Sparrow asked curiously.

Villia raised a slim, grey brow at him and wrinkled her nose in distaste. "Your file said the human police smelled it at all the scenes, but couldn't find any residue to identify it? That's because it binds to oxygen molecules in order to find its way more quickly through the bloodstream. It doesn't settle and stick to the furniture, it remains in the air like a thinly scattered mist."

She shook her head and eyed the carpeted flight of stairs up to the second floor. "That's where it happened. Pain and horror. The atmosphere up there is thick with it. That's where she spent her final moments, and that's where I should cast my spell."

Villia's wiry frame took on a transparent cast as she shifted into a partial spirit form and drifted up the stairs. Sparrow had seen her do it before. She was literally using every cell in her body to analyze the air.

It was a highly specialized ability that took a great deal of concentration. He waited until she reached the landing before he followed her up with silent footsteps.

She glided unerringly down the darkened hall toward Heather Peter's bedroom, her nebulous silhouette wavering as she collected data. Sparrow kept his distance, and by the time he entered the room behind her, she had returned to solid form.

"Anything?" he enquired, taking in the sage green walls and rows of bookshelves.

"Yeah, a headache," she mumbled as she squeezed the bridge of her nose between her bony forefinger and thumb.

Sparrow reached into the inner pocket of his sports jacket and pulled out a tiny, drawstring pouch of healing dust that Lorien had given him. He tossed it to Villia, who gave him a grateful look as she caught it. She tilted her head back and sprinkled a silvery pinch of it over her eyes, sighing with immediate relief.

"High grade stuff," she said appreciatively as she handed the pouch back to him.

"Courtesy of my soul mate's faerie guardian," he replied with a faint smile.

"Your soul mate's a lucky girl," she said with a chuckle. "Unlike the one who lived here," she added soberly. "Her terror is the strongest essence lingering in the air of this house. Whoever killed her scared the piss out of her first."

"You read the file," Sparrow remarked quietly. "He raped her and strangled her."

The mage shook her head. "Terrifying, to be sure, but that's not what I mean. This woman was mentally tortured. It's as if he hooked into all of her deepest, darkest fears and made her believe they were coming true."

Sparrow frowned. "A death djinn could do that to one of his charges. Can you tell if her soul was intact when she died?"

Villia shook her head. "Not without seeing the body."

Sparrow grimaced. He hated sneaking into human mortuaries. He almost always ended up having to erase some poor attendant's memory.

"Did you get anything about the piece of shite who did this to her?" he asked.

Villia blew air into her hollowed cheeks. "There's an...imperceptible something. I can't put my finger on it," she said in frustration. "It's like he barely spent any time here. She definitely suffered in this room. But maybe he blinked her somewhere else to torture her?"

Sparrow nodded slowly. "It would explain why there's so little sign of a struggle. Perhaps he did the worst of it elsewhere, and then gave her just enough Morpheus to subdue her so he could finish her off quietly in her bed."

"It's a theory," the mage replied with a halfhearted shrug. "Let me cast this spell to see if I can magnify her last words."

Villia closed her eyes and began murmuring an incantation. Her low-pitched voice and the soft hum of the air conditioning unit were the only sounds Sparrow perceived. But those sounds gradually expanded in his ears, until he felt as if they would overtake his brain.

He winced as the pressure built in his head, feeling time slow painfully. Villia's voice rose as she completed the spell, the increase in volume almost unbearable to his senses.

Then suddenly she was silent. Sparrow's ears popped. The air conditioning faded from his awareness. And the dense ball of noise inside his head collapsed into a vacuum that sucked only the fading resonance of dead sounds into his eardrums.

"No! Please stop!" The woman's cry reverberated inside his head, so full of pain and fear that his breath left him in a rush.

"It's not real," she panted, *"NOT REAL,"* she reiterated forcefully, as if desperate to convince herself it were true.

Then she screamed. It was a piercing shriek unlike anything he'd ever heard—an embodiment of mindless terror. Sparrow cringed against the sound, unable to stop his hands from flying to his ears, though it did nothing to help.

Abruptly her screaming stopped, to be replaced by a helpless, choking gurgle. Her struggle for air went on and on, making him clench his jaw so tightly he thought his teeth would crack. Then finally the woman fell silent and the mage spell faded away.

The blessed normalcy of the A/C unit's hum returned to Sparrow's ears. He looked over to find Villia's expression grim, her parchment skin almost the same ashen grey as her eyes.

"I don't know if that told us anything," she said in a reedy voice, "except that we need to catch this bastard. Before he does the same thing to another poor woman."

Chapter 11

Scarlett hovered awkwardly in the small, bright space between the elevator and Sydney's front door. She hadn't been able to reach Pat all day. And she didn't think he'd appreciate it if she told his office it was an emergency, just because it made her uncomfortable to show up at Sydney's unannounced.

She took a breath and knocked loudly, unsure if Sydney would be able to hear her over the wild guitar strumming beyond it.

The music decreased in volume and there was a rustling on the other side of the door. Then it opened in a rush, and Sydney stood in the frame, her animated russet eyes looking Scarlett up and down.

"Wow," she exhaled. "You look amazing!"

Scarlett felt her cheeks heat beneath the other woman's scrutiny, and glanced self-consciously down at her attire. She didn't know where she and Grey were going for dinner, so she hadn't known whether to lean toward casual or dressy.

Her signature style was a black leather vest, jeans and a ponytail. She'd opted to keep the vest, replace the jeans with a chic pair of fitted slacks, and to wear her hair down. It had been a good decision, if Sydney's expression was anything to go by.

"Thanks," she mumbled.

"Come on in," Sydney invited with a wave. "I take it you have a date with Grey tonight?"

Scarlett nodded as Sydney closed the door behind them. "He said he'd pick me up around 6:30. He asked if you could let the front desk know he's coming. If you don't mind," she added hesitantly.

"Of course I don't mind," Sydney replied, grabbing the phone from its base before she dropped onto the couch. As soon as she hung up she asked, "So how was your workout this morning?" Her grin was unabashed.

"Good," answered Scarlett as she lowered herself onto the loveseat. She looked over to find Sydney watching her expectantly. "Um, good," she repeated. "Grey was a good student. Better than I expected."

Sydney nodded slowly, nibbling her lip to hide a smile. "And how was breakfast?"

"That was good also. Very nice. We sat out on the terrace overlooking the beach."

Sydney sighed. "You're going to make me pry, aren't you?"

"What do you mean?" Scarlett asked warily.

"I *mean*, I want you to tell me if you kissed him again," Sydney cajoled.

"Oh. That. Well, yes, we did."

"And was that 'good' too?" Sydney asked with a raised brow.

Scarlett relaxed into the cushion, unable to help the grin that spread across her lips. "Yes," she breathed, "it was."

"Now we're getting somewhere," Sydney muttered. "Did you discuss any of the things we talked about last night?" she asked gently.

"Not...directly," Scarlett replied. "But we agreed that we should talk about what happened."

"That's a good start," Sydney said, smiling. "Your hair looks nice down, by the way."

Scarlett reached up to smooth her hand over its length. "Really?"

Sydney nodded. "It softens your face and brings out the green in your eyes. You know," she added, tilting her head, "I think I have the perfect necklace to go with those earrings. Do you want to try it on? You don't have to wear it if you don't like it."

"Uh...yes, thank you," Scarlett replied, touched by the other woman's generosity.

"No problem. It's in my room." Sydney motioned for her to follow, leading her through a kitchen stocked with shiny silver human appliances, and down a short hallway.

Scarlett did her best to ignore her discomfort over intruding into Sydney's private space.

"Your room is beautiful," she complimented, taking in the huge canopy bed with gossamer silk curtains draped from its burnished cherry-wood frame. The carpet was lush and thick beneath her booted feet, the space enveloped with soft creams and dark blues.

"Thanks," replied Sydney, opening midnight satin drapes to let in the late afternoon light. The sliding glass door behind them led onto a balcony with an ocean view.

"My ex-husband gave me this necklace," she mused, crossing the room to a niche with a mirrored wall above a vanity sink. She bent to open a side compartment in a wooden jewelry stand, and rummaged around inside.

"You mentioned your ex-husband before. Are you two still...friendly?" Scarlett asked, uncertain if her question would be welcome.

"We see each other now and then." Sydney chuckled. "Actually, he and Angelica are dating. You met her—she's the succubus who works as a maid here."

"She's *dating* him?" Scarlett asked in disbelief.

"It's okay," Sydney reassured her. "Our divorce was painful, but sometimes what we think we want isn't really what we need. I think Angelica's a better fit for him. And I know Sparrow's a better fit for me."

"I...that's good," Scarlett replied haltingly. "It's just that I've never heard of a succubus *dating* anyone."

"Oh, right!" Sydney laughed. "Sometimes I forget how unusual Angelica is. I don't really know any other succubi."

"I've known a fair few," Scarlett commented. "And if what you say is true, your friend is unlike any I've ever met."

"Variety is the spice of life, right?" Sydney proffered with a shrug. "My friend, Sunny, is actually seeing a couple of incubi that Angelica introduced her to. Though I'm not sure if they're exclusive with each other.

"Ha, here it is!" Sydney held up a thin gold chain with a single diamond pendant worked between the links. "Try it on," she urged, offering it to Scarlett.

Scarlett gingerly accepted the necklace, lifting her hair and fastening it behind her neck as she gazed in the mirror. The chain was so fine that it was nearly invisible, only the intermittent shimmer of gold glistening against her skin above the diamond. The gem rested in the hollow between her collarbones, reflecting the light with a brilliant sparkle that made it appear as if a tiny star floated there.

"I know it's not the same teardrop shape as your earrings," Sydney apologized. "But I wanted you to see it anyway. Don't feel like you have to wear it if you don't want to."

Scarlett cleared her throat. "It's beautiful," she whispered. "I would love to wear it. Thank you."

"It really does look great on you." Sydney's reflection beamed at her in the mirror.

"I'm, uh, not very good at this girly stuff," Scarlett admitted quietly.

"Neither am I," Sydney replied, holding Scarlett's gaze. "I think it's because neither of us are that it works."

Scarlett chuckled and turned away from the mirror, frowning as she spied a tawny leather chair through the half open door of the closet. It looked out of place, and far too large for the space. "Isn't that the chair from your living room?"

Sydney winced and sucked air through her teeth, making a pained sound. "Yes," she mumbled guiltily. "Sparrow and I wanted to make sure you and Grey sat next to each other at dinner. Are you mad? Please don't be mad."

Scarlett pointed a finger at the other woman, schooling her expression into careful blankness. "That was a clever trick, sister. I'm going to have to watch out for you, aren't I?"

"It was a meddlesome attempt at matchmaking," Sydney said contritely. "And I apologize."

Scarlett watched Sydney fidget for a moment longer and then shook her head. "Don't fret about it," she chided, grinning as she moved to grab the chair. "Here, I'll help you put it back where it belongs."

Sydney scooted around the other side of the recliner so they could lift it together. "You enjoyed that just now, didn't you?" she speculated. "Watching me squirm?"

Scarlett bit her lip. "Perhaps a little."

Sydney laughed. "Of the two of us, I think *you're* the one to watch out for."

∞∞∞∞∞∞∞∞∞∞

Grey glanced at the time and tapped the speed dial on his cell phone.

"Hey Captain America, anything to report?" chirped Liza.

"I was just about to ask you the same thing, Lizzie. You get any hits on the supernatural angle?" he asked as he checked his reflection in the mirror and brushed a speck of lint from his charcoal grey slacks.

"Not unless you count the fact that all six victims had *Vampire Diaries* in their tv queues," she replied drily.

"Vampires?" Grey repeated, frowning when he noticed the fabric of his new black silk shirt was puckering around the collar. He'd paid a ridiculous price for the damned thing at the gift shop downstairs, and he didn't have time to exchange it before his date with Scarlett.

"Popular tv show," Liza explained. "Two vampire brothers, one's a sweet good guy, the other's an irresistible bad boy. They're doomed to forever have the hot bodies of eighteen year olds, but they've lived for more than a century, so women of all ages can drool over them without feeling weird about it."

Grey laughed. "Is that it? They all watched the same tv show?"

"Nothing else worth mentioning," Liza said regretfully. "Three of the vics made purchases at small new age-y type shops in their area within the last couple of months. But the shops are all independently owned and there's no connection between the items purchased: a book on faeries, a goddess-themed calendar, and a pair of crystal earrings—all from different distributers.

"What about you? Anything interesting turn up on your end?"

Grey sighed. "I met with the lead detective from the Sheriff's office this morning—decent guy—and briefed his team on the profile. Spoke with the lab techs and spent the rest of the afternoon at the crime scene. Same herbal scent was in the air, but still no id on it. I noticed the vic owned several books on supernatural topics, but maybe I'm just grasping at straws there."

"Maybe, maybe not. I'll keep looking into it," Liza promised. "One other thing. A call came through on the hotline from some woman in California who's claiming a serial killer is after her, a Marianne Thornton."

Grey could practically see Lizzie rolling her eyes through the phone, and he couldn't help but smile. So many tips came through the hotline on a daily basis that it wasn't humanly possible to check them all. Fortunately a good portion of them were easily dismissible, such as the ones involving alien conspiracies, Big Foot sightings, and other similarly ridiculous claims.

"I'm sure she's just some crackpot, but I thought I'd mention it because she insisted on speaking with you personally."

Grey's brows rose. "I wonder how she got my name."

"I don't know," Liza said with a grimace, "but she claimed to have some sort of psychic connection to Heather Peters."

Grey grunted in disbelief. He wasn't completely closed off to the possibility of there being unexplainable phenomena left in the world. But in his experience, people who contacted the FBI claiming to have a direct connection with such phenomena usually had a few screws loose.

He shook his head and fidgeted with his collar, wincing as the sharp edge of a cardboard tag jabbed into his neck. "Damn it," he muttered under his breath as he glanced at the clock and fumbled with the shirt's stiff new buttons.

"I know," Liza apologized. "But I texted you the info in case you want to follow up on it."

"No, it's not that," he assured her. "I want to hear what she has to say, crackpot or not. It's just that I'm late and I forgot to cut the price tag out of my shirt."

There was a brief silence, and then Liza drawled, "It's dinner time. And you're late. And you're wearing a new shirt. Who is she?"

Grey snorted. "Has anyone ever told you that you should be a detective?"

"Out with it, Grey," Liza demanded. "I deserve to know if you've found some rich Palm Beach sugar mama, and you're planning on retiring early. Lord only knows who they'll partner me with next."

"Hardly," Grey said with a chuckle. "She's a cop I met down in Key Largo."

"You suave devil," Liza accused with a grin. "You must have made some impression for her to drive all the way up there for a date."

"It's a long story. And I really am running late," he said as he shrugged his now-tagless shirt back on and re-buttoned it.

"Fine," she huffed. "I'll talk to you tomorrow. Just remember to wrap it before you tap it," she added, hanging up on his answering groan.

∞∞∞∞∞∞∞∞∞∞

"Come on in, Grey," invited Sydney as she opened the door to the penthouse. "Make yourself at home. I'm just switching out some laundry, and Scarlett will be out in a minute."

She shot him a smile and disappeared into a small utility room off the kitchen.

Grey wandered toward the living room and looked past the sprawling balcony, taking in the view of ocean waves gently lapping against the shore beneath the setting sun. He loved the green serenity of Virginia's forests, but there was something to be said for Florida's breezy tropical warmth.

He felt, more than heard, Scarlett enter the room behind him. He turned to find her lingering just outside the adjoining hallway, watching him. A wave of desire punched him hard in the gut.

She was so damned gorgeous, she literally took his breath away.

He'd desired women before, of course. But he'd never felt such a visceral reaction for anyone in his life. It was as if some deep part of him recognized her on a level so basic that he feared he'd never be able to get her out of his system again.

"Hey there, beautiful," he said softly.

Her lips rose in a tentative smile as she moved toward him, thin silk molding her toned thighs and supple leather hugging the curves of her breasts. He wanted to pull her into his arms and kiss her senseless, but settled for a chaste brush of his lips against hers.

"How was your day?" he asked.

Her smile seemed to slip, but was back in place so quickly he wondered if he'd imagined it.

"Typical vacation," she replied lightly. "Wondered around the hotel and took a walk on the beach."

In actuality, she'd taught one beginning, one intermediate, and two advanced swordsmanship classes today. And during her last sparring round, she'd been so preoccupied by thoughts of her upcoming date with Grey, she'd allowed old Aedan to slip beneath her guard and get in a good strike.

The grizzled veteran had looked as surprised as she did. And her ribs still smarted.

"That sounds restful," Grey replied with a grin.

"That's one way of putting it." Scarlett's lips twisted in a smirk. "How was your day?"

Grey shook his head. "Guy's still out there, so pretty unsuccessful."

Scarlett saw the frustration and guilt that cut across his chiseled features, and her eyes softened. She wished she could tell him it wasn't his fault—that the playing field was tipped against him because his quarry wasn't even human.

Instead she said, "Well, let's grab some dinner, soldier. You can get back in the fight tomorrow."

Grey chuckled. "That's the best advice I've heard all day. You said you wanted hotdogs, right?"

Scarlett lifted a brow and he laughed.

Grey watched Scarlett's face light up as she took in the colorful interior of the restaurant he'd chosen. The walls were painted in bright murals, with funky knick-knacks in shades of orange, turquoise and purple littering the privacy dividers between the booths.

They reminded him of the souvenirs found in every tourist shop in Mexico. But combined with the secluded seating arrangements and dim lighting from hanging lanterns, the restaurant gave off a cheerfully relaxed vibe.

"What a lovely place," Scarlett murmured as they settled into the thick cushions of a corner booth. She hadn't been to many human restaurants, and this one was decorated unlike anything she'd ever seen.

As soon as the hostess left their table, their server was waiting to take their drink order.

"Do you like margaritas?" Grey asked.

Scarlett nodded. That was the drink her brother, Doyle, usually served when he made tacos.

"We have a two-for-one special on our frozen strawberry, mango or lime margaritas this evening," offered the waiter.

Grey waited for Scarlett's preference, but she only blinked at the server in confusion.

"I think we'll just have them the old fashioned way," he told the younger man. "Do you have a favorite tequila?" he asked Scarlett.

"Uh, no. You choose," she replied. Doyle had learned to make the drink during his days as a bartender at a human restaurant in Dublin. But she'd never paid attention to how he made it or what type of liquor he used.

"Two Sauza margaritas, on the rocks," Grey told the waiter, "salt for me, how about you?" he asked Scarlett.

She smiled and nodded yes. That one she knew the answer to.

A busboy dropped off chips and salsa as the waiter left with their order. Scarlett reached to dip a chip, then closed her eyes and hummed a happy sound as she took a bite.

"Mmm…the crisps are still warm and the salsa tastes like tomatoes from the garden," she commented blissfully.

Grey knew he was grinning like an idiot, but he couldn't help it. Her pleasure was intoxicating. And her unique blend of strength and vulnerability was becoming an addiction.

Just that morning she'd shown him more sword fighting techniques in one lesson that he'd seen in all of his Marines instruction combined. Her skill and discipline were admirable. Yet here she was, treating the simple enjoyment of a dinner out as if it was a first time experience.

"What?" she asked, another chip arrested halfway to her lips. He was looking at her like she'd done something unusual again.

Her heart sank as she wondered how much longer she'd be able to blame her lack of human realm experience on their difference in nationality.

"Nothing," he replied quietly. "It's just that I keep realizing you're the most amazing woman I've ever met."

A blush colored Scarlett's cheeks, but she was saved from replying when the waiter dropped off their drinks and asked it they were ready to order.

"We need a couple more minutes, man," Grey said amicably.

Scarlett sipped her margarita, her eyes widening as she scanned the menu. "I've eaten lobster tacos before."

She figured it was a safe bet that Grey wouldn't find her admission too strange. She'd been to the roadside taco stand near Doyle's place in Key Largo many times, and nothing on their menu ever had lobster in it.

"I haven't either," Grey replied with a grin. "Do you want to try them?"

"I don't know," she said doubtfully. "I'm rather fond of the plain old ground beef ones in a crispy shell. That's what my brother used to make for dinner whenever I needed cheering up."

"The brother whose wedding you beat me up after?" he teased.

"I thought you might have forgotten about that, since this morning's more recent beating," she replied, popping another chip in her mouth.

"Ouch," Grey said, his eyes gleaming with humor. "Not going to let me hold our first meeting over you anymore, then?"

Scarlett shook her head slowly, nibbling her lower lip to keep her smile at bay. Her tongue darted out as if to soothe the nip, and Grey's stomach tightened in response.

He wanted to lean across the table and brush his own tongue across that sweet little indention in her bottom lip. He wanted to trace it and tease it until she opened in response and took him inside her mouth.

Scarlett's eyes flared with heat and she inhaled a shaky breath before sipping some of the icy liquid from her glass.

Not for the first time, Grey felt as if she could tell what he was thinking. And was as affected by it as he was.

He cleared his throat and reminded himself that he wasn't in any hurry. Tonight was about them getting to know each other better.

The waiter returned to take their orders, after which Grey made an effort to focus on conversation, rather than her delectable lips.

"So, is your brother a good cook?" he asked, returning to their previous topic. "Can he make anything other than tacos?"

Scarlett snorted. "The only other meal Doyle cooks is breakfast. And I'd wager more than a few ladies have been missing his omelets since my sister-in-law came around."

Grey laughed. "Bit of a player, was he?"

"Might as well have been his own tourist attraction."

She rolled her eyes and Grey grinned. "Do you like his new wife?"

Scarlett looked thoughtful. "Violet is…good for Doyle. She makes him happy. And I feel as if I haven't really given her the chance she deserves. I mean to get to know her better."

"It's always hard when someone you're close to finds their other half," Grey said with a nod of understanding. "You wonder if that person is right for them, but you know you can't do anything about it, even if you think they're not."

Scarlett studied him in bemusement. "That's very true. I don't easily trust people. And two of my best friends have found their soul mates in the past few months. My brother with his wife, and Pat with Sydney."

Grey tilted his head at her in curiosity. "Do you believe in soul mates, Scarlett?"

She flushed, taking a sip of her drink to cover it. For her people, soul mates were a reality. Mated sidhe couples bore physical proof that their union was destined. When a sidhe found his or her mate, the magical Aegishjalmur tattoo that they received upon coming of age appeared as a twin image on their mate's body.

It had been many years since she had dared hope that such a thing would happen for her. Yet she had no doubt as to the existence of the soul mate connection.

Humans were different. Their mortal lives were short and they were given no such proof, therefore many of them dismissed the idea of soul mates as a faerie tale. Which was sad, in a way, because karmic law provided that certain human relationships were just as destined as her people's soul mate connection.

She realized that Grey was still waiting for her response, and decided to be as truthful as she could. "I do. I don't believe it happens for everyone, but I believe that it does happen."

His answering smile was slow, and so sexy it took her breath away. "I hadn't pegged you for a romantic. But when I see a couple like Sparrow and Sydney, or an elderly couple that still holds hands and looks at each other like they're the only two people in the world...I can't help but believe in soul mates too."

Scarlett blinked at him. Everything about him continued to surprise her. He respected her strength without being threatened by it. He shared his own vulnerability without fear.

And the mere fact that she felt so drawn to him, despite him being human, was the biggest surprise of all.

The waiter brought their dinners and left with a warning that their plates were hot. Grey located the lobster taco in his sampler combo and cut it in half. Scarlett grinned as he placed a piece on her plate next to her ground beef ones.

"Now we can both say we've tried it," he told her with satisfaction.

They spent several comfortably silent minutes tackling their food. Then after a while, Scarlett said, "So, you never mentioned if you have any brothers or sisters."

Grey gave her a lopsided smile. "No. I'm an only child."

"Did you miss not having a sibling growing up?" she asked curiously. She couldn't imagine not having had Doyle around.

"I guess I watched my friends with theirs, and wondered what it might be like," he answered in a measured tone. "But my mother never had any interest in marriage or having more children."

Something about the way he said it sounded strained, and she peered at him, trying to figure out why.

He looked down at his plate, chewing slowly. He was about to tell her something he'd never told anyone. And the only reason he could come up with for doing it was that he wanted her to understand him. But, perhaps more importantly, he needed her to know that he was capable of understanding her.

"Remember I said I didn't know my father?" he asked, catching her eye once more.

She nodded.

"That's because my mother didn't know who he was. He attacked and raped her. They never caught him."

Scarlett gasped, waves of shock flashing through her. "I'm so sorry, Grey. How old were you when you found out?"

"She managed to keep it from me until I was twenty," he said with a mirthless chuckle. "My whole life she told me that my father was a deadbeat who ran out on her.

"But I'd been in the military for two years and was working toward a career with the FBI. And she knew that my parentage could come up during their background check and psych eval. She didn't want to take a chance on me finding out the truth from some clinician reviewing my file."

"Goddess, that must have been awful. For both of you," Scarlett said with a wince. She realized belatedly that most humans weren't used to addressing their deity in the feminine, but he didn't seem to notice.

"Yeah," he agreed in a hoarse voice. "I went from hating my dad for abandoning us, to hating him for an entirely different reason."

Scarlett reached across the table and squeezed his hand. "You're lucky you had such a strong, remarkable woman for a mother."

He threaded his fingers through hers, rubbing his thumb lightly over the pulse point at her wrist. "It amazes me that she never once made me feel like I was unwanted while I was growing up," he mused. "God knows, if it had been me, I don't think I could have stood the reminder of an attack like that.

"I asked her once why she kept me, and she admitted that she'd considered abortion. But her family was poor and very religious, and she had no idea who to talk to about it."

"I don't know that I could have done what she did," Scarlett mumbled on a tight swallow. Although pregnancy was possible between a sidhe and a human, she had been too young for it to be a concern after her own rape. But if she *had* somehow gotten pregnant, there was no doubt in her mind that she would have terminated it.

Grey shook his head. "No one would ever have the right to expect you to. My mother's decision was born from a blend of desperation, stubbornness and religious faith. I can't say I'm disappointed she made that choice," he said with a grim smile, "but I don't believe any woman should be forced to keep an unwanted pregnancy, regardless of the circumstance."

Grey released her hand to take a bite of taco, trailing his fingertips across hers in a way that left them tingling after the absence of his touch.

"So, I'm a little out of practice," he remarked several moments later, "but I'm fairly certain that was too much information to lay on someone during a first date."

Scarlett laughed. "I believe that rule only applies if you've not already had your arse kicked by the other person on two different occasions," she drawled with a deliberate thickening of her accent.

"Well, that's a relief," he said, grinning at her. "Does that mean I haven't scared you away from the possibility of coming back to my room for a nightcap? I managed to get my hands on a bottle of twenty year old Midleton 1991," he dangled.

It was a rare single cask Irish Whiskey. He had no doubt Scarlett would appreciate it, and he was eager to share a glass with her.

"I have no expectation of more than a drink," he added quietly, holding her gaze to make sure she understood. "Anything that does or doesn't happen between us will always be your choice."

His direct honesty slid past her defenses and sent a warm and jittery sensation straight into her core. It was part nerves, part anticipation of the pleasure he offered…if she was brave enough to take it.

She tried to shake off the intensity of her reaction as the waiter stopped back by the table and reached over to collect their plates. "How about some fried ice cream for dessert?" he suggested.

Grey looked to Scarlett and she shook her head.

"Another round of margaritas then?" the young man cajoled as he swept up their empty glasses.

"No thanks," Scarlett replied in a throaty tone, "I'm saving my appetite for a dram of whiskey later."

The look she gave Grey made him go hard beneath the table.

<u>Chapter 12</u>

Scarlett reclined on the couch in Grey's hotel room, watching as he pulled the bottle of twenty year old whiskey from its hinged wooden box and set it on the coffee table. She smiled when, next to it, he set a small bottle of spring water, and a pair of glasses that were properly tapered at the top.

"Would you like some ice?" he asked.

She lifted a brow at him, her eyes glittering with humor.

"Found that question funny, did you?" he observed as he sat beside her and stretched out his legs, his charcoal slacks molding his muscular thighs in a curiously distracting way. "I see how you are."

"And how's that?" she asked, openly grinning as her gaze travelled to his face.

"You're a whiskey snob."

She scoffed at him with mock outrage. "Why? For not wanting to numb my tongue and dull the flavor with ice?"

"Some people like a cube or two," he defended. "They say the cold mellows out the alcohol burn and opens up a new flavor profile."

"Bollocks," she snorted. "If you can't handle the burn, stay out of the whiskey. Besides, I don't see *you* adding ice."

"Personal preference," he replied with a shrug.

"Well, no one from my village would be caught dead adding ice to a fine Irish whiskey," she informed him. "They'd be chased out of the pub."

"I see," he replied, slowly rolling up the sleeves of his black silk shirt to reveal the smooth caramel flesh of his corded forearms. "So you come from a long line of whiskey snobs."

The unhurried movement of his fingers as they turned his cuffs was oddly mesmerizing, and it took her a moment to realize that he'd slurred not just her, but her entire village, with the 'snob' label again. Her eyes narrowed and flew to his, to find them simmering with laughter and something deeper—a patient but heated invitation.

"Just pour the whiskey," she said breathlessly.

Grey chuckled and leaned forward to break the seal on the bottle. "One finger or two?" he asked in a soft voice.

"Just one to start, neat," she requested.

He poured two identical glasses and handed her one as he settled back into the cushions beside her.

"It looks like melted butterscotch," Scarlett murmured as she held it up to the light.

"Mmm," Grey sounded in reply, appreciating the way the light glinted in her strawberry blonde hair far more than the way it illuminated the liquid in her glass.

He watched the thick fringe of her lashes flutter down over her sea-green eyes as she lifted the glass to her nose and tested the aroma.

"What do you smell?" he asked softly, captivated by the dreamy look on her face and the tiny spark of diamond fire nestled in the delicate hollow between her collarbones.

"Oak and vanilla," she replied without hesitation, an unhurried smile spreading across her face as she continued, "and so much ripe fruit… peaches, apricots, melon…honey," she added, the lilting brogue of her voice as enticing as the nectar she identified.

"There's more, but I can't quite put my finger on it." She frowned in concentration, making him want to reach over and smooth the pucker from her brow.

Instead he joined her in trying to distinguish the layered elements of the whiskey's complex nose. He smiled suddenly. "Think of the more exotic tropical fruits," he hinted.

"Kiwi?" she said finally, sounding both surprised and delighted.

Her enjoyment was contagious, and Grey's grin widened.

"Let's taste it," she urged with relish, taking a sip and rolling it across her tongue, allowing it to linger there with her eyes closed.

She drew a slow breath through her nose, the creamy swell of her breasts rising beneath supple black leather and a lacy whisper of silk. The graceful length of her neck tightened as she swallowed at last, letting the spirit slide down her throat.

"Mmm, Grey, that's lovely," she murmured, her voice gone husky.

Grey shifted and stifled a groan as all the blood in his body rushed to his cock. "You're lovely," he told her quietly.

Her eyelids flickered open and her gaze held his as she enfolded her glass between her palms, warming it. He couldn't tell if the color in her cheeks was from the liquor or his compliment.

Grey took a belated draw from his own glass, allowing the whiskey to coat his tongue and settle against his palate.

"Hints of all the flavors found in the nose," she commented in a roughened tone. "But it has some orange and spice to it as well."

Grey nodded, savoring the burn as he swallowed. "Ginger and cinnamon," he offered in agreement.

"And a trace of caramel and dark chocolate," she added, smiling as they both took another taste.

After a few moments he supplied, "It has a nice finish, warm and earthy. Want to see if a splash of water opens it up a bit?"

Scarlett shook her head, cradling the glass just below the sexy little indention in her bottom lip. "Not just yet. Sometimes I find that if I keep sipping it full strength, my taste-buds find their way around the sharper edges and I don't need it."

"Damn, woman," Grey exhaled in admiration. "Irish secret military, a sword fighting master, and a connoisseur of fine whiskey to boot. You know you're one-of-a-kind, right?"

Scarlett's blush was definitely his fault this time, and the knowledge gave him a dizzy rush of satisfaction.

"What's your favorite whiskey to keep on hand for day-to-day?" he asked her curiously.

"Old Proudfoot," she answered without needing to think about it.

Grey frowned. "I've never heard of that one."

Scarlett stiffened and he wondered if he'd offended her. But then she cleared her throat and explained, "It's a small distillery near my village. Their 10 year blended is an old family favorite and my Da sends me a bottle now and again."

"I'm sure it beats anything we get here in the States," he said with a wistful grin. "I have got to get over to your side of the pond one of these days."

Scarlett's smile seemed almost sad as she replied, "It's a beautiful place. I think you'd enjoy spending time in my village. And my cousins, Quin and Thom, would love you."

"Really?" he asked dubiously, thinking they wouldn't like him at all if they knew the sorts of fantasies he'd been having about their cousin. But he wanted to know more about Scarlett's family, so he said, "Tell me about them."

"Quin is a bear-sized oaf," she described with an affectionate snort. "But he's incurably sweet and has a quick wit. And Thom is a young know-it-all with blonde curls and a mouth that jabbers on long after he should have the sense to shut it."

Grey laughed at her forced glower. She obviously loved her cousins, regardless of any annoying tendencies. "You miss your village and your family, don't you?" he asked softly.

She studied him over the rim of her glass, an unfathomable look swirling in the depths her eyes. Then she tipped the last of the golden liquid between her lips and shook her head slowly before answering, "I'm not missing anything right now."

Grey's heart hammered in his chest at her admission. He nodded toward the bottle and asked, "Would you like another?"

She shook her head again, leaning forward to place her empty glass beside his on the coffee table. Then, with the fluid grace of a jungle cat, she turned and straddled him, settling lightly onto his lap.

Grey groaned as his growing erection pulsed beneath her. His hands came up to rest against the lean curves of her hips and he tilted his head back to look into her eyes. Her expression was heart-rendingly uncertain as she whispered, "Is this okay? I haven't really done this before…"

Shock prickled across his nerve endings and he struggled to find words that wouldn't make him sound like a complete idiot. Finally he lifted a hand to cup her cheek and managed, "Scarlett, you've never…?"

Her delicate skin flamed with embarrassment and she tried to look away, but he wouldn't allow it.

She swallowed and replied in a small voice, "Never willingly."

He expelled a rush of air, his jaw clenching until the muscles along the sides began to jump. "How old were you?" he asked tightly.

She hesitated, his raw anger unnerving her.

He took a deep breath, brushing his hand down the length of her hair as he made an effort to calm himself. "Please baby, you have to talk to me about it, just a little," he entreated.

She gave a jerky nod and replied, "I was sixteen. There were two of them."

His hands made involuntary fists, his knuckles cracking before he was able to force them open again. "Do you know who they were?" he asked in a deceptively quiet tone. "I think I need to kill them."

"I think Pat already took care of that," Scarlett assured him on a shaky laugh.

"Good," he growled. "I knew there was a reason I liked him." Vigilante justice wasn't usually Grey's style, but in Scarlett's case he would have made an exception.

He reached up to feather his thumb across her temple, smoothing some stray strands of hair to rest behind her ear. "So in all the years since, you've never been with anyone?"

Scarlett nibbled her lip, feeling achingly vulnerable. "I never wanted to before."

Grey's chest tightened with a conflicting tangle of desire, guilt, sorrow, and some other emotion he wasn't quite ready to identify. He wanted to kiss her so badly that it was hard to breathe. But he was afraid that if he rushed things with her, they'd both regret it.

"I have to ask, baby, are you sure?" He searched the sea-green depths of her eyes for some sign that he wasn't about to fuck things up beyond repair. "Why now?"

Scarlett was embarrassed by his sudden hesitation. She'd been afraid of this—that as soon as he found out what happened, that she'd never been with anyone else, he might not want to be with her. She didn't believe he was some fool who thought her tainted, but neither could she offer him the uncomplicated sexual relationship he was probably used to.

"I know I freaked out on you last night," she admitted, wounded pride shining in her eyes, "and I understand if this is just too complicated for you."

She started to pull away and Grey shook his head, caging her with his arms. "Whoa, baby, hang on. That's *not* what I said."

He waited until he caught her gaze again. "I want you, Scarlett," he told her in a heated tone, "more than I've ever wanted anyone in my life. Every time I see you all I want to do is touch you. I'm hard for you right now." He punctuated the confession with a gentle thrust of his hips that made her gasp.

"My desire for you isn't what's in question here," he asserted. "And I'm never going to view making love to you as a complication. An honor and a privilege—most certainly a pleasure—but never a complication."

His honesty and the glint of humor in his eyes made tears well in hers. He reached up with both hands to brush them from her cheeks.

"My only concern here is doing what's right for you," he said softly. "I don't want to rush you, or do something that might trigger a panic attack like the one you had last night."

Scarlett nodded and took an unsteady breath. "I want you too."

Something deep inside Grey reacted to those words with such force that he had trouble following what she said next.

"I don't know why now, after all this time," she confessed. "And I don't know if there can be anything between us beyond this. All I know is that I need for you to touch me. And I think I can be okay with it as long as...I don't feel trapped beneath you."

She winced as she said it, like she was afraid he'd be put off by that being a condition of their love-making.

Grey's eyes widened as his brain caught up with her meaning. "Baby, you're saying you want to be on top?"

"If that's okay," she affirmed, encouraged by his tone.

"Scarlett, honey, that is the sexiest request I've ever received," he said with a chuckle. "If it were up to me, you'd always be on top."

A heady rush of relief coursed through Scarlett at his words. She gave him a luminous smile and lowered her head to skim her lips against his.

The caress was achingly light, but it was enough to send lightning streaking across Grey's nerve endings. When she started to withdraw, he caught her head with his hand, threading his fingers through her hair and gazing into her eyes as he pulled her back.

He rubbed his lips gently against hers, his senses starved for her. He kissed across her delicate upper lip with fluttering brushes of his mouth, shifting to her plump lower lip and catching it softly between his so that he could graze its sensual little indention with his tongue.

When he deepened the kiss, stroking inside her mouth with leisurely thrusts, it awoke a primal rhythm within Scarlett.

She melted into him, her arms sliding around the solid expanse of his shoulders as her hips pressed down into the rigid warmth of his thighs.

She could feel his thickening length through the gauzy silk of her slacks, and it sent a wave of mind numbing need rolling through her core.

She strained against him, seeking the tantalizing friction and heat of his body. Grey groaned and circled his hips upward into the vee of her thighs as he devoured her mouth. His fingers found the top button of her leather vest and worked it free, his thumbs smoothing over the cresting swell of her breasts before moving to free the next fastening.

Her nipples pebbled beneath her silk camisole, and she whimpered into his mouth as his thumbs found them and stroked them into hardened little peaks before returning to free the third and final button.

He cupped the weight of her breasts through her whisper of lingerie, caressing lightly as he gentled their kiss. She trembled at his touch. She had always assumed that the nipple was the most sensitive part of the breast. But the soft brush of his fingertips along the sides and lower curves was the most exquisite sensation she'd ever felt.

With a final taste of her mouth, he pulled back and captured her gaze, his dark eyes smoldering with heat. "Everything I do is for your pleasure, Scarlett," he said in a hoarse voice. "If I do anything that you don't like, just tell me and I'll stop."

She nodded and moistened her kiss-bitten lips. "And what of your pleasure?" she asked throatily.

The smile he gave her was sinful. "Your pleasure *is* my pleasure."

Grey dipped his head to her breast, and she was lost as the flat of his tongue laved slowly across the dampening silk, caressing the curves his fingertips had grazed only moments before. The meaning of his words spun in her brain and her thoughts turned hazy as raw desire sizzled through her bloodstream.

He lapped at her nipple with slow, broad strokes, the pressure of his tongue and the rasping of the heated silk making her shudder. She slid one hand up the back of his head to hold him close, his skull trim like roughened velvet against her palm.

Grey's fingertips skimmed lightly down her stomach and glided beneath the waistband of her slacks and panties. His thumb unerringly found the tiny nub of her clit and pressed there as he drew her nipple between his lips to suckle.

Scarlett's head dropped backward on a muttered, "Ah, Goddess," as a rush of liquid passion left her wet between her thighs. His tongue circled her nipple, his thumb mirroring the movement below, and she whimpered at the intensity of the sensations coursing through her.

She wasn't unfamiliar with the mechanics of sexual pleasure, but she'd never had a strong urge to explore such things on her own. Apparently she'd been missing out.

Grey's thumb slid lower, gliding through the silken dew between her open thighs, and he shuddered beneath her. "God, baby, you're so wet," he groaned against her breast.

He lifted his mouth to hers once more, his tongue stroking hers as his hands slid beneath her ass. "Wrap your legs around me," he murmured, never breaking their kiss as he stood and walked them to the bedroom.

Setting her gently on her feet, he reached for the edge of her camisole and slowly slid it up the sensitized flesh of her stomach and breasts before lifting it over her head and dropping it to the floor. His eyes holding hers, he unzipped her slacks with the same unhurried movements, hooking his thumbs over the waistband to push them down the lengths of her legs.

"You are so damned beautiful," he whispered reverently, dropping to his knees before her and smoothing his palm over the black lace that covered the crisp blonde hairs of her sex.

Looking up at her he said, "Spread your legs for me, baby," his voice making an enticement out of the command.

She did as he asked, and he leaned forward to kiss her through the lace, drawing his tongue languidly up the satiny panel of fabric that was already damp with her desire for him. When she gasped and swayed on her feet, his palms moved to cup the cheeks of her ass, steadying her as they held her to his mouth.

He kneaded and parted the toned globes, adding another dimension of sensation as his tongue retraced its path of liquid fire up between her thighs. He teased and nipped her tender flesh through the fabric, pressing up into the shallow valley between her labia, caressing her there with unhurried strokes.

Her fingers tightened against the back of his head and she moaned, her thoughts dissolving into incoherence as her body was consumed with feverish waves of heat.

He urged her backward until her legs hit the end of the bed and she collapsed into a sitting position on the edge. Grey moved between her thighs, his body spreading them wider, and cupped her face in his palms. "Doing okay, baby?" he asked softly.

She tried to speak, but no sound passed her throat, so she swallowed and gave him a dazed nod. Grey grinned and captured her lips with his before trailing his mouth down over her breasts and stomach. His tongue dipped into her belly button, feathering kisses around it as he murmured, "Lift up, baby."

He worked her panties down her hips and over her legs, tossing them aside before smoothing his palms back up the insides of her thighs. He held her gaze as he slowly spread her wide and lowered his mouth to her once more.

His tongue teased and lapped at her, drawing her cream from her soft folds, and Scarlett sank back onto her elbows as she watched him. Her breath came in short bursts and deep tremors of need echoed through her. The flesh beneath his mouth began to throb and she inhaled sharply.

Grey looked up with concern in his eyes. "Scarlett?" he asked.

"I ache," she gasped huskily.

"I can fix that," he whispered, reaching up to brush his thumb over her nipple. Keeping his eyes locked to hers, he fastened his lips around her clit, tonguing it gently as he trailed a finger through her soft folds, gathering her wetness on his fingertip before sliding it inside her.

She tightened reflexively against the invasion, but the width of his shoulders held her thighs open. His finger withdrew to caress her inner lips, gathering more of her honey before plunging inside to stroke her intimately once more.

The sweet, sliding friction of his touch transformed the ache into ecstasy, and she groaned in wonder as her body bloomed for him, straining to take him deeper.

Still holding her gaze prisoner, he ground his tongue against her clit and withdrew from her body, sliding two fingers up through her moisture and working them both into her at the same time.

Scarlett murmured a plea in Gaelic, her vision blurring as his fingertips stroked and coaxed, gliding faster into her heated sheath. An extraordinary feeling began to build deep within her, a tiny ball of pleasure spinning and expanding. It gathered momentum, rolling outward in all directions, rippling through every cell and nerve ending until her body and mind could no longer contain it.

Scarlett cried out Grey's name, surrendering to the first orgasm she'd ever experienced as she fell backward onto the bed.

When Scarlett finally opened her eyes, Grey was standing at the foot of the bed, still fully clothed, and watching her with an expression of reverent awe. She stretched languidly and smiled at him, too relaxed to be embarrassed by her nudity. For the first time in her life she felt…sexy.

He sat beside her and handed her a fresh glass of whiskey, trailing his fingertips down her side as she propped herself up to take a sip.

"That was amazing, baby," he said in a quiet voice.

Scarlett grinned at him over the rim of the glass. "I think I'm the one who should be saying that."

Grey shook his head, unsure how to explain without sounding like a besotted fool. As he'd touched her, he'd felt her pleasure as if it was his own. He'd started to come just from watching her orgasm. Not that he wouldn't have expected the sight to be arousing, but he'd actually felt as if he experienced it with her.

"Trust me when I say that it was just as good for me as it was for you," he assured her.

She ran her tongue along her bottom lip, spreading the tingling warmth of the liquor, and he went instantly hard again. He'd never seen anything sexier than Scarlett, stretched out naked on his bed, drinking twenty year-old Midleton.

"I want to see you," she told him in a whiskey roughened tone. "All of you."

Grey expelled a harsh breath and placed her glass on the nightstand, seizing her mouth in a heated kiss. She tasted of wood-fire and spice, lush fruity overtones blooming on her tongue like piquant drops of rain.

She reached for the tiny buttons of his shirt, her nimble fingers working them through the stiff buttonholes with remarkable speed. Peeling the black silk from his thick shoulders, she broke their kiss and leaned back to look at him.

She'd seen him in his fitted cotton tank during their workout, and it had been obvious that he had an amazing body. But the sight of his bare flesh gleaming dark bronze over the tight muscles of his chest and well-defined abs made her pulse quicken and her mind go slack.

She brushed a thumb over one of his flat, dusky nipples, enthralled by the way he trembled beneath her touch. When she swept her tongue across it, he groaned and clenched his fists against the sheets. Scarlett moved lower, trailing her lips across the firm contours of his stomach. His skin was warm and smooth against her tongue, tasting of salt and a unique essence that was all Grey.

His abdominal muscles rippled as she trailed her fingertips along the inside of his waistband, finding the hidden fastening of his tailored slacks and releasing it.

She unzipped and tugged, pulling the fabric past his firm buttocks and down his muscled thighs, revealing black boxer-briefs that were stretched taut over his erection.

Her eyes rose to his, brimming with desire, and an uncertainty that was so unlike her it made his chest ache.

"Touch me, Scarlett," he rasped. "If it feels good for you, I guarantee it will feel better for me."

Her answering smile was slow, and so seductive it could have made an angel fall from grace. He forgot how to breathe as she lowered her mouth to his cock and licked a fiery path up his hardened length, chafing softly against the thin layer of cotton that restrained him.

Her tongue repeated its wicked progression, her lips wrapping around the swollen outline of his head when she reached the tip. Suckling gently, she tasted the musky elixir of his pre-cum through the dampened fabric.

Grey released a hoarse shout and dragged her up his body. He plundered her mouth with a savage kiss, pulling her thighs apart so that she straddled him.

Scarlett broke away, giving him a questioning look. She'd sensed the pleasure she was giving him with an awakening instinct she didn't know she possessed. "Why did you stop me?"

Grey framed her face with his palms, his expression stark with need. "I'll never last if you keep touching me that way with your mouth, baby."

He smoothed his thumbs over the soft wisps of hair at her temples, nipping and teasing at her lips until she opened to him. Sliding one hand down her back, he began a slow, rocking thrust with his hips, pushing up into the silken valley of her sex.

Scarlett moaned and echoed his movements, grinding downward against him in a rhythm that was every bit as provocative as her mouth had been. Grey shuddered, overwhelmed by the wild sensation of their mingled pleasure, and fought not to release in his underwear like a teenager.

He gentled his thrusts and murmured, "Scarlett, baby, do you want me inside you? It's okay if you're not ready…"

She closed her eyes and muttered something low and fast in Gaelic, then said in a husky tone, "I want you inside me, Grey. Please."

His heart stuttered at her words, and he lifted off the bed to pull away the last piece of fabric that separated them. The first slide of her slick, heated folds against his rigid flesh nearly undid him as he reached for the box of condoms in his nightstand.

She blinked at the little foil packet in confusion as he started to rip it open. "What's that for?" she whispered.

He gave her an odd look. "It's not that I think either of us have anything," he explained haltingly. "I just assumed…are you on birth control?"

Scarlett's eyes widened in comprehension. "No. I mean, no, we don't need that."

Grey hesitated, and his refusal to take a careless chance on bringing a child into the world unlocked a deeper facet of her desire for him.

"Just trust me," Scarlett said with a soft smile. "I'm not fertile now."

Something akin to sorrow flashed across his gaze as he wondered if her trauma had made her sterile. He nodded his head and tossed the condom back on the nightstand, claiming her lips with a sweet possession that promised to make them both forget everything but the heat and passion they shared.

Grasping her hips, he settled her against him, hissing at the way her delicate cleft embraced his thickened shaft. He slid himself back and forth slowly between the swollen lips of her vagina, brushing the sensitive nub of her clit with each pass, until he felt her liquid nectar begin to flow around him.

Scarlett's breath came in short gasps, his movements stealing her ability to think as fissions of mind-numbing sensation radiated throughout her body. And at the center of it all was an inexplicable, burgeoning need—to feel him more, to feel his touch deepen—that threatened to shatter her control completely if it wasn't sated.

She whimpered into his mouth, her kiss turning desperate. Grey slid his palms beneath her ass, spreading her open and lifting her so that the slickened knob of his cock was positioned at the entrance to her body.

He pushed into her with an unhurried thrust, gliding slowly up through her tight, velvety channel until her hips met his and he was seated deep inside her. The pleasure was so profound that his vision went dark and stars swirled in the waiting satiny blackness. He shook his head and tried to speak, but only a rumbling groan escaped his throat.

Scarlett nibbled at his lips, whispering, "Oh Goddess, Grey please… more."

He lifted her again, sliding her up the length of his shaft and pulling her back down with greater force. Scarlett let out a keening little moan, experimentally using her thigh muscles to duplicate the movement. She murmured a throaty plea as she realized she could take control of the rhythm.

She pushed herself up, savoring the fullness and the heated glide of him as his thickened head slipped through her, stretching her inner walls until she almost withdrew from him completely. Her muscles clenched in protest at his loss, and her body released a rush of liquid, as if it wept for her to take him back inside.

With agonizing leisure, she slid back down his shaft. The sensation of him filling her curled up her spine and rippled out into her extremities, until the entire surface of her body vibrated with pleasure. A flush warmed her skin and a soft whimper left her throat as she repeated the movement faster.

Grey rocked back against the headboard as she began to ride him, her beautiful eyes glazed with desire as her hands pressed into his shoulders for leverage. He pumped up into her as she came down, thrusting deep, and a cry of assent broke from her lips as she drove the pace harder.

Her inner muscles gripped him as a flood of her honey washed over his cock, easing his passage through her tightening sheath. He reached down to massage his thumb against her clit, and she bucked against him, her entire body trembling as her orgasm began to roll through her.

Grey took control once more, driving up through her clenching channel, intensifying and prolonging her climax, before he finally took his own release with a hoarse shout of ecstasy.

Scarlett collapsed bonelessly against him. For a long while he held her there and simply enjoyed the intimate press of her weight and the warmth of her skin against his.

Then, when he regained control of his limbs, he slid them both down the mattress. Slipping out of her body, he rolled to his side, still holding her within the circle of his arms. She gave a drowsy murmur as she turned and snuggled her tight ass right up against his groin.

His pulse leapt and, to his surprise, he began to stiffen again. But she was already taking the slow, even breaths of sleep. He chuckled quietly and reached over to dim the light, not wanting to darken the room completely in case she awoke disoriented.

He yawned and smiled, thinking he was the luckiest man alive. Gently brushing her hair aside to reveal the intricate tattoo inked between her shoulder blades, he studied it with lazy interest.

It was beautiful and a fittingly unique choice for Scarlett, with its complicated Celtic knot work and curious snowflake design. It drew him in, its green color vivid and intriguing.

Grey closed his eyes and leaned forward to skim his lips across it. The warmth of her skin lulled his senses as a curious tingling vibration caressed his mouth, like a faint electrical current. His lids flickered open and he blinked as the ink seemed to shimmer with an emerald glow.

But when his eyes refocused, it was gone.

Telling himself he must have imagined it, he shook his head and dropped a soft kiss on Scarlett's nape. Then he drifted off to sleep.

Chapter 13

Grey sat in his rental car outside the austere governmental complex that contained the Medical Examiner's office and the morgue. The sky was heavy with impending rain and a dreary blanket of clouds trapped the summer heat in a stagnant mass of air.

He rubbed his throbbing temples, unsure if his headache was from the weather, caffeine deprivation, or sheer aggravation. Whatever it was, he sincerely regretted not staying in bed with Scarlett this morning.

So far today he'd had to deal with a prickly homicide sergeant, a boneheaded morgue attendant, and a criminally negligent drive-through employee. And it was only noon.

He suspected the sergeant's annoyance was spurred by an internal conflict with his detective, rather than by Grey's actions. But uncooperative locals never helped a case, so Grey made the effort to smooth things over nonetheless.

After that waste of time, he'd come by the morgue to view the victim's body, and discovered that she had been 'misplaced'. When they finally located her, the attendant refused to admit he'd made a mistake—despite the fact that a homeless man seemed to be missing his toe-tag, and Grey's female vic wore one labeled '*John* Doe'.

And, maybe worst of all, he suspected the vacant-eyed employee at the drive-through had given him decaf by mistake when he'd stopped for his mid-morning coffee.

He rubbed at his temples again, thinking longingly of fine whiskey and Scarlett lying naked in his bed.

Now, God help him, he was about to return a call from some whack job in California who claimed to have a psychic connection to his Virginia victim.

He'd been searching for a possible paranormal connection between the vics, but this was ridiculous. It merely illustrated his desperation, and failure to make headway on the case, that he was willing to talk to the woman at all.

The phone rang three times before a soft, jittery voice answered, "Hel... hello?"

"Hello. This is Agent Greyson Derrington calling for Marianne Thornton."

"Oh, thank God," breathed the voice. "This is Marianne. Thank you so much for taking the time to call me back."

Grey frowned. She didn't sound crazy. She sounded terrified. "Yes, ma'am. I received a message that you think you have some information regarding a serial murder case that the FBI is investigating."

"Yes, I…I think that the man who murdered Heather Peters is after me."

"Did you know Heather Peters?" Grey asked.

"Uh, no. I'm sorry. I didn't," she replied shakily.

Grey waited for her to elaborate, but she remained silent. "Ma'am, has someone threatened you?" he questioned.

"Marianne. Please call me Marianne." She let out a small, weary sigh. "No, Agent Derrington, I haven't been threatened, exactly. And I know how insane this is going to sound. But Heather contacted me night before last. She told me you were working her case, and I didn't know who else to call."

A chill crawled up between Grey's shoulder blades. "Pardon?" he said in a quiet voice. He was irritated that such an obvious fabrication had spooked him. She was either an excellent liar, or she truly believed that she'd spoken to a dead woman.

"Heather kept a dream journal," Marianne said in a rush, as if afraid he would hang up on her. "She said you read it when you were at her house."

"How would you know that?" he demanded.

He immediately regretted betraying an emotional response. Christ. There were only so many ways she could know about him reading Heather Peters' journal. And one of them included her being connected to the killer.

Grey took a calming breath and asked her the question he should have asked, "Do you know who killed Heather, Miss Thornton?"

There was a beat of silence, and then she replied, "I know Heather started having terrible nightmares before he killed her. I know he used some kind of drug to keep her asleep. I know you had someone pick up her pet fish so they wouldn't die." Marianne gave a teary laugh. "She thanks you for that.

"And I know you probably won't believe me until it's too late," she added in a sober tone. "But he stalks us in our dreams. I don't know how, but he does. And he's coming for me next."

She swallowed audibly. "I don't know how much longer I can stay awake, Agent Derrington."

Grey was still reeling from the fish thing. There was no possible way she could know about that, unless this was Liza playing some kind of practical joke. But this was too tasteless, even for her.

Of course Marianne might know about the fish if she, or someone she knew, had been watching Heather Peters' house…but that still didn't explain the fear in her voice.

"Miss Thornton, have you left California at any time during the last week?" he asked finally.

"No," she answered in surprise.

"Would you be willing to answer a few more questions down at your local police station?" he inquired.

"You think I'm involved, don't you?" she replied on a helpless laugh. "I'm not. And they're just going to think I'm crazy. But as long as they give me caffeine, I'll answer whatever questions you want."

"Good. I appreciate your cooperation," Grey said, hoping she didn't disappear in the wind as soon as they got off the phone. "Are you currently at your home address?"

"Yes, I'll be here," she confirmed tiredly.

"I'll make a call and have a patrol car pick you up. Feel free to ask the officer for identification before opening your door."

"I'll do that," she replied. "But when this guy comes for me, it's not going to be in a patrol car while I'm awake. It's going to be while I'm asleep, in a nightmare that he creates.

"So if I'm the next body you find, Agent Derrington, please remember what I told you. Because he's not going to stop until you make him."

She hung up and Grey slowly lifted the phone away from his ear, shaking his head in disbelief. *What the hell kind of Freddy Krueger bullshit was she selling?*

Dream killers and communicating with dead victims. But whatever her deal was, he needed to get to the bottom of how she knew about the journal and the fish.

It was unnerving how convinced she'd sounded, though.

He speed dialed Liza.

"If it isn't my favorite man in black," she drawled into the phone.

He smiled. "If it isn't my favorite goddess of the interweb."

"I should totally black hat your system for that noob slur," she said with a snort. "Luckily you also referred to me as a goddess, so you remain in my good graces."

"I have no idea what any of that meant, but I have a feeling that being in your bad graces would be terrifying, Lizzie."

She laughed. "What's up Captain America?"

"I need you to work your magic cross country and have a patrol car pick up that woman who called the hotline from California, Marianne Thornton. She should be waiting at home. Tell them she's a person of interest in a federal murder investigation and that we'll be sending someone by to question her."

"The psychic lady? You're messing with me," she scoffed.

"Nope," he replied. "Heather Peters spoke to her from the grave, and I need to hear what she had to say."

"No problem. Should I call Bill Murray and see if the Ghostbusters are available to question her?" Liza asked cheerfully. "*Crackpot*," she added on a muffled cough.

Grey chuckled. "You have no idea how much I wish I was kidding. But

I spoke to her, and she knew things that only someone who'd been around Heather Peters' house would know."

"Like what?" Liza demanded.

"Like the fact that I found Peters' dream journal while I was there, and read about the nightmares she had before she died," he replied with a resigned sigh.

Liza made a vexed sound. "Grey, I know how frustrated you are with this case…"

"And I know exactly what you're thinking," he interrupted in a long suffering tone. "But she knew about the fish too, Lizzie. She knew I asked you to come get them so they wouldn't die. How the hell do you explain that?"

Liza sucked in a breath. "I don't know, Grey. Hidden cameras?"

"Now *that* is one of the many reasons I love you," he replied, grateful for her logical perspective. "Send a team over there to look for them. Now. She, or someone she knows, had to be watching me when I was at that house. And unless they were perched on a grassy knoll with binoculars and a listening device, cameras make a damn sight more sense."

"Okay," Liza said doubtfully, "but if they're savvy enough to spy on the FBI with hidden cameras, they've probably been removed by now to keep them from being found."

"You're probably right," Grey acknowledged, "but it's worth a shot. Have the team start with the vic's bedroom. Also have them look at vantage points outside that have a view into the bedroom. That's where I was when I read the journal and spoke with you on the phone about picking up the fish."

"You got it," Liza replied.

"And I still want Marianne Thornton picked up for questioning. But not because she's psychic," he added drily.

"You have no idea how relieved I am that your pot hasn't cracked," she said with a grin. "Who's going to question her? Are you hopping a flight to the west coast, or are we briefing someone from a field office over there?"

"I haven't decided. Let's see if we find anything at the Peters house first. Thornton agreed to go in willingly, but let them know she's not free to go until we've questioned her."

Grey hesitated. "And tell them to make sure she gets plenty of coffee, snacks, or whatever else she needs to keep her conscious while she waits."

"Got it. Don't starve the witness," Liza chirped. "Anything else?"

"That's it for now. Just keep me posted," Grey replied.

"Always. But before you hang up, I found something odd while I was dotting the i's and crossing the t's."

"What's that?" asked Grey.

"In your report you stated that you spoke with," she paused, then read from her screen, "an officer Patrick Sparrow from PBPD and an officer Scarlett Thresher from KLPD at the scene of the Palm Beach murder."

"That's right," he confirmed.

"Well, I checked, and there are no officers with either of those names working for PBPD or KLPD. I even checked with the counties to see if they were with the Sheriffs, but they'd never heard of them either. Are you sure you got those names right?" she asked.

Grey's heart sank into his stomach. "I…Are you sure about that, Lizzie?" he asked, even though he knew better. Liza never made those kinds of mistakes.

"I'm positive, Grey. No law enforcement agency in Florida has any record of those names. You must have written them down wrong," she said confidently.

When he didn't respond after a moment she asked, "Grey, are you there?"

"Uh, yeah," he answered hoarsely. "I'm sure it's fine. I probably just got the names wrong, like you said. I'll check back over my notes and let you know."

"Sounds good. Glad that's not the same KLPD lady friend who drove all the way up there to get a piece of you last night," she teased.

Grey forced a laugh and hung up before Liza's keen bullshit detector went off.

What possible reason could Scarlett and Sparrow have for lying to him about their identities? And what else had she lied to him about? The useless decaf he'd drunk churned in his gut, making him nauseous.

This day just kept getting better and better.

∞∞∞∞∞∞∞∞∞

Scarlett waved to Quin as she left the training center after her last class of the day. She crossed the village square toward the footpath that led back to her cottage, smiling as she inhaled the minty fragrance of the pennyroyal carpeting the apothecary's lawn. The afternoon sun shone brilliant on the meadow beyond, turning the white clusters of yarrow into patches of summer snow against the grass.

Scarlett felt like she was floating on air. She couldn't wait to see Grey again tonight. And the strangeness of actually wanting to return to the human realm was a giddy sensation.

They'd made love again this morning before he left for work. The memory of his slow drugging kisses, and the way he'd thrust up into her body with deep unhurried strokes, was enough to make her shiver despite the warmth of the sun.

She drifted past the tall, blooming stalks of foxglove that lined her front path, and made her way into the cool interior of her cottage. She grinned as she noticed that the black slacks and under-things she'd tossed onto her bed earlier had been laundered and were folded neatly on her dresser.

As she stepped into the shower, she thought about taking another trip into Seelie City for a visit to *The Queen Bee*. Bradan had been extra helpful since her last trip, and he'd already polished off most of Cybele's special rosemary infused honey.

Luckily there were still a few biscuits left, as well as a good portion of the creamed vanilla honey that Scarlett had discovered she liked.

She pulled her damp hair into a casual ponytail, threw on a vest and jeans, and padded barefoot into the kitchen for a snack. The tea kettle was already humming. "You're the best, Bradan," she murmured to herself, knowing the brownie would hear her.

She was just sitting down to a mug of strong, hot tea and a plate of biscuits with honey, when she heard an insistent tapping at the window. It sounded like an over-large bumblebee dashing itself against the glass. She turned with a frown to find Lorien hovering on the outside and rapping her tiny fists against the pane.

Scarlett gave the faerie a bemused look and motioned for her to come inside.

Lorien appeared above the table, her wings sifting purple dust into Scarlett's honey jar as she gasped, "Sydney sent me. It's Grey. You'd better get to the penthouse quick."

Scarlett's heart skipped a petrified beat, and she blinked to Sydney's living room before it—or her mind—could catch up.

Chapter 14

Grey sat stiffly on the loveseat he'd shared with Scarlett, waiting for Sydney to finish making her phone call in the other room. When she returned, she sat across from him on the couch, looking worried.

"Sparrow's on his way," she told him with a smile that did nothing to settle the anxiety in her eyes. "Um, can I get you something to drink?" she asked, starting to stand again.

He shook his head curtly and she dropped back onto the cushion. She pulled a throw pillow into her lap and began fidgeting with the fringe.

"What about Scarlett?" he demanded.

"I couldn't get hold of her, but isn't she supposed to meet you back here soon?" she answered in a placating tone.

He checked the time on his cell, unsnapping the lock on his gun holster with a subtle movement as he replaced the phone. "Not for another hour," he replied.

He couldn't believe that Sydney had anything to do with the murders. Or Sparrow or Scarlett for that matter. But neither could he explain their presence at his crime scene and the badge Sparrow had flashed when he'd claimed to be PBPD.

Maybe he just didn't want to believe it. The unsub impersonating a police officer would explain the victims letting him into their homes without a struggle. And a female accomplice would help establish trust with the vics.

His mind flashed to the way Scarlett had panicked the first time they'd kissed, and how her reaction had reminded him of vets with PTSD. Then he thought of the way she'd bloomed for him last night after her stirring request that they make love with her on top.

He shook his head to clear it. No. There was no way she could be involved. If anything, with her advanced combat training and the trauma she'd been through, it would make more sense for her and Sparrow to be vigilantes.

She'd practically told him that Sparrow had murdered the men who'd raped her. And he understood the impulse. God knew if he'd been able to find any clear evidence in his mother's case, he would have had a hard time not using his resources to make her rapist disappear from the face of the earth.

There was a knock at the door and Sydney jumped to her feet. Her relief was palpable as she raced to open it and leapt into Sparrow's embrace. He held her in his arms and stroked her back in a comforting gesture.

But his impassive gaze held Grey's as he looked past her into the living room.

"Sydney, baby," Sparrow said quietly, "why don't you wait in the other room while Grey and I have a chat."

"No," Grey stated flatly. "I'm sorry, but I need both of you to stay where I can see you."

Sparrow's eyes hardened and he gave Grey a warning look, but his smile for Sydney was gentle as he steered her back to the couch.

"The only reason I'm not charging you with felony impersonation of a police officer, and dragging your ass to jail right now, is because I need some answers first," Grey said in a tight voice.

Sydney's resigned glance at Sparrow told Grey that his accusation came as no surprise to her.

"I'm only going to ask you once," Grey gritted. "Why were you and Scarlett at my crime scene?"

Sparrow inhaled slowly, as if trying to decide how much to say. "It's not what you think, brother, I can promise you that."

Grey's jaw tightened. "I believe we've established that what I *think*, when it comes to you and Scarlett, is irrelevant. What I need now is the truth."

Sparrow let the silence fall heavy between them, and Sydney finally broke it with a softly pleading, "You have to tell him, Sparrow."

Something akin to regret flashed in Sparrow's gaze as he replied, "I'm sorry, baby, I can't."

"Of course you can," she argued. "You told me."

A hint of amusement crossed his expression as he replied, "You were already ass deep in trouble with Balthus. And you're my soul mate."

"Grey needs your help too," she insisted with a meaningful look. "And what about Scarlett?"

"There are a lot of reasons this isn't the same, baby, not the least of which include his ties to your government," he said, his tone apologetic but resolved. "And Scarlett knew what she was getting into."

Though they were being deliberately vague, the undercurrents of their exchange made it clear to Grey that the vigilante theory was the most likely scenario.

"Look, man," Grey grated, "I'm going to give you one last chance to come clean with me. If this is what I think it is, and you weren't involved in the commission of a crime when you flashed me that fake badge, the only thing I have you on *so far* is a misdemeanor. Don't add obstruction of justice to that charge."

Sparrow gave him a rueful smile. "You're one of the good guys, brother. And I truly wish I didn't have to do this. But I'll make sure you get the credit when we catch your killer."

Sparrow's words and Sydney's gasp of denial tripped an alarm in Grey's brain. He had his gun out in a flash, but Sparrow was…simply no longer there.

Grey blinked at the empty space beside Sydney, his disbelief making him sloppy for the split second it took Sparrow to get him in a headlock and disarm him. Grey had no idea how Sparrow managed to bend the laws of physics and get behind him that fast.

It wasn't humanly possible.

"Sorry, brother," Sparrow murmured as he pulled out the little pouch of black dust he kept for emergencies like these.

It would erase Grey's memories of any contact he'd had with denizens of the faerie realm, leaving his mind malleable to the explanations Sparrow left in their place.

Sparrow only hoped it didn't leave Grey as addled as the mortuary attendant he'd had to dust earlier. The man had been so confused he'd mis-tagged the Palm Beach vic's body as a "John Doe" and put her back in the wrong bunk...

Chapter 15

Scarlett arrived in the middle of Sydney's living room with a distinct lack of grace. She yelped in pain as she stubbed her bare toe against the rough driftwood base of the coffee table.

Her discomfort was forgotten as her entire body went numb with panic at the sight of what Pat was about to do to Grey.

She dove for Pat's hand, knocking his fingers out of the way before he could sprinkle memory erasing dust over her lover's head. The black powder fell harmlessly into the cracks of the sofa cushions, but she knew there was more of it in that damnable little pouch of his.

"Pat, no!" she shouted. "You can't do this!" She tried to push Pat out the way while shielding Grey with her body.

Grey grunted as Sparrow's muscular arm tightened around his neck like a constrictor squeezing a rat.

He thought he might have been able to get out of the man's choke hold if he'd had another minute to collect himself. And if Scarlett hadn't leapt on top of him.

After appearing out of thin air.

Christ. They must have drugged him. Hallucination was the only possible explanation.

Pat swore at Scarlett in Gaelic. "Letty, he knows we lied to him about being with the human police. This has become too complicated."

"I can make him understand," Scarlett pleaded. "His entire life has been about secrecy. Our secret will be just one more he has to keep."

"I'm sorry, Letty, but we can't take that chance. He's a human government agent," Pat said firmly. "You have to let him go."

Scarlett shook her head in denial, her sea-green eyes brimming with unshed tears. "I can't, Pat," she whispered brokenly. "He's the only man I've ever...and it will be as if I never even existed for him. I can't lose him that way."

Pat gaped at her, inadvertently squeezing Grey's neck tighter. "Are you telling me you shagged him already?" he demanded in English.

"Sparrow!" Sydney reprimanded.

He cast a penitent gaze at Sydney, releasing his hold on Grey when the man let out a weak gurgle. Sparrow watched as Scarlett ran gentle fingers over Grey's bruised throat, murmuring words of comfort.

"You nearly choked him to death!" she accused, her eyes flashing angrily before she returned to fussing over Grey.

"*Do you love him, Letty?*" Pat asked her softly in their own tongue.

She stilled, her expression twisting with aching uncertainty. "*I don't know. I've never felt this way about anyone.*"

Pat drew a surprised breath. He should have seen it before. It was written all over her face. He smiled slightly and shook his head. "Do you have any idea the amount of shite I'm going to be in with the Seelie Court for letting a human FBI agent walk around with full knowledge of our existence?"

Sydney chuckled. "At least confidentiality is part of his job description."

Grey drifted back to consciousness to find Scarlett hovering over him, and Sparrow sitting by Sydney's side once more. He was pretty sure the heated exchange between them had been Scarlett talking Sparrow out of killing him. But things were a little hazy because the bastard had choked him out.

If he survived this, Sparrow was going to pay for that one. But he needed to tread carefully—the man still had his gun.

"Relax, Letty, I haven't done any permanent damage," Pat said blandly. "He's awake now. Aren't you, brother?"

Grey opened his eyes and narrowed a venomous gaze on Sparrow. "What did you give me?" he asked hoarsely. "I was hallucinating."

Sparrow smirked, and Sydney elbowed him in the ribs hard enough to make him grunt.

"You haven't been drugged, and you aren't hallucinating," Sydney told Grey softly. "Sparrow and Scarlett aren't exactly…human."

Grey pinned her with a disbelieving look. "Okay," he said calmly. *Jesus. He'd thought she was the sane one.*

"I'm so sorry I had to lie to you," Scarlett said in a tight voice. "I wanted to tell you the truth so badly, but we're forbidden to reveal our existence to humans."

Grey blinked. There was that word again. *Humans.* "Okay, I'll bite. If you're not human, then what are you?"

"We're sidhe," Scarlett explained with a thread of desperation in her voice, "a race of immortal warriors from the faerie realm. Our world exists alongside yours, but hidden by a veil of separation."

"Faerie realm," Grey echoed faintly.

"I know this is a lot to take in, brother," Sparrow said. "But we're here because—that serial killer you're hunting? He's not human either. And without our help, you're never going to catch him."

Grey pressed his face into the heels of his hands. "Okay, so, let me get this straight," he said, sighing and lifting his gaze. "You're telling me that you're not human. My unsub isn't human. And you were going to, what? Kill me because I found out you weren't really police officers?"

Scarlett gasped a horrified, "No!"

Sparrow laughed. "No, brother, I was just going to tinker with your memory a bit. We're not savages."

"Right. Of course not," Grey replied in a reasonable tone. "Mind if I get my gun back then?"

Sparrow shook his head, his expression equal parts disappointment and amusement. "I'd be glad to return it. As soon as I'm sure you can see Lorien over there."

Sydney and Scarlett followed Sparrow's gaze to the faerie sitting on the glass coffee table, tiny bare feet swinging over the edge. She grinned and waved, her color shifting dress sparkling in the fading rays of daylight that shone through the sliding glass door.

Grey looked confused, obviously still unable to see her. "Who is Lorien?"

Scarlett's face fell. "You don't believe a word we've said, do you?"

She sounded so genuinely hurt that Grey's heart squeezed inside his chest. His eyes found hers, and he couldn't help reaching up to graze his fingertips across her soft cheek. If she was conning him, part of him wanted to let her.

Hell, most of him wanted to let her.

"Scarlett, baby," he said on a pained groan, "I can't take much more of this. If you two are vigilantes, going after this sicko for what he's doing to these women, I get that. After what happened to you, I can't really blame you.

"But if you want me to believe this other craziness you're spinning, you're going to have to give me some proof. Otherwise, just do what you're going to do with me."

"Vigilantes?" Scarlett repeated, sounding bewildered.

"You have to admit, it's a heck of a lot more plausible than a magical realm that exists alongside ours," Sydney said with a chuckle.

"Enough," Sparrow declared, standing up. "I'm putting this poor bastard out of his misery. Ladies, we'll be right back."

Grey gave him a dubious look. Then, before he could react, Sparrow had disappeared and reappeared behind him again. Sparrow wrapped both arms around his shoulders, and everything went dark.

Suddenly Grey was plummeting through space so fast that it felt like his stomach couldn't catch up. He tried to breathe, fighting panic when he couldn't seem to get any air into his lungs...and then it was over. He landed on spongy ground with a soft thump, his knees almost collapsing beneath him.

Sparrow's arms steadied and then released him. Feeling dizzy, Grey looked around in disbelief. He was on a grassy plateau, the setting sun capping a nearby mountain.

Wildflowers bloomed in a profusion of color, and the air was filled with the buzz of insect wings. Hundreds of huge dragonflies with vivid, jewel tone bodies hovered and darted about him.

A handsome chestnut horse grazed several yards away, and Grey blinked, staring hard at it. He had to be crazy. It looked like the damn thing had wings.

It tossed its head in their direction.

"Evening," Sparrow greeted with a nod.

"Evening," it replied in a low rumbling voice before returning to its grazing.

Grey's knees did collapse then. "Holy fuck," he mumbled as his ass hit the soft, springy turf.

"So, this is the faerie realm," Sparrow said conversationally, "and that's a pegasus."

Grey nodded, still staring at the winged talking horse.

"This is where Scarlett and I come from. And just so you know, she is the *only* reason I didn't go inside your head and scramble your memories today."

Sparrow crouched down and looked him in the eye. "She likes you. A lot. And if you hurt her, I'm going to scramble a lot more than your memories. You feel me, brother?"

Grey nodded again, starting to remember why he'd liked this guy in the first place. "I feel you."

Sparrow smiled and extended a hand to help him up.

"Just one more thing, though," Grey added as they both stood.

Sparrow gave him a questioning look, and Grey threw a hard right cross into Sparrow's cheek.

"Don't ever touch my gun again."

Sparrow's head rebounded on his neck from the force of the punch. He reeled for a moment, dazed. Then he shook it off, working his jaw back and forth as he probed it gingerly with his palm.

"I deserved that," he admitted, as he pulled the gun from a seemingly invisible pocket inside his jacket and handed it back to Grey.

Grey holstered it, looking askance at Sparrow's close-fitting jacket. There was no way Sparrow's pocket could have concealed his .357 Magnum. "I'm not even going to ask, man."

Sparrow grinned. "Sometimes that's best. Ready to get back to the ladies?"

"I don't know." Grey lifted a brow. "Does it involve you hugging me again?"

"What can I say, brother? You're a sexy man. I can't keep my hands off you." Sparrow's lips twitched with humor as he threw his arm around Grey's shoulders and blinked them back to Sydney's living room.

Grey struggled to keep his feet as they touched down on the textured carpet after another gut twisting journey through the void, or whatever the hell it was. His gaze automatically searched for Scarlett.

What he saw didn't help his efforts to remain standing.

Her bare foot was lifted in the air, and a tiny, winged woman hovered above it. The creature pulled a little pouch from somewhere inside her color-shifting dress, and reached to sprinkle some silvery dust over Scarlett's pinky toe.

Scarlett sighed in relief. "Thanks, Lorien. I hit it against the table so hard I think I broke it."

"Any time," the tiny woman said with a smile, fluttering down to stand on the glass tabletop beneath her. Her violet eyes looked beyond Scarlett to find Grey staring at her in astonishment.

"Well hello there, handsome. I guess your and Sparrow's little jaunt did the trick." Her laughter was like the tinkling of wind chimes.

Scarlett twisted around, jumping to her feet when she saw him. She looked like she wanted to rush into his arms, but she held herself back.

"I saw a pegasus," he murmured, unable to take his eyes from the... "Faerie?" he blurted, watching the iridescent flicker of her wings and the eye befuddling colors of her dress. "Are you a faerie?" he asked Lorien breathlessly.

"I'm a sprite," Lorien replied with a gleeful expression, "which is a type of faerie, yes."

"Right," Grey said faintly.

Sydney gave Sparrow a reproachful look and padded over to Grey, taking his arm and leading him back to the solid comfort of the sofa.

"I know exactly how you feel," Sydney assured him, gently pushing him to a seat next to Scarlett. "Sometimes faerie folk can be a little insensitive when it comes to how shocking it is for us humans to find out about them."

Sparrow snorted. "He seemed pretty okay with it a few minutes ago, when he slugged me and demanded his gun back."

Sydney's concerned gaze flew to Sparrow, taking in the bruise forming on his jaw. She frowned, looking back to the purpling contusions on Grey's neck.

"It looks like you both need some healing," she replied in irritation.

Lorien sniggered and darted up to sprinkle the silvery dust from her pouch over Grey's neck. He froze, following her with his eyes. A warm, tingling sensation spread across the area, like soft sunlight seeping into his skin, and the throbbing soreness dissipated.

"Thanks," he muttered, watching in bemusement as she zipped over to Sparrow to do the same for his jaw.

"Are you okay?" Scarlett asked in a cautious tone.

Grey turned to her, uncertain how to respond. Snippets of the conversations they'd had, flashes of their heated passion, and a hundred unanswered questions rolled through his mind.

"I thought you might be able to understand," she ventured in a halting voice, "since you've had to keep so many secrets yourself."

He cleared his throat. "This is, uh, a little more intense than any of the secrets I've been keeping."

"I know," she said helplessly. "I'm sorry."

He nodded, trying to appear reassuring. But his sane and logical world view had just been flipped on its ass. And the dust was still settling.

He looked from her to Sparrow. "You said before that the serial killer I've been chasing isn't human," he said, grasping onto the one solid thing that he knew would focus his mind.

"That's why going after him has been like chasing a ghost," Sparrow affirmed. "And it's why you're going to need our help to catch him."

"What is he?" Grey asked.

Sparrow shook his head, pacing the floor in front of Sydney's corner bar. "I'm still working on that one."

Grey frowned. "Well, how do you know he isn't human?"

"The night you and Scarlett met down in Largo," Sparrow answered with a nod in her direction. "She smelled a distinctive herbal odor on you."

Grey's eyes widened. "That smell has been at every scene. But the lab hasn't been able to identify it."

"It's a sleeping draught made by our people," Scarlett told him quietly, "a fast acting and very potent one, called a Morpheus potion. The reason I attacked you that night was because, when I smelled it on you, I was afraid you'd try to use it on me."

Grey blinked at her in dawning understanding. "You thought I was going to knock you out and hurt you," he said, his voice a blend of compassion and remorse.

Scarlett gave him a sideways smile. "I thought you might *try*," she corrected. "Even if you'd gotten the drop on me, you'd have needed quite a bit of Morpheus to keep me under. Years of insomnia have given me something of a tolerance for it."

Grey laughed, her hint of cockiness somehow making him feel as if the world was beginning to right itself again.

"So my people couldn't identify it because it has magical properties," he guessed. "But if it was made by your people, doesn't that mean one of your people could be doing this?"

Scarlett cast a troubled gaze toward Pat, who answered, "It's possible, of course. But the sidhe don't fit the profile for this type of crime. And anyone from our realm could get their hands on a Morpheus potion. No, it's far more likely that a being with a different set of powers than ours is responsible."

"Different how, what type of powers?" Grey asked.

Sparrow sighed. "The type of power to get inside someone's mind and control their thoughts. I had a mage associate of mine go over the Peters house today. She told me that Heather Peters died in terrible fear—and not just the fear that came from being attacked. She said it was as if the woman was made to believe all of her worst fears were coming true."

"A death djinn could do that to one of his charges if he wanted, couldn't he?" asked Sydney.

"That occurred to me too," Sparrow replied. "But we examined the two most recent victims' bodies, and both of their souls were intact when they died. A death djinn couldn't control someone like that unless he had possession of their soul."

Grey shook his head and blew out a breath. "I am really trying to follow you guys here, but you just keep throwing weirder things into the mix."

"Sorry, brother," Sparrow said with a grin. "I guess with us, once you're in, you're *all* in."

"I'd love to see my tech analyst's reaction to my notes on this case after talking to you," Grey replied drily.

Sparrow smirked. "Unless you want me to pay him a visit with some memory dust, I wouldn't recommend it."

"She's a *she*, and please don't mess with her mind. She's got mad skills, and I need them."

Sparrow chuckled.

"So you don't think it's a 'death djinn'," Grey repeated the term with distaste. "What other kinds of beings could be doing this?"

"The list is long, brother," Sparrow answered soberly. "Just like humans, any number of citizens from our realm can go bad. And as far as mind control is concerned, there are many different ways to do it.

"Our current working theory is that the killer is knocking his victims out with a Morpheus potion in the human realm to keep them docile, and then transporting them to the faerie realm to carry out the attack. That would explain why you haven't found any signs of a struggle."

Grey nodded, his brain working double time to incorporate the new information with his existing frame of reference for the case. He sucked in a breath as he remembered his earlier conversation with Marianne Thornton.

"Is it possible that the killer could be controlling his victims from inside their dreams?" The question made him feel foolish, but in light of what he'd learned today, he owed it to Marianne to find out.

Sparrow gave him a considering look. "What makes you ask that?"

Grey described Heather Peters' dream journal and his exchange with Marianne Thornton.

"That sounds like an incubus," Scarlett murmured.

Grey gave her a questioning look.

"They can control dreams," she explained, "but it's usually for the purpose of fulfilling fantasies. They have a natural psychic link to the sexual desires of mortals, and take sustenance from a mortal's heightened energy and emotions during sex."

"Some of them have been known to join forces with the Unseelie Court, though," Sparrow said thoughtfully. "It's not unheard of for them to be involved with the soul trade and other questionable activities."

"Sunny is seeing a couple of incubi," Sydney offered. "Do you think they, or Angelica, could help?"

"Who's Angelica?" asked Grey.

"You met her," Sydney replied with a smile. "She works here at the hotel as a maid. And she also happens to be a succubus."

"Succubus?" Grey echoed in disbelief.

"Succubi and incubi are the same race of beings, but succubi are female and incubi are male," Sparrow explained. "I'm concerned about this Marianne Thornton, though. If our killer is an incubus, and he's after her, she's in serious danger—especially if she falls asleep."

Grey's cell phone rang and he held up an apologetic finger when he saw that it was Liza. "Excuse me, I need to take this."

He rose and maneuvered his way around the loveseat before striding down the hall to shut himself inside the guest bathroom.

"Hey Lizzie, what's up?" he asked, softening his voice out of habit so that no one would overhear him.

"Company?" she asked.

"Nothing gets past you," he replied with a smile.

"Well, just calling to let you know that the team found zero, zilch and nada with regard to the hidden camera agenda," she said, disappointment coloring her tone.

"Huh," he sounded, resisting his instinct to bring her in on the newest developments in the case. "What about evidence of someone watching from vantage points that look into Peters' bedroom window?"

He asked the question, even though his mind had already discarded that theory and started to accept the possibility that Marianne was telling the truth about Heather Peters speaking to her from beyond the grave. He didn't want to make Liza suspicious by not asking for the results of all the angles he'd asked her to pursue earlier.

"Nothing there either, G-man, I'm sorry." The note of failure in her voice made him feel guilty as hell. But even if he could tell her the truth, she would never believe it.

"Thanks, Lizzie," he said softly. "There's a logical explanation for how Thornton knew about the journal and the fish. We'll find it."

"I know," she replied with an exaggerated sigh. "I just wanted to be right about the hidden spy camera angle."

Grey chuckled.

"So, uniforms picked up Thornton and they're holding her at the local police station. What do you want to do about questioning her?" she asked.

"Still working on that," Grey replied. "They can hold her for forty-eight hours. I'll get back to you after I look into a couple of other things."

"'Kay. Did you have a chance to look over your notes for the names of the officers you met at the crime scene there?" Liza asked.

Grey massaged the bridge of his nose with his thumb and forefinger. "I'm sorry, Lizzie, I haven't had a chance yet."

"No worries, Captain America. Just let me know when you can. You know how the higher-ups love their paperwork."

"They'd fall apart without all that red tape," he joked half heartedly. "I'll let you know soon, I promise."

He hung up and paced back to the living room, feeling like a traitor for lying to Lizzie. To his surprise, a blonde in a French maid's uniform was sitting in the arm chair with her back to the sliding glass door. Sydney's fluffy black cat was stretched across her lap, purring in contentment.

He recognized her as the woman who'd let him into his room the other night, which meant she must be the succubus. Sparrow was wasting no time bringing her up to speed on the case.

"Sorry to interrupt," Grey interjected, "but I'm having an issue with a report I filed stating that I spoke with Pat Sparrow of the PBPD and Scarlett Thresher of the KLPD at the Palm Beach crime scene.

"Do you have anything in your bag of tricks, *other than mind erasing*," he warned with a glare, "that will explain the two of you not showing up in our system?"

Sparrow chuckled. "No problem. Magically 'editing' human law enforcement records is part of our basic training in the Seelie Police Academy."

"Comforting," Grey echoed derisively. "I'd appreciate it if you could get that done posthaste. My tech analyst is waiting for me to correct the names before the report gets sent up the chain."

"I'll fix it tonight," Sparrow assured him.

"Create a plausible reason for your names not showing up in the first place," Grey advised. "She's like a dog with a bone if something rouses her suspicion."

"It won't be a problem," Sparrow promised with a grin.

"My other issue is Marianne Thornton," Grey continued. "I have her..." he trailed off as he realized that the maid was staring at him.

Perhaps beaming at him was more accurate. The smile she leveled at him was bright enough to signal boats coming into shore.

"Uh, hi. Angelica, right?" he said uncertainly.

She nodded, her blue eyes luminous enough to mesmerize.

"It's nice to see you again," he told her, purposely focusing his gaze on Scarlett. He didn't know how succubi worked, but this one definitely had some kind of mojo going on.

"It is so nice to see you again also, Mr. Derrington," she said with barely concealed excitement. "You and Scarlett were magnificent last night. Your passion permeated the entire hotel. It was a thing of beauty and inspiration."

Scarlett's face turned bright red and she sank lower into the leather sofa cushions, as if she wished they would swallow her whole.

Sydney's hand flew to her mouth like she was trying to stifle her laughter, and Lorien didn't even bother to hide her sniggering. Sparrow just shook his head and muttered, "Better you than me, brother."

Speechless, Grey dropped to a seat beside Scarlett and squeezed her fingers in commiseration. What had she told him before...that succubi and incubi were linked to the sexual desires of mortals?

Right. Probably best to ignore this the same way he'd ignored Sparrow's magical gun concealing jacket.

"Uh, thank you," Grey replied, clearing his throat as he changed the subject. "I heard Sparrow updating you on the case. Do you think it could be an incubus committing these crimes?"

Angelica's face fell. "These are terrible atrocities. I hate to believe that one of my people would be capable of such a thing. Yet I know this is only naïve and wishful thinking on my part.

"I would very much like to speak with the woman who told you she is being hunted in her dreams. If it is indeed an incubus, I can help her to guard her dreams from him."

"Good." Grey nodded. "And that's actually the next thing I wanted to talk to you about," he said, transferring his gaze to Sparrow.

"I have Marianne Thornton sitting in a police station in California, waiting to be questioned about her involvement with the case. In light of this," his gesture encompassed the room at large, "I obviously no longer want anything she says to go on record.

"But that leaves me with the problem of explaining how she knew about certain events that occurred at Heather Peters' home, and why her knowledge is no longer of concern to the investigation."

"I can alter any records you need altered," Sparrow reminded him. "You said she called your hotline claiming to be a psychic? I can make it appear that she's consulted on police cases before with success. You can report that she claimed to have a couple of visions before her psychic trail went cold."

Grey sighed. "Lizzie will never believe that. She won't stop digging until she figures out how Marianne *really* knew what happened at the Peters' house.

"Not to mention everyone in the unit will be calling me *Mulder* for the next year," he added on a grumble.

"Who's Lizzie?" Scarlett asked, noting the familiarity in his voice when he spoke of the woman.

"She's my tech analyst," Grey explained. "But she's also my partner. We've worked side by side on this case for over three months. And she has an uncanny ability to tell when someone is lying. I've had to lie to her twice today, and I can promise you that she already suspects something is up."

Grey rubbed at the five o'clock shadow on his jaw in frustration. "I have no idea how I'm going to pull off the rest of this investigation without telling her the truth."

"You can't, brother," Sparrow said, a note of steel in his tone.

"I get that," Grey replied. "I just haven't figured out how I'm going to manage it yet. You have to understand, man, we trade updates at least twice a day. And she's a friend."

"Doyle told his business partner, Manny, about us," Scarlett murmured.

Sparrow gave her a warning look. "Manny isn't an FBI agent. He runs snorkeling tours in the Keys. And Doyle only told him because he needed Manny to cover for him when he had to blink off of a boat full of tourists. Not to mention Manny was dating a merrow at the time."

"I told Sunny," Sydney added quietly.

"Again. Not an FBI agent," Sparrow reiterated with thinning patience.

"You can't ask him to keep this secret from every other human in his life," Sydney insisted in a calm voice. "It's not realistic, and it's not fair."

"And I've already taken a huge risk letting Grey in on it," Sparrow argued. "If too many mortals with high level ties to the human government find out about us, the Seelie Court could view it as a threat to the veil between our worlds."

"What does that even mean?" Sydney asked with a grimace.

Sparrow took a deep breath and shook his head. "Baby, I'm not saying these things to be argumentative. The Seelie Court is convinced that chaos will disrupt the balance between good and evil if the veil drops. And if they believe the veil is in danger, I have no idea what they're capable of doing in order to protect our secrecy."

Lorien mumbled, as if she wasn't entirely sure she wanted them to hear her, "Every human who knows about us gets one free pass to confide in another human."

Five sets of eyes flew to the sprite sitting on the edge of the coffee table.

"Where did you hear that?" Sparrow demanded.

Lorien sighed in irritation, darting upward to hover at everyone's eye level. Orange dust leaked from her wings, making sparkling little piles on the glass tabletop below her.

"The guardians asked the Faerie Council to petition the Seelie Court about it when more and more of our human charges started becoming aware of us. The Court agreed, but swore us to secrecy because it's not something they like to encourage."

She narrowed her tilted violet eyes threateningly. "So if any of you ever say you heard it from me, I'll sprinkle every pair of underwear you own with fire dust from now 'til eternity."

"If that feels anything like sitting in warming gel and being spanked with a flogger, it could be more pleasurable than you imagine," Angelica said in a thoughtful tone.

Lorien glared at her.

"Don't worry," Angelica said reassuringly, "I still won't tell anyone."

Sparrow gave Lorien a doubtful look. "Are you sure about this? Even if every human who knows only tells one other human, the secret of our world could spread exponentially."

Lorien shrugged one tiny shoulder. "The guardians felt the exception was necessary and sprites hold a lot of sway with the Seelies. Besides, only a small percentage of our charges find out about us, so I'm sure the Court assumed that clause wouldn't be invoked very often."

"It looks like you're in luck, Grey," Sydney said with a smile. "You can tell your partner if you feel it's necessary."

"Though I still don't think it's a good idea unless you absolutely have to," Sparrow cautioned.

Grey snorted. "Yeah, I'm not looking forward to that conversation. If you thought I was a hard sell, just wait 'til I try to convince Lizzie there's a secret magical world that exists alongside ours. She's going to require some serious proof.

"And if I don't get it right the first time, I'm liable to find myself off the grid and locked up in a mental hospital under whatever name she decides to give me."

Scarlett's sea-green eyes narrowed dangerously. "I'd convince her myself before I let anything like that happen."

Grey's lips twitched with humor. "I believe you would, baby," he murmured.

Something loosened in Scarlett's chest at his words and the way he looked at her when he spoke them. It was as if the air in the room had been too thin ever since Pat had tried to dust his memory. And only the small dimpled smile Grey gave her now allowed her to breathe fully once more.

Tears of relief pricked behind her eyes, and she blinked them back. He searched her gaze, his own eyes softening as he reached up to cup her cheek. She tilted her face into his palm, struck by the sense that her thoughts were somehow laid bare to him.

And that even if they were, it was okay.

Sparrow cleared his throat. "So we've established that it won't be the end of both our worlds if your partner finds out about us," he reiterated. "Now we need to figure out what to do about Marianne Thornton."

"Right," Grey breathed, reluctantly pulling his hand from Scarlett's cheek. Every cell in his body wanted to carry her down to his room and make love to her until he forgot how he'd almost lost her today.

He shook his head and forced himself to focus. "I need an excuse to get Marianne out of that police station and question her off record. One that will satisfy Lizzie," he said, thinking aloud. "It's probably best if Angelica gets to her soon, though, so she has some protection if there really is an incubus after her."

"Just give me the address and I can be there as soon as you let her know to expect me," Angelica agreed with a nod.

"Good," Grey said. "It should take six or seven hours for me to fly to California…" he broke off, frowning at Lorien's burst of laughter.

Sydney rolled her eyes and sent Grey an apologetic look. "What she means is—you don't have to fly commercial anymore. Now you have access to instant transportation, courtesy of *faerie air*," she told him with a smirk.

Grey's eyes widened in comprehension. "You mean you can just," he snapped his fingers, "whisk me right there?" he asked with a glance at Scarlett.

"Well, I'm not really supposed to, but Pat can," Scarlett replied, smiling at his disbelieving expression.

"Why aren't you supposed to?" he asked her curiously.

"I'm a private citizen. Pat has clearance to use magic like that in your realm because he's a Seelie Police detective," Scarlett replied.

"Oh. I just assumed…" Grey hesitated, "I mean, with your martial arts training and everything…" he trailed off, looking puzzled.

"My people are warriors. Everyone begins sword training at age eighteen," she explained, regretting the lies that had built up between them.

Grey nodded slowly, digesting that new piece of information. He was eager to ask her more, but he'd have to wait until later when they were alone.

"Okay, here's what we're going to do," he said, switching gears back to the business at hand, "I'm going to call Marianne and tell her that the police will escort her home and that I'll meet her there with a couple of my associates, and not to speak to anyone else about the case.

"The tricky part is going to be Lizzie. I'm thinking that, barring you pulling her into your realm and introducing her to a pegasus," he said with a dry look at Sparrow, "the only way she's going to buy any of this is if I convince her I'm working with a secret branch of the agency that's above her security clearance.

"And it would help if you could do your thing to make your names come up as police officers while she's on the phone with me. Lizzie's practically a savant with computers. If she thinks you're able to hack the system and she can't figure out how, she'll believe me when I tell her you're above her pay grade."

"No problem," Sparrow agreed. "I'll feel better if you can swing that story instead of revealing us to her."

"I'll do my best. But I'm pretty sure she records our conversations for her notes," Grey added, "so it would be great if you can make sure she's unable to record this particular conversation. The last thing I need is one of my superiors listening in while I tell my tech analyst that I'm working with a non-existent secret division that can alter law enforcement records."

"I'll do you one better," Sparrow offered. "You can use my phone to call her, and no human device will be able to id the number or record anything you say. Your phone company records won't even show that a call was received on her end."

"Perfect," Grey replied, feeling better now that they had a plan. "I'll let Marianne know what's going on first, and then we'll tackle Lizzie. Let's do this."

Chapter 16

Burr searched the murky twilight of the dream plane for the little blonde, cursing in frustration at his inability to find her. He'd been waiting for his newest plaything to start dreaming again for almost two days.

He knew he'd scared her with that graveyard nightmare. But none of the women he'd played with had gone this long without sleeping so early in the game. Not even after he'd injected their worst fears into their dreams for nights on end.

The last one had been terrified of small spaces. Not his favorite fear—it didn't leave a lot of room for creativity. Stuck elevators and shrinking basements were about the best he could come up with, but they'd done the job.

The final nail in her coffin had been trapping her in a coffin. He giggled at his own joke. She was gibbering with mindless panic by the time he joined her inside it and the real fun began.

The one before that though...she'd been afraid of spiders. He shivered with pleasure as he remembered her screams. Spiders could scurry and bite and crawl into crevices in the body where they weren't meant to go.

Spiders he could work with.

He had some entertaining ideas for the blonde's reanimated corpse fear too. He scanned the teeming multitude of dreamers for her energy signature again, rage fogging his mind with dark heat when he still couldn't find her.

Burr lashed out, slamming his fists into the glittering balls of soul light that surrounded him. The faint gasps of the pathetic humans echoed through his ears as they were jerked violently awake.

He closed his eyes, chest heaving in agitation as he tried to calm himself. Maybe he should take this as a compliment. Maybe he'd perfected his art so well with the graveyard nightmare that she couldn't bear to fall asleep again.

Surely she wouldn't be able to resist the call of slumber much longer though. Unfortunately, he hadn't established enough of a connection yet that he could follow her into her realm and see what she was up to while she was awake.

He would remedy that as soon as the bitch came back to him.

She was playing hard to get, and it was starting to piss him off. If she didn't watch it, she was going to ruin their sport.

He hoped to get at least another week of entertainment out of her before their endgame. But he wouldn't be able to control himself if she kept making him this angry...

∞∞∞∞∞∞∞∞∞∞

"Hello?" Marianne slurred the greeting into the phone as if she was only half conscious.

"Ms. Thornton, this is Agent Derrington. Are you still at the police station?"

"Yes," she affirmed, sounding a little more alert.

"Listen, some new information has come to light, and I would prefer to speak to you at your home. Would that be alright?" asked Grey.

"Um, I guess," she agreed in a hesitant tone.

"I'm going to send you home in a patrol car and meet you there. I'll be bringing a couple of my associates along to speak with you as well. I would prefer it if you didn't discuss the case with any of the other officers, okay?"

"Can you meet me soon? I don't know how much longer I can stay awake." Her voice sounded teary and panicked.

"Ms. Thornton…Marianne," he corrected softly, "I know you're afraid. But I'm bringing someone with me who can help you. Ask for a cup of coffee before you leave the station, and we'll be waiting at your house when you get home. I promise."

Uncertain silence filled the phone-line. "Okay," she murmured finally, as if she was too tired to argue.

"Okay," Grey repeated with warm reassurance. "We'll see you soon."

He hung up and dialed Lizzie from Sparrow's phone, thinking the device looked surprisingly similar to his own.

"Liza McKenzie," she greeted crisply.

"Hey Lizzie, it's Grey. Are you alone in your office?"

"Oh, hey Grey. You didn't come up on caller ID," she said in a distracted voice. There were rustling noises in the background, like she was shuffling papers and closing drawers.

"And yeah, I'm alone, why? Are we having phone sex? If so, hurry up and tell me what you're wearing. It's almost time to go home."

"Cute." Grey snorted. "Before you go, can you do me a favor and have a patrol car take Marianne Thornton home?"

"Okay," she replied, sounding nonplussed. "What happened there? Did you have someone from a field office question her?"

"Not exactly," Grey answered, grimacing at the fabrication he was about weave for Lizzie. "She'll be questioned, but not under the jurisdiction of our department."

"Whose jurisdiction then?" she asked.

Grey sighed. "I came across some deeply classified information, and if I share it with you, you can't put it in any of your reports. If that makes you uncomfortable, let me know, and I'll leave you out of it."

"Are you kidding?" Liza exclaimed. "Have you met me? I'm offended it even occurred to you that I'd choose to tattle in a report over playing secret agent with you."

Grey smirked at her annoyed grunt. "I had to offer you plausible deniability."

"Plausible…gah! Give me a break. I'm not the one who breaks out in a cold sweat every time I lie, Captain America. I knew something weird was going on with you today. Out with it already!"

If you only knew how weird, he thought.

"Make the call to send Marianne Thornton home and then we'll talk," Grey told her. "I'll wait while you do it."

Liza's huff was cut off with a click as she placed him on hold. She was back in two minutes with an impatient, "Done. Talk."

Grey took a deep breath and said, "I'm working with a secret branch of the agency. Knowledge of their existence is above both our security clearances. But they've made an exception because they think this killer may be someone inside their own department."

Liza whistled softly.

"They have technology like you've never seen, Lizzie. I'm using one of their phones, which is why I didn't show up on your caller ID. And if you try to record this conversation, nothing I say will come through."

"How is that even possible?" she scoffed. "Hang on…"

He heard her fiddling with something in the background, then a clear audio playback of her impertinent phone sex question. It was followed by silence, and then her asking about whether he'd had someone from a field office question Marianne. There was more silence, and then Lizzie's next response. It was as if Grey's half of the conversation had been erased.

She turned it up louder, continuing to listen to the sound of her own voice, interspersed with dead space where Grey's should have been. Finally she stopped the recording with an excited, "Holy crap. How do they do that?"

"I have no idea," Grey replied. "But want to see something else cool?"

"Does a bear shit in the woods?" she retorted.

Grey chuckled. "Those two officers from my report who didn't show up in the system as PBPD and KLPD—check their names again for me."

He heard the click of her keyboard.

"Still not there," she said smugly.

Grey gestured to Sparrow, who typed something into a tablet-sized device that he pulled from the same impossible pocket where he'd kept Grey's gun.

Sparrow nodded and Grey said to Liza, "Okay. Now check again."

"Seriously?" she intoned. "There's no way they can hack two separate high security systems that quickly…oh Peter, Paul and Mary, yes they can.

"Who the hell are these people?" she demanded, sounding torn between frustration and admiration.

"I can't tell you much more than I already have. But they're flying me out to California to talk to Marianne Thornton because they have evidence that she really might be this guy's next victim.

"They think their own technology may have been used either on my phone, or at the Peters house, and that's how Marianne knew about the journal and the fish. They think she's been in recent contact with this guy and that she's in danger."

"Jesus," Liza echoed. "When are you going? Does she have some kind of protection detail on her until you get there?"

"We're leaving as soon as I get off the phone," Grey said. "They have their own transportation, and it's faster than your average private jet."

"Is it a Cessna Citation X?" she guessed eagerly.

"Nope, faster than that," Grey replied with a grin.

"How much faster? That's the fastest private jet in the air!" Liza stuttered.

"Let's just say we'll be there by the time the local police get their act together and drive her home," he replied.

"What? I'm the tech analyst! Why are *you* the one who gets to play with all the cool toys?" she complained.

"You don't know the half of it, Lizzie," Grey said with a shake of his head.

If she was this excited over the lie, he couldn't wait to see her face if she ever learned the truth.

∞∞∞∞∞∞∞∞∞

Marianne Thornton lived in a one-bedroom apartment in suburban Santa Monica. Her cramped but tidy flat was on the second floor of a tree shrouded building with mottled red and grey masonry that looked as if it was constructed from century old clay.

Grey stood at Marianne's sliding glass door and looked out onto a balcony so small it hardly seemed worth having. Its weathered wooden planks looked none too sturdy either. Although he could see the allure of stepping out onto it and being able to touch the leaves of the nearest eucalyptus.

The shaggy-barked trees dotted the lawn surrounding the building, adding to the historic feel of the charming little neighborhood.

"I can't believe this is real," Marianne said faintly. "Are you sure I'm not dreaming? I don't suppose you'd tell me if I was."

Angelica smiled gently at her. She had traded her French maid's uniform for skintight jeans and a clingy pink top that fell just short of their low-slung waistline. She still looked like she belonged in a Frederick's of Hollywood catalog.

"You are not dreaming yet, I promise you." The succubus reached across the batik-draped surface of Marianne's compact dining room table and squeezed her hand reassuringly. "But I would like your permission to join you when you do. There are lucid dreaming techniques I can show you that will keep an incubus from entering your dreamscape."

Marianne nodded dazedly. They hadn't been able to get much information out of her. She was so sleep deprived that she seemed almost to be in a trance.

"I would also like to draw some protective wards around your bed. They will only work, however, when you sleep within their boundaries. This means you cannot fall asleep anywhere else. You must take all of your rest in your own bed."

Angelica held Marianne's gaze to make sure she understood, her brows knitting at the disoriented look in the girl's eyes. She turned her concerned gaze on Sparrow, who was watching their exchange from across the table.

"I must work quickly," she murmured. "Marianne is completely exhausted. Keep her awake as long as you can, but bring her to the bed immediately if she loses consciousness."

She blinked out and, after a moment, Grey heard her rustling around in Marianne's bedroom. It was the only other room in the apartment, and mere feet from the space occupied by the table.

He watched the blonde girl's wan expression, noting the fact that a woman disappearing into thin air in front of her hadn't seemed to register. He moved to the chair Angelica had vacated, just as Sparrow scooted his own chair closer to her.

"Marianne," Grey said loudly, "we need you to stay with us for just a few more minutes, okay sweetheart?"

He reached for her hand, chafing it between his palms to get her blood flowing. It remained limp in his grasp.

Sparrow leaned in and pressed the back of his hand to her cheek, closing his eyes and muttering something in Gaelic. Then his eyes shot open and he cursed.

"Angelica," he called grimly, "you need to hurry. She's trapped in a *mara*."

Chapter 17

Burr sneered at the whimpering boy who lay crumpled on the pavement at his feet. Skinny and pale, with overlarge teeth, the gangly teenager was a perfect specimen of everything he hated about the human race.

He was feeble and weak, a useless bag of flesh and bone taking up space in an even more useless realm of mortal existence. Rather than try to defend himself, he looked up at Burr with soft eyes that pleaded for mercy.

Burr didn't believe in mercy. No one had ever shown him any. Even the name his mother had given him was meant as a cruel reminder that he was nothing but a thorn in her side.

He narrowed his gaze as the boy tried to curl into a protective ball. His lanky, awkward limbs curved around his bruised ribs in an attempt to shield them from the steel-toed boots Burr had conjured for his beating.

The boy's cheek rested against the curb, spittle clinging to those giant buck teeth as he cried and gasped for air. Burr smiled and nudged the teen's head to the side with his boot, positioning those ugly teeth against the gritty surface of the curb.

Then he lifted his foot and stomped hard on the back of the boy's head. Malicious satisfaction ricocheted through him at the muffled scream and spray of blood that spurted from the boy's mouth.

Burr inhaled the boy's pain and fear, feeling calmer and more in control than he had in days. He stepped out of the boy's dreamscape and back into the twilight of the dream plane. It only took him a moment to realize that the little blonde had finally come back for him.

He reached out, drawing the shimmering ball of her soul light into his hand. He closed his eyes and stepped into her dreamscape, thinking how lucky they both were that he'd been able to burn off some of his rage and hunger before seeing her again.

This next stage of the game was delicate. Restraint was needed. He'd have to give the little slut what she craved so she'd open herself up to him enough that he could follow her into her waking realm.

Then, and only then, would he be able to show her how things really were. How he held control over her fears, and her desires meant nothing when weighed against his own. How she existed solely for his pleasure.

Before the end she'd understand one simple truth.

That he owned her.

∞∞∞∞∞∞∞∞∞

"What the hell is a *mara*?" demanded Grey, his hands moving to grasp Marianne's shoulders. He gave her a jolting little shake, but she remained unresponsive.

"It's an induced state of sleep paralysis," Sparrow explained, sweeping the girl up into his arms and carrying her to her bedroom as Angelica had instructed. He laid her on the bed atop an old, hand-stitched quilt that looked as if it had seen better days.

Angelica knelt at the foot of the bed. She held something in her palm that Grey couldn't quite see and was using it to trace symbols on the floor. They glowed faintly at first and then winked into invisibility.

The succubus sang softly beneath her breath as she inched her way around the perimeter of the bed. Her voice was soothing, its cadence reminding Grey of a lullaby.

"How is she in sleep paralysis? She was just sitting at the table, talking to us. Is it the incubus?" Grey asked in alarm.

"She must have been so tired she nodded off with her eyes open." Concern etched Sparrow's features as he brushed the girl's hair out of her face. "And yes, if I had to guess, I'd say it's the incubus. A *mara* isn't a natural phase of sleep. It's a highly suggestive state that lies somewhere between sleeping and waking.

"It can be used to communicate with a mortal on a deep subconscious level, like hypnosis. Hallucinations can be induced, either calming or frightening ones, depending on the purposes of the *mara*.

"It can even be used to keep a mortal paralyzed during a possession. I fear what this incubus intends..." Sparrow trailed off as Marianne began to moan and tremble, her slight form undulating rhythmically against the bed.

Grey frowned. She looked and sounded as if she was in the throes of pleasure rather than pain. His gaze flickered to Sparrow, who watched her with an expression of dawning comprehension.

Angelica continued to sing softly and draw strange symbols, as if she was unaware of the disturbing scene taking place above her. Having moved past the foot of the bed, the room's mirrored closet doors reflected the slim curve of her back as she kneeled on the side opposite where Grey and Sparrow stood.

Grey prayed that, whatever she was doing, she finished it soon.

"He's using the *mara* to give her sexual pleasure," Sparrow murmured. "It would feel far more real to her than if he merely did it in her dreamscape. I'll wager that's how he's gaining their trust and getting them to invite him into their waking realities."

"Can he hurt her in the *mara*?" Grey asked.

Sparrow tilted his head. "Yes and no. Right now he's still on the dream plane. He can only create the illusion of physical contact there. But if he gets her to invite him here, he can do whatever he wants."

"How do we catch him if he shows up?" Grey asked, automatically unsnapping the lock on his holster.

"That'll certainly slow him down," Sparrow said, not missing Grey's reflexive action. "But our best bet is in Angelica's hands. If I'm not mistaken, she's weaving a trap into those wards."

Grey nodded, his skin prickling with edgy awareness. He'd yet to face an enemy that couldn't be taken down with a few well-placed strikes and a .357 Magnum.

But if singing and symbols were what it took to end this nightmare, he wasn't complaining.

Angelica's voice rose in a lilting melody as she reached Marianne's wooden headboard, her movements fluid and graceful as she traced glowing symbols in a rising line up the wall. Grey had never heard a sound so pure, yet so seductive at the same time.

He could easily imagine the legends coming to life, and sailors steering their boats onto the rocks, mesmerized by her siren's song. A glance at Sparrow's slack expression told him the other man wasn't unaffected either.

Grey closed his eyes, an unbidden image of Scarlett coming into his mind. Her toned thighs trembled against his hips as she took him deep within her body. Her beautiful face flushed as she rose above him, riding his length, her tongue darting out to moisten that sweet little indention in her bottom lip…

A strange reverberation filled his ears, a discordant counterpoint to the fantasy and the angelic strains that had conjured it. He blinked in confusion just as Sparrow shouted, "Watch out!"

All hell broke loose in the cramped space of Marianne's bedroom.

Grey looked up in time to see a compact man with brown hair and a narrow back lunge for Angelica. He knocked a tiny orb of light out of her hand, sending it flying through the air to sail over a still sleeping Marianne.

It rebounded against the dresser, hitting the tile floor with a crack and rolling beneath the bed. Angelica growled a vivid expletive that shook Grey out of his stupor.

Her delicate fist flew into the man's nose with a surprisingly vicious thud, and she blinked out while he was recovering. Grey realized two things in that moment: the man must be the incubus, and Angelica hadn't had a chance to finish her wards.

Grey drew his gun as the man's small, mean eyes narrowed on Sparrow and he leapt for Marianne.

"Oh no you don't," Sparrow snarled, surging forward onto the bed to shield the girl. He body-checked the shorter, wiry man with the heft of his shoulder, sending him tumbling to the floor.

Grey half rolled across the bed, trying to get a shot at the incubus. But the man had disappeared by the time his feet hit the rumpled throw rug on the other side.

A glance at Sparrow revealed a long sword held ready in his grip. Fiery red characters sizzled angrily down the length of its double-sided blade.

"Nice weapon," Grey remarked as he scanned the room, muscles taut and wary.

"Wait until you see Scarlett with hers," Sparrow replied, his gaze sweeping the span of mirrors for any sign of movement.

Grey didn't have time for the carnal heat that surged through his veins at that image. "Do you think the bastard's coming back?" he asked.

"I doubt he'll give up so easily," answered Sparrow. "He tried to blink out with her before. Almost succeeded. I need to keep physical contact with her until those wards are complete."

Something rustled beneath the bed, and Grey vaulted backward toward the dresser, landing in a crouch as he leaned down to peer through a gap in the blue dust ruffle.

He grunted as searing pain ripped across his back. Rearing up, he threw his elbow behind him, the hard boney point ramming into soft tissue and eliciting a howl from his attacker.

Grey rolled onto the torn flesh of his back, ignoring the pain and holding his gun steady as he searched for a clean shot. Gleaming metal claws, still wet with his blood, flew at his face from the shadowy corner between the dresser and the wall.

He jerked out of the way, his spine wrenching at an unnatural angle as he twisted and shot. The crack of the bullet was impossibly loud in the close confines of the room. His ears rang with the aftershock as he pushed off the dresser to gain distance from his assailant.

"Filthy human," spat the incubus as he doubled over, pressing his hands against his side. Blood bloomed in a bright red stain through the torn cloth beneath his palms.

It was then that Grey saw the wicked device that had slashed open his back. On one fist, the incubus wore a modified gauntlet with inch long metal claws protruding from each knuckle. It looked like something from a medieval weaponry exhibit.

Grey was almost relieved to discover that the creature bled red and didn't actually have metal claws sprouting from his fingertips.

Light exploded throughout the room, like a hundred flashbulbs going off at once. Grey squinted against the blinding onslaught, his narrowed gaze catching the afterimage of the unbroken line of symbols that circled the bed and disappeared behind the headboard.

Marianne groaned and started to sit up, her green eyes going round with fright as she took in the chaos surrounding her.

Burr cursed, realizing that the meddlesome succubus must have completed the wards while he wasted time on the sidhe and the mortal. He sneered at Grey, whose projectile human weapon was still leveled at him, and then blinked away. He hated to flee, but he obviously needed to regroup.

"Damn it," Grey swore.

"Was that him?" Marianne asked, her voice cracking with terror and exhaustion.

"Yes, but you're safe now, sweetheart," Sparrow replied soothingly. "Agent Derrington wounded him. And Angelica's protective wards will keep him away from you."

He straightened from the mattress, sending his sword back to its ethereal sheath. Directing a solemn grin at Grey he said, "Nice shot, brother. Remind me to heal that back before Scarlett sees you, though. Otherwise she's liable to kick my ass."

"Would you mind releasing me?" Angelica's muffled voice drifted up from beneath the bed.

Sparrow spoke a single word, the look on his face hovering between surprise and mirth. Angelica appeared next to the footboard, her clothing disheveled and bits of fuzzy dust speckling her hair.

"Caught in your own trap?" Sparrow asked, his expression carefully blank.

Her cheeks pinkened to almost the same shade as her shirt. "At the time, I did not see any other option."

Sparrow nodded in sympathetic amusement. "I don't suppose you recognized him?"

Angelica came as close to glaring as Sparrow had ever seen her. "You mean because we're the same race? No. I don't suppose I did."

"Are you sure he's gone?" Marianne asked in a timid whisper.

Angelica's eyes softened as they travelled to the frightened girl. "As long as you remain within the wards that surround this bed, he cannot harm you."

Marianne took a shuddering breath, her gaze still wavering with uncertainty.

Angelica modified her voice with a soothing suggestion and added, "With your permission, I will stay with you this night. I will extend the wards to the rest of your home, create a protective talisman for you to wear, and meet you in your dreamscape to teach you some lucid dreaming techniques that will give you more control when you are on the dream plane."

Marianne nodded, the wrinkles in her brow smoothing away.

"Very good," Angelica replied with an encouraging smile. "You have nothing to worry about, Marianne. Right now, the most important thing is for you to get some much needed rest. And I will join you in your dreams shortly, okay?"

The girl nodded again, her sleepy eyes touching on both Sparrow and Grey before they fluttered closed. "Thank you," she murmured as she drifted into slumber.

"I need you to exempt me from the wards so that I don't get trapped again," Angelica said quietly to Sparrow.

"Of course," he replied, his gaze heavy with respect at the way she'd handled the terrified girl. "We'll come back to question her after she's had some rest. I appreciate all of your help, Angelica. And I apologize if I offended you before."

The succubus shook her head, her expression grim. "The only thing that offends me is one of my own people profaning our gift for bestowing sacred pleasure with a use so heinous and monstrous."

Chapter 18

"Come on. We're going for a walk on the beach," Sydney said, her tone brooking no argument.

Lorien had blinked out to babysit her nephew not long after the boys' and Angelica's departure. And Scarlett's anxious pacing was beginning to drive her a little bonkers.

Scarlett paused and looked up at her in surprise. "What if they come back?"

"I'll leave a note on the coffee table," Sydney replied, already scribbling their intended destination in large letters on a yellow notepad.

She proceeded to the door, slipping on some flip-flops in the entryway and holding up a second pair while giving Scarlett an impatient look. Scarlett huffed out a worried breath and joined her.

"But what if I miss Grey and he leaves?" Scarlett protested as they stepped onto the elevator.

Sydney's lips quirked upward in a sympathetic smile. "It's going to be okay. He's going to get over you lying to him, and it's going to be okay."

Scarlett's uncertain eyes searched hers. "How can you know that? Everything between us has been a lie. I didn't get the chance to explain..."

"I know, because I saw the way he looked at you," Sydney interrupted as the smack of their flip-flops echoed through the lobby. "Even in the midst of all his confusion, he still looked at you like you were the only person in the room."

That eased a small fraction of Scarlett's tension. "He must feel as if I made a fool of him, though," she said unhappily.

Sydney sighed as she opened a glass door and skirted around a waiter carrying a tray of drinks out to the pool area. "Did Sparrow ever tell you how I 'forgot' to tell him I was married when we first got together?"

"What?" Scarlett asked in surprise. "No. How could you forget something like...never mind. It doesn't matter. You and Pat are soul mates. You could have forgotten to tell him you were an imp-troll hybrid wearing a glamour spell, and you still would have ended up together."

Sydney raised a brow and looked askance at Scarlett. "Have you ever seen an imp-troll hybrid?"

"'Twas a figure of speech," Scarlett shot back, her accent thickening in her agitation. She knew she was being a blaggarding whiner, but she couldn't seem to stop herself.

"Look how beautiful it is," Sydney murmured, gazing out at the waves breaking gently beneath the gathering dusk.

Scarlett made an effort to shut her mouth and followed Sydney out onto the wooden planks of the platform leading down to the beach. The breeze teased strands of hair free from her ponytail, coaxing them to flutter softly against her cheek. She inhaled deeply, drawing in the mineral essence of the salt air and the tranquility it offered.

Sydney paused at a bench built into the banister at the bottom of the ramp. They both abandoned their flip-flops to a row of other discarded shoes before opening the gate and stepping down into the sand.

It still held the sun's warmth, and Scarlett hummed with contentment as it sifted between her bare toes and massaged the soles of her feet. She trailed after Sydney, down toward the water, where moisture packed the loose grains into a cool clay that held the shape of her footprints.

"Feeling any better?" Sydney murmured as she bent to pick up a tiny, perfect whelk shell that had miraculously managed to wash ashore unbroken.

Scarlett sniffed. "Are you trying to manage me, human?" she demanded, a reluctant smile hovering at the edges of her lips.

Sydney snorted. "I'm trying to be your friend, you stubborn sidhe woman." She sniggered because the two words sounded funny together— she-woman, like the opposite of he-man.

"What's so funny?" Scarlett asked in exasperation.

"Well, when I was little, I used to watch this cartoon called He-Man," Sydney explained. "And he had a sister named She-Ra who had her own cartoon. But I always wondered why they didn't just call her She-Woman. I mean, it would have made sense, right?"

Scarlett shook her head. Her brother Doyle watched cartoons sometimes. From what she'd seen, they were terribly silly. "You are the strangest human I've ever met."

Sydney nibbled her lip. "But you do feel a little better, right?"

"I don't know," Scarlett hedged, narrowing her gaze on the other woman. "It usually takes a good fight to really make me feel better."

Sydney laughingly took a step back, the incoming surf splashing up onto the rolled cuffs of her jeans. "Sorry. I'm afraid walks on the beach and ridiculous banter are all I have to offer."

"I suppose that will have to do," Scarlett replied with a sigh. "Do you know how to make tacos? Those usually make me feel better too."

"Of course I do," Sydney scoffed, returning to Scarlett's side and meandering along as she scanned the shoreline for more shells. "But I'm better at ordering them from the Mexican place down the street."

Scarlett chuckled.

"You were wrong before, you know," Sydney commented idly.

Scarlett frowned at her. "About what?"

"Not *everything* between you and Grey has been a lie. Just the superficial stuff," she said with a shrug.

"Right," Scarlett huffed. "Just the stuff about my job, my life, oh and let's not forget the very existence of my world."

"Trivial," Sydney insisted with a small smile. "All of that stuff is like this shell," she said, holding up the little whelk. "It's armor and decoration. Life and love reside in the soft stuff hidden beneath. And that's where you and Grey connected."

Sydney's eyes lit up and her smile widened. Scarlett realized why when she heard Pat's deep drawl behind her.

"Good evening, Ladies. We got your note."

Scarlett spun to find him standing there next to Grey.

"How was California?" Sydney asked.

Both men's faces turned somber at the question.

"It's definitely an incubus," Sparrow replied. "We got there just in time to save the girl, but he got away. Angelica's still with her."

"You'll catch him," Sydney assured, threading her fingers through his.

"Did he come through to this realm?" Scarlett asked. "You know if he was able to get a physical lock on you he might retaliate." She cast a worried glance toward Sydney.

Sparrow pulled Sydney to his side, his arm tightening around her reflexively. He reached into his pocket and pulled out a black leather cord with a metal medallion that resembled a small coin.

"I don't know if we had enough contact for him to manage that," he said gruffly. "But Angelica made a warding talisman for Sydney. And Grey too," he added with a nod at the matching medallion around the other man's neck. "Just in case."

"Good," Scarlett murmured with a nod.

"Thanks," Sydney said as she slipped the cord over her head and tightened its adjustable knot.

"Now how about you call it a night and blink us back to my penthouse?" Her smile was all for Sparrow, and the invitation in her voice was unmistakable.

Sparrow's eyes heated, but he paused to flick a questioning glance at Scarlett and Grey.

"Scarlett was just telling me how much she enjoys walking on the beach," Sydney invented with an unapologetic grin. "Right before you got here she was saying she wasn't quite ready to go in yet."

"Oh yeah, that's right. I was," Scarlett corroborated in a dry tone.

"No reason not to enjoy it while you're here," Sydney said cheerfully as she pressed the tiny whelk shell into Scarlett's palm. "Have fun and we'll see you guys later."

Pat blinked them out, leaving Scarlett and Grey alone at the shore's edge.

The moon rose on the distant horizon, as if emerging from the ocean itself. Its incandescent brilliance melded with the glow that spilled from the sprawling hotel grounds, lending Scarlett enough light to clearly see his features.

She frowned as she noticed the dark, irregular stain marring the cloth of his shirt just above his shoulder. She reached out to trace it with her fingertips, side-stepping to get a better look at his back when she felt a tear in the fabric.

"What the devil happened here?" she exclaimed. "It looks like you were clawed by a damned dragon!"

"Sparrow took care of it. It's fine," he insisted, trying to turn toward her again.

She refused to cooperate, remaining glued to his back with a stern, "Stay put and let me see," as she gingerly lifted his ruined shirt.

He closed his eyes, shuddering at her touch as her fingers gently explored the contours of his shoulder blades and the length of his spine.

"The incubus had a fist weapon. Funnily enough, Sparrow said it was called a dragon claw," he remarked with grim humor. "The bastard grazed me with it, but the wounds weren't too deep. Sparrow was able to heal them with the same dust Lorien used on us earlier."

Scarlett finally lowered the shredded cloth and moved to face him once more. Her gaze searched his, her eyes swimming with regret.

"I'm so sorry I lied to you," she said quietly. "I hated every moment of it."

He reached up to smooth an errant wisp of hair from her cheek. Cupping her face in his palm, he brushed his thumb across her mouth to still the quivering uncertainty there.

"You didn't really hate *every* moment, did you?" he teased.

She tried to smile through the tremble in her lips. "Are we okay?" she whispered.

"Scarlett, I don't see how you could have done things any differently than you did. There are still some gaps that I wouldn't mind having filled in with the truth.

"But none of that changes the fact that you're the most amazing woman I've ever met." Holding her gaze, he parted her lips with the pad of his thumb and leaned forward to taste her.

She sighed into his mouth, drinking in his breath as if she was starving for him. His own kiss turned hungry, his tongue rasping against hers in a desperate rhythm. Scarlett pressed into his chest, aligning her body with his as she tried to get closer.

It wasn't close enough.

She swept his leg and he fell to the damp sand with a grunt, her full weight atop him. Spreading her thighs she straddled him, rocking her hips into his as he joined their hands and stretched their arms above their heads.

Scarlett writhed against his length, moaning as his heat and the friction of their clothing teased her breasts into sensitive peaks. Grey claimed her mouth, his kiss mastering her despite his submissive position.

The incoming tide rushed around them, the foamy water rising above Scarlett's knees as they sank into the shifting sand. The sea-spray infused Grey's lips with a hint of salt as they moved feverishly against hers.

He tasted lush and wild on her tongue, engulfing her senses like a rainstorm overtaking the sky. The tide rose higher, washing around them and soaking them both.

Grey released her hands, banding his arms around her and lifting them into a sitting position. "I think we should go back to my room," he whispered against her mouth.

Scarlett grinned. "What's the matter, soldier? Afraid of a little water?"

He licked at the droplets that clung to her skin, following them down the smooth column of her throat to the hollow between her collarbones. Lingering there, he slowly kissed his way down to the soft valley between her breasts.

Scarlett gasped, her head dropping backward as her brain shorted out with pleasure.

"Not at all," he murmured, rotating his hips upward into the wet vee of her thighs as his tongue flicked out to trace the inner curve of her breast. "As a matter of fact, I was going to suggest we take a bath."

"A bath?" she repeated faintly. It took her a moment to grasp the meaning of the word. "Together?" She blinked at him, her eyes cloudy with passion.

"Mmmhmm," he hummed lazily against her tingling flesh. "How else am I going to soap the salt from every inch of your beautiful body? Of course, I'll have to go over my work with my tongue to make sure I don't miss anything."

She swallowed, muttering something in Gaelic. In a husky voice she said, "I'm breaking the rules. Just this once." Then she blinked them directly to the Jacuzzi tub in his hotel room.

Grey exhaled in surprise as they reappeared with her straddling him inside the deep, oversized spa. At least she'd managed a relatively soft landing atop the gel mat affixed to its surface. Chuckling, he reached to turn on the tap, making the water hot but not scalding.

"I've been wanting to get you into this tub since I first saw it," he growled. He pushed to his feet, her legs sliding down his until she stood before him.

He lowered his head to kiss her, his fingers releasing the buttons of her vest and pushing it from her shoulders. He frowned as he dropped the stiffening black garment to the floor.

"I'm afraid we've ruined your leather," he apologized, his hands moving to the edges of her camisole and slipping it up over the flat plane of her stomach and the ripe contours of her breasts. He lifted the thin scrap of material above her head, his palms skimming the lengths of her arms and making her shiver.

"Faerie dust will fix it," she replied in a breathless voice as her trembling fingers unbuttoned his ruined shirt, revealing the smooth, caramel skin beneath. She drank in the sight, the firm expanse of his chest and shoulders a marvel of nature to her.

"Really?" he murmured as he flicked open the top button of her jeans and slowly slid the zipper down. "Faerie dust heals clothes too? That's interesting."

He shimmied the tight denim over her hips, capturing one of her nipples between his lips as he bent to push the damp fabric, and the slip of lingerie beneath, past her thighs. He lingered at her breast, suckling and lapping at the taut peak with his tongue.

Scarlett moaned, the warm, rising water caressing her feet and calves as his mouth worked its wicked magic on the flesh he'd uncovered above.

"What else can it do?" he asked as he trailed lower, fluttering kisses over her belly. The stubble on his jaw abraded her skin gently, feeling sexy and masculine against her softness.

"Hmm?" she sounded, having lost the thread of their conversation.

"Faerie dust," he clarified as he lifted one of her legs, and then the other, to pull her jeans the rest of the way off. "What else can it do?"

He reached for a small bottle on the ledge of the tub and dumped its contents into the heated water where it rushed in from the tap. An amazing smell permeated the room with the steam. Scarlett closed her eyes, breathing in jasmine, citrus, and a pleasant hint of something spicy.

"Well, what you're talking about is healing dust," she replied faintly. "But faerie dust is a general term that can refer to any dust preparation created by the magic of the sprites. Or it can simply refer to the dust that falls from their wings."

A low hum rose up and Scarlett's lashes fluttered open as the water began to simmer and froth around her bare legs in a soothing massage. Foamy white bubbles grew thick on its shimmering surface, obscuring the floor of the tub beneath.

"Fascinating," Grey intoned, his tongue flickering out to tease the bud of her clitoris, his breath heating her sensitive flesh as his rumbling voice resonated against her. "But you didn't really answer my question. What can it do other than healing wounds and fixing clothes?"

Scarlett's knees nearly collapsed at the overload of sensation. His hands landed on her hips, steadying her, as he rose to strip off his now-soaked pants. His grin was puckish as he relinquished them with a soggy splat to the discarded heap next to the tub.

Scarlett narrowed her eyes at him, suspecting that his queries were only meant to toy with her while he drove her mindless with his touch. She smoothed her palms down the muscular contours of his abs, shaking off her haze of desire with difficulty.

Leaning forward, she trailed her lips across his bare chest, her tongue darting out to taste his smooth, salty skin. He groaned, his pecs leaping beneath the tantalizing torment, and she smiled.

"Grey," she murmured, kissing and licking at his flat nipple. "Let's play a game."

He sucked in a tight breath and framed her face with his hands, gently pulling her lips up to his. "I'm not sure I can survive whatever game you've concocted in that diabolically brilliant brain of yours," he replied, his dark eyes gleaming with humor as he tried to capture her mouth.

She teased and nipped at his lips, refusing to allow him to deepen the kiss. "Don't be a spoilsport," she admonished.

Rubbing her naked body down the length of his, she lowered her hand into the silky, oiled warmth of the water. Then, straightening slowly, she circled her moistened fingers around the widening crown of his erection. "I'll make the rules simple enough for even the most thickheaded soldier," she whispered in a sultry voice.

Grey shuddered in her grasp, a fierce shockwave of pleasure rebounding through him. Scarlett laced the fingers of her free hand through his and pulled him down to kneel on the soft mat in the sunken tub. The foamy bubbles swirled and parted around them as they sank together into the fragrant, welcoming heat.

"You seem to have some questions about my world," she said, skimming her lips over the angular planes of his jawbone and chin.

"Ask me whatever you want," she offered, placing open mouthed kisses along the corded length of his neck. His pulse raced beneath her tongue, and she suckled at the skin there, feeling his cock jump against her palm in reaction.

"What makes it a game?" he asked hoarsely, reaching to pull the loose band from her ponytail and comb his fingers through her hair.

She kissed lower, lingering at his nipples before moving down to trace the molded definition of his abs with roving caresses of her lips. The sinuous line of her back elongated into a smooth plane of satiny skin, her delectable ass rising in a tempting curve just beyond.

He reached to palm one rounded globe, but she stopped him with, "You have to keep your hands to yourself and your mouth free to ask questions."

He grumbled in protest but lowered his hand, his stomach muscles rippling beneath her sensual exploration as she added, "I, however, get to do whatever I want with mine." She held his gaze as she flattened her tongue and slowly extended it to cushion the head of his penis.

"God, Scarlett," he shuddered the words out, his voice strained and rough. She felt his dizzying rush of pleasure echo through her as she swirled her soft, wet tongue around him, gathering the salty pre-cum from his tip.

"You wanted to know what else faerie dust can be used for?" she said in a throaty tone, her lips hovering at the taut mahogany crown of his shaft.

Her warm breath and the vibration of her speech on his flesh robbed him of thought, and he let out a muffled groan, his cock jerking involuntarily against her lips.

"There are many different kinds of faerie magic," she murmured, taking him into the heated cavern of her mouth and allowing him to slide over her tongue until he bumped the back of her throat. The water had risen to submerge his heavy sac, and she reached down to cup it in her palm, watching his reaction as she grazed her fingertips along the tight rounded skin.

She shivered with shared pleasure as his eyes rolled closed. She repeated the movement, lightly grazing with her fingernails this time, as she withdrew her mouth and released his head from her lips with a soft pop.

"One interesting thing to note is that the dust falling from a sprite's wings will change color with his or her mood," she continued informatively.

A low, incoherent moan escaped Grey's throat as she trailed her tongue along the underside of his shaft, starting at the base and working her way leisurely up to the tip.

The water was high enough now that it spilled into her mouth and bubbles sloshed over the edges of the tub. Much to her delight, Grey didn't seem capable of noticing, so she reached to turn the tap off herself.

Taking him in her oil-softened palm, she stroked his length, watching in fascination as clear liquid beaded at his head. She brushed her thumb across it, holding his gaze as she slowly lifted her hand to her mouth to taste it.

Fire blazed in Grey's eyes and he let out a growl as his hands flew to her shoulders and he tried to pull her up to his lips. She chuckled and dodged out of his grip with a splash.

"Uh, uh, uh," she sounded, "that's against the rules."

Breathing hard, he clenched his hands and folded them behind his back, as if he didn't trust himself in the face of her temptation. His gaze devoured her flushed cheeks and her breasts, kissed by the damp curled ends of her strawberry blonde hair.

Scarlett's heart beat faster at the sensual heat and promise burning in his eyes. "Sprites can use their own dust to influence other beings," she said huskily, "for example, as a sleep aid, an intoxicant, a stimulant, and many other things."

She walked forward on her knees through the swirling warmth of the spa, stopping only when she was close enough to feel his breath on her face. Tingling energy wavered and leapt between them, as if tiny arcs of lightning connected their skin.

"They can also make their dust into more complicated preparations," she whispered, "like healing dust, or the transport powder they use to blink things from place to place."

Unable to help herself, she leaned in a fraction and brushed her lips over his, pulling back before she could get lost in his kiss. "Sprites may be small, but they are mysterious and powerful. Much of their magic lies hidden as a closely guarded secret known only within their own society."

Her fingertips skimmed over the words 'Semper Fidelus' tattooed across his shoulder. *Always Faithful* was the translation he'd given her.

A curiously empty feeling pricked her heart as she compared its meaning to her own Aegishjalmur tattoo's inextricable ties to her people's soul mate connection.

Grey saw the troubled look cloud her gaze and broke the rules of her game. Pulling one hand from behind his back, he stroked her soft cheek with his knuckles.

Instead of chastising him, she leaned into his touch, squeezing her eyes shut as she struggled to shake off her sudden melancholy.

"Do you have any more questions about faerie dust?" she asked quietly after a moment.

Grey shook his head solemnly.

"You must have other questions about my world, though," she murmured, a smile trembling at the corners of her lips.

He studied her face, a bevy of questions tumbling through his head. But only one seemed to matter at the moment. "What made you so sad just now?"

She swallowed, her smile becoming tenuous. "That's not technically a question about my world."

He searched her gaze, and her breath hitched in her throat as she realized she was afraid of how deeply he'd see into feelings she wasn't yet ready to put a name to.

"Rain check?" she asked, with a forced grin. "I'd rather not talk about things that make me sad right now."

He nodded, but the look he gave her was perceptive enough to tell her that he saw through her avoidance.

"I don't ever want to do anything to make you sad," he murmured. He released the hand still behind his back, reaching to graze both sides of her face with the lightest of caresses.

Scarlett's breath quickened and her pulse turned erratic at the sheer tenderness of the words and the gesture. He leaned forward, his face blurring in her unsteady vision, as he brushed his lips across hers, slowly, back and forth.

She whimpered against his mouth, little puffs of air escaping her lips as a sharp longing rolled through her, devastating her senses. A low, aching tremble of emotion shook her core.

Inexplicable tears pricked behind Scarlett's eyes, but before they could overtake her, Grey claimed her lips with a shatteringly gentle passion that swept them away.

His mouth moved over hers with a soft surety that transformed her desolate longing into a cresting wave of desire. His touch fueled a steady, building warmth within her, replacing the hollow emotion with life and need…and love.

And there it was—the feeling she had tried so hard not to identify. She loved Grey. She kissed him back with slow, ravaging abandon, allowing all of her defenses to crumble into dust beneath the patient onslaught of his mouth.

Grey felt the change in her as she melted into him, her kiss turning sweet and wild. She allowed him to lower her into the warm embrace of the water, and he groaned at the feel of her silky skin sliding against his.

The soft weight of her body settled atop his lap below the swirling surface. Grey slid his hand up her back, his fingers massaging the delicate curve of her spine as she arched beneath his touch.

His other hand played over her side, his thumb sweeping up the elegant span of her belly to trace the outline of her breast. Scarlett shuddered against him and he felt her pleasure reverberate across his nerve endings in slow, heavy waves.

She circled her hips, her supple movements enchanting him into a dream-like haze as she shared his breath in the fragrant, steam-clouded room.

"Grey, make love to me," she whispered into his mouth, her plea slipping between his lips like ripe, luscious fruit.

He mirrored the circle of her hips, his hands sliding down to hold her above him as he glided through the velvety folds that harbored the entrance to her body. The slick, honeyed invitation of her desire beckoned him further, and he slowly pushed the wide dome of his head inside her, matching the shallow thrust with his tongue.

Scarlett moaned thickly, rocking against him as she tried to take him deeper. But he held her in place, massaging the globes of her ass with his fingers and spreading them apart. The sensation echoed through her thighs, widening her cleft for him as he withdrew and then pushed back inside, stretching her tight little opening once more.

A keening sound escaped her throat, and Grey absorbed it along with her mindless surge of need, as he repeated the slow, superficial thrusts of his cock and his tongue. Her inner muscles rippled around him, seducing him deeper, and he couldn't find the strength to resist any longer.

He lowered her down onto his lap, pushing up to seat himself fully inside her. His hands lifted to span her hips and one thumb slid over to press rigid little circles against her clit as he began to move within her.

Already hovering on the edge of orgasm, the sensation of taking his full length into her body after his teasingly shallow thrusts sent her flying. Grey swallowed her cries, stroking up through the rhythmic tightening of her muscles. He pushed her past ecstasy, into a realm of sensitivity and awareness that transformed her every nerve ending into a live wire.

As if he knew, his hands left her hips and began a slow skim of her body as he allowed her to take him at her leisure. She balanced her palms on his shoulders, rising higher on his shaft as his fingertips grazed down the slender groove of her spine.

Her breath rushed from her lips as she slid down onto him, his hands lifting to test the weight of her breasts and lingering there to softly stroke her curves.

She rose again, and his fingers skimmed down the lengths of her arms, lightly circling the sensitive pulse points at her wrists. The synchronicity of his touch and his kiss, combined with the caress of the simmering water against her skin, transcended pleasure.

A second orgasm began to rack her body, starting low in her belly and rippling outward to quake through every muscle with shocking intensity. It left her trembling like a leaf, but it felt so amazing that she couldn't bring herself to care.

Again, he continued to push up into her tightening channel, urging her to ride him through her climax as he captured her mewling gasps in his mouth.

Grey was lost in her. He marveled at finding the control to keep going after the sublime satisfaction of Scarlett coming on his cock.

The pleasure was so intense by the second time that he could barely breathe, and his capacity to think so impaired he was afraid his brain had melted.

Every brush of her fingertips against his skin as she pressed her weight into him; every stroke of her slick, velvety inner walls around his shaft; every soft swirl of her tongue against his—heightened his senses past the boundaries of intoxication.

He felt her euphoric abandon as she came for him, her ecstasy echoing through him until he didn't know whether it was hers or his own.

It was magic. *She* was magic. And it wasn't just the sex, though making love to her filled him with a reverence more profound than any he'd ever experienced.

It was more than that. Somehow he'd managed to fall in love with her in less than a week. It was insane. He wouldn't have believed it was possible.

But it was undeniably true.

And he was terrified that he had nothing to offer a strong, beautiful woman who held the secrets of a magical, hidden world at her fingertips. Nothing but the pleasure he was giving her now.

Grey slowed his thrusts, sliding his hands over her thighs and lingering at the soft curves of her knees before exploring the smooth expanse of her calves. He canted his hips, encouraging her to take more of him inside her, as his fingers circled the fine bones of her ankles and his thumbs slipped down to gently massage her insteps.

Scarlett moaned, aftershocks of bliss still quaking through her core as he pushed her higher with the deepening strokes of his cock. Her shuddering intensified with the press of his fingers against her feet, as if he'd completed some arcane circuit of sexual energy between them.

Delirious with the pleasure, she murmured softly against his lips, over and over, begging for him to take his release inside her. She couldn't understand his lack of response, until finally she realized she was speaking in Gaelic.

"Grey, please, come for me," she exhaled, her tongue twining with his.

When he still didn't react, she wondered if she'd forgotten how to speak English. Framing his strong jaw with her palms, her hips still undulating helplessly against his, she broke their kiss and tried again.

"Grey," she whispered, gazing into his dazed eyes. Their color reminded her of melted chocolate and for a moment she lost herself in their sweetness. Shaking off her stupor, she managed, "Come inside me, *mo ghrá.*"

Heat sparked in his gaze as he focused on her. His hand came up to pull gently at her hair where it fell over her shoulder, his knuckles grazing her nipple. Scarlett shivered and her breath left her in a quiet gasp.

"One more time, baby," he rumbled. "Let me make you come one more time."

Scarlett's brows drew together at his pained expression. She shook her head, unable to contain her feverish sigh as he buried himself inside her with deep, unhurried strokes.

"Goddess, Grey," she panted, "every time you move like that, it sparks another mini-climax for me. Please, *mo ghrá*, I want to feel you release inside me. Let me pleasure you too."

Grey groaned, his eyes falling closed as his hips ground upward into hers. "Baby, your pleasure *is* my pleasure," he rasped.

"Then give me what I want," she whispered seductively, knowing he was holding back, and determined to make him lose control.

"Come for me, Grey," she coaxed, tightening her inner muscles around him as he pushed inside her.

"God, Scarlett, baby," he exhaled, his voice strained to breaking as he increased the rhythm of his thrusts.

She brushed her fingertips over his lips, milking his shaft with her channel as she murmured, "I want to make you lose control the way you make me lose control, *mo ghrá*."

He let out a strangled moan as he plunged into her faster.

"That's it, Grey," she cried, meeting his frenzied thrusts as a dizzying wave of ecstasy rushed through her, stealing breath and thought as it broke against her consciousness and sent her spiraling into oblivion.

When Scarlett's eyes fluttered open, she was lying on Grey's bed wrapped in fluffy, white towels. She had a vague recollection of him lifting her from the tub and gently drying her before carrying her to the bedroom.

She heard voices speaking softly above the hum of the air conditioning, followed by the creak of the hotel room door swinging shut. Grey padded barefoot back into the bedroom, a large tray balanced between his hands with four dishes stacked atop it, each covered with a silver dome.

"You're awake," he noted with a grin.

The thin white spa robe he wore was belted loosely at his trim waist, the neck falling open to reveal smooth, darkly bronzed skin and a glimpse of his muscular chest. Angelica's talisman hung low between his chiseled pecs, and he made the leather cord with its little round medallion look infinitely sexy.

Scarlett sat up and tucked a towel around her breasts as he started to lay the dishes out in a line across the coverlet of the bed.

"What's this?" she asked in surprise, inhaling the rich, savory aromas drifting from beneath those silver lids.

"I thought you might be hungry since we skipped dinner, so I ordered room service," he explained, handing her a bottled water and a roll of silverware in a linen napkin. "I wasn't sure what you'd want, but I didn't want to wake you, so I picked out a few things I thought you might like."

"Mmm, I'm starving." She smiled and traced her bottom lip with her tongue, eliciting an inward groan from Grey. "Let's see how well you've come to know my tastes."

He chuckled and uncovered the first dish. A giant soft taco had been flattened and cut into four pieces, then nestled on a bed of shredded lettuce. Small dishes of sour cream and salsa lay to the side.

"Cheese quesadilla," he identified, moving to lift the lid on the next dish.

Scarlett plucked a triangle of quesadilla and took a bite. It was warm and crispy on the outside, filled with soft, melty cheese on the inside, and she hummed happily as she reached to dip it in salsa.

Grey lifted a brow at her, his hand hovering above the second dish. "Do you even want to see the rest?"

Scarlett nodded her head in vigorous affirmation, sea-green eyes dancing with laughter as she took another bite and allowed a long, stringy piece of cheese to stretch out between the quesadilla and her mouth.

Grey settled onto the bed and tipped his head, giving her a mischievous look. "In that case, let's play our game. For every satisfactory answer you give me about your world, I'll uncover another dish."

Scarlett made a disgruntled noise as she chewed, waiting until she swallowed to exclaim, "You'd use food against me when I'm starving?"

Grey snorted. "Considering the way you teased me earlier, baby, you're getting off easy."

She fluttered her lashes at him. "You didn't like it, soldier?"

He reached forward to grasp one of her wrists, bringing her fingers to his lips. Holding her gaze, he pulled each one slowly into his mouth to lick the salsa and sour cream from them. Scarlett's heart slammed into her ribs with each sensual drag of his tongue.

"I liked it," he said huskily, smiling as he released her. "But you owe me three thorough answers for three dinners. And you can work on the quesadilla while you're answering the first question."

"Fine," Scarlett agreed with a breathless nod. "Ask away."

Grey snagged a piece of quesadilla and chewed thoughtfully as he studied her.

"Well?" she drawled after a minute when he still hadn't moved to ask his first question.

"I'm having trouble deciding what to ask," he admitted. "Three questions aren't nearly enough to tell me everything I want to know about you."

Scarlett chuckled. "You're the one who set the rules," she teased. "And the quesadilla isn't going to last much longer. You'd better hurry, or you might have a hunger revolt on your hands."

Grey grinned. He was sure she'd be willing to answer more than three questions. But he was enjoying the game and wanted to ask the best three he could come up with.

"Okay," he said finally. "This is a multi-part question."

She blew a raspberry at him. "Are you trying to cheat already?" she demanded.

"I told you I'd require thorough answers," he replied with a shrug. "But if you want to forfeit the game before it even starts…" He hid a smile as he began to stack the covered dishes back onto the tray.

"I will blink all three of those back to the faerie realm and leave you here dinnerless if you even try it," she warned on a laugh.

"Now who's a cheater?" he accused with mock outrage. "I'm going to have to remember how unscrupulous you get when you're hungry."

Scarlett snorted. "Go ahead and ask your several-questions-unfairly-rolled-into-one-question," she mocked as she took the last quesadilla triangle, flashing him a look that dared him to object.

Grey's eyes crinkled in amusement as he replaced the dishes in a line across the middle of the bed.

"Originally you gave me a cover story about being in a secret branch of the Irish military," he said slowly. "Today you said your people are warriors who begin sword training at eighteen, and that Sparrow's a detective and you're a private citizen."

He narrowed his gaze on her. "What do you really do, and what did you mean by 'warriors'?"

She blew out a breath. "I know I invented this silly game," she began, her voice losing its flippant tone, "but I want you to know that lying to you was never a game to me. I...care for you...Grey, and I wouldn't want you to ever believe that I enjoyed keeping the truth from you."

"Shhh," he hushed, reaching for her hand and giving her fingers a gentle squeeze. "I know that, baby. I understand you couldn't tell me about your world. And I want you to stop feeling guilty about it." He smiled and gave her a pointed look. "Okay?"

She responded with a tentative nod.

"This game is an excuse for me to discover things about the most amazing woman I've ever met." He kissed her fingers before releasing them. "Not to mention I love playing with you. And I care for you too, Scarlett. Very much," he added softly.

Her heart gave a strange leap, feeling as if it was expanding inside her chest.

"Now answer my first question, woman," he insisted, his lips curling upward.

Grinning like an idiot, she began with the easiest part. "I teach sword fighting techniques in my village, and sometimes to visiting students from other villages as well."

"So that's your job," he said, his voice filled with sudden understanding. "No wonder you were so good at it during our lesson."

She nibbled her lip, looking pleased at his compliment. "Every sidhe completes advanced sword training to ensure we're skilled enough to properly use the soul bound swords each of us learns to summon at the age of eighteen," she continued.

"And many of us go on to continue our martial training in other styles, since every adult sidhe is eligible to be called to war by the Seelie Court, should it become necessary."

Grey shook his head, trying to absorb all of that. "The Seelie Court... they're the ones who are so concerned about the veil between our worlds and too many humans finding out about you?"

Scarlett nodded in assent. "They're our highest governing body and are responsible for keeping the balance between good and evil in check."

Grey whistled softly. "Good and evil, that's heavy stuff. How often do they call your people to war?"

Scarlett tipped her head to the side with a half smile. "Fortunately, not often. The last time was during the Unseelie uprising almost two hundred years ago."

"Sparrow mentioned the Unseelie Court when we were discussing the incubus," he recalled.

"Most of the peoples of my world are aligned with either the Seelies or the Unseelies. The Unseelies strive to create chaos and upset the balance between good and evil. Every once in a while they revolt against the Seelies and try to seize control."

"So that's what the uprising two hundred years ago was about, and the Seelies won," Grey assumed.

"Yes," Scarlett confirmed with a sad smile, "but many were killed in the battle, including Pat's father."

"I'm sorry to hear that," Grey murmured. He paused for a moment, his brows drawing together as if he was having trouble with the math.

"That would mean Sparrow's at least two hundred years old," he deduced in a halting voice.

Scarlett nodded, an odd, expectant expression hovering in her eyes.

Grey held her gaze, his own eyes widening. "And the two of you grew up together."

Scarlett nodded again, tracing the backs of her teeth with her tongue while she waited for it to sink in.

"Immortal," Grey breathed in disbelief. "You didn't just say your people were warriors before. You said they were *immortal* warriors. How old are you, Scarlett?"

She tented her palms over her face, peeking at him through her fingers. "A hundred and ninety-five," she whispered, her muscles tense as she waited for his reaction.

His mouth fell open as he shook his head in speechless wonder.

"Do you think I'm too old for you?" she asked on a rushed exhalation, her voice a tangle of uncertainty.

"Oh, baby," he chuckled softly, leaning forward over the line of silver-domed plates to pull her hands from her face and cradle her cheek in his palm.

"I think you're too amazing for me. I still think I might wake up to find this has all just been a dream. I mean, sure, a hundred and ninety-five makes forty seem like a bit less of a hurdle," he said with a spark of humor in his eyes.

"But knowing your age doesn't change the way I feel about you. You're beautiful and sexy, inside and out, and an arbitrary number has nothing to do with that."

She swallowed, tilting forward to meet his lips with her own. She kissed him softly, with gentle brushes of her lips and the tender nudge of her tongue against his. It was a quiet expression of emotion that wasn't meant for the sibilance of words.

But as she slowly withdrew, that unspoken emotion swirled thickly between them, as if waiting to be gathered and coalesced into speech.

Scarlett cleared her throat and gave him a lopsided smile. "Wasn't that three questions already?" she asked shakily.

"I just have one more for now," he murmured, reeling from the indelible impression her kiss left on his heart. "Can I see your sword?"

Scarlett let out a huff of laughter. "Really?"

Grey nodded, the look in his eyes heated and eager. "Oh yeah."

She unfolded the lightly tanned lengths of her legs, letting the towel fall from her naked form as she rose to stand beside the bed. The high curve of her breast lifted in a tantalizing motion as one toned arm reached behind her back, and she made a teasing show of pulling her soul bound sword from its intangible sheath.

Grey lost his ability to breathe as she stood unclothed before him, the bright golden blade of her sword rippling with fiery green runes as she gripped it with an easy confidence that he found staggeringly sexy.

Her tongue dipped down to touch the indention in her lower lip and she sent him a heavily lidded smile as she whispered, "I see you've brought your sword to bear as well."

He followed her gaze to the jutting swell pushing at the thin cotton beneath the loosely knotted sash of his robe. "Baby, you are so damned sexy," he growled, his palm finding the outline of his erection and stroking along it.

Scarlett's eyes flickered like candle flame, glued to the motion of his hand. Her delicate skin grew flushed and her breath left her parted lips in little puffs above the sharpened tip of her sword.

"Do you like that, Scarlett?" he asked her softly, his fingers curling to delineate his shape beneath the cloth.

Her gaze flew to his, simmering with heat as she nodded.

Grey closed his eyes and took a deep, dragging breath. "Christ, baby. If it's possible to die from sexual arousal, you're going to be the death of me."

He smoothed his robe and gathered his control with effort. When he reopened his eyes, Scarlett was grinning at him.

"Are you still hungry?" he asked gruffly.

"Starving," she admitted.

"Then let's uncover these before they get too cold to eat," he suggested, placing his hand safely on one of the silver domed dishes.

"Thank you for showing me, though," he added softly. "Your sword is beautiful."

"Thank you. So is yours," she murmured, her lips curving teasingly as she re-sheathed her magical weapon.

"You are a menace, woman," he accused, pulling the lids from all three plates in quick succession.

Scarlett rewrapped her towel and settled onto the bed with relish, too hungry to argue his verdict.

Chapter 19

Burr swore and jerked against the burn of the fire orchid powder as he forced it into the small hole left in his side by the human's projectile. It seared his flesh, sizzling into his bloodstream as it did its work.

He knew he wasn't in mortal danger. But he'd decided to purify the wound in case the cursed human had added something nasty to his weapon.

The man was obviously working with the sidhe and the succubus, so who knew what sorts of spells might have been used to alter his conventional human equipment.

Breathing past the pain, his eyes took in the ramshackle interior of his 'family' home. Out of habit, he avoided looking at the plaque high on the wall that proclaimed the only other birthright his bastard father had left him—his misbegotten last name, *Downy*.

When the fiery agony began to subside, he rose from the spindly wooden table where he sat. It rocked beneath his weight on its uneven legs and he slammed his fist down onto its scratched surface with an angry thud.

He was losing control. He wasn't normally bothered by the broken-down furniture dotting the decrepit shack. What use did he have for physical comforts, when he was able to create all he could ever want in dreams?

That was a lesson he'd learned at a young age when his father had dumped him here, after his whore human mother had abandoned him. His magic had been too strong for him to remain in the human realm, and his very existence was an embarrassment to his full-blooded incubus father.

Left to fend for himself in the dingy confines of the secluded cabin, he'd begun to discover exactly what his magic could do. And it had been a welcome revelation.

He stepped past an empty, overturned bucket that had lain there so long he'd forgotten its original purpose. He reigned in his temper, forcing himself not to kick it. His booted feet ground against the old layers of grit embedded in the uneven surface of the ancient wooden floor planks.

Stooping over a long, mounted board that served as a shelf, he squinted into the dim light as he scanned through its rows of curious contents. He chose a small chipped black bowl, a stoppered vial of clear liquid, and an unwieldy lump wrapped in a stained threadbare cloth. Then he returned to the table.

Pouring some of the liquid into the bowl, he unwrapped the cloth from his dragon claw. He dipped the weapon into the clear solution, swirling carefully so that it washed over each blade. The liquid turned cloudy, taking on a rusty tint, and Burr smiled at his success.

He had no doubt that the amount of blood he'd salvaged from the human was enough for him to find the man in both the dream plane and the physical realm.

Staring into the surface of the bowl, he focused his rage on the dark-skinned man. The man who had somehow managed to involve a gods-be-damned sidhe warrior and an interfering succubus bitch in his games. The man who had stolen his latest playmate right out from under his nose.

He'd been so looking forward to savoring the little blonde's terror as he cloaked himself in the guise of a rotting corpse and ripped her clothes off, holding her down to take his pleasure…

Burr shuddered, breathing heavily as he squeezed his eyes shut and tried to let go of the fantasy. She was lost to him now. And it was all the dark human's fault.

He gritted his teeth and affixed his gaze on the bowl to scry with renewed hatred and concentration. Slowly, the liquid began to whorl with energy, and a murky twilight reflection of the dream plane came into view.

He watched as thousands of tiny, flickering soul lights drifted past. They disappeared into the depths of the shallow bowl, giving the impression that, if he touched the surface, he could reach down into eternity.

Gradually the scrolling movement stopped and a single twinkling light began to grow larger, as if it was rushing up at him with great speed from far below. It expanded, blocking out the glimmering multitude surrounding it, and Burr fixed it in his mind's eye as he shifted reality and followed it into the dream plane.

When he reappeared in the nebulous landscape of dreams, he zeroed in on that same glowing ball of light. Its energy signature was unmistakable from both his scrying and his brief physical contact with the human male.

Unsure exactly what he planned, only knowing he was intent upon revenge, he reached out to grasp the man's soul light in his palm.

An unearthly scream of warning resounded throughout the dream plane, loud enough to pierce the dreamscapes of countless nearby humans and send them jerking awake.

Burr cried out as the man's soul light burned the astral flesh from his palm, and then winked out of existence in the dream realm as the man awoke in his own realm.

His entire being vibrating with rage, Burr shifted back to reappear inside his decrepit little cottage. This time he did kick the damned overturned bucket, sending it flying to smash against the wall.

How dare that good-for-nothing bitch of a succubus ward the humans' dreams from him! First the blonde slut, and now the dark-skinned man. He had half a mind to go after her with the rare spelled-silver knife he'd used to kill his father.

The thing had cost him a fortune in trade, and it would please him greatly to get another use out of it. Killing immortals was generally a messy, but swift, affair. It required destruction of the heart or removal of the head. This particular knife, however, was one of the few methods that provided a more lingering, unpleasant death.

But first things first—it was time to pay the dark human a visit in the flesh. He returned to sit in front of his scrying bowl, working to focus his turbulent anger on the man's location in the human realm.

∞∞∞∞∞∞∞∞∞

Grey awoke with a start, a strange fading wail echoing through his ears, like a remnant from a rapidly dissolving dream. Suppressing a shiver, he pulled the soft, heavy comforter higher over his and Scarlett's bare shoulders.

Settling deeper into the fluffy pile of pillows, he smiled as she murmured sleepily and nestled closer against his side. His eyes scanned the dim room, the narrow sliver of light from the crack in the bathroom door revealing nothing out of place.

Scarlett's slow, even breaths and the gentle hum of the air conditioner lulled him back to sleep within minutes.

He did not see the compact form of a man appear suddenly, crouching in the shadows between the armchair and the drawn curtains that concealed the balcony.

Burr remained motionless, but for the intermittent blink of eyes that burned with hatred beneath a shock of dull brown hair. He simply watched and listened, wanting to ensure the man slept before he approached and dosed him with the Morpheus potion.

He cocked his head as he realized he heard the sounds of two people breathing with the quiet, measured rhythm of slumber. Rising with care, he approached the bed. A female sidhe lay beside the man, her flawless skin glowing in pale counterpoint to his darkly bronzed flesh.

An idea began to form in Burr's mind. It was dangerous, but if he took the necessary precautions, it would be far more rewarding than his original plan.

Torturing and killing the man would have provided a lackluster thrill, seeing as Burr had no sexual inclination toward other males. The beautiful female sidhe, however, was an entirely different prospect.

It was risky. Most sidhe were skilled warriors and possessed powerful magic. But if he kept her drugged with enough Morpheus potion, it shouldn't be a problem.

Her end wouldn't be as satisfying with her unconscious, but the idea still possessed an attractive sense of retribution. The dark-skinned man had stolen his plaything from him; now he would return the favor.

Noiselessly, Burr crept around the side of the bed and pulled out a vial of

Morpheus with a premeasured dropper. Careful not to shift the mattress with his weight, he leaned over the sidhe woman's sleeping form.

Her face was tipped upward, her lips parted slightly as if awaiting his kiss. He smiled at the thought as he pulled the dropper from the vial and gently squeezed its contents into her mouth. The pungent herbal odor of the tincture rose up to coat the air like rancid oil.

Grey's nose twitched as he hovered at the edge of sleep, pulling him back toward consciousness. Scarlett's body was pressed into his side, warm and reassuring, but something felt wrong in the room. His eyelids flickered open, snapping wide as he discerned the shadowy figure leaning over her.

He let out a strangled shout, trying to pull her beneath him so that he could shield her with his body. But he was too late. The incubus grabbed hold of her and blinked out, leaving behind only tousled bedcovers and her lingering warmth on the mattress.

A paralyzing feeling of loss and panic like he'd never known seized Grey's heart. He leapt from the bed, a choking cry of despair and helplessness ballooning in his throat, catching there as he tried to remember how to breathe and think.

He stumbled toward the phone on the nightstand, his jerky movements knocking the receiver to the floor. He bent to retrieve it with a gravelly curse, his hands trembling so badly he could barely dial '0'.

"Tenth floor penthouse," he grated harshly before the operator could recite more than a word of her polite, rote greeting.

Thankfully she didn't question his rudeness or the fact that it was after two in the morning. The phone rang five times before a groaning Sydney picked up. "Hello?" she croaked, sounding irritated.

"Scarlett's gone," he panted.

Grey's voice was so splintered by pain and fear that Sydney didn't need to ask questions to know something terrible had happened. "Oh goddess," she breathed, tears springing to her eyes as she met Sparrow's concerned gaze and handed him the phone.

"Grey?" Sparrow said sharply.

"The incubus," Grey rasped, "took Scarlett."

"I'm coming," was all Sparrow said before the line went dead.

Grey bent double, holding his arms tight to his body as he tried to keep himself together. If this had been any of the other sickos he'd put behind bars, he'd have known exactly what to do. The bastard would have never gotten close enough to touch his Scarlett.

But that was because they had all been human, like him. Not magical, like Scarlett.

A low, keening moan escaped his throat. She should have been with someone of her own kind. He was fucking useless to her. And because of him, she was going to die in torment, suffering just as his mother had to bring him into his useless existence.

Sparrow blinked into the room and his eyes found Grey, his brows drawing together at the human's obvious agony. He was curled in on himself, his despair so thick and heavy in the air that it tightened Sparrow's gut into knots.

He flicked on the light switch and grabbed a bathrobe from the chair, draping it over Grey's bare back as he lifted him upright with difficulty and helped him stagger to the bed. The distinctive green tattoo between Grey's shoulder blades caught Sparrow's eye, and his mouth flattened into a grim line as he recognized it.

"Brother," Sparrow said in a roughened tone, "I know you're inside out right now, but I need you to pull it together. For her sake."

Grey lifted his head, breathing hard through clenched teeth as his desolate gaze burrowed into Sparrow. "How do we find her?"

"We start with Marianne Thornton," Sparrow asserted briskly. "She should be rested enough to speak coherently, and she may remember something we can use."

Grey nodded and rose from the bed, his movements mechanical as he yanked on a pair of jeans from a suitcase that rested atop the dresser.

"Sydney's calling her friend, Sunny, who knows a couple of incubi that might be able to help," Sparrow continued. "Angelica knows them as well, so she may be able to contact them if Sunny…"

Sparrow fell silent as Grey violently ripped Angelica's medallion from his neck and hurled it across the room. Grey met his eyes in the mirror above the dresser, jaw tight and chest heaving in agitation.

"Why the hell didn't you insist Angelica make one for Scarlett too?" Grey demanded, his voice low and bitter.

The accusation in Grey's tone was a merciless punch below Sparrow's belt. He bit back a retort, fueled by his own pain and anger that one of his oldest friends had been kidnapped by a psychotic incubus while under Grey's watch.

But at least Grey had found something other than despair to drive him forward, even if it was misplaced anger.

"The talisman only kept him out of your dreams, and we don't dream the same way you do," Sparrow replied with restraint. "It didn't guard against him blinking out with you. You'd have needed Angelica to draw wards around the bed for that."

Grey squeezed his eyes shut and his fist hit the top of the dresser hard enough to make the wood buckle. "I'm sorry," he grated.

Sparrow recognized the guilt in his voice, and knew damn well it was only partially due to Grey lashing out at him. "There's no reliable way to predict what a maniac will do. In your line of work, you know that."

Grey remained mute as he pulled a t-shirt from the suitcase, turning sideways to glance in the mirror as he pushed his arms into it. He couldn't help remembering the vicious weapon the incubus had used on him.

He silently swore to whatever deity was listening that, if he got Scarlett back unharmed, he would worship at their altar for the rest of his miserable life.

Narrowing his eyes, he twisted his shoulder closer to the mirror, the t-shirt arrested in his grip as he made ready to pull it over his head.

"What the hell?" he murmured, staring in consternation at the green Celtic knot-work tattoo inked high between his shoulder blades.

"Recognize it?" Sparrow asked as he rose from the edge of the bed and joined Grey by the mirror to inspect the design.

"It's the same as Scarlett's," Grey identified in shock. "What does it mean?"

Sparrow smiled slightly for the first time since Grey's panicked phone call had woken him. "It means welcome to the family, brother. You can ask Scarlett all about it when we get her back safe and sound."

Chapter 20

"I don't know what else I can tell you," Marianne said, wringing her small hands in her lap as she frowned across the table at Grey and Sparrow. "When he came to me in my dreams, he looked…different than the man who was in my bedroom earlier. It was as if he matched his appearance to my fantasies."

Angelica, who sat in the chair beside her, placed a comforting hand on Marianne's shoulder. "That is perfectly normal. Succubi and incubi can sense the sexual desires of mortals and we are able to alter our appearance to reflect whatever image you are attracted to."

"Did he speak to you about anything in your dreams, or take you anywhere that you didn't recognize?" Sparrow questioned.

Marianne shook her head. "No, he only came to me in my bedroom. And the things he said to me were," a blush rose in her fair cheeks, "you know, seductive kinds of things."

She paused as she tried to recall if there was anything more, shrugging her shoulders in helpless frustration when she couldn't. "I even recognized the places where he gave me nightmares. It was like he pulled them from my mind."

"Do you think you can contact Heather Peters again?" asked Grey, struggling to keep his voice level, though he was screaming inside at their lack of progress. "Maybe she remembers something."

The petite blonde's eyes swam with guilt and sorrow. "I'm so sorry this happened to your friend, Agent Derrington," she whispered.

"Grey," he corrected, her sympathy almost his undoing.

"Grey," she murmured, looking down at her lap and sighing softly as she continued, "I don't want to get your hopes up. My ability to speak with the dead has never been something I could control. They've always come to me out of the blue."

Her gaze lifted back to Grey's, and his stomach tightened at the tiny spark of cautious determination in it.

"But my grandmother's spirit seems to find me when I need her most. And she's always come through to me the strongest when I sit by her grave. So maybe if you take me to where Heather Peters is buried?" she suggested uncertainly.

Grey groaned. "She's still at the morgue. What if we could get you in to see her body?"

"No," Sparrow interrupted, shaking his head in agitation, "if she lingers anywhere it won't be in that cold, transitory place. She'll be at her home, where she lived and died."

Marianne took a deep breath and nodded. "Okay. Take me there. You saved my life, and I'll do whatever I can to help you."

"Thank you," Grey said softly, earning a pained smile from her.

"Angelica, can you check in with Sydney and see if you can help find your and Sunny's incubi friends?" Sparrow asked.

"Of course," she said.

"We'll meet you back at Sydney's when we're finished. If you can't find them, try to bring another one of your people along. If Marianne can contact the Peters woman, maybe she'll remember something that one of you will recognize."

Sparrow directed a reassuring smile at Marianne. "I'm going to transport Grey to Ms. Peters' house now. I'll be back for you momentarily. Don't be frightened, okay? I promise we'll keep you safe."

"Alright," Marianne agreed breathlessly.

Less than five minutes later, Marianne, Grey and Sparrow were standing in Heather Peters' darkened bedroom. The moon, long past its zenith, hung low in the sky. It was barely visible through the silhouetted trees beyond the second storey window.

Marianne shivered, her chill having little to do with the temperature. The dead woman's house emanated a desolate emptiness that felt as if it would swallow her whole.

Sparrow strode over to the window, his footsteps sounding softly against the wooden floor. He murmured an incantation, then turned and motioned to Grey. "You can flip the lights on now. No one will see us."

Even Sparrow's confident voice was hushed in the waiting silence, as if in deference to the house's oppressive aura of sentience.

Marianne drew a relieved breath as light filtered through the stained glass globe beneath the ceiling fan, revealing soothing, sage green walls and casting warmth into the shadowy corners of the room.

Her relief was short lived as both Grey and Sparrow turned to her expectantly. She swallowed past the tightness in her throat and approached the unmade king sized bed, placing her hands against the mattress as she gingerly sank to a seat on its edge.

She closed her eyes, and willed the whispering voices to fill her head. The slow whir of the ceiling fan and the imperceptible sigh of the house settling were the only sounds that met her ears.

She squeezed her eyelids tighter, trying to trigger the appearance of the black dots that sometimes filled her vision when the voices came to her.

Nothing happened.

"Heather?" she whispered softly. "Are you here? I need to speak with you."

The only thing she perceived was the painful anticipation of the two men who waited nearby with misplaced faith in her ability.

Focusing all of her concentration on the memory of Heather Peters' voice warning her about the man coming after her in her dreams, she made one last effort.

"Heather," she said more forcefully, "I need your help. The man who killed you has kidnapped another woman. He's going to do the same things to her that he did to you, unless you can help us find him."

She waited with baited breath for some kind of acknowledgement from the other woman's spirit.

But there was nothing.

Slowly she opened her eyes and looked up at Grey and Sparrow, her gaze laden with regret as she shook her head in defeat.

"Are you sure?" Grey asked, his voice stark with disappointment.

Marianne blinked back tears. "I'm so sorry. They've always been the ones to initiate contact in the past. I've never purposely tried to talk to anyone other than my grandmother."

"It's okay, Marianne," Sparrow assured her tiredly. Mediums had never worked for him before; he shouldn't have expected this time to be any different. "It was a long shot, but thank you for trying. We'll take you home now."

Marianne knew it wouldn't be okay, though. Not for their friend.

She rose from the bed reluctantly, letting out a squeak of fright as a book fell from one of the shelves along the wall and smacked loudly against the hard wood floor.

A strange expression crossed Grey's face as he strode over to pick it up. "It's Heather's dream journal," he said in a stilted tone. "The exact same thing happened to me the last time I was in this room. The journal fell off the shelf for no apparent reason."

Sparrow slowly scanned the bedroom, looking for some sign of paranormal activity, afraid to hope that the book falling was anything more than a coincidence.

Suddenly Marianne swayed dizzily and sank back onto the bed with a gasp. The two men rushed to her side, waiting to catch her if she collapsed, but hesitating to touch her otherwise.

It was as if they shared the unspoken fear that physical contact would break her tenuous connection with the dead woman's spirit. They hovered over her, waiting, hardly daring to breathe.

Marianne sat rigid on the edge of the mattress, eyes moving rapidly behind closed lids. She cocked her head to the side, as if listening to something only she could hear. Then she smiled, her posture relaxing as she exhaled.

"She's here," she murmured, her voice taking on an eerie singsong cadence. "What do you want to ask her?"

Sparrow chuckled in disbelief, and Grey felt the knot in his chest loosen for the first time since Scarlett had disappeared.

"Ask her if she can tell us anything that might identify her attacker," Sparrow prodded with cautious optimism, "something he said, a name, a place he took her that she didn't recognize…"

"Tell her the smallest detail could make a difference," Grey added hoarsely.

Marianne was silent for long moments. Her face turned pale and drawn, and she whimpered softly as tears began to roll down her cheeks.

Grey glanced at Sparrow in concern and tentatively placed his hand on her shoulder. "Marianne? Are you okay?"

She nodded blindly, tears leaking faster from beneath her closed eyelids. "He hurt her so much," she whispered.

She sniffled, listening in silence a while longer before she spoke. "He had her so drugged that she didn't know what was real and what wasn't. He never told her his name. But she thinks he took her to a cabin in the woods."

Marianne swallowed, her voice turning rough. "It was small and old and dirty, just a wooden shack as far as she could tell. And she could hear nighttime forest sounds, like trees rustling and maybe an owl and crickets and other insects and, oh god, the spiders. They were everywhere, scurrying and biting…

"She doesn't know if they were real or not," she hiccupped on a sob.

"Tell her they weren't real," Sparrow said grimly.

Marianne nodded, a pall of misery and horror shrouding her expression.

"He said terrible things to her, nasty things about his mother, and about all human women being whores."

"He could be half incubus, half human," Sparrow muttered to himself.

Marianne took a shuddering breath her forehead creasing in concentration. "There was a plaque on the inside wall of the cabin. The word *Downy* was engraved on it."

"Was there anything else on the plaque?" Sparrow asked intently.

Marianne shook her head. "No, just the one word."

"Could it be a name?" Grey demanded eagerly.

"Maybe. She doesn't know," Marianne murmured. "That's all she can remember."

"Thank her for her help," Sparrow said gratefully. "We need to get this information to Angelica and her friends as quickly as we can."

"And tell her we'll make him pay for what he did to her," Grey added in a gravelly tone, gently squeezing Marianne's shoulder in reassurance.

Marianne listened in silence for another minute, the corners of her lips lifting in a sad smile. "She wants to thank you again for making sure her fish are taken care of. They were her pride and joy."

Grey nodded, his throat working convulsively against his sorrow for Heather Peters and his overwhelming fear for Scarlett. "Tell her she's welcome," he managed unevenly. "But we need to go now."

Chapter 21

Scarlett frowned in uncertainty as she stumbled over a rut in the wide, dirt-packed road. Gas lanterns sat atop poles at long intervals along the deserted thoroughfare, their intermittent puddles of light doing little to illumine the cloud-darkened night.

The air was thick and damp, a lonely chill cutting through the heavy mantle that lay between dusty earth and hidden sky. The fecund stench of horse manure filled her nostrils, mingled with sweet traces of fresh hay.

A hint of something oily and herbal intertwined with those natural scents for a moment, seeming out of place, and tugging at a memory that faded away as quickly as it had appeared.

A strange disquiet filled Scarlett and she pulled her wrap tighter around her shoulders, hurrying toward the sidewalk that ran alongside the wheel-rutted road. She stepped up onto the uneven paving stones, blinking down at the tight bodice and long skirts of her dress in the dim light.

She was having trouble remembering how she'd gotten there. But the vacant street indicated that it must be quite late, so it made sense that she should be heading home. A low clatter rose up in the distance and she halted, her searching eyes identifying the approaching outline of a carriage drawn by two horses.

Scarlett stepped further from the curb into the pooling shadows at the mouth of an alley, the fine hairs on the back of her neck prickling in warning. For some reason, the thought of being seen by whoever was in that carriage terrified her.

Her breath caught in her throat as the clip-clop of hooves drew closer, slowing as they neared her hiding place. The carriage gently bounced forward on its springs as the driver pulled up on the reins, settling back into place as it rolled to a stop.

Just as Scarlett was about to flee blindly down the alley, a dainty foot emerged from the side door, followed by several frilly layers of petticoats. A nervous woman glanced up and down the street, waving the carriage on its way as she silently entered one of the doors along the front of the three-storey brick building.

Scarlett exhaled in a rush, her pulse pounding unaccountably loudly in her own ears. She smoothed her skirts with shaking fingers and stepped out of the alleyway. Her head jerked cruelly backward and she muffled a scream as she instinctively used her body's momentum to twist sideways and look behind her.

A young man of about eighteen stood in the shadows, lounging against the side of the building. He wore an embroidered silken vest and a fine linen shirt with ruffles at the neck. His blonde hair was greasy above an even greasier smile.

The silken length of her hair was wrapped around his fist.

"Hello, whore," he whispered, putrid alcohol fumes wafting over her face.

Scarlett's heart stopped and she froze in his grasp as time slowed and horror stripped her of the capacity to think.

A second face loomed pale out of the darkness beside him. A slightly older man with shabbier clothes grinned at her. "Join us for a drink and a game of cards at my place. We'll show you a good time, sweet thing."

Scarlett's heart slammed into her ribs as memories gripped her and the neurons in her brain fired frantically.

She shrieked with mindless rage and fear, striking out at the younger man with a vicious elbow to the face and somehow yanking herself from his grip. Though from the sting to her scalp, she was sure she left a good bit of her hair behind, wrapped in his filthy fingers.

Then she ran as fast as she could down the deserted sidewalk.

Panting hard, more from fright than exertion, she blinked the sweat from her eyes and tried to remember the way to escape. She knew it was something simple, but the memory hovered just out of her reach.

Scarlett sobbed in frustration as she tripped on a jutting paving stone that had been dislodged from its mooring. The air flew from her lungs as she landed on her stomach, her palms grinding into the rough, gritty planks of an unkempt wooden floor.

She blinked in confusion as reality shifted around her. She was in a house that she hadn't seen for almost two hundred years, laying at the feet of the two men she'd been trying to escape.

She moaned in denial and scrambled away from them, only to find herself at the feet of another man. Relief spiraled through her in dizzying waves as she looked up and recognized Pat.

He frowned and stepped away from her, as if he couldn't bear to touch her. "I told you not to sneak back here and see this man," he reprimanded. "I warned you that he was bad news and you didn't listen. You deserve this."

He nodded grimly at the other two men and strode out the door, slamming it behind him and leaving her there.

Sick horror gripped Scarlett, reaching deep inside her to rip at her soul. His betrayal devastated her on such a visceral level that she gagged, almost losing the contents of her stomach to the grimy, splintered floor.

Hands fastened around her bare ankles, her skirts snagging on jagged wood and riding up over her knees as she was dragged backward.

Scarlett screamed, releasing all of her anger, fear and pain into the sound as she struggled wildly, kicking her feet at the men with every ounce of strength she possessed. The air wavered before her eyes, rippling out in widening swells until it broke against the walls of the room.

The walls billowed and reality shifted once more as she found herself lying naked on the dusty wooden floor of a dim, squalid shack. A foul taste coated her impossibly dry mouth, and she was so groggy and disoriented that her limbs wouldn't obey her brain's command for them to move.

Her bleary eyes drifted to the side as she discerned a hand resting on her forehead. There beside her sat a compact man with an oval, gently freckled face. His brown hair was close-cropped on the sides, longer on top, and looked as if it might turn curly if allowed to grow.

She studied him in a daze, reaching for some hint of familiarity. A distinct dimple created a small cleft in his chin below lips that rested in a flat, even line. His eyes were close-set above a nose that ended in a slightly upturned tip.

He might have been handsome, if there wasn't something so terribly off about him. And then she realized what it was—he was the incubus Grey and Pat had been hunting.

Burr's brow furrowed as he lost control of the dream just when it was starting to get good. The sidhe bitch was feisty. And her fear had been gratifyingly easy to pull from her mind, since it was based on actual memories from her past and not the illogical phobias that so many humans seemed to have.

He refocused his concentration, reaching for the threads of the dream he'd woven so he could pull her back into it. But he couldn't seem to get a grasp on her subconscious. His eyelids flickered open and he grunted in surprise to see hazy, sea-green eyes looking back at him.

Impossible.

There was no way she could be awake after the amount of Morpheus he'd given her. He stared at her in shock. Panic flooded her gaze and she groaned, struggling to get away from him.

Noting that her paralysis was beginning to wear off, he leapt from the floor and ran to his jumbled shelf of supplies. Somewhere among them was a fresh vial of Morpheus...

Scarlett broke out in a cold sweat, fear gripping her in its unrelenting talons. She had no memory of how she'd gotten there. But she'd seen Grey's reports, and she had no doubt as to what would happen to her if she didn't escape.

She willed herself to blink away. It was such a simple action. She'd done it thousands of times before. But whether it was a residual effect of the Morpheus, or the cold fear shivering through her muscles, her magic was paralyzed along with her limbs.

Scarlett watched the incubus paw through the cluttered contents of the shelf in dread. Whatever he was looking for couldn't be good news for her.

Her stomach cramped in protest as she strained against her body's malaise, weakly managing to lift her arms from her sides to cover her bare breasts.

She closed her eyes and tried to center her breathing the way she did before a sparring match, concentrating fiercely on summoning her sword.

She reopened her eyes to find herself still weaponless as she lay unclothed and vulnerable on the floor of the dingy shack. And worse, the incubus appeared to have found what he was looking for. He was measuring some liquid out in a dropper that was almost certainly meant for her.

The pungent aroma of Morpheus curled throughout the room, and Scarlett heard herself whimper in fear. Her tolerance to the potion had saved her once, but she doubted the incubus would allow such an oversight again.

She turned her head and squeezed her eyes closed against the sight, a hot knife of despair piercing her heart. She thought of Grey, and how beautiful their fleeting romance had been. In their short time together, he'd healed her in places that had been broken for almost two centuries.

She almost smiled as she remembered the way he'd looked at her as she summoned her sword for him, standing naked and unashamed next to the bed where they'd made love for the first time.

"Open wide, sweetheart," the incubus murmured from somewhere above her.

Her eyes flew open, her heart hammering as the cold fear in her blood twisted into burning anger at his sadistic need to control and torment her.

Kneeling over her, he positioned the dropper between her tightly closed lips. He smiled at her resistance, his soft palm coming up to caress her cheek. Abruptly his mean close-set eyes turned hard, and he dug his fingers into her jaw with bruising force as he tried to pry it open.

Scarlett's eyes flashed with her hatred for him and everything he represented. Then she snapped her eyelids shut against him. Envisioning the heat in Grey's gaze as he watched her summon her sword, she made one final attempt to call her soul bound weapon into her grip.

The muscles in her wrists and arms tightened reflexively against a familiar weight as something warm and wet sprayed across her face and neck. Her eyelids fluttered open to meet the bewildered gaze of the incubus as he hovered above her, impaled on her golden sword.

With her lips set in a grim line, she gathered her strength and slowly twisted her blade into his rotten heart. The Morpheus potion dropped from his nerveless fingers, rolling across the gritty floor, as he made a gurgling noise and life faded from his body.

"Bastard," Scarlett whispered vehemently.

Burr knew it was true. His father had never let him forget it. It was sadly unsurprising to him that it was the last word he'd ever hear.

A shudder rippled through Scarlett, tears of shock and relief springing to her eyes as she realized he was dead. Morpheus still coursed through her system, but she found the energy to push him off of her, using her sword as leverage.

She pulled the blade from his chest with difficulty, only sheer tenacity allowing her to call forth a cleaning spell to rid it of his filth. Her muscles quaked with tremors and tears leaked down her face as she realized she didn't yet have the power to blink away from the horrible place.

Then, suddenly, Grey and Pat were there. Pat swore as he took in the sight of Scarlett kneeling, shivering and nude, alongside the bloodied incubus.

Grey pulled her up into his arms, shielding her with his body, while Pat conjured a blanket and handed it to him to wrap around her. A split second later Angelica appeared, followed by two striking dark-haired incubi with identical aristocratic features.

Grey held Scarlett close, rubbing her back and murmuring words of comfort as he tried to shelter her from the throng of bodies crowding the cramped space.

"Did you do this, Letty?" Pat asked gently, pointing to the lifeless incubus that lay crumpled at their feet.

She nodded, her teeth chattering so hard she wasn't certain she could speak.

"Good," he replied grimly.

"Did he hurt you, baby?" Grey asked softly. The agonizing guilt and sorrow in his eyes left her breathless.

"N...Not l...like that," she stuttered.

His jaw tightened and he swallowed audibly as he crushed her to him. "Thank god," he whispered brokenly. "I never would have forgiven myself if you'd had to go through that again, Scarlett. When he took you I," he closed his eyes, his throat working convulsively, "I was so afraid I'd never get the chance to tell you how much I love you."

Scarlett lifted a shaky hand to touch his cheek. "Are you k...kidding?" she demanded haltingly. "You sh...should have kn...known I'd k...kick his ass."

A chuckle rumbled through Grey's chest, tangling with a sob as it ripped from his throat. "You're right, I should have, baby. You're an amazing, brave, ass-kicking woman."

Scarlett managed a tremulous smile as she looked up at him. "I l...love you too."

Grey leaned down and kissed her softly, a butterfly brush of his lips against hers. Scarlett closed her eyes and sank into his embrace, her body still trembling with aftershocks.

"Sparrow's going to blink you out of here, and I'll be right behind you," he murmured, looking at the other man for confirmation.

Sparrow nodded, flicking a disgusted glance over the scrying paraphernalia on the table and the body on the floor. "We'll take care of this mess later."

He aimed a grateful smile at Angelica and her incubi friends who'd recognized the name 'Downy' and helped them to find the cabin.

Then he gathered one of his oldest friends into his arms and blinked her away from a scene that was eerily similar to one he'd found her in almost two hundred years ago.

Only this time, she was lucky enough to have been able to save herself.

Chapter 22

Marianne dreamt of the graveyard. A sanctified hush lay over the weathered shrine. She wandered amongst its stoic granite congregation, her fingertips trailing across the familiar lichen-spotted faces of stone.

A breeze stirred the ancient trees, sending their curly beards of moss swaying gently above her. A sense of peace stole through her, winding around her heart and loosening the tight knot of fear coiled inside.

Marianne cocked her head as she realized that she wasn't alone. A slight woman in a cornflower blue dress stood beneath a massive oak. She stooped over a heart-shaped tombstone, a wistful expression on her careworn face as she flattened her frail palm against its rose-tinted surface.

"It's still the prettiest memorial in the whole cemetery," she murmured in satisfaction, vestiges of her Kentucky roots woven throughout the syllables.

"Grandma?" Marianne whispered as she approached. She'd never stopped hearing her grandmother's voice, but she hadn't seen her since her death almost ten years ago.

The elderly apparition straightened to her full height, still diminutive next to Marianne's petite five-foot-two frame. "Mari child," she greeted softly, the faded green of her crinkled eyes sparkling with warmth.

"Oh, Grandma," Marianne whimpered, dropping to her knees and wrapping her arms around the tiny woman's waist. Her tears soaked into cornflower blue cotton, darkening it to a patchy indigo.

"Shhh, it's okay child," her grandmother soothed, smoothing trembling hands over Marianne's hair, just as she had when Marianne was little.

"You did good, Mari. You helped bring a bad man to justice."

Marianne raised her face to look up at her grandmother with tear-stained eyes. "I did?"

Grandma smiled and nodded. "He'll never hurt another poor girl again." Then she patted Marianne on the shoulder and said, "Stand up, child. There's someone I want you to meet."

Marianne rose slowly, clinging to her grandmother's soft, age-lined hand. There, leaning against the wide oak trunk, was a young woman about Marianne's age. She had a short cap of red hair that framed a round face with pixie-like features.

She shot Marianne a mischievous grin as she pushed off the tree and came to stand beside them. "Hey," she greeted. "Nice to finally meet you face to face."

"Heather?" Marianne breathed.

"Yup," the girl confirmed. "Pretty cool, huh? I didn't know I could talk to you in your dreams. But apparently it's, like, a one time thing. Just to say goodbye."

"Goodbye?" Marianne echoed questioningly.

Heather nodded, her gaze turning faraway and dreamy. "There's this shining sea of light," she murmured. "It's been calling to me, but I was so lost and angry after…" she shook her head as if shedding an unwanted memory and smiled. "Anyway, I think I'm ready to go into it now."

Grandma squeezed Marianne's hand in the surprisingly strong grip of her own. "It's my time too, Mari."

Marianne's troubled eyes flew to hers.

"I was so worried for you when I passed, child," Grandma sighed. "You were far too young to deal with this ability you have, and your mama just couldn't understand. She put you through so much out of her own fear."

Grandma made a tisking sound and reached up to pat Marianne's cheek. "You survived it though, Mari. And you've grown into a strong, beautiful young woman. But I've been lingering here for so long now, under the excuse of watching out for you, that I'd almost forgotten I'm supposed to move on."

Marianne's breath hitched as the meaning of her grandmother's words sank in. "Oh, Grandma, I'm so sorry," she said achingly.

Her grandmother interrupted her with a frown, "Now don't you fret about it, child. It was my choice, and I won't have you taking responsibility for it."

Grandma smiled abruptly, the expression taking years off of her aged face. "And besides, you're going to be okay now. I can feel it, Mari."

The unwavering conviction of her words shook Marianne to her foundation with the certainty that they were truth.

"It's time to go," Grandma said, joy and excitement shining in her eyes. "I love you, child."

Marianne nodded, tears blurring her vision as she hugged her grandmother. "I love you too," she said in a choked voice.

The dream faded and Marianne woke to the soft warmth of her grandmother's quilt tucked around her. Tears overflowed her eyes, streaming down her cheeks and past the gently upturned corners of her lips as she whispered the word *goodbye*.

<u>Chapter 23</u>

Grey peeked quietly into Sydney's guest room to check on Scarlett. She was still sound asleep, recovering from the effects of the Morpheus potion and the exhaustion of her ordeal.

He closed the door with care and returned to the living room. Sparrow reclined on the couch with a steaming mug of coffee, late morning sunlight spilling through the wall of sliding glass to brighten the dull gray of his newspaper.

"Sunny says it's chilly in Paris," Sydney commented from the dining room table, where she sat working behind her laptop.

She paused to yawn and stretch her arms above her head until her spine released an audible pop. Sparrow cringed at the sound and she sent him a mocking look as she continued, "So don't forget to bring a jacket."

"Yes, my *anamchara*," he answered, drawing the Gaelic endearment out with a low, silky cadence.

Humor and shared intimacy sparked in Sydney's gaze as she held Sparrow's. The smile lingered on her face as she turned to Grey.

"Are you sure you and Scarlett don't want to join us for a late supper and a night in the most romantic city in the world? We're staying at the Hotel Amour," she cajoled, playfully waggling her eyebrows.

Grey chuckled. "It sounds incredible, and hopefully Scarlett will forgive me for declining, but I think I'd rather have her all to myself this evening."

"Of course," Sydney said quietly, nodding in understanding.

"Hey man, can I use your phone again?" Grey asked, tipping his chin at Sparrow. "I need to call Lizzie and give her a heads up on what's about to happen."

"Sure, brother," Sparrow replied, tossing him the phone.

Grey caught it smoothly between his palms. "I hate to do it," he said regretfully, "but she'll be more likely to accept the lie if I remind her she's been technologically outmatched."

Sparrow grinned sympathetically as Grey padded back up the hallway to make the call in the privacy of the guest bathroom.

"Liza McKenzie," her clipped tone greeted.

"We got him, Lizzie," Grey breathed, not needing to feign the satisfaction and relief in his voice.

"Grey?" she chirped in disbelief. "Holy crap, you did? What happened?"

"He came after Marianne Thornton, and we were ready for him," Grey replied simply. But the lie stuck in his throat as an image of Scarlett flashed through his head, trembling as she knelt beside the dead incubus.

He shook it off and continued recounting the story he and Sparrow had worked out. "The guy was a high level black ops agent, gone rogue. He didn't officially exist, so they're creating an identity for him now.

"My report will say that I followed up on a connection you found between the victims ordering candles online from a website based out of West Palm Beach, Florida. The site is MagickWicks.com and it'll be registered to Carlos Jameson."

He gave her the spellings and rapid keyboard clicks on her end were followed by Liza's abrupt, "That website doesn't exist."

"Not yet," Grey agreed, "but it will have existed for over ten years by the time I file the report. The reason it won't have caught our attention earlier is that some of the victims' purchases will go back that far."

Liza made a dubious sound. "They're going to have to alter a lot of records to make this airtight if anyone goes digging."

"These guys are thorough, Lizzie," Grey assured her. "By the time you go looking for these connections tomorrow, everything will be in place and nothing you report will be a lie."

"I cannot believe I'm being talked into shady dealings by your upstanding Captain America ass," she said drily. "Somehow I always envisioned I'd be the one to corrupt *you*."

Grey snorted. "The official story will be that I went to his home and smelled the herbal odor from the crime scenes as soon as he opened the door. I'll say he fled back into the house when I identified myself. I gave chase, and narrowly escaped being killed when the paranoid fuck accidentally tripped one of the explosive booby traps he'd set up around his house."

"Are you calling him a paranoid fuck in the report?" Liza asked in a guileless voice.

"I'll probably leave that part out," Grey intoned sarcastically.

"I've never heard you use the word 'fuck'," Liza mused. "I don't know whether to be proud or worried at this sudden descent into common morality."

"I'm sure it's only temporary," Grey said in amusement.

"One of us, one of us," Liza chanted, "gooble gobble…"

"O-kay then," Grey drawled loudly, "moving along. His body will be burned beyond recognition." *Well, not his body, but that part of the cover-up wasn't for Lizzie's ears.*

"When I call in backup, and the bomb squad diffuses another purposely conspicuous trap, we'll find trophies from each of the victim's houses and strands of their hair melted into the herbal candles he's been making."

"That's just disturbing," Liza remarked. "What weirdo came up with that?"

"I think I saw it on an episode of *Criminal Minds* once," Grey invented with a smirk.

"Oh," she replied thoughtfully, "I like that show."

"I'm glad you approve," Grey said in a solicitous tone. "Now like I said, you won't have to lie in any of your reports. Just take a look further back into the victims' credit card purchases tomorrow and you should find the website on all of them. Let me know when you find the connections and I'll set things in motion on my end."

"*Fine*," Liza articulated the word with exasperation. "But I think it's only fair that, in repayment for my silence, I get a play date with the tech analyst from your secret branch. I want to see her toys."

"Lizzie," Grey warned, "you know that can't happen."

She huffed in annoyance. "Will you at least put in a good word for me?"

"I'll do my best," Grey deferred with a grin.

It was good to know he could bring Lizzie in on the truth if he had to. But he was considering saving his one free pass to reveal the faerie realm to his mom. Besides, at this point Lizzie would probably be disappointed to discover the secret was magic instead of technology.

"Okay," Liza agreed with a thwarted sigh. "Got anything else for me? I have a meeting in a few minutes."

Grey paused and then asked, "How are Heather Peters' fish doing?"

"Great," she answered in surprise. "They all made the transition beautifully. I haven't lost a single one."

Grey smiled. "Thanks Lizzie. I'm sure she would have appreciated it."

"No problem, Captain America," she murmured, her tone soft and genuine. "I'm sure she would have appreciated the fact that you got the fuck who took her away from them."

"It wasn't me who got him." Grey swallowed guiltily as he thought of Scarlett taking on the incubus alone.

"Save it for someone who doesn't know how hard you've been working to catch him, Grey," Liza replied gently.

She hung up before he could respond.

Chapter 24

Scarlett awoke with late afternoon sunlight streaming through the slivers in the blinds. Soft pillows and bedding surrounded her, cushioning limbs that felt heavy with pleasant lassitude. Grey's reassuring weight pressed against her side, and she inhaled his clean scent of soap mingled with warm male skin.

He was propped up against the headboard, jeans riding low on his hips as he typed into a computer that rested against his thighs. One dark brow was furrowed in concentration, and his tight cotton tee molded his muscular arms and chest.

He looked so breathtakingly sexy that it took her a moment to realize they weren't in his hotel room. They were in Sydney's penthouse, in the room where she and Sydney had fallen asleep together that first night.

And then it all came rushing back.

The steady rhythm of Scarlett's breath sped up, and Grey glanced over to find her watching him. An uncertain smile spread across his face as he put his laptop aside.

"How do you feel?" he asked softly.

"Okay," she replied, her voice cracking in her dry throat. "Thirsty."

He handed her a glass of water from the nightstand. "This should still be cool," he murmured.

She sat up and accepted it gratefully, drinking half in one swallow. Sipping slowly at the rest, she looked around the room. She noted in bemusement that she wore a long, pink sleep-shirt with a faded picture of a kitten imprinted on the front.

"Are Pat and Sydney here?" she asked.

"No, we're alone," Grey replied. "They're meeting Sydney's friend Sunny in Paris for the night. We were invited, but I wasn't really up for it. I hope you don't mind."

Scarlett shook her head as she took another drink. She frowned at Grey over the rim of the glass. "I don't remember anything after Pat blinked me out of there."

"You had a lot of the Morpheus potion in your system," Grey explained, his eyes searching hers. "You passed out from the drug and the exhaustion of fighting its effects.

"Sparrow brought you here because he and I needed to figure out details. Lorien waved her wand to clean you up, and gave you something to help you rest peacefully while the drug worked its way out of your system."

Scarlett nodded, allowing his words to percolate through the spaces in her memory and fill in the blanks.

"Scarlett," he spoke her name with gentle authority as he reached for her free hand and threaded his fingers through hers. "You said back at the cabin that the incubus didn't hurt you 'like that'.

"Baby, I need you to tell me exactly what that means. I know you weren't wearing clothes when he took you, but he had you alone for a couple of hours, and you were drugged. Even if he didn't rape you, if he kissed you, or touched you intimately, or forced you to touch him, I want you to tell me.

"I know you don't want to think about it, but it's important that we deal with…"

Scarlett set the water glass on the nightstand and turned to face him, placing her fingers against his lips to shush him.

"He didn't," she whispered firmly, holding his gaze until she saw the tension leave it as he accepted her words.

She smiled slightly as she removed her fingers from his lips. Then she took a deep breath and continued, "He would have. He was working up to it. But he was having too much fun poking around in my head and playing with my fears."

Grey's eyes narrowed. "What do you mean, playing with your fears?"

"He was a sadistic bastard, Grey," Scarlett replied with a wince. "He found my memories from my rape and tried to make me relive it in a dream that he was controlling. He tried to make me believe Pat thought I deserved it."

A sound like a low growl escaped Grey's throat.

"But I woke myself up before it happened." She released a fractured sigh. "It was awful. And I was terrified. I was paralyzed, and my magic froze, and I thought I was going to die."

Grey pulled her into his chest. "I'm so sorry, baby," he groaned, his voice breaking with emotion.

Scarlett wrapped her arms around the solid comfort of his body, and took a moment to feel his strength envelop her, as she matched her breath to the beat of his heart. "But you saved me," she murmured.

A desolate chuckle rattled through Grey's chest. "Baby, you saved yourself. I was pretty damn useless. And if I was an amazing, magical woman like you, I'd be seriously considering what the hell I was doing with a man like me."

Scarlett leaned back and gave him a disgruntled look. "A man like you?"

"A man who couldn't even manage to keep you from being kidnapped when he was sleeping right beside you," he clarified softly.

"Baby, has it occurred to you that if you'd been with someone who had magic like yours, he would have been able to keep you safe? You wouldn't have had to go through what that goddamned incubus put you through… *Oof.*" He exhaled in a painful rush as she punched him hard in the gut.

"You are a giant idiot," she sputtered. "Just like Quin. Men. You can't even help it, can you?"

Grey stared at her in bewilderment.

"I haven't spent nearly two centuries learning to defend myself just so I could turn the responsibility of my safety over to you," she told him, her accent thickening in her anger.

"If I'd've been sleeping next to some random sidhe bloke, and that incubus decided to take me, he'd have had just as little chance as you of following wherever the bastard blinked us to.

"And I'd've had far less chance of finding the strength to break through my magical block for the first time in my life, and summon my sword despite my panic, so that I could defend myself like the warrior I'm supposed to be."

Tears sparkled in Scarlett's sea-green eyes as she glared at him. "That was all because of you, Grey," she said, her voice beginning to fray around the edges.

"You think you have no magic? You made me fall in love with you after a lifetime of panic attacks whenever I got too close to humans.

"It was you I thought of when I was trying desperately to summon my sword in that goddess forsaken cabin. The expression on your face when you asked me to summon it for you after we made love."

Scarlett swallowed, her voice gone hoarse and reedy. "You unfroze my magic after almost two centuries, when nothing else could. That's *your* magic. And it's more powerful than anything I've ever felt.

"So don't give me that bollocks about me being better off with somebody else…"

Grey silenced her with his mouth. Cupping her nape in his palm, his fingers brushed through her silky hair as the heated demand of his kiss stripped her of words.

His tongue teased at the seam of her lips and she moaned, opening for him and pushing back with her own. Her hands fisted in the snug cotton of his t-shirt, pulling him closer as she claimed the warmth and passion he offered.

He reached up to enfold one of her hands in his, pressing it against his heart. It beat steady and true beneath her palm. The abiding rhythm wound through her, like the eternal waves of the ocean rushing onto the shore.

"I don't ever want to picture you with anyone else," he murmured against her lips, brushing and tasting with gentle heat.

"And I love your strength," he breathed softly into her mouth, "but I'll never stop wanting to be the one who saves you if you need saving."

Tears spilled down her cheeks and he kissed them away, returning to her mouth to nip and caress as his hands moved to frame her face. She felt his lips stretch in a smile against hers, and her eyes fluttered open to find his damp with his own tears.

He leaned back a fraction to look at her, his deep gaze drawing her in with its quiet warmth. "It's too late to change how I feel," he whispered. "I love you, and I'll always want to keep you safe. I'll carry your mark for the rest of my life—on my body, and on my soul."

A question flickered in her eyes, and he slowly pulled away, muscles flexing as he lifted his shirt up over his head and stripped it from his arms. He twisted one thick shoulder to show her his back, eyes glued to her face as he watched for her reaction.

Scarlett gasped, fingers flying to her parted lips as she exhaled in quick, disbelieving bursts. For one painful moment she wondered if it was a cruel joke. If he'd gone to a human tattoo artist in a misguided attempt to honor her.

But no. The design was perfect and the inking smooth, as if it had resided there for years. She reached out to brush her trembling fingertips across the emerald green warrior's mark, and felt only the sleek, unblemished warmth of his skin.

Her eyes reluctantly drifted away from the Aegishjalmur and found his. "Oh, Grey," she said softly, the words a mere ruffle of air.

"What does it mean?" he asked, searching her gaze for some inkling of how he should react to the sudden appearance of her tattoo on his body.

"It's…faerie magic. It's how my people know when we've found our soul mate." She swallowed, falling into silence.

He said he loved her, but those were just words spoken in the fever of emotion. This was a lifetime commitment engraved in indelible ink.

The corners of his mouth twitched and something she couldn't identify glowed in the depths of his eyes. "You're my soul mate?" he asked in a probing tone.

Scarlett nodded, afraid to speak.

He hesitated, a small frown furrowing between his brows. "And the fact that I'm mortal and you're not?"

"Our life-forces are bound together now," she replied huskily. "You'll share my immortality for as long as we both live."

"Which could be hundreds of years, or more?" he speculated.

She nodded again.

An unhurried smile transformed his expression, revealing his sexy little dimple. "I get to love you forever," he rumbled in a heated tone.

"Forever," she confirmed on a whisper.

"I was going to do that anyway," he whispered back. He reached to tuck her hair behind her ear, his fingertips lingering to trace the fragile shell as he watched her with tenderness shining in his gaze.

"Show me," she murmured, leaning forward to stroke his lips with languid need, her kiss fed by the slow burning passion he fueled in her blood.

Grey shifted her atop him, her night shirt riding up around her hips and leaving her bare to his touch.

He deepened the caress of his tongue as his hands glided up the smooth flesh of her thighs. Finding her center with his thumb, he traced the delicate seam of her labia, already moist with her honey.

Her moan of pleasure shimmered through their kiss as he massaged her clit with her own wetness. Reaching to unzip his jeans, he gradually worked them over his hips as he slid his thumb back down through her soft folds. He dipped inside the lush haven of her body, gathering her cream and gliding up to circle her tiny bud once more.

Scarlett's fingers found his freed erection, and Grey sucked in a breath as she caressed his sensitive head and stroked his length.

She tightened her thigh muscles and lifted, positioning him at the slick entrance to her passage. Then, breaking their kiss so that she could watch his face, she unhurriedly lowered herself onto his shaft.

Grey groaned long and low, his senses intoxicated with her as she allowed him to slowly stretch and fill her, taking him all the way to the hilt. She teased his lips with hers, her hips tilting in a drowsy rocking motion against him, as she held him seated fully inside her.

"Grey?" she murmured dreamily.

"Yeah, baby?" he panted, his blood on fire for her.

"Slide down the bed with me." She pulled the nightshirt up over her head and tossed it to the side.

His gaze arrested on her bare breasts, he cradled her ass in one hand and used the other to push off the headboard until he was lying flat on his back with her astride him.

Scarlett skimmed her fingernails over his chest, circling the flattened peak of his nipple before folding herself down to trace it with her tongue. Grey's hand tightened on her ass and he pushed up into her with a reflexive thrust, making her gasp with pleasure.

Scarlett kissed his neck, trailing her lips up over the pulsing vein until she reached his ear. Grey shivered and bucked beneath her as she gently suckled his earlobe, struggling to remain still beneath the teasing onslaught of her mouth.

"I want to feel your heat and weight over me as you push your cock inside me," she whispered into his ear.

Grey went stock still, his cock throbbing within the satiny grip of her channel as if it understood her words. He reached up to brush her hair back from her eyes, capturing her gaze with his as he asked, "Are you sure, baby?"

Scarlett nodded and smiled. "Mmm…so very sure."

Grey's heart beat double time as he seized her lips in a devastatingly gentle kiss, rolling her beneath him with care so that he remained buried within the warm refuge of her body.

Then, with easy measured thrusts, he finally began to move inside her. Scarlett released a musical sigh as her head fell backward onto the mattress and she arched up to meet him.

Grey's forearms cradled the sides of her head, his thumbs brushing her temples as he kissed her softly. He slid deep inside her, withdrawing in slow counterpoint to the sweep of his tongue against hers.

He surrounded her and filled her, engulfing her with heat and passion, until every cell of her body overflowed with pleasure. She shuddered beneath him, mini-tremors of release coursing through her as she met him thrust for thrust.

Grey shifted his weight, reaching back to coax her thigh higher up his hips. She moaned against his lips as the movement opened her to him, her ecstasy swelling with his as he suddenly glided deeper inside her.

His kiss grew wild, his tongue tangling with hers, and her trembling intensified as he pumped into her slick, tightening channel with heavy strokes.

Scarlett cried out as Grey pulsed inside her and spilled his seed, her own orgasm catapulting her into nirvana alongside him.

Grey rolled over, pulling her into his arms as he collapsed against the pillows.

"I've been keeping it to myself because I couldn't explain it before," he murmured. "But I can feel it when my touch pleasures you. Is that part of our soul mate connection?"

"Mmhmm," Scarlett hummed, smiling against his chest.

"Now that's what I call a perk," he said on a relaxed exhalation. "What other sorts of secrets have you been holding out with?"

"None," Scarlett replied with a slumberous chuckle. "You know all of my secrets now."

"Somehow I doubt that, baby," Grey said in amusement.

"It's true," Scarlett insisted.

"Well, I'm holding some secrets back," he informed her nonchalantly.

Scarlett lifted her face to scowl at him. "And what does that mean?"

Grey shrugged, his dark eyes sparkling with merriment. "Forever's a long time. A guy's gotta keep some mystery about him."

Scarlett's gaze narrowed threateningly. "I could make you tell me, you know."

"Here we go again," Grey intoned, shaking his head in disappointment. "I knew you were a bully."

Scarlett snorted, her expression turning mischievous. "I have other ways," she said in a sultry voice, sliding her hand down the muscular contours of his stomach and cupping him in her palm.

Grey groaned as need spiked in his blood. "I've always heard that you catch more flies with honey than with vinegar," he remarked hoarsely, dragging her up to his lips.

"Tell me all your secrets, Grey," Scarlett coaxed against his mouth.

He shook his head slowly, grinning as he nipped at the little indention in her lower lip. "Sorry. They're classified."

"Please?" she breathed, rubbing the length of her body against his.

"Alright," he relented on a roused exhalation, rolling her onto her back in one smooth movement that had her gasping and laughing.

His fingertips skimmed over the softness of her cheek. "I love you. And I'm the luckiest man in the world," he admitted.

"Shhh, don't tell anyone," he warned as he claimed her mouth.

Epilogue

One Month Later...

"Do we have special plans for this honey I'm supposed to bring?" Grey asked in playful curiosity.

Scarlett laughed. "We do, but not those kinds of plans. It's a gift for my roommate. He's got a bit of a sweet-tooth."

Grey gaped at her. "I'm just now hearing that you have a roommate, and it's a *he*?"

"Jealous?" Scarlett drawled with an impish grin.

Grey raised a dark brow. "It's a cat isn't it? You're trying to get me all worked up over a cat."

Scarlett sputtered with hilarity. "Have you met many cats with a sweet-tooth, then?"

Grey shook his head at her, the gleam in his eyes promising retaliation.

"You'll see when we get there," she said teasingly. "So let's go."

Scarlett wrapped her arms around him, excitement brewing in her heart as she blinked him to her home in the faerie realm for the very first time. It had taken a month, but the Seelie Court had finally approved her petition to use simple magics in the human realm, and given her permission to transport her soul mate to the faerie realm.

Grey strove to regain his bearings as they reappeared inside a small, homey cottage that vibrated with an aura of green, growing things. Flowers sprouted haphazardly from a motley assortment of vases throughout the rustic wooden interior. Some of their colorful heads were beginning to droop, but the imperfection only added to the charm.

Large windows claimed a place on every exterior wall, flooding the space with natural light. A tiny kitchen lay off to the side of the main living area, bright yellow curtains framing the window above the sink. A tea kettle whistled on top of a stove that was neither electric nor gas, but appeared to be fueled by some synergy of magic and flame.

"Do you like it?" Scarlett asked with tentative enthusiasm.

"I love it," Grey replied, grinning at her. "It feels like home."

Scarlett's smile was pure sunshine. "I'm glad," she said softly.

"We're supposed to be at the village pub in a few minutes," she added in a breathless rush, "but let's have a quick cup of tea before we go."

Grey followed her to the little café set in the corner of the kitchen and lowered himself onto one of two carved wooden chairs. He placed the jar of comb honey he'd brought in the center of the table, while Scarlett brought the kettle over and poured steaming tea into two glazed yellow mugs.

She broke the seal on the jar and spooned honey into both, handing him one as she dropped into the other chair. "Tell me that's not the best tea you've ever tasted," she said as she sipped hers with a contented sigh.

Grey chuckled, wondering what she was up to as he took a swallow. His brow lifted in surprise. He wasn't usually a tea drinker, but she was right, it was delicious. Earthy and strong with bright, floral notes brought out by the honey.

"It really is the best tea I've ever tasted," he agreed, impressed.

Scarlett grinned as if he'd done something praiseworthy, and then leapt up from her seat leaving her mug mostly full. "Now we have to go or we'll be late," she exclaimed cheerfully.

She was on the front stoop by the time he stood, calling behind her, "Just close up on your way out, if you don't mind."

Grey hurried after her, perplexed by her erratic behavior. As he pulled the door shut behind him, a tiny man with brown parchment skin and bat-like ears beamed at him from the closing gap. He wore a cloth cap with a large button sewn onto it, and tufts of white hair poking out beneath.

When the door clicked shut he was gone. Grey blinked in amazement, wondering if he was imagining things, as he ran down the front garden path to catch up with Scarlett.

"Well, that wasn't weird at all," he said drily as he drew alongside her.

"Did Bradan show himself?" Scarlett asked eagerly.

Comprehension dawned in Grey's eyes. "Was that little man your roommate?"

"He did show himself!" Scarlett said, laughing in delight. "That means he likes you."

"Glad to hear it," Grey replied, still baffled. "What kind of faerie is he exactly?"

"Bradan is a brownie," she explained, leading them onto a narrow footpath that cut across a meadow of snowy white flowers. "Brownies are hearth faeries. They choose a home and take care of the domestic chores without complaint as long as the owner of the house doesn't allow their honey supply to dwindle.

"But they're very shy and they rarely show themselves. He must have liked your gift and the fact that you complimented his tea." Scarlett grinned. "Not to mention, I've been talking up your visit for the past month."

"Wow," Grey breathed. "So let me get this straight—you live with a little man who cleans your house in exchange for honey?"

Scarlett looked askance at him, her lips twitching with humor. "I'm actually very lucky. It's considered a great honor for a brownie to take up residence in your home."

"No, I get that," he agreed amiably. "I'd be honored too. Where do I sign up? I'll keep the pantry stocked with nothing *but* honey, provided I never have to clean another bathroom."

"I don't know," Scarlett contended. "I've always thought there was something sexy about a man bent over scrubbing a toilet."

"Like I said," Grey replied, "I'd be happy to clean your bathroom."

Scarlett smirked.

"Wait," Grey said suspiciously, "does this mean I need to be jealous of Bradan after all?"

"Brownies *are* said to be unusually well endowed, considering their size," she teased.

"You're a menace," he growled, playfully swatting her ass before she could hop out of the way.

Scarlett laughed, hooking her arm through his as they approached the village. "That's the training center where I teach."

She pointed out the large open air arena in the middle of the thoroughfare. "Maybe we can have a sparring match later," she suggested.

"If it's your plan to get me drunk and then kick my ass in front of all your friends and family, I'd appreciate a warning," he said drolly.

"I do have a surprise for you," she told him, nodding to people in greeting as they passed, "but that's not it."

"Really?" he asked, gazing at the colorful storefronts that surrounded the training center on every side. "Because that sounds like it would be right up your alley."

She tightened her hold on his arm, inching closer to him so that she rubbed against his side as they walked.

"I was just planning on having a drink and introducing you to a few people," she murmured, studying him from beneath lowered lashes. "But I'm not opposed to working some sparring in if you're in the mood for foreplay later."

Grey gave a shout of laughter. "Only you could make getting drunk and getting my ass kicked sound sexy, baby."

Scarlett smiled, pulling him to a stop as she lifted onto her tiptoes to give him a quick kiss. "We're here," she said, tilting her chin up at an old-fashioned wooden sign that hung out from the side of a building.

Its freshly painted surface portrayed a long-stemmed pipe and a pint of ale, and proclaimed:

Sweet Edith's Pub
Est. 1889

As they stepped inside the dim dark-wood and brass interior, Grey was surprised to feel a flutter of nerves at the prospect of meeting Scarlett's kin. But his fears were instantly allayed when he saw Sparrow and Sydney sitting at the sprawling, polished bar.

"Hey guys!" Sydney greeted with a wave, reaching to hug them both.

Sparrow smiled, kissing Scarlett's cheek and shaking Grey's hand with a comradely, "Hey brother."

Only two more people sat at the bar—a boy in his late teens with longish blonde curls and the burgeoning muscles of youth, and a giant bear of a man with shaggy orange hair and more of his skin tattooed than not.

"My parents are sorry they couldn't be here to meet you today," Scarlett murmured, "but they had a previous engagement with my brother and his wife. So this will just be casual drinks with a few people."

Scarlett led him over to the bar's other occupants. "Grey, this is my cousin Quin," Scarlett said, introducing him to the giant, "and this is my cousin Thom." She squeezed the younger man's shoulder affectionately.

They both shook Grey's hand, their smiles open and friendly.

"So you're the human peeler who's stolen our Letty's heart," Quin boomed with a grin.

"Speak English Quin," Scarlett scolded. "He means policeman," she clarified for Grey.

"No worries," Grey assured them in amusement. "And the heart stealing was mutual." He cast a tender glance at Scarlett.

Scarlett threaded her fingers through his. "As you might have guessed from his excess of ink, Quin is our village's tattoo master."

"Cool, man," Grey said with a nod, eyeing Scarlett as she became uncharacteristically fidgety.

"I recently had him do a little work for me," she continued, sucking in a nervous breath as she pulled up the short sleeve of her fitted tee. "This is your surprise. I hope you like it."

Grey stared at the new ink that spilled across her shoulder in curving script, spelling 'Dílis i gCónaí'. The words were unfamiliar, but the style of the letters was an exact replica of his 'Semper Fidelus' tattoo.

"It means 'Always Faithful' in Gaelic," she translated softly. "Sydney said it might not be appropriate for me to wear a Marines tattoo. But since wearing my Aegishjalmur wasn't really your choice, I wanted something that would be comparable without causing offense."

The uncertainty in her gaze, combined with the sentimentality of the gesture, nearly broke Grey's heart. "Baby," he murmured in disbelief, "that is the single most beautiful and touching thing anyone has ever done for me."

Tears flooded her eyes and he pulled her into his chest. "I'm so glad you like it," she whispered.

"I love it. Thank you." He leaned down to give her a quick kiss, but the sweet warmth of her lips drew him in. Captivated, he lingered to taste her, gently brushing his tongue against hers.

"A round of Old Proudfoot for everyone!" Thom called, his voice enthusiastic, though it cracked partway through the word 'Proudfoot'.

Grey pulled reluctantly away from Scarlett at the reminder that they weren't alone.

Quin clapped Thom on the back. "You're thick as manure and about half as useful, son. Way to interrupt the moment. Are ya even old enough to drink?"

Thom blushed and Scarlett sent him a sympathetic smile as she clung to Grey.

"Old Proudfoot sounds good," echoed Sparrow. "Put mine on Letty's tab."

Scarlett scoffed at him.

"Big, sappy puddle of goo," was all he said.

Scarlett's eyes widened as she remembered their bet when she'd visited him at his office what seemed like a lifetime ago, and it was her turn to blush.

Sydney sniggered. "He's been waiting to do that for a month," she confided.

"A round o' Proudfoot it is, an' it's on the house," the bartender announced.

"Thanks Aedan," Scarlett said in a heartfelt tone as the grizzled sidhe made swift work of pouring seven whiskies. "Aedan isn't just our bartender," she told Grey, "he's also one of our oldest, most accomplished warriors."

"Nice to meet you, sir," Grey said with a respectful nod.

Aedan snorted. "It's Aedan ta ya, young man. Me sweet Edith'd be spinnin' in her grave ta hear ya callin' me sir."

"Sorry, Aedan," Grey correctly warmly as he accepted the glass of whiskey. "I noticed the pub is called Sweet Edith's. Was that your wife?"

Aedan's smile was wistful as he replied, "Aye, close enough. She was me soul mate, like you an' young Scarlett here."

"I'm sorry for your loss," Grey said quietly.

Aedan nodded brusquely. "Aye. Yer a good lad." He moved to polish the bottles along the rear of the bar with a worn cloth, though Grey was certain they didn't need it.

"Ya' know, there's an old sidhe tradition," Aedan said, turning back toward them with a glint in his eye. "Our newly mated males make a toast ta their soul mates, thankin' them fer the unique gifts that they bring inta their lives. Edith always loved that tradition."

"That's beautiful," Sydney said softly.

Scarlett gave Grey a guilty look. "You don't have to, it's not..."

"Hush, Letty," Sparrow interrupted, grinning at Aedan, "let the man speak."

"Let's hear it, man," Quin urged Grey. "Don't ya want to hear it, Thom?" he demanded, jostling the silent youth with his elbow and nearly knocking him off his stool.

Sparrow sent Scarlett a mocking grin.

Aedan raised his glass and lifted his chin at Grey.

Grey inhaled sharply, taking a sip of whiskey for courage and silently thanking Scarlett for not inundating him with more people this first trip to her village. "Okay. Well I'm thankful that I somehow ended up with the most gorgeous, amazing swordswoman in two realms. That's pretty unique."

Everyone chuckled and clinked glasses before taking a drink. But Aedan's expectant gaze didn't let Grey off the hook.

He acknowledged the old warrior with a nod. "But Scarlett's real gift to me is that she's someone I can truly share my life with," he added quietly.

"Because of who and what she is, I can tell her about my day without feeling like I'm betraying the oaths I took for my country. And that's something I never thought I'd find, and never realized how lonely I'd be without. So I thank her for that."

Sydney made an 'Aww' sound, and the men murmured, "Here, here brother," as they all clinked glasses again and took another, more solemn drink.

Scarlett fought tears for the second time since entering the pub and leaned into Grey to whisper, "Thank you, *mo ghrá*." She kissed his cheek and smiled. "But you should probably know, that toast isn't really an old sidhe tradition."

Grey narrowed his eyes and looked up at Aedan, who was watching him with an unrepentant grin. Sparrow and Quin burst out in laughter.

"Well it should be," Sydney defended, "it was beautiful."

"'Twasn't really a lie," Aedan maintained, topping Grey's glass off with another finger of the excellent whiskey. "When Edith worked behind this bar, she loved nothin' more than ta tell that story an' hear a young man make that toast."

Leaning forward, he pierced Grey with an astute look. "An' now I know that our Letty's heart is in good hands. So welcome ta the family, brother."

He reached a sinewy hand across the bar and firmly shook Grey's palm.

"*Sláinte*," said Aedan, his lips curling upward as he raised his glass again. "Ta Scarlett an' Grey. May ya be always faithful ta one another."

"To Scarlett and Grey," everyone echoed enthusiastically.

Scarlett leaned into him. "Though I'd love to show you where I work," she whispered for Grey's ears alone, "I think I've decided I'd rather have my foreplay in a bed than a sparring ring today."

Grey gave her a slow, heated smile. "Anything you want. Your pleasure is my pleasure, baby."

The End

Dear Readers,

If you enjoy my books, I'd truly appreciate it if you would take a quick moment to add positive reviews online at Amazon.com, B&N.com, and/or your Goodreads.com shelf. Your recommendation is the best advertising!

Want to know how Sydney and Sparrow got together? Following the *Afterword*, you'll find an excerpt from their story, *A Risky Proposition*, Book 1 of The Third Wish Duology. I hope you enjoy it!

- Dawn Addonizio

Afterword

1-800-656-HOPE is the National Sexual Assault Hotline. It is an automated 24 hour a day system that anonymously connects callers with the nearest available Rape Crisis Center (RCC) in their area. It is operated by the Rape, Abuse and Incest National Network (RAINN), which is the largest cooperative anti-sexual-assault organization in the United States, partnered with over 1,100 Rape Crisis Centers throughout the country. You can find more information on RAINN's website, www.rainn.org/get-help, where you can also connect to their Online Hotline and talk to someone via their anonymous instant messaging interface.

If you are suffering the effects of sexual abuse, whether a recent experience or a past trauma that is haunting you, please take advantage of these resources and talk to someone. It's anonymous. It's free. And it can help. Whether you talk to someone or not, know this: It's not your fault, and you are not alone. It is estimated that someone in the United States is sexually assaulted every two minutes, and that at least 10% of all rape survivors are male.

Rape can take many different forms. Less overtly violent forms, where no weapon is used and no obvious physical evidence of the attack is left on the body, often leave a survivor feeling as if they cannot report the attack or even consider it a rape. They are left trying to silently deal with the very real psychological trauma of an event that they don't feel justified to label as traumatic. Like all survivors of rape, they are at significantly increased risk for depression, drug and alcohol abuse, PTSD, and thoughts of suicide. All forms of rape are an inexcusable violation. No means no—always—even if you are in a relationship with someone. And if you are too young, drunk, drugged, sick, or intimidated to say 'No', no one has any business trying to initiate a sexual act with you. Inability to consent is NOT consent.

In the United States, the first Rape Crisis Centers were created in the early 1970's. It is interesting to me that the advocates for these centers were considered by many to be "radical" feminists, who were forced to redefine rape in more "radical" terms in order for it to be taken seriously by law enforcement, the medical profession and the criminal justice system. These advocates argued that rape is a symptom of patriarchies and the subordinate roles and oppressions created by them. They worked to redefined rape as an act of violence rather than sex, and theorized that rape would only become obsolete in a society where men and women had equal status. This theory can easily be expanded to include the necessity of equality between peoples of different race, creed and sexual orientation. None of this seems particularly radical to me, though some would argue that laying the blame on the patriarchal nature of our society unfairly places blame on men in general. It's possible that it is a sweeping generalization to presuppose that all patriarchal societies support a climate in which the subordination of a victim includes their "feminization" by an abuser who views his- or herself as being superior, aka more "masculine". I'm uncertain as to whether we can know for sure, having never lived in anything other than a patriarchal society.

I would, however, offer this: Men have long held the power roles in our society in massively disproportionate numbers to women. And gender roles are so intrinsically ingrained in our culture and our psyches, that it would naturally follow for us to subconsciously equate power with masculinity. This idea does not place the blame at the feet of men as a gender; it places it upon the very fabric and structure of the society in which we live.

Whatever the root causes of rape, the history of Rape Crisis Centers in our country is an anti-establishment one, in that they were forced to work against hospitals and other social service providers in order to advocate for survivors. Fortunately the movement has come a long way with regard to politicizing the criminality of rape, and the current social climate provides for more cooperation with mainstream organizations that can offer recourse for survivors of this crime.

Yet even with increased education and awareness, widely accepted statistics reflect that one out of every six females and one out of every thirty-three males in the U.S. will be sexually assaulted in their lifetime. To add some alarming perspective, think about your family and friends. Chances are, someone you are close to will be, or already has been, sexually assaulted. And if that's still too abstract to break your heart, apply those numbers to the school classroom of a child you love.

And the sad truth is that it's probably much worse than that. Those numbers only account for reported incidents, and it is estimated that more than half of rapes go unreported. If I'm reading the data correctly, that puts the real numbers at *greater than* one in three women and girls, and one in sixteen men and boys. I opted to round up for the guys because their incidence of not reporting attacks tends to be higher due to the gender stigma associated with a man admitting he's been raped. Not to mention I've read some research reflecting that far more men have experienced sexual abuse than even these numbers imply.

Some argue that the numbers are largely inflated, and that one purpose of this inflation is to frighten women and to keep them feeling powerless, vulnerable and at the mercy of men. I have no trouble believing that men who want to keep women powerless would use such an unconscionable tactic. But my own experiences, along with those of family members and friends, also make it disturbingly easy for me to believe that the numbers are not inflated at all.

Despite the fact that rape remains the most under-reported crime in America, Rape Crisis Centers have made huge strides in altering our perception of sexual violence as a country. Although the level of cooperation varies by community, and the system is not always perfect, the goal of Rape Crisis Centers remains to support survivors of rape— physically, emotionally and legally. They are there to help, and are staffed by compassionate, trained volunteers who are happy to give advice, or to simply lend an ear.

Regardless of our country's need to continue improving how we handle both the survivors and perpetrators of rape, the U.S. is leaps and bounds ahead of many other countries, particularly those where strong taboos are attached to sex and sexuality. In some countries it is not uncommon for rape survivors to be disowned by family and friends, not permitted to marry, divorced by their spouse, or even killed. I include this not to diminish the struggles of rape survivors in our own country—one person's suffering is not invalidated by the suffering of another—but to point out the wide spread urgency of this problem.

"Don't teach your daughters not to step out into the night. Instead, teach your sons better." I saw this in a photograph, printed on a sign held by an anti-rape activist marching at a rally in India. It struck me as a particularly poignant truth. And though women are not always the victims, and men not always the perpetrators, it reflects the reality that only by educating new generations to view other human beings with more respect can we stop the cycle of violence.

Rape is a terrible personal violation that results in far reaching effects— physical disease, mental anguish, emotional distress, social anxiety, intimacy issues and spiritual confusion can all stem from a sexual assault, and can last throughout a survivor's lifetime. If you are a survivor of rape, in any of its forms, help is available. Talk to someone supportive. Channel your pain and anger into creative or physical pursuits that you enjoy. Be kind to yourself.

Silence can be as crippling an enemy as the attacker who violated you.

1-800-656-HOPE
www.rainn.org/get-help

This is a conglomeration of easily obtained information that is reiterated across multiple sources, interspersed with my own thoughts on the subject. I apologize if you feel I've misrepresented or left out anything significant, as that certainly was not my intention.

   ~Dawn Addonizio

An excerpt follows from *A Risky Proposition*, Book 1 of The Third Wish Duology. This is Book 1 of a two-part series that tells the story of how Sydney and Sparrow got together. I hope you enjoy it!

What would you do if a sexy djinn offered you three wishes? Before you get too excited, you'd better read the fine print—because the price for pleasure could be your eternal soul.

When Sydney Corrigan tries to forget her problems with a night out in exclusive Palm Beach, the sinfully handsome Balthus is only too happy to help. Unfortunately Balthus is no ordinary man. He's a death djinn intent on claiming her soul.

Luckily Sydney has her faerie guardian on her side.

Not to mention Pat Sparrow, an exceedingly hot Irish detective who would love nothing more than to discredit the death djinns and show Sydney what real pleasure is all about...

<u>Chapter 1 of *A Risky Proposition*</u>

"What the hell am I doing here? Ugh, I wish I was dead," I muttered as I shoved the ladies' room door open with more force than necessary. A dark-haired man at a nearby courtesy phone jerked his head in my direction. I looked down and quickened my step through the doorway, my pale cheeks heating in embarrassment.

I wasn't usually prone to such outbursts, but I had just found out that my husband was cheating on me.

Jeremy and I had been married seven years and I'd thought everything was fine between us. We still talked...laughed...had semi-regular sex. Money was okay. We could have used a little extra, but who couldn't?

And he had to go and screw it up by sleeping with some vapid little tramp that made eyes at him at the office.

I fought a fresh bout of angry tears as I stomped from the restroom and crossed the ritzy hotel lobby in search of the bar. My heels struck a sharp echo against the polished marble tile and I pushed my long brown hair past my shoulder, doing my best to ignore my discomfort over the near-indecent length of my cocktail dress.

Relief coursed through me as I escaped the naked space of the hotel foyer and made my way into an intimate corner lounge. I positioned my short skirt beneath me on the burgundy leather of a barstool and glanced up as the bartender approached from the dim wooden depths of his post.

He gave me a mocking look as I tugged at my hem. "What can I get for you this evening, madam?" he sniffed.

My expression hardened and I ordered a Grey Goose martini, foregoing a 'please' and my usual ready smile. I wasn't in the mood for his attitude. So what if he worked for one of the most exclusive hotels in the country?

My lack of friendliness seemed to have the opposite effect on him. His frosty demeanor warmed as he handed me my drink, and he was downright solicitous as he offered me a choice of two crystal bowls filled with bar munchies. Sad that being rude actually makes some people treat you nicer.

I sighed and sipped the icy vodka, realizing that this encounter wasn't helping my current, less than favorable, view of humanity. I managed to swallow without pulling a face, which would have ruined the sophisticated image I was attempting to cultivate.

No one here had to know that I was in a place I would normally never go, wearing a dress that was far more revealing than anything I would normally wear, drinking a drink I would normally never order.

I picked up the frilly pick with the olives and slid one free with my lips, chewing slowly as I glanced around the bar to give myself a break from the alcohol.

A couple sat in a booth off to one side. A generous sprinkle of salt and pepper dusted the man's hair at his temples. The obviously younger woman had not an ounce of fat on her, with platinum blonde hair and a red dress that clung to her tanned, surgically enhanced curves like a second skin.

Blech. His wife of fifty years, and the mother of his children, was probably waiting for him at home while he was out hoping his wealth could buy him a newer model.

A maddeningly fair voice in my head insisted that my opinion of men might be just a bit skewed at the moment. I nearly stuck my tongue out at it.

A guy closer to my age, several barstools down from me, caught my eye and raised his glass in a friendly salute. His eyes twinkled as if we were sharing a joke and I found myself smiling back at him. He made a questioning motion toward the seat next to me.

I gave a shrug of assent and he picked up his glass and moved to join me. Polite, but confident; I liked that. There wasn't anything not to like about his looks either—tall, lean and muscular, with chestnut hair and vivid green eyes. No sign of a wedding band.

That was lucky for him. I was in the mood to perform a Bobbitt on the next married guy who showed signs of cheating.

"Good evening. My name is Balthus." His voice was rich and cultured, with a faint accent that I couldn't put my finger on.

"I'm Sydney." I smiled and took his extended hand, wondering what kind of parents named their kid Balthus.

I had a firm handshake. Some men seemed to take it as a challenge and squeezed my hand painfully in return. But Balthus' grip was almost sensual, lingering for just a moment longer than necessary before he released me.

"Balthus—that's an interesting name," I commented, trying to ignore the tingling sensation that traveled up my arm at his touch.

"It's a family name," he explained, his mesmerizing eyes never breaking contact with mine. They appeared molten, almost as if flames burned within their depths.

If there was such a thing as vampires, they'd probably have eyes like this guy's, I thought.

"I'm pleased to make your acquaintance Sydney," he said in a velvet tone, "and I appreciate you allowing me to join you. Solitary drinking is never as entertaining as imbibing with a companion."

Ooh bonus—cute and well-spoken. I shook my head and chuckled at myself. Vampires—what a crazy idea! Besides, he was far too tan to be anything of the sort.

"Are you staying here at the hotel?" I asked.

"Yes. Just for the weekend, on business."

"And what type of business are you in?" I took a small sip from my glass, giddy that I was actually doing this: sitting in a posh bar, drinking a high-end martini, making small talk with an attractive stranger. I really hadn't been sure that I could pull it off. Years of faithful marriage can make for rusty flirtation skills.

"Oh, mostly trading and commodities," answered Balthus with a vaguely amused gleam in his eyes. "And what do you do, Sydney?"

"Well, a little management, a little advertising, a little bookkeeping," I responded with a dismissive wave. My job truly wasn't that interesting.

"Like a free-lance consultant," he surmised.

"I guess you could call it that." I grinned. It sounded better than

Administrative Assistant, or any of the other titles I usually gave myself when people asked me what I did for a living.

"And are you here on business, or do you live in the area?" He took an easy swallow from his glass.

"I actually live about a half hour's drive away, but I work here on the island."

"And what is a beautiful woman like you doing here alone on a Friday night?" His voice was warm, but his smile was deliberately teasing. "Where is your husband this evening?"

"What makes you think I'm married?" I asked, playing along with a surprised tone.

He reached over and softly traced the faint tan-line on my ring finger. I forgot how to breathe for a moment as pure electricity crackled between us. It sent waves of awareness traveling across my skin and my gaze involuntarily jumped to his, finding a knowing look behind the heat in his eyes.

I took a gulp of vodka to steady myself, and as an excuse to look away. After seven years of monogamy, I wasn't used to even entertaining the sorts of feelings I was beginning to have about this man. My fingers played nervously over the stem of my martini glass as I decided how to respond.

"We're separated," I said finally. Not officially true, but I promised myself that it would be soon enough. Oh, Goddess—what were we going to do with the house? I shoved back a fresh pang of hurt at Jeremy's betrayal and looked up with shielded eyes to find Balthus staring at me.

"And what was it that separated you?" he asked, his voice just above a whisper.

My brow furrowed as I thought about whether I wanted to discuss this with a complete stranger. I supposed I was already well on my way past reckless this evening, considering the skimpy dress and the hotel bar. And talking to Balthus was cheaper than therapy—although not much, at Palm Beach drink prices.

"He no longer possesses the qualities that I require for a relationship to work," I muttered.

A lazy smile spread across Balthus' face, its effects on my body stealing my breath once more. "And what might those qualities be?" His voice brushed over me like an intimate caress.

I hesitated, inhaled, and then said in a rush, "Respect and loyalty, for starters." I attempted to even out the breathless defiance in my tone.

His eyes held mine for a long moment, as if he was drawing the truth from me. They bathed me in heat, leaving me unable to look away.

"How could anyone be disloyal to you?" he asked, almost as if he was talking to himself. I could detect no guile in his manner, and the question hit so close to the center of my pain that I felt tears prick at the backs of my eyes.

Shit. I shouldn't have started talking about this.

Balthus broke our eye contact and cleared his throat, then took a long draw from his glass. I was embarrassed that he felt the need to give me a moment and I made a valiant effort to swallow back my tears.

"You know," he said, staring down into the ice-cubes at the bottom of his glass, "there is one sure way to forget about that type of disloyalty." Balthus' gaze captured mine again and the teasing warmth in his eyes, combined with his slow, sexy grin, seemed to help dislodge the lump in my throat.

"I'll admit," I began unsteadily, "I wish I could forget about my problems, even if only for a night. But don't tell me that you're suggesting I...reciprocate my husband's disloyalty with someone I just met," I continued in a chiding tone. "I hardly think that would do anything but complicate matters further."

Balthus laughed then—a deep, rich bass that seemed to resonate throughout my entire body. "Oh, Sydney, you are delightful," he chuckled with a shake of his head. "I think I'm going to enjoy getting to know you better."

"Oh really?" My brows rose at the assuming tone of his statement. A prickle of unease touched my spine, but I shrugged it off and told myself that I was being childish. I just wasn't used to interacting with men this way.

"That is, if you'll consent to conversing with me for a while longer," he replied smoothly. "You don't seem to be enjoying your drink." He pointed to the now-warm liquid that still filled half my glass. "Share a bottle of champagne with me?"

I hesitated as an increasingly fuzzy corner of my brain warned against accepting his offer. But my reserve faded and my inner alarm bells dissolved into a pleasant, carefree haze. Champagne sounded fun! And I was here to have fun, right? And to forget about...something.

Frowning, I looked up to find Balthus' expectant gaze centered on me. "So what do you say, Sydney?"

I blinked and gave him an uncertain smile. "Champagne sounds good." I suddenly felt as if I'd been holding my breath for hours and was finally letting it all out in one big rush. The relief was dizzying.

Balthus shot me a devilish grin and signaled the bartender.

An hour later I found myself a few shades past tipsy, and laughing merrily at something Balthus was saying as I accompanied him up to his tenth floor penthouse in a heavy marble and bronze elevator that opened directly into his private outer foyer.

As I waited for Balthus to unlock the penthouse door, however, that annoying, rational inner voice intruded once more. I scowled as it pierced my cloud of contentment, demanding to know what the hell I was doing getting drunk and going to some strange guy's hotel room. This was not normal behavior for me. Maybe I should slow things down and forgo Balthus' offer of a nightcap...

My thoughts stalled out as Balthus turned to me with a disarming smile and beckoned me through the door.

I trailed behind him, gaping at the most luxurious hotel room I'd ever seen. Balthus strolled forward into the suite's sitting room and halted behind an elegant freestanding bar trimmed in tawny leather and burnished metal rivets that matched the room's over-stuffed leather sofas.

Everything in the space, from the speckled fawn carpet to the ultra-modern fixtures to the Impressionist style paintings on the walls, had been chosen with exquisite care and taste. But it all paled in comparison to the breathtaking ocean panorama visible through the room's wall of expansive sliding glass doors.

"This view is incredible!" I made my way across the plush carpet toward the sprawling balcony. "Do you mind if I open the door?"

"No, go right ahead." Balthus indulged my enthusiasm. "Would you like another glass of champagne?" he called.

I turned, prepared to politely refuse, just as he popped the cork and began tipping some into a delicate crystal flute. My refusal died on my lips. I shook my head and found myself agreeing to a drink I knew I didn't need as I wandered out onto the balcony.

The night was warm, but the penthouse was high enough that the breeze took the edge off the heat. I breathed deeply, the tang of salt from the ocean air helping to clear my head. I leaned over the railing, enjoying the feel of my wind-tousled hair teasing the sensitive skin on my bare shoulders.

I felt Balthus' presence behind me and turned to accept one of the chilled crystal flutes he held. He gently reached to tuck a few strands of hair behind my ear, his fingertips gliding down my neck to linger warmly on my shoulder. His touch amplified the sensations I had already been enjoying, and I had to close my eyes and force myself to remain still against the wave of desire that blossomed through me.

"It's beautiful here," I prattled.

"It certainly has its charms," Balthus agreed with a smile. "I come here quite frequently, actually."

"This penthouse is fantastic. I wish I could live here." I shivered with growing anxiety.

Balthus' fingers tightened on my shoulder and I felt that odd prick of unease in my spine again. But then his fingers began a slow massage, dissolving away my tension as if by magic. He took my glass from my nerveless hand and placed it beside his on a nearby table.

"Why not?" he whispered. "Surely a woman as lovely as you deserves to live in such a beautiful penthouse. What else do you wish, Sydney?" he asked, his breath softly stirring the hair near my temple as he moved closer.

I leaned into the warmth of his body. "I wish…" Hmm…I was sure I wished a lot of things…but I could only seem to think of one desire as I stared up into the fiery depths of Balthus' eyes…

"That's enough," a disembodied voice interrupted from the darkness. The words I had been about to speak died on my tongue.

A man appeared, as if he had melted away from the shadows of the wrap-around balcony to assume solid form.

I froze, furious with myself for having been so stupid as to go somewhere this private with a man I'd just met. Actually, it was more terror desperately trying to work its way up to fury—until I noticed that Balthus looked every bit as stunned as I did.

Holding onto the small morsel of relief provided by that, I clutched at his hands where they rested on my shoulders, trying to dissolve back into him and away from the other man.

My relief was short-lived as my gaze shot to the man's hand. He was pointing something at us. My breath caught in my throat and my brain screamed *Gun!* Panic swelled, excluding all other thought. Yet for some reason, my eyes kept trying to break in and signal my brain that something was off.

I didn't know much about weapons, but the one this man was holding looked rather odd. It seemed to be made entirely of tarnished bronze, and the finger loop at the back looked more like a handle than a trigger.

"Miss, step away from the djinn."

I had the distant thought that the stranger's tenor brogue sounded Irish. He stared at me expectantly, impatience tightening his features when I didn't immediately obey his command. My brain finally kicked into gear as I realized that, despite my attraction to Balthus, I didn't know him well enough to stand between him and a bullet. The thought eased my guilt as I began to inch away from him, my mind registering distractedly that the stranger had called him…the djinn?

I didn't get far before Balthus' grip tightened painfully on my shoulders.

"Stay where you are Sydney," he commanded. His cultured voice belied the unpleasant manner in which he held me. "She is mine, by right." He glared at the other man.

I stiffened, not liking the sound of that at all. "Um, I'm not sure what's going on here," I began, raking Balthus with an indignant glare, "but I really wish the two of you would just…"

"SHUT UP!" growled the man with the gun. "Not one more word if you value your pathetic life at all!"

My mouth snapped shut at his vehemence. "Ow!" I gasped as Balthus' fingers dug deeper into my shoulders, my own fingers scrabbling helplessly against his in an attempt to pry them out of the indentions I was sure they were making in my skin. It felt as if they were beginning to burn brands into my flesh. My panicked gaze flew to the man in front of us as his voice rang out with authority.

"Balthus of King Moab's tribe of the Ifrit djinn, in the name of Impellier, I sentence you to imprisonment for crimes against the Realm. In the name of Impellier, I summon you into containment until such time as the Realm sees fit to free you." He broke into the lilting syllables of a strange foreign language, his words taking on the tone of a well-practiced chant.

Not that I understood much of what he'd said in English.

But I did notice that, as the man continued speaking, Balthus' grip on me weakened. I took the opportunity to duck away from him and scramble back into the corner between the wall and the railing of the balcony, as far away from the both of them as I could get without taking a dive off the tenth storey.

The bizarre, chanting man blocked the escape I longed for—back inside the penthouse and into the elevator, down and away from this stupid, over-priced hotel full of assholes.

This whole night had been a mistake.

"She is mine by right!" Balthus insisted, a note of pleading breaking through his demand.

His words might have galled me more, if I hadn't been so damned scared, and if my brain hadn't started to register the fact that Balthus seemed to be…fading. His legs were going smoky and transparent, and the phenomenon was spreading slowly up his body. I blinked as my obviously damaged mind tried to convince me that the Balthus-smoke was drifting toward the barrel of the gun that the other man was pointing at him.

No. Not a gun, I realized. It was an old-fashioned, metal oil lamp. I couldn't do anything but stare—it was either that, or pass out. Come to think of it, unconsciousness might have been preferable, but I'd never been the type of girl to swoon.

"Sparrow, she's mine!" Balthus let out a thin, petulant wail, the smoky remains of his upper body drifting toward the opening in the lamp's spout and disappearing, as if he was being sucked into it by a vacuum.

"Shut it, Balthus," the man replied, sounding irritated. "You know damn well that if she'd completed the contract, you'd have already claimed her."

And with that, Balthus' smoky head vanished, and he was gone. I felt a mad giggle rise up into my throat as I watched the last of him get sucked into the narrow metal spout. My eyes rose disbelievingly to the stranger's face. He was gazing intently at the lamp, making a complicated hand gesture over it and whispering a series of unintelligible words.

Then he tucked the lamp into a pocket inside his jacket, where it disappeared without leaving so much as a lump or a crease. Surprising, but hardly worth comment after what I'd just witnessed. That task completed, he focused his attention on me.

I was hoping he'd have forgotten my presence, but no such luck. All the air left my lungs and the old phrase 'like a deer in the headlights' suddenly took on a very personal meaning. I searched desperately for a third option to my innate fight or flight response. I was trapped in the corner with him blocking the door, and somehow I didn't think I'd come out on top in a contest of strength.

The man had about a foot on me and he looked *solid*.

His eyes pierced mine for a long moment, and then he waved over the railing. "If your life means so little to you, you could just jump."

Then he turned and went inside the penthouse.

A Risky Proposition is available now in print or e-book!

My novel *Passionate Magic* tells the story of Scarlett's brother, Doyle, and his soul mate, Violet. I hope you enjoy it!

- Dawn Addonizio

Passion...

When Violet Hendrickson takes a tour in The Florida Keys and meets sexy boat captain, Doyle Thresher, the attraction is instantaneous. The warm summer sun, the mystique of the ocean, and the charming, chiseled Irishman are more than she can resist.

Magic...

But something evil is lurking beneath the waves, lying in wait for Violet. And when she nearly drowns on Doyle's boat tour, he knows it's no ordinary accident. In order to keep her safe, he will be forced to reveal his most deeply held secret.

Will Violet be able to accept the magical truth of his identity? And will he be able to convince her of the existence of the evil that hunts her...before it's too late?

About the Author

Dawn Addonizio lives in South Florida with her wonderful husband, who is a science teacher, and their beloved menagerie of pets.

When she's not working her day job, or staring into space, she spends her time writing fantasy and making jewelry, wine accessories, and all manner of other sparkly things.

You can visit her store at DawnsBoutique.Net, "like" her on Facebook/D. Addonizio, and read some of her musings at DAddonizio.blogspot.com. You can also follow her on Twitter @DawnAddonizio